Literary Pasadena

The Fiction Edition

PROSPECT
·PARK·
BOOKS

PASADENA, CALIFORNIA

Published by Prospect Park Books
969 S. Raymond Avenue
Pasadena, California 91105
www.prospectparkbooks.com

Distributed to the trade by
Consortium Book Sales & Distribution
www.cbsd.com

Library of Congress Cataloging in Publication Data has been ordered. The following is for reference only:

Literary Pasadena: The Fiction Edition; edited by Patricia O'Sullivan; foreword by Michelle Huneven.—1st ed.
    p. cm.
ISBN 978-1-938849-09-1
1. Short story—Authorship. 2. Pasadena, Calif. I. O'Sullivan, Patricia. II. Huneven, Michelle.

First Edition: April 2013

Book design by Kate Hillseth
Printed in the United States of America

Contents

Editor's Note

As a bookish young girl growing up in frosty central Connecticut, I had only one conception of Pasadena. Entering my living room every New Year's Day was an astonishing assemblage of beautiful smiling young women with perfect teeth, riding floral floats in the sunshine. They might have been my age but I presumed unquestioningly that they had never encountered flannel, corduroy, acne, heartbreak, or the thick Russian novels that allowed me to simulate an intellectualism that I neither felt nor articulated. My misimpression persisted when later, as an effete New Yorker, I dutifully did my part to espouse the widely expressed view that New York was the center of all universes that mattered to me: artistic, musical, theatrical, and certainly literary.

My adopted city has a population of less than 150,000, yet Pasadena looms large in the imagination of writers and is home to many. In these pages, you will find mothers, bikers, teachers, con artists, screenwriters, killers, and yes, beautiful young girls with perfect white teeth. You will encounter some writers you know well and others who deserve discovery. My debt of gratitude to each and every one of them cannot be overstated, including those writers who were disappointed by our selection. I am especially obliged to bestselling novelists David Ebershoff and Lian Dolan for allowing us to excerpt the two books that must be included in any discussion of Pasadena's contemporary literary representation, to Naomi Hirahara for helping spread the word about the project, and to Michelle Huneven, whose early and continuing support provided the catalyst for its success. And although publisher Colleen Dunn Bates envisioned this project many years ago, she generously allowed me to shepherd it into existence with the invaluable help of the ever-insightful Jennifer Bastien. It has been a privilege, an honor, and a revelation.

For New York is not the capital of the literary universe. This quiet space exists wherever an author lifts a pen or types a key, wherever a child sounds out first written words, wherever a community gathers to celebrate stories, wherever a reader opens a book or boots up an e-reader, wherever booksellers devotedly curate selections, wherever a small independent press enthusiastically takes on the task of sharing beautiful stories by local authors—it is Pasadena.

Patricia O'Sullivan
Pasadena, California

Foreword

Before I could start my third novel, I needed to decide where to set it. I had in mind a mid-size western city with an old downtown hotel and summer heat. Boise and Spokane were ideal but too far away from my Altadena home. I actually flew to Sacramento one weekend, scouted for the right hotel, and found it, too. I drove through neighborhoods where my characters might live—I was searching for a certain configuration of driveway and bushes. Several would do. But I worried: Could this really be where my imagination would live for the next three to five years? Back home, I fretted and procrastinated. Months passed, and I still didn't start my book. Yet while I dithered, in some back corner of my brain, a novel was amassing like an egg on an umbilical rope.

And then the obvious hit. Why not set it right here, in Pasadena, Altadena, La Cañada Flintridge? I could repurpose the Castle Green for my own use—I was writing fiction, after all! Certainly, the summers had triple-digit temperatures. I had no trouble finding driveways hedged in oleander thickets. Suddenly, all my research lay in easy driving distance. The seasonal birds and weather could be ascertained from my own window.

Some years later, when the novel came out, I gave a reading at Vroman's, Pasadena's long-surviving independent bookstore. During the Q & A afterwards, an audience member asked how much the Pasadena setting had determined my characters—or could the story have happened anywhere? I briefly tried to picture my heroine in Boise or Sacramento, but failed: she lived in the chateau-style apartment behind Euro Pane bakery; her best friend grew up privileged in the San Rafael hills; she dated an Art Center painting instructor, then married an older man with horse property in La Cañada Flintridge. She was *formed* from Pasadena clay.

I was fascinated, then, to see how Pasadena has similarly shaped and formed so much of the writing in this anthology. The Crown City's literary landscape is a geography that hovers at a slight kilter to the actual: the iconic landmarks, familiar street names, stores, and schools drift through these pages like manifest content in dreams. Strangers to Pasadena who read this book will accumulate, as through osmosis, an uncannily intimate, insider's sense of the Rose City. They'll know, without a formal civics or history lesson, that the city was settled by wealthy, sun-drunk midwestern industrialists in the late 1800s, and that today the population is demographically diverse and multilingual, and that the north-south main drag, Lake Avenue, refers to no known body of water.

Pasadena locals will enjoy small, pleasurable shocks of recognition as the iconic crosses path with the humdrum. We too pass the Rose Bowl on our way to drop our kids off at school, the Norton Simon en route to the Orange Grove Von's, which (who knew?!) is the secret budget supermarket for Linda Vista and San Rafael matrons. And oh my god—remember the turquoise-and-black tile at the Rialto theater? Remember the Rialto, and revival house theaters, period? Also, one can't help but glean a few practical tips: The Kitchen for Exploring Foods is the go-to caterer, the Aquatics Center is the place to swim. For camellias and azaleas, there's that world famous nursery up on Chaney Trail in Altadena.

In the literary landscape of Pasadena, we are allowed glimpses into history, into crimes as they're underway, into the souls of the citizens; we're privy to family conflicts, cute meets, and adultery, to the struggles of mothers, to real estate obsession, and to age-old secrets.

Pasadena and environs don't figure into every work of fiction in these pages. The collective imagination of our writers ranges far afield geographically and formally. You'll find speculative fiction, fantasy, crime writing, and just plain beautiful prose, some of which takes place in Texas, Orange County, or some other parallel universe. But all the authors have breathed the air, drunk the local water, and sat alone at their keyboards somewhere in the gently sloping lap of the San Gabriels, within a few miles of the Rose Bowl.

Pasadena, it turns out, is an excellent place to write. The proof is in the disproportionate number of published and celebrated authors, past and present, who've called the city home. Our literary forebears include Charlotte Perkins Gilman, Zane Grey, Harriet Doerr, Octavia Butler, Charles Webb, and Richard Vasquez, to name a few. This anthology presents only a sliver of the area's practitioners: there are also poets, memoirists, screenwriters, comedy writers, historians, philosophers, and biographers laboring within the local zip codes.

Here, we're far enough off the beaten path—a continent away from the publishing hub of New York City, and just far enough from Hollywood's manic buzz—to escape the clamor and pressure of those industries, and that makes it easier to focus on the work at hand.

If the writing life is grounded in solitude and silence, it helps to have beauty nearby. Pasadena's Arroyo and mountains, its fine architecture and old trees, the year-round sunshine and blooming foliage, feed the imagination and the soul.

But Pasadena is no cultural backwater. At various times in my life, I've driven three miles downtown to see Saul Bellow, Joan Didion, Bob Dylan, Julia Child, Ian McEwan, Jane Goodall, the Dalai Lama... Pasadena's two large, bookstores, the independent Vroman's with its ample parking lot, and Old Town's vast Barnes & Noble, bring in a steady stream of writers from all over the country. Caltech, Occidental College, and the Huntington Library and Gardens all have stellar lecture series. Many writers, scholarly and literary, do research at the Huntington Library, and a tramp through the gardens there should be prescribed for every writer's stiff neck or temporary block. I've taken breaks from my desk and visited the small, world-class Norton Simon Museum to gaze at Zurbarán's luminous lemons and lock eyes across the centuries with Rembrandt's self-portrait.

The secret, I'm afraid, is out. Writers are everywhere around Pasadena, and somehow, we find each other: I myself live next door to a book-writing historian on one side, a playwright on the other. I've met writers at readings, in coffeehouses and cafes, across the broad oak tables in the main branch of the Pasadena library. I spot them, drumming on keyboards, scribbling surreptitiously into Moleskines, barking voice memos into smartphones. Just a few weeks ago, at the Little Flower Cafe, I saw a man reading W.G. Sebald's *The Emigrants*. "That's one of my favorites," I said, and we started chatting. He was a writer, of course. A fiction writer, who, like me, needed a break from his desk and came out, with some hope, perhaps, of running into a kindred soul for a bit of conversation—the odds of which, in Pasadena, are pretty darn high.

Michelle Huneven
Altadena, California

Petrea Burchard

Portraits

K AREEN RAN HER FINGERS through her silver-gray coif. She resisted pulling her own hair.

"I won't pay a late fee. I mailed that check a week early. It's not my fault your staff couldn't get around to entering it on the computer." Kareen was short of breath.

The voice at the other end of the line argued something about applying payments by 5 p.m. on weekdays.

"Fine," said Kareen. "You may cancel the card."

"Mrs. Sorensen, we don't wish to lose you as a customer..."

"Cancel the late fee or cancel the card. I have other cards."

"Okay, Mrs. Sorensen. I'll be happy to cancel the late fee for you. Just give me a moment."

"Thank you." Kareen sighed. It worked. It would not work again next month.

The call finished, Kareen replaced the receiver. The morning's meeting with the lawyer had left her shaken. She stared at her folded hands, trying not to panic. Age flowed blue in her veins. Her manicure was growing out. There would not be another manicure. There would not be more shopping on credit. There would not be much at all.

She heard a soft rustling. Had Arleta been listening? The maid dusted the gilded frame of a painting on the wall across the salon.

Kareen had once found the room refreshing, with its mint green walls and tall windows. Now the high ceiling felt oppressive.

"Credit card companies," said Kareen. "They'll bleed you dry."

"I try to keep credit cards to a minimum," said Arleta.

Was she mocking? Maybe.

"You've never let a man handle your money, have you, Arleta? You've been smart."

"True."

"I wasn't smart." It was not unusual for Kareen to speak openly with her maid. She trusted Arleta to be discreet.

"I guess not."

Kareen rubbed her hands together. "I don't suppose it will be a surprise when I tell you I can't pay you this week."

Arleta stopped dusting and turned to face her employer. Her parted lips told Kareen she'd been wrong. Indeed, it was a surprise.

"I didn't know it was that bad," said Arleta.

"Yes. But next week…"

"No. No next week." The maid dropped the feather duster right there on the sofa.

Kareen stood from the armchair, an involuntary motion. "I'll figure something out."

"Call me next week." Arleta walked out of the room.

Kareen followed. "I can't manage this place without you."

"I can't manage my kid without a paycheck, Mrs. S." On her way to the pantry for her purse and sweater, Arleta took off her apron and let it fall on a kitchen chair.

"Arleta, wait."

Arleta grabbed her things and headed for the front door.

Kareen hurried back to the salon. She could think of nothing else to do. She lifted a painting from its hook on the wall, the same painting Arleta had been dusting. It was a portrait of a man, Kareen had no idea who, perhaps some relative of her dear, departed jerk of a husband. She trotted after Arleta and caught up with her at the door. "Maybe this is worth something. Please take it."

Arleta stopped in the shade of the porch and turned. She gave the painting a disdainful look and heaved an exasperated sigh.

"I'm sorry," said Kareen, fighting tears. She and Arleta were not friends, nor were they master and servant. They had been partners in the house, moving around each other on quiet days, chatting sometimes about Arleta's little girl, sharing lunch Kareen made for the two of them in the kitchen.

"I'll pay you as soon as I can." She extended her arms, holding the painting, knowing it was not nearly enough.

Arleta took it.

Kareen examined a small tear in the sleeve of her off-white silk blouse. It was at the seam. She could fix it. Breathless, she searched the bottom of the pantry for the sewing kit and came up empty. Arleta had probably found a better place for the kit, a logical place. Kareen would find it eventually. For now, she put on a sweater.

Arleta parked the Ford on the downhill slope of Nithsdale Road, half a block west of San Rafael School. The uphill walk to the front entrance should not have been a challenge for a woman of 32. Cleaning a rich lady's home was tiring, but losing her job was exhausting. She joined the other parents in front of the school as she always had, but everything was different. Now she was unemployed.

She should not have walked out like that. She should have tried to work something out, especially since the rent had gone up. Again.

Seven-year-old Linda came running, her dark brown ponytail flying, two impossibly blond kids in tow, all three of them waving colorful construction paper and shouting complete sentences in what sounded to Arleta like perfect Spanish.

"Hicimos el arco iris!"

"Tengo cola en el pelo!"

"Maestro me dio una estrella!"

Being of Mexican descent and speaking almost no Spanish was an embarrassment to Arleta. She wanted better for her daughter. She placed her palm on Linda's shoulder to steer her toward the car. "That's a nice rainbow," she said. "What have you got in your hair?"

"Glue, momma, I told you."

"You'll have to teach me Spanish."

"Tengo cola en el pelo."

"What does that mean?"

"I've got glue in my hair."

Kareen turned the Lexus north onto Orange Grove Boulevard. Ordinarily, she'd drive to the Pavilions across from the Assistance League. Or she'd send Arleta. This day she continued north, past Colorado Boulevard and the Gamble House, across the 210 Freeway into northwest Pasadena. She rarely stopped in that neighborhood, only passed through, and she had no fear of being recognized. None of her friends would venture this far.

She was surprised to find the Vons grocery store as clean and almost as well-stocked as the Pavilions in her neighborhood. The prices were lower and there were more black people, but those were the main differences. She found herself overdoing the friendliness—one doesn't grin and say hello to strangers at the grocery store—so she concentrated, wandering the aisles, searching for peanut butter and canned soup, trying not to be noticed in her sunglasses and scarf.

She'd been right to come here. She was finally being smart. Too little, too late, maybe. Maybe it took the bastard's death to wise her up.

She was pleased to find decent fish. Those steaks looked all right, too. There was no filet mignon. They had that at Pavilions. Her mouth watered when she thought of the last time she'd eaten a filet at the Raymond. It would be a long time before she'd have another fifty-dollar steak, or even a ten-dollar steak, for that matter. She'd need a boyfriend to get a meal like that. Or a girlfriend. The thought made her giggle. She placed a family pack of hamburger in her cart.

"Kareen, fancy meeting you here!"

Oh god. It was Franchetta from the Showcase House committee. Franchetta's copper hair sat above her freckled brow like a puffy beret.

"I could say the same of you!" said Kareen, her heart pounding.

"We're the smart ones, aren't we? It's a little out of the way but the prices are so much better."

Kareen drew in a breath. Had everyone been smart except her?

"Will we see you at the next meeting?" Franchetta eyed the salmon fillet. "We missed you last time."

Kareen hesitated. "I don't think I'll be available this year."

Franchetta went pale. "Oh. Of course. Forgive me, I'm so sorry. I wasn't thinking." She placed her hand on Kareen's arm.

At first Kareen wondered what Franchetta meant. The woman seemed truly upset.

"Thank you. I'm fine," said Kareen.

Franchetta thought for a moment. "I don't know how we'll manage without you. You're so good with the vendors; you always get the best deals. But do what you must, Kareen. We'll be there when you need us."

She must have been referring to Archer's death, Kareen thought. "Yes. Thank you."

Kareen realized with a pang that she would never go back to the committee. She loved the social life, but on the west side of Pasadena, serving on fundraising committees meant money.

After a spaghetti dinner at the small kitchen table, Arleta washed Linda's hair in the kitchen sink. At bedtime, she pulled up the blanket, kissed her daughter good night, and turned off the light.

She shuffled into the living room and plopped down on the sofa. The painting rested beside her, basking in the golden light of the second-hand lamp. She lifted the portrait onto her lap. Just some guy, she thought. Some old, white guy dolled up in a Mexican cowboy outfit. It wasn't even a good painting.

She should have refused it, should have had some pride, tried to negotiate something else. Kareen Sorensen said Arleta had been smart, but where were the brains behind this? She'd been an idiot. She had walked out of Kareen's house because of her pride, stopping just long enough to accept this raggedy old picture.

She hadn't been smart about men, either, no matter what Mrs. S had said. She'd been as much a fool as Mrs. Sorensen had, except Mrs. Sorensen was left with a house full of antiques and she was left with a child. She had quit school and run off with the first guy who gave her a chance to get out of the house. And look where that had gotten her.

She would go to Merry Maids in the morning, then Molly Maids, then the Cheery Cleaners, and whatever else was out there. She would fill out the forms, call the numbers, pound the pavement. She had no reserves, no time to waste.

And if she had to find another place to live, that painting was not going with her.

The light bulb had gone out in the kitchen. Kareen dug through the pantry shelves in semi-darkness, cursing: *I let the maid do every damn thing and now I can't find a goddamn light bulb. I let the idiot manage the money and he cleaned me out. I even let someone else do my goddamn fingernails. Well, screw that. At least I know how to change a goddamn light bulb.*

She slammed the pantry door. She would find a light bulb in the morning. She left the kitchen and stomped up the stairs without turning on the light, not because there was no bulb but because it would save on the electric bill. In the master bathroom she turned on a light just long enough to find her manicure kit.

She sat on the window seat at the bedroom's bay window, where she'd spent many comfortable hours reading when she'd had the leisure to do so. But she'd never read a book on finance, never even so much as glanced at the checkbook or the bank statement, had no idea she was broke until Archer died and the lawyer gave her the news.

She found the nail file in the kit and allowed the moon to light her work.

This was not entirely Archer's fault. It was hers, too. She should have paid attention. And she should have had her own means, beyond her inheritance, should have created a business using her talents. What would that be, she wondered? Could she do that now? The one thing she was good at was organizing fundraisers, and she was too ashamed, too afraid people would find out she couldn't make a donation herself.

She could not sell the house. She'd grown up there, as had her father and grandfather. The giant Victorian had been in her family since the beginning, built on land her people had owned since Pasadena was settled in the 1870s. It's not possible to sell one's history.

She would die one day, not far in the future—ten, twenty years maybe—and she had no one to leave the house to, no family left who cared about it. What's a legacy anyway? It doesn't mean anything to anyone except the person whose legacy it is.

The next morning, Kareen stood staring at her unmade bed. She had never made a bed, but how hard could it be? It was a matter of simple logic. She carried the pillows to the window seat and returned to stare at the bed once more. She tugged at the sheet to straighten it, then padded around to the other side to smooth it. The sheet was uneven. She pulled, disgusted with herself. How had she lived more than six decades and not learned to make a bed?

When she finished, her bed looked far less perfect than the tidy confection Arleta made of it every day. Kareen decided to leave it as it was for the time being. Her molars ground in spite of herself.

She gave up after a week.

She closed the upstairs and moved into a downstairs guest room. In order to avoid running the air conditioner she'd been leaving the windows open for a breeze and could not keep up with the dust. Maintaining the house was much more difficult than she had anticipated.

Still, she tried to keep the downstairs livable. One didn't have to mop the kitchen floor every day, thank goodness, because doing so left her back aching. Cleaning the tops of things required climbing onto a chair, and her balance wasn't so good anymore. She decided that unless she expected a tall visitor she would leave the dust up there.

But she didn't expect visitors. When the phone rang she let the machine answer, and returned calls when she was certain no one was home. She'd leave a message. "Nice of you to call. I've been so busy."

It was important that she maintain personal cleanliness. It was important that she smell good. It was important that no one could tell by looking at her that she was scrimping. She avoided going out.

There was some social security. She could figure out how to make it on that. She hadn't been smart, but she could learn.

Arleta waited on the sidewalk in front of a house on North Hudson Avenue. She and the other Cheery Cleaners, who did not seem cheery but just tired, had been dropped off at 2 p.m. Their ride was supposed to come at 5:00. It was 5:41.

The other women she'd worked with that day sat at the curb, chatting in Spanish. You'd think the homeowner would allow them to wait on the porch or even on the sofa, and maybe he would have, but it was against company policy. When you're finished working, you have the client sign the form, you give him his copy, then you wait outside.

This Cheery work wasn't what Arleta was used to. Neither was the pay. The house they'd cleaned was cute. Simple. Nicer than her rental. But not like Mrs. Sorensen's imposing Victorian on the west side. Arleta missed the place. One day she would live in a mansion like that, or at least she should. Linda should. A home like that, with an attic and back stairways, built-ins and stained-glass windows, would be heaven for a kid.

When she finally got home she propped her sore feet on the coffee table and sipped a Bud Light, staring at the old guy in the Mexican hat.

Kareen decided to let the back yard go. It was fenced in. The hedge was high. No one would see. However, the front had to be mowed. The hard part was convincing Enrique. He had his pride.

"It will be a *jungle!*" With arms waving, he demonstrated grass growing as high as the sky.

"Enrique, I'm a widow now. I have to make some changes."

"I'm sorry, Mrs. Sorensen."

"Thank you."

"But you *can't* leave it," he said, opening his palms in supplication. "It's gonna get *bad*. Let me do it every other week. I'll cut your bill twenty-five percent."

"I need you to cut it fifty percent."

"You're gonna get *rats*."

She did not want rats.

"Once a month, then. Fifty percent plus ten dollars."

"Aw…"

"That's what I've got," said Kareen, leaving him on the sidewalk.

Arleta found a parking space on Mentor Avenue. She was tempted not to pay the meter but couldn't take the chance, especially on a Saturday; the cost of a parking ticket was a hundred times more. She walked west on Boston Court to the corner of Lake Avenue, clutching her package.

Arleta had always been able to provide for herself and her daughter. She managed by being careful. She had never before set foot in the likes of the Art & Antiques store. She adjusted her print blouse, tucking it in at the waistband of her black skirt. She felt dampness there, sweat. Inhaling deeply, she pulled her shoulders back before stepping across the threshold. She would not allow a clerk to read nervousness on her.

For a moment she stood, dazzled, surrounded by caramel-colored wood, golden candlesticks, and gleaming crystal. The walls were lined with paintings much more beautiful than the one tucked under her arm. Her resolve almost melted.

"Good afternoon," came a chilly voice from the back of the store. A tall man of elegant posture stepped out from behind an ornate black cabinet that looked to Arleta like it was trimmed with real gold. The man was a study in beige: beige suit, beige shirt, beige skin, beige hair. Everything about him was neatly pressed, parted, folded, and combed. He waited. He did not smile.

"Good afternoon," said Arleta, remembering not to grin too

broadly. She hesitated, her chest feeling hot. "I wonder if you can price a painting for me."

"I'll be pleased to take a look," said the man, sounding anything but. His expression was skeptical. Arleta suspected he'd seen one too many.

Kareen's arms ached, but it felt good to work up an appetite, then sit on the sofa and wolf down a hamburger. She needed a shower, but she was too hungry to let dinner wait.

She'd taken down all the paintings in the salon, then washed the wall. She knew it was crazy, but it had long been a fantasy of hers to see what that wall would look like without all those awful old pictures.

She loved everything about the house but the paintings. She loved her quiet street, her privacy, her discreet neighbors. She loved the oak floors, the doweled railings, the gingerbread, the turrets on either side of the porch. She loved the porcelain tiles, the clawfoot tub, the rippled glass in the windows. The furnishings her family had collected over more than a hundred years were treasures to her. She might have to sell the Tiffany lamps but they mattered less than the lived-in stuff: Grandpa's chair, Great-grandmother's vanity set, Father's footstool.

Why she didn't love the paintings as well, she didn't know. She couldn't remember a time when they hadn't stared down at her from the walls of the salon. They'd always hung in the same places. Periodically, the painter would come. He'd cover the furniture with plastic, take down the paintings, paint the walls the same, mint green, then rehang everything exactly as it had been before.

Mostly, there were portraits—some were of her ancestors who had settled Pasadena in the nineteenth century. Some she guessed were of their contemporaries, and Archer had added a few. Other paintings were of early Pasadena. When she removed them from their hooks to wash the wall, she found handwritten labels on the backs: "Arroyo, '98 dry season," "Library and new palm trees," "Henry Millard and bees." Most of the paintings were signed, the names unfamiliar.

Kareen stifled a burp. She would accept no complaints from her body. The hamburger was fine; she just wasn't used to it. She gazed at the wall. No matter how hard she wiped, the marks remained: darkish blocks where the paintings had been, lighter mint green faded around them. Dark squares or no dark squares, she preferred the empty space. The cluttered walls had overcrowded her.

The paintings stood in regimented lines on the floor, leaning against the sofa, stacked on the furniture. She would put them in storage. There was room in the basement. She'd explored it while doing laundry that afternoon.

A buzzer rang. The first time she'd heard it she'd panicked, thinking the house was on fire or someone was breaking in. But it was only the dryer.

She pushed herself to stand. Her body ached. It made her angry that sixty-seven felt so different from fifty-seven. One last load of laundry and she would put her feet up. Read a book, maybe. Or sleep.

Kareen pulled the string to turn on the basement light. The string broke in her hand and the light did not come on.

"Damn."

Frustration rose in her esophagus like bile. She breathed hard. It was only laundry. She was careful to hold the handrail, taking each step one at a time. The basement wasn't completely dark. From the ground-level windows, light floated in like ancestral ghosts, selecting this box and that old suitcase on which to rest. Archer's things. She had never known what was in them and she didn't care. She might give them to the Salvation Army. Or she might go through them to see if there was anything worth selling. Either way, she'd get rid of it all. That would make room for the paintings.

She found the dryer door with her fingers and pulled the handle. Light spilled from the opening, illuminating the wicker basket, which she filled with warm, dry clothes.

A favorite sweater, shrunken to doll size, ruined. She'd neglected to read the tag. She had never before appreciated how much one had to know, what an education one needed, simply to run a house.

She lifted the basket. A deep, awful spasm tore through her back and bent her, sending her sideways. Unable to let go of the basket in time to brace herself, she fell hard beside it, banging her head on the cement floor.

Each attempt to move was answered with more wrenching of her back, making it worse.

I will not, she thought. I will not despair.

The doorbell rang.

Arleta waited. She rang again. She knew the signs. Kareen was home. Maybe she was in the shower. Or maybe Mrs. S didn't want to see her.

She rang one more time, then turned and walked down the steps and along the sidewalk to her car.

A deep breath, a measured pace. Kareen pulled herself up the stairs with the help of the railing and by biting her lower lip so hard she tasted blood. But she made it. She looked through the small window in the front door in time to see Arleta.

Arleta, the one person she wanted to see, was walking away from the house. Kareen knew by the bit of gold glistening on the bumper of Arleta's car that the sun was setting.

With effort, she pulled the door open and called out, "Arleta." Soundless.

Arleta did not hear, could not have heard. Still, as she opened the car door, she looked up. Without speaking, she closed the door and retraced her steps. She was carrying a package under her arm. She frowned.

"What happened?"

"Not my day. You're dressed up."

"Here, come on."

Kareen took Arleta's offered arm.

In her skirt and pumps, Arleta looked like a lady from an office. She helped Kareen to the sofa in the salon and propped her up with pillows. She brought painkillers from the upstairs medicine cabinet. "Man, it's dusty up there!" cleaned the blood from Kareen's lower lip with a damp cloth, and made them each a cup of tea.

Kareen refused to call the doctor. "I'll know by tomorrow if it's more than a pulled muscle."

Arleta agreed with only the slightest reluctance. Eager to get down to business, she perched across from Kareen at the edge of the pin-striped armchair and pulled the painting out of the bag.

The joy that had lifted Kareen with Arleta's arrival dissolved. "You don't want it."

"Listen. No. This is worth something."

"That's why I gave it to you. I felt I owed you…"

"It's some historical guy. Worth a lot. Like maybe half a million dollars."

For a second, Kareen lost her breath. Her chest felt hot.

"The guy at the antique store knew the painting right away. This is Don Benito somebody. Did you know everybody used to speak Spanish around here?"

Kareen knew. With imposing eyes, Don Benito stared at Kareen from Arleta's lap. "You could have sold that painting for a lot of money."

"Yeah, but I'm smart, like you said." Arleta looked around the room. On either side of her, legions of paintings lined the floor. More paintings languished on the chairs and rested atop the antique commode. "Kareen. I want to make a deal."

"Go on," said Kareen, noting but not minding Arleta's use of her first name.

"Your paintings, your negotiating skills, my strength, my energy."

"My…?"

"You own the product, but I'll be doing the footwork, so I'll take a cut."

"My…negotiating skills?"

Arleta leaned back and turned on a lamp. "I could have sold that painting, but not like you. The look on the guy's face when he saw it. When he said he'd give me two hundred thousand, he was sweating.

I think he was low-balling me, but I wasn't sure what to say next. So I told him I'd think about it."

Kareen had negotiated with gardeners, credit card companies, caterers, and florists. She'd never thought of it as a skill. But Arleta might be onto something. "Good for you. Sweat is a sure sign. And you didn't take the first offer. When you go back he'll offer more."

Arleta laughed. "When I go back I'll have you with me."

Kareen smiled. It sounded like fun.

"Look," said Arleta, "you need a roommate. I can take care of you and the place."

"You have a little girl."

"She's a good kid. Mostly she's in school."

"It's not a deal-breaker." Just for a second, Kareen pictured a child running through the back yard. "Let's say you both live here rent-free, plus you get ten percent of sales."

"Ha."

"Twenty?"

"Fifty."

Arleta's eyes glowed in the lamp light. Kareen was having fun, too.

"Thirty and we can talk," said Kareen.

"Thirty-five. I'm cleaning the house *and* taking care of you, remember?"

Neither was a fool, not anymore.

"You're a good negotiator, too," said Kareen.

"I learn from the best."

Kareen raised her teacup. Arleta raised hers. They clinked.

"Thirty-five it is," said Kareen, feeling joy for the first time in as long as she could remember.

"We renegotiate in one year." Arleta winked.

Kareen didn't like those paintings, not one of them. She never had. Her back ached. Her nails were cracked. She put down her cup and reached out to shake Arleta's hand.

Lian Dolan

Helen of Pasadena, an excerpt

IDEN AND I HAD debated the merits of a shirt and tie most of the morning. I thought he should wear one for the Ignatius interview. He disagreed. "Mom, it looks like I'm trying too hard," he argued.

"A shirt and tie simply says you care. You'll have to wear one every day for four years when you get in. What's the big deal about wearing one to the interview?" I hissed in that special mother hiss. Honestly, his moods were all over the place these days—understandable, given that he'd lost his father recently. But why, why, why pick a fight over a shirt and tie? I pulled the car into the school parking lot, observing the high ratio of Mini Coopers and old Volvos in the student spaces.

Compared to the lush, green surroundings of his elementary school, Millington, Ignatius was as urban as Pasadena could manage. The old stone buildings, originally a Jesuit seminary and retirement home constructed in the 1920s, were covered in ivy and jammed up against a freeway onramp. A small chapel, with a stained-glass window featuring the names of Jesuit colleges, stood off to the right. The pool and sports fields rolled out beyond the chapel, an endless rectangular strip of green and concrete alongside the freeway. A brand new football stadium, complete with a million-dollar turf field, press box, and deluxe locker rooms, was at the far south end of the campus. (One very loyal, very successful former third-string quarterback had donated the entire stadium. Benchwarmer's revenge, my husband, Merritt, had laughed at the dedication ceremony.)

The campus was not beautiful, but it reeked of tradition: the broad stone steps in front where students gathered in the morning; the worn wooden crucifix touched for luck by a thousand boys a day as they entered the gates; the drafty dining hall where the seniors led grace before meals. Ignatius, despite its Catholic heritage, was the closest institution Southern California had that could compare with the elitist Eastern prep schools of Massachusetts and Connecticut. The big difference was that it wasn't elitist.

The children of the rich, the poor, the immigrants and the powerful of all colors and creeds came to Ignatius from all over Los Angeles County. Long before prep schools grew endowments to cover financial aid for needy students, Ignatius had prided itself on a "write the check" admissions policy. If the son of a gardener or cop or mechanic was deemed qualified to attend, some alum would simply write the tuition check on behalf of that student for four years. It started sixty years ago with Father Michael at the helm and continued today with Father Raphael. The beloved Jesuit would scan the alumni directory and pick up the phone. The lawyer or real estate mogul or judge would never meet the kid he sponsored. And the student hoped to someday repay the debt in the same way. It was quiet and discreet, and it built the most loyal alumni in the area. Most Ignatius Crusaders considered their high school allegiance to be even deeper than their college or fraternity connection.

I wanted Aiden to have that connection. I felt like I could still give him that, even if so much else in his life had changed.

As I redid my lipstick in the rearview mirror, I took one last stab at Aiden. What was wrong with him? "It would be a sign of respect to school tradition to wear a tie."

"Fine. Just…whatever, fine." And he put on the tie and a dramatic scowl.

Super. A terrific day to come down with attitude.

And it got worse from there.

Hank Pfister, the director of admissions, ushered us into his cramped office. Humility in all things, the needlepoint pillow on the couch advised. So I've learned lately, I thought.

"So Aiden, what are you reading in English this quarter?" Mr. Pfister offered up as his first question. I knew that he knew exactly what an eighth-grade student at Millington would be reading this quarter: *Romeo & Juliet* and *To Kill a Mockingbird*. Twenty-five boys from Millington had applied to Ignatius; Aiden was the last to be interviewed. Only about a half dozen would get in. Aiden was a legacy and decent kid who had just lost his dad, but his grades were not good. He needed this interview. I got the sense that Hank Pfister knew that, too.

I appreciated the softball question.

"Umm, umm..." Aiden started, not looking up from the floor for a second of eye contact. Then the fidgeting began, leading to the chair twisting. "Umm, Romeo and, umm, Juliet. That's pretty good. And then that one about the lawyer dude defending the African-American guy. The Mockingbird one."

The lawyer dude? Shakespeare is "pretty good"? Who is this kid?

"Oh, Aiden," I fake-laughed, hoping to diffuse the growing discomfort in the room. "I'm glad you think William Shakespeare is *pretty good.*"

"Tough audience," Hank Pfister responded, playfully jerking his head toward my son. God bless you, Mr. Pfister.

Then playtime ended.

"If you can't understand a single word the guy writes, how great can he be?" Aiden snapped, his voice full of defiant energy now. "I could read that crap all day long and still it wouldn't make any sense. What's the point?"

There is no sound in the world quite as deafening as the sound of all hope leaving a room. *Please, Aiden, please pull it together.* But I could see that he was just getting started with his Angry Young Man phase.

We struggled through another ten minutes of questions and answers. Even the routine questions about water polo failed to elicit a civil response from my son. Eventually, it was Mr. Pfister and me talking about Aiden while Aiden checked his imaginary watch. We carried on the charade, including handshakes and wishes of good luck, until the end of the interview, but we all knew one thing for sure: this Aiden was not Ignatius material.

My mother was very good at silence. It was her greatest parenting asset. Of course, it made me crazy as a kid, when she would call out in front of my friends for "a moment of silence and meditation" if we got into an argument over the rusty trampoline in our backyard. "Let's all close our eyes and take a deep breath. Exhale the dark energy," my long-haired mother in the flowing skirt would instruct my bewildered church-going friends. "Breathe in the light."

She would remain very still for about a minute while my friends tried not to laugh and I tried not to die of embarrassment. Then she'd return to the moment with a big smile and a solution. I think the solution was that the horror of the mediation made everyone involved in the "dark energy" completely forget what the fight was about. Nevertheless, we were all calmer, and the trampoline play continued without incident or need for further meditation.

But I was never more grateful for the lesson of silence than on the way home from Ignatius. The fifteen-minute drive felt like fifteen hours. Aiden and I did not exchange a single word. I did my best to breathe out the dark energy; he stared out the window, barely breathing at all.

Both Tina and Candy had texted me with the same "How'd it go?" message. I wasn't ready to answer that question yet. I turned the phone off. I could hear my mother's soothing voice, "Let it go. Breathe out and let it go."

When we arrived back at our house, the "For Sale" sign was being hammered into the front yard in advance of the weekend open house by a couple of guys on Rita the Armenian's team. "Tasteful typeface and classy colors!" realtor Rita had promised. I'm sure the neighbors would appreciate the art direction. I turned off the ignition and sat for a second. So did Aiden.

"Aren't you going to say anything?" he challenged when we finally got out of the Audi.

I can't remember a time when I'd ever had less to say, except maybe when Merritt told me about his affair with Roshelle Simms. Or when the accountant told me that our money was gone. I couldn't possibly comprehend what had just happened, so I certainly had nothing constructive to say about it. I simply stated the obvious.

"I guess you really don't want to go to Ignatius. I thought you did. We'll figure something out."

Aiden's face registered surprise, as if he'd expected me to rip into him upon our arrival home. And certainly, if he'd behaved like that in front of Merritt, there would have been serious consequences: yelling, accusations of letting down the family name, no computer or cell phone for a week. But in the few last months, I'd lost all sense of how to measure the importance of events. Was blowing the Ignatius interview less important or more to Aiden's life than having to sell his house? Who knew? I wouldn't know for decades the impact of Merritt's death on our lives, so I certainly wasn't going to jump to conclusions now. "Let's just order pizza so we don't mess up Emilia's clean kitchen."

"Mom, I'm sorry. I messed up. Are you mad at me?" That was the most emotionally complex thought Aiden had uttered all afternoon. Acknowledgment, apology, acceptance of responsibility.

"No," I said truthfully. Saddened, disappointed, scared, but not mad. "No, I'm not mad. We'll figure it all out."

David Ebershoff

Pasadena, an excerpt

Mrs. Cherry Nay wasn't from Pasadena, nor did she pretend to be, but by 1944 she knew as much about the city as anyone born at the Arroyo Seco's lip. Her name as a girl hadn't been Cherry, and certainly it hadn't been Nay, and when she arrived in Pasadena on New Year's Day 1920, she quickly shed a few pounds from her past. Cherry walked with small strong legs and a sturdy gait, her pistol-gray curls shooting from her head. Since the outbreak of war, the simple, colorless clothing she had worn all her life had become fashionable among the women of Pasadena; over the years, Cherry had begun to blend in in other aspects too. She was forty-one, and only once in her life had she lied about her age: when she was seventeen, she told the editor at the *Star-News* that she was eighteen and a half; during this interview she also embroidered her experience reporting society gossip, inventing a story of lurking in a hibiscus to catch a railroad heiress in illicit arms. On the spot, the editor had hired Cherry, and she'd worked for him for more than ten years, stringing for the *American Weekly* insert too, eventually becoming a well-known and sometimes feared columnist. But long ago, Cherry Nay had given up that sort of life. Now she and her husband, George, ran Nay & Nay, real-estate brokers and development. She left the development to George and handled the residential sales, and over the years Cherry had learned that a real-estate broker could uncover as much as a reporter, often more. Because she no longer considered herself a snoop, she tried not to peer into the yawning drawers in her clients' bedside tables, but there they were, open like infant coffins, offering her a full view into their lives, the Bible next to the sleeping pills. Ever since her childhood, Cherry had taken pride in her ability to piece together a person's life with only a few scraps of information, a Holmesian skill she put to use throughout her day. Back in 1930, she had first met George at a City Hall hearing over the proposed motor parkway, six lanes of concrete he and the others wanted to pour along the bottom of the arroyo. George had an attractive, muscular build and pretty, almost girlish blue eyes, and he carried a volume of Marcus Aurelius shoved up under his arm. He looked like the type of man who was prone to yelling, but in fact he spoke softly, choosing his words with care. He was determined to build the parkway, and he told the hearing in nearly a whisper that he wouldn't give up until the concrete had dried. At the time, Cherry had known nothing else about him, but just this was enough for her to be able to imagine his entire life; and it was enough for her to know she wanted to give up reporting—"It's a dirty business," she predicted George would say one day—to become Mrs. Cherry Nay.

But on this December morning in 1944, all that felt like another life, one she had reported on, filed, and tossed away. She had a near perfect memory, recalling everything of the years when she had signed her columns "Chatty Cherry," but there was an uncomfortable, tele-scoped distance between that woman and Mrs. Cherry Nay, who had to get across town for a nine o'clock showing at the Rancho Pasadena. The seller was a man by the name of Bruder; she had known him since she was a girl, and she liked to think that if she had done any good as a journalist, it had been with him. He was selling the old orange ranch, 160 acres, a place where quite a few things had happened in the last generation, and as Cherry drove west on the Colorado Street Bridge—"Suicide Bridge," they'd been calling it since it opened years ago—she promised herself not to get bogged down in its past. That was the trouble of a perfect memory: at any time it could flood Cherry, the dam loosened by the scent of orange blossoms on the breeze or the way the morning light cut into the hillside, and especially when she drove down the coast to Baden-Baden-by-the-Sea. Cherry hadn't spent much time at the rancho herself, but her old friend Linda Stamp had seen her life change there, end there too, and in some ways, Cherry had to admit, her life as well had turned the corner because of the Rancho Pasadena. Cherry preferred to keep herself removed from the narratives of others, but in this case she hadn't entirely succeeded, becoming a bit player in a larger story, a fact she was reluctant to admit, especially to herself.

Her appointment was with a man named Blackwood, whom she knew of but had never met. George, who had gone to Washington to draw up contingency plans for the real estate of German cities, had warned that Blackwood was a small-timer; "a bit of a looky-loo," George had written in one of his nightly letters. Yet few others had called about the rancho—it had become something of an anachronism by 1944—and Bruder had reminded Cherry that he was anxious to strike a deal: "Do what you can to relieve me of it," he had said. The pain in his voice would be apparent even to those less observant than Cherry Nay.

On the telephone, Mr. Blackwood had spoken in a somewhat childlike voice, one that Cherry had found sincere, and she pasted this observation to her developing profile of Andrew J. Blackwood.

She was driving quickly through the Linda Vista hills, where the live-oaks canopied the streets and the scent of run-over skunk hung noxiously in the dewy morning; she was in a hurry to reach the house and open things up prior to Mr. Blackwood's arrival. And at precisely the same time that Mrs. Cherry Nay was turning her key in the door of the Rancho Pasadena mansion, the Imperial Victoria was crossing Suicide Bridge, the morning sun burning in Andrew Jackson Blackwood's rearview mirror.

On the seat beside him was the advertisement from the *Star-News*:

EVERYTHING FOR SALE

BEAUX-ARTS MANSION

100 ACRES OF ORCHARDS

60 ACRES OF GROUNDS

YOUR OWN ARROYO!

THE RANCHO PASADENA

LAST CHANCE TO OWN A PIECE OF CALIFORNIA HISTORY!

He had had to phone twice, eventually securing an appointment with George Nay's wife. Mrs. Cherry Nay had given him directions in a friendly but distracted voice, as if she had just realized she had lost something, a diamond ring down the drain or something of the sort. Blackwood interpreted this as an encouraging sign that he was dealing with a birdbrain. But her directions had proved topographically precise, including that the asphalt would end at a black walnut, and that the street would become a white dirt road, and that at the road's end there'd be a gate covered in wild cucumber. "A dirt road? In Pasadena?" This had brought a ripple of hope to Blackwood, who wondered if much of the rancho remained undeveloped, a crude piece of arid scrubland. Over the telephone he had inquired about the price, but Mrs. Nay had said, "Now, Mr. Blackwood! You know as well as I that I'd never give that out over the phone."

Over the years, Blackwood had heard surprisingly few stories about the ranch and its family, the Poores. As far as Blackwood knew they all were dead now, Captain Willis Poore the last to go, a heart attack last year while doing calisthenics on his terrace, or so Blackwood had read in the obits. The captain's wife, a woman by the name of Lindy, who, according to the *Star-News*, wasn't from Pasadena, had been dead for a number of years; his sister, Lolly, too, a girl who had once kept the largest rose garden in Southern California. The obit had gone on to say that the rancho "had seen its best days pass," and Blackwood had made a note to keep his eye on the auction block. The rancho sprawled at the western edge of Pasadena, tucked between Linda Vista and Eagle Rock in a small valley that most people didn't know how to find, including Blackwood. He thought, vaguely, that he had heard Stinky say that the family had something to do with the founding of Pasadena; but Stinky also added that the Poores weren't a Caltech family, that was certain. "Goodness, now take a look at this," Stinky had said on the telephone. "I'm looking at a 1925 Valley Hunt Club roster, and sure enough, here they are. Captain Willis and Miss Lolly Poore, Junior Members."

The dirt road was in bad shape, toothed coyote brush and thickets of poisonous buckeye creeping into the car's path. Blackwood drove carefully, worried about his paint job, making his way up the chaparral hill. The rains had left everything blindingly green, the deerweed in bloom with tiny butter-colored flowers and the sagebrush tipped with yellow blossoms. Vines of Pacific pea climbed the live-oaks, their ovate leaflets shimmering in the December wind. A row of bluish leaves sprouted from the road's center hump, an early sign of a poppy trail. The car continued its climb, and the pitch of the road steepened. Soon the ceanothus and the lilac and the twisted-trunk madrone were nearly choking off the car's path. The morning's blue shadow pressed the side of the hill, a chill touching Blackwood's neck, and he thought about turning around. But at last the car approached the tall black gate. As Mrs. Nay had said, vines of wild cucumber twisted through the wrought iron; Blackwood got out and shoved the gate, and to his surprise it opened easily, as if a hand were pulling it from the other side. It was warm from the sun, and he dragged it across the road; dust rose in a line that seemed to mark the rancho's boundary, a border to another world.

Back in his car, Blackwood continued up the hill, switchbacking through thickets of holly berry and pink-veined laurel sumac and minty eucalyptus. He was listening to the Saturday "True Stories" program on KHJ, and just as the actress on the radio whispered in a panic "I think there's someone in the house!" reception was lost. Blackwood stretched to fiddle with the dial, and to his great disappointment the white plastic knob snapped off in his hand. The road turned sharply, but Blackwood, whose eye was on his dash, failed to turn with it, and

the Imperial Victoria's front wheels ran off the road and the car tee-
tered over the edge. With no time to spare, Blackwood's frightened
foot found the brake; he was on the verge of a terrible plunge into the
arroyo below.

Yet when put into reverse, the car performed for Blackwood. With
sweaty palms he steered back onto the road. He mopped the moisture
from his face and, reminding himself that caution was the developer's
guide, continued up the hill. Beyond the bend, the one he had almost
missed, the road crested and the wildbrush fell away and before him
was a wide, untended lawn surrounded by tight-budded camellias and
yews and fan palms swaying high above. The grass needed reseeding,
but immediately Blackwood began to tally the acreage. The great lawn
alone must have added up to nine or ten.

The road skirted the lawn, and soon the dirt gave way to pavement,
a strip of white concrete cracked and sprouting branchlets of ricegrass.
Blackwood reached for his hat with the maroon band and the tiny
golden feather, propping it on his head, and it was then that he saw
the house. The Poore House, as Mrs. Nay had referred to it on the
telephone, dwarfed the mansions on Orange Grove—"Millionaires'
Row," they used to call it long before Blackwood moved to town. The
house seemed to Blackwood even bigger than the Hotel Vista, but
that wasn't possible; in its heyday the Vista could sleep five hundred.
Blackwood thought about how Pasadena's richest citizens, tucked behind hedgerow and hairy-leafed arroyo willow and pillared gate, called
their Mediterranean villas *casitas*, their slate-roofed palaces *cottages*,
their Greene & Greene redwood mansions *bungalows*. "It's how they
are," Stinky had remarked, in his analytically detached way. "There's
no economic rationale for denying one's wealth, the way some people
do around here. But it wasn't always like this. A generation ago it was
just the opposite, everyone flaunting about. Things change, don't they,
Blackwood?"

Blackwood would have to present himself to Mrs. Nay as unim-
pressed, not letting on that he'd never seen an estate like the Pasadena;
as if he were used to surveying private kingdoms. She had described

the mansion as Beaux-Arts, but it was more than that: it was a twisted California mélange of Italian villa and Andalusian farmhouse and French château, three stories, plus attic, whitewashed with a red pantile roof supported by a cornice decorated with escutcheons bearing navel oranges and bobcat heads. A wide terrace ran along one side of the house, its chipped balustrade topped with marble urns potted with dying yucca—Blackwood guessed this was where Captain Poore had fallen dead. Creeping ficus jacketed the eastern half of the house, tangled with a dying passion-fruit vine.

Blackwood drove through the portico's narrow columns and parked the car. He saw no one and heard only the chime of the yew leaves and the calling jays. In the distance, the Sierra Madres were limey yellow in the early sun, their peaks protected by snow, and it occurred to Blackwood that he had found a private world separated from the rest of Pasadena. It was not altogether impossible that they'd be asking too much for the Rancho Pasadena; right away he'd have to get the price out of Mrs. Nay.

"What are you talking about?" said Cherry Nay. "You haven't even seen the place. Let's not talk about prices until I've shown you around." She was the forty-and-over ladies' tennis champion at the Valley Hunt Club, and ten years of rushing the net—how Cherry Nay loved to volley and smash an overhead!—had worked her skin into a supple brown leather. In person there was nothing birdbrained about Cherry, and she sensed that her very presence had surprised Blackwood, as if the most apparent facts about her didn't add up easily: her girl-size body and her sun-worn face and her old lady's hair and her pleasure, and enviable skill, in assembling information and relaying it with authority. She had a habit of closing her sentences with the firm statement *And that's just the way it is,* and she said this now as she told Blackwood that since he had bothered to come out to the ranch, he might as well stick around for the tour. "Now let's see this big old house!" She said this with the giddiness that had greeted Blackwood on the phone, and he was disappointed in himself for misjudging her; he wasn't dealing with a rube at all.

They moved down the gallery that ran the length of the mansion. The house was empty except for a row of gilt-legged chairs draped in muslin and, at the base of the main staircase, a six-foot marble statue of Cupid blindfolding a half-robed woman whose bare stone breasts caused Blackwood to avert his eyes, a modesty Cherry noted as she explained, "The owner is selling everything as is."

The house had been built in 1896, she said, for a land speculator and orangeman by the name of Willis Fishe Poore I. "Carved out of the old Rancho San Pasqual. It replaced an earlier but also grand mansion," she said over her shoulder, moving quickly, assuming that Blackwood could take everything in at her rapid pace. What Cherry was careful to keep to herself was that Bruder had called from the village booth early this morning and asked if she knew anything about a man named Andrew Jackson Blackwood; he'd been poking around Condor's Nest, Bruder had said, and Cherry, careful not to lie, had said that she'd never met Mr. Blackwood. "Is he a serious fellow?" Bruder had inquired. "There's something about him that makes me think he might be the one." Cherry had said she would try to find out. She hadn't revealed that Blackwood would be inspecting the Pasadena in a few hours, and Cherry somehow understood that it would be best for her to mediate. She knew she had something to gain by keeping each man away from the other for as long as possible, allowing information to transmit through her.

"Willis Fishe Poore?" said Blackwood.

"The first."

"The first?"

"Mr. Poore, as I'm sure you know, was one of Pasadena's founders. He kicked off the Indiana Colony back in 1874. Not that George and I care about those things—whose homestead was here first and all that rigmarole of the past. But as I'm sure you know, there are those around town who take great pride in their antecedents." When the house first rose on the hill the ranch totaled 2,500 acres, but that was long ago, said Mrs. Nay. Now the Pasadena was a not-unimpressive 160: 60 acres for the estate and its gardens—"what's left of them"—and

100 acres set aside for the orchards, half dead and the other half gone wild, producing oranges as black and filmy as coal. "The spreading decline hit during the Great Drought back in 1930, doing the grove in once and for all. It's too bad, really. It was mostly navel, that was the crop. But there was grapefruit, tangerine, cherimoya, mandarin, apricot, blood orange, peach, walnut, sapota, and Kadota fig. It was quite a place, Mr. Blackwood." Once there'd been a staff of six gardeners, Japanese men in green rubber boots who swept the lawn with bamboo rakes. In the house there'd been secretaries and chambermaids in lace pinafores and a seamstress and, later, a chauffeur who parked the cars in the converted stable. It took Willis Fishe Poore four years to build the house, and thirty mules to level the hilltop and dig the trout pond and clear the two acres for the thousand rosebushes. The house resembled the Château Beauregard, said Mrs. Nay. "Elmer Hunt—you've probably heard of his nephew Myron—transformed it into a…I suppose the best description is a California *castillo.*" There was a bowling alley in the basement and a billiard room where Mr. Poore used to gamble with his ranch hands and a loggia off the portico where delicate Arcadia orange trees, planted in porcelain saki barrels, blossomed so sweetly that Lolly Poore, Mr. Poore's daughter, once collapsed from the onslaught of their perfume. There were twelve bedrooms, each with a view of the orange grove, and eight baths—"The first full-service in Pasadena, George always reminds me to point out"—plus a back wing big enough for a staff of twenty-four.

"But those days are over," said Mrs. Nay. "Nobody lives like that anymore." She doubted Blackwood intended to live like that. He could turn out to be the type of man who would raze everything, denuding the hill even before he had a plan of what to do with it. It was a shame, really, and although Cherry wasn't a sentimental woman she held out a tiny hope that someone would come along and roll a carpet down the hall and replant the groves. Nothing wrong with keeping a little bit of history alive, Cherry liked to say.

On the landing between the first and second floors, they looked out the window toward the North Vista and its dolphin fountain, now dry and cracked, and a camellia garden reclaimed by a bramble of red-berried toyon. From this view, Cherry realized, the ranch appeared rather forlorn, as if it were straining to expose its true sadness to its visitor.

"How long has the house been empty, Mrs. Nay?"

"A year or so. But it was on the decline for quite some time."

"Like so many properties around town, Mrs. Nay. They say Pasadena isn't what it used to be."

"I suppose you're right, Mr. Blackwood. When was the last time anyone built himself a mansion? Years ago, probably 1929 or 1930 at the latest. I can remember when they went up two a week."

Blackwood sensed an opening, although he didn't understand where it might lead him. He said, "You mustn't forget the war, Mrs. Nay."

"Of course, Mr. Blackwood. I don't want you to think I'm not do-ing my part. We save our cooking fat in a tin can like everyone else, and the cook and I have learned more cottage cheese recipes than I ever thought possible. I'm not complaining. Surely the war will end one day, but I have a strong feeling Pasadena will never be the same."

"Nothing will be the same, Mrs. Nay."

"That's true, Mr. Blackwood." And then, "And that's just the way it is." She paused before saying, "But that's not why we're here. There's plenty more to see, Mr. Blackwood! Note the Diana statue. That comes with the house as well."

She was having a hard time piecing Blackwood together; he was both rough and sophisticated, confident and self-conscious, adolescent and middle-aged. She knew he wasn't from Pasadena, and she knew that his application for membership at the Valley Hunt Club had been rejected. The same was true for the Athenaeum over at Caltech, even his friend Stinky Sweeney hadn't come out full-hearted on Blackwood's behalf; and the Playhouse had voted not to elect him to its board. But Cherry's sympathy for outsiders far surpassed her husband's and that of most of the people she knew, and she wanted to take Blackwood's hand and advise him to stop trying: some people will pass through the gates, and some never will.

On the terrace, she pointed out the orange grove and the ranch house and the outbuildings. "It comes with all sorts of picking and packing equipment. If you're interested, if you're serious, Mr. Blackwood, I will supply you with an inventory."

He felt obliged to say, "I am serious, Mrs. Nay."

Her finger traced the property line: "From that hill with the fire scar in its side to that one shaped like a camel's hump, including that little arroyo over there."

"What's that noise?" asked Blackwood.

"What noise?"

"That whirring noise?"

The two stood on the terrace, its red Welsh tiles casting a glow about their feet.

"That's the parkway, Mr. Blackwood."

"Is it *that* nearby?"

"Yes, it's just beyond that first hill over there. Captain Poore, who was Mr. Poore's son, sold some of his land to the men who dreamed of paving the Arroyo Seco with a six-lane road." She failed to mention that one of those men was her husband.

"I suppose you can hear it night and day?"

"I'm afraid so. They say a thousand cars use it every hour." She and Blackwood exchanged a look that they both understood to mean that the parkway's proximity would knock something off the price; she held private the thought that the parkway had made her and George very rich. "Except for the automobiles, we really could be stepping back in time, couldn't we, Mr. Blackwood."

He thought her a handsome woman, small and mulish, like the few lady professors scuttling around Caltech. He thought to ask, "How about you, Mrs. Nay? Were you born in Pasadena as well?"

She said that she was from Baden-Baden-by-the-Sea, and that George was from Bakersfield. "We're both upstarts in Pasadena, but we've done all right for ourselves. We've been over on Hillcrest for the past ten years and we've seen the changes, Mr. Blackwood. And we know the next ten will bring even more." She was of two minds about what she did in real estate—ushering in progress and stamping out the past—and sometimes it was as simple and innocent as shepherding a bungalow with a swing on its porch from one generation to the next, but other times, especially with George's deals, it meant deciding that the past should come down altogether: choosing one hundred tiny new houses over a citrus grove.

Blackwood noted that in the past several years the changes had been especially rapid: the Hotel Vista converted into an army hospital, the candied-fruit shops on Colorado Street boarded up, and a dozen Orange Grove mansions abandoned in the night and turned into rooming houses, or pulled down by rat and ivy. A nearly imperceptible brown veil hung over the rancho's valley, blurring the landscape like one of the *plein-air* paintings that hung in the ballroom of the Valley Hunt Club—or so Blackwood had heard.

"And what's that over there, Mrs. Nay?"

"What?"

"That white structure at the far edge of the grove? Is it a folly?"

"Not at all. That's the mausoleum. They're all buried there, the whole family."

"Who?"

"The Poores. Most recently Captain Poore. He followed his wife and sister by more than ten years." And then the memory washed over Cherry and she said, although she didn't intend to, "She was an unusual woman."

"Who?"

"His wife."

Continuing her tour, Mrs. Nay explained that the library's mahogany paneling had come from a manor outside Windsor, pried from the walls of a cash-poor earl and crated to California by the Duveen Brothers. The roller shades were drawn and the seams in the herringbone parquet collected dust, and the room was gray and vacant, except for the six thousand books on the shelves. "The present owner chose not to take them. He says he doesn't like to read another man's books.

He's not from Pasadena, Mr. Blackwood. Or, I suppose he is, but not like anyone else."

"How do you mean?"

"He was an orphan. Raised at the Children's Training Society, out by the old City Farm. It closed a while back now. You probably don't know it. There's no reason you would."

"I'm afraid not." Blackwood pulled a volume of Gibbon from the shelf and found a bookplate that read, *This book belongs to the library of Lindy Poore, 1930.* The pages were heavily underlined and annotated. On the inside of a schoolroom edition of *The Three Musketeers* he found a signature, written over and over, *Sieglinde Stumpf.*

"Sieglinde Stumpf?"

"What's that, Mr. Blackwood?"

"Who's Sieglinde Stumpf?" He pointed to the signature.

"She was the mistress here."

"Here?"

Mrs. Nay nodded, and her hand fell to his wrist. Sometimes Cherry would say to George that she hadn't thought about Linda Stamp and Bruder in years: "It feels like someone else had known them, not me..." But in truth, a day didn't pass when she didn't turn over the details, the stones of the story tumbling and polishing in her mind. "Tell me, Mr. Blackwood. Is it the house or the land that interests you?"

"Both, Mrs. Nay."

"Do you have any intention of preserving things as they are?"

"No plans yet, Mrs. Nay. But anything is possible. I'm most interested in what's best for the property. And for Pasadena."

"I was hoping you'd say that," she confessed. "We shouldn't rip up every last thing, should we? On most days, I find the past a useful thing to keep in mind. I had a gentleman in here who had an idea to turn the mansion into a halfway house. Another fellow wanted to build an apartment complex where the roses are. You can't imagine what he had planned for the orange grove. Still, the present owner has little reason to seek preservation. If it were up to him, he'd tear down the whole thing. He says the only thing the mansion could be used for is a home for old ladies."

"A home for old ladies?"

"That's what he says, and I know he's probably right. But I'm sure you can see this is a one-of-a-kind. In the end I am a realistic woman, Mr. Blackwood, and my only hope is that the future owner thinks carefully before he raises his ax."

"There aren't many people who can take on a mansion and one hundred and sixty acres just for themselves these days, are there, Mrs. Nay? Few people set themselves up as barons anymore."

"That's what the present owner says." In the dim library, her eye gleamed and she made a little swing with her arm, as if she were on the tennis court.

"Did you mention who the present owner is? Is he Captain Poore's heir?"

"I didn't mention the name, Mr. Blackwood. He has asked me not to say."

"I understand."

"But he is an unusual man." She said this to test Blackwood, to fillip the crystal of his interest to hear how it rang.

"Is that so?"

"I've known him for years and years." She added, "He once worked the orange ranch here."

"And now he owns it all?"

"It's a long story, Mr. Blackwood. Mr. Bruder's history is complex." She knew that the revelation of Bruder's name would startle Blackwood. Cherry wanted to grade his resourcefulness, to see if he was the type of man who could stitch together a story with the little scraps she had meted out.

"Mr. Bruder?" said Blackwood, pressing his lips together so as not to give anything away. He peeled back the window shade: the small valley lay before him, the hills fighting off the fiery reach of the new houses, the roof tiles as orange as flame and the fresh roads the color of smoke. What was the likelihood that it was the same man? On the other hand, what was the likelihood that there were two? "Do you have any idea why Mr. Bruder is selling?" asked Blackwood.

"As I said, it's a long story."

"I have time."

"I really shouldn't say. After all, I'm representing the seller."

"It would help me in my decision. And my decision might be for the good of things in Pasadena." Cherry didn't say anything, and Blackwood tried again. "Who is this girl named Sieglinde?"

"Which Sieglinde? There are two." Cherry checked her watch. She didn't know why she felt the need to tell the story, but it pressed at her from beneath her skin, an angry fist punching out. Like Blackwood, she sensed that an era was coming to an end, and perhaps she wanted to set things straight before the world moved on. And unlike Bruder, Cherry had never made a promise to keep a secret; and oh! how from the day she first heard Bruder's name she had known he would change their lives. Now they were allies of a sort, she and Bruder, hooked together to a past that was receding quickly. She had recounted the story to George early in their marriage, and he had said, his lips gentle upon her forehead, "Cherry, I'm glad you've given up newspapering. It makes you ponder such horrible truths."

"Should we pull a couple of chairs onto the terrace?" she said to Blackwood. "Beneath the coral tree?"

"After you, Mrs. Nay."

The transition from the library to the white sun erupted a flash in Blackwood's eyes. For a second he couldn't see, and then his pupils readjusted and Mrs. Nay was waving her hand, "Over here, over here."

On the breeze was a lingering scent of citrus. The past blossomed on its sturdy stalk. The memory carried Cherry upon its sweeping flood and she said, but not to Blackwood, "Where to begin, where to begin?" She hesitated, and then, with her eyes sealed, said, "Where did the trouble first begin?"

Dianne Emley

The Last Wife

"I TOLD GARY THAT if he tried to leave me, I'd kill him." Kiki Sumner laughed and took a sip of her martini. "He knows I'd do it, too. I told him that I'm not just his third wife, I'm his *last* wife." She enjoyed being outrageous.

Betts Engleford playfully slapped Kiki's toned arm. Little that came out of Kiki's mouth surprised her anymore. Betts knew that Kiki's larger-than-life persona hid an underlying insecurity. The look on Kiki's face as she watched both their husbands fawning over their shapely new associate, Annabelle, made Betts believe that there was a glimmer of truth in Kiki's threat.

"Kiki, you know that Gary is completely devoted to you."

"And I'm totally devoted to him but—let's put it this way." Kiki raised her index finger, displaying a manicured hand and enough gems to skirt being over the top. Straddling that fine line had become her brand. "Gary's worth a lot more to me dead than divorced. If we divorce, I get a tiny settlement according to the pre-nup, but if Gary dies, his will leaves me well provided for." She let out a throaty laugh. "Looks like a loophole to me."

Betts and Kiki were peering out from behind drapes beside French doors that were opened to the slate terrace of the Sumners' newly renovated manse off of Linda Vista, overlooking the Rose Bowl. Kiki had drawn Betts from a group engaged in conversation to point out Gary standing with Betts' husband, Paul, on the terrace with Annabelle. Both men were clearly in her thrall.

The Sumners were hosting a holiday party for the employees and spouses of Crown City Partners which everyone called CCP. Paul Engleford and Gary Sumner had founded the highly regarded Pasadena venture capital firm after earning their MBAs at USC where they'd met. It had been a rough year for CCP. The firm had eked out a profit after Paul and Gary had completed a painful downsizing and reorganization that included bringing in Paul and Betts' son, Matthew, who Paul, eyeing his own retirement, was grooming to be managing partner. They'd also hired Annabelle Hill, who they'd touted as bringing a fresh perspective into the stodgy firm. The pretty twenty-eight-year-old was an unlikely candidate. She didn't have the stellar work and educational background of Crown City's traditional entry-level associates. What she did bring to the table, in addition to sex appeal, was a deep-pocketed client, her former employer, The Merton Group, run by Carl Merton, whose investments had helped keep CCP afloat over the past year.

Kiki was suspicious that there was more behind the hiring of the leggy brunette than the company line spouted by Gary and seconded by Paul, especially because Annabelle was hired out of the blue without the partners' normal, thorough vetting process. Betts hadn't shared with Kiki, nor would she, that she also found Annabelle's presence in the firm deeply unsettling.

Shadows were lengthening as the day drew to a close. The pleasantly warm daytime temperature was cooling nicely at the cusp of the evening. A waiter was illuminating votive candles on outside tabletops and along the deck railing. Another waiter was lighting candles inside the house. Other help circulated with trays of hors d'oeuvres, wine, champagne, and sparkling water.

Kiki had hired The Kitchen for Exploring Foods to do the party, not risking engaging anyone other than the go-to caterer for savvy, well-heeled Pasadena hostesses. She was still uneasy in her role as a boss's wife. Even though she had fun with her flashy persona, she wouldn't take chances with a high-profile event. She didn't have Betts' easy confidence as a hostess. Betts often cooked and served at her parties, bravely trying out recipes for the first time, with only her longtime housekeeper to help with clearing dishes and glasses and Paul manning the bar.

"You know what my dear momma from Savannah, Georgia used to tell me," Kiki began. "She'd say, 'When a man marries his mistress, he leaves a job opening.'"

Kiki followed up with what Betts was thinking but was too polite to say. "Gary was separated from his second wife when we were dating, but I'll confess to some hanky-panky before the separation—after I punished him with dead-lifts and drop squats." She'd been Gary's personal trainer and was fifteen years his junior.

Betts smiled cryptically. Her mother, Sarah Ludlow, had taught her to listen, ask questions about others, and say little about herself or her own views. Because of that, she was known as a good conversationalist.

Kiki went on. "I know Annabelle's not married, but is she involved with anyone?"

"I don't know."

Gary's booming laughter reverberated all the way inside the house. He was a big man—a former college football player—with a barrel chest and a salesman's personality. He'd begun shaving his head when he'd started going bald and his bald pate gave him a hipster look. He was CCP's idea man.

Paul was the firm's numbers guy—sedate, conservative, and content to let colorful Gary have the spotlight—but their business relationship was showing strain. The recession had hit the firm hard and it was affecting their decades-long friendship. Not helping matters was Gary's tendency to be a spendthrift, which had worsened after he'd married Kiki five years ago.

Betts watched Paul sip his gin and tonic and then lean toward Annabelle to make a comment. Paul was tall and lean. He kept in shape by swimming daily, either at the Rose Bowl Aquatics Center or in their backyard pool. His wavy, strawberry blond hair was just starting to show gray at the temples, but he still looked boyish and nerdy, an impression heightened by his tortoiseshell glasses.

Annabelle also leaned in until her full lips were almost touching Paul's face. She was fetching in a figure-hugging sheath in a bold, multi-color print that set off her tan. Red high heels flattered her legs. The clothes were expensive and Annabelle wore them well but gave them a whiff of trashiness. It was in the way her lush hair cascaded over her shoulders, the pout of her lips, and her habit of lowering her eyelids with their fringe of fake lashes. The whole package was overtly sexual in a way that Betts, schooled in proper behavior at cotillion and by her own strict mother, couldn't pull off if she tried. She had tried and ended up looking as if she was going to a costume party.

Annabelle laughed at whatever Paul had said, pressing her fingertips against his hand, letting them rest there long enough for the gesture to turn from friendly to seductive.

Betts watched as Paul gave Annabelle a crooked smile. Betts knew that smile. "Annabelle's flirting with Paul too, Kiki, and he clearly doesn't mind, if that makes you feel better."

Kiki made a dismissive noise. "Betts, you can be absolutely certain that *you're* the last wife. You and Paul are a perfect team and you're both still having fun. Matthew and Jessica are great kids—adults, I should say—and doing so well. You and Paul make it look easy and Lord knows it isn't."

"Thank you." Kiki might have seen Betts' bright blue eyes darken if she hadn't been so caught up in her own drama. "Takes a lot of compromise. Knowing when to speak and what to say and when to keep your mouth shut."

"How many years have you been married?"

"Thirty." Betts was trim and attractive at fifty-three, but the years spent golfing, horseback riding, and gardening in the California sun had taken a toll on her skin. She kept herself up but wasn't the type to bother with cosmetic dermatology or plastic surgery.

"This isn't any of my business, but do you and Paul have a pre-nup?" Kiki asked. "I imagine your parents would have insisted, with your family money and all."

Betts came from old money, the solid kind—from land and transportation—and the quiet kind. The Ludlow family fortune entered the public eye through philanthropic largesse—a Ludlow Pavilion at Huntington Hospital, Ludlow buildings at Caltech, PCC, and USC, and Ludlow scholarships and fellowships.

Betts and Paul lived comfortably but not flashily in a well-maintained, hundred-year-old colonial home in Pasadena's Madison Heights neighborhood. Their biggest luxury was their Lake Tahoe compound, which was perfect for family get-togethers. Paul and Betts' pleasures were simple—spending time with family and friends and watching USC Trojan football from the longtime Ludlow family block of seats.

Betts' patient smile conveyed her answer to Kiki, who said, "Right. None of my business. I'm a nosy big-mouth and you're sweet to put up with me. Besides, you and Paul are indestructible."

Betts gazed at her husband and said quietly, "People change."

Kiki let the thread drop when she was again distracted—the party planner had stepped from the dining room and signaled to her.

"Time for dinner." Kiki downed the last of her martini, pulled an olive from a toothpick with her teeth, and dropped the toothpick into a potted fern. She began promenading, tapping her big diamond ring against the rim of the crystal glass to sound a chime as she announced, "Dinner is served in the dining room."

Betts beamed when her son, Matthew, came up and offered his arm. She took it and gave it a squeeze. "Where have you been?"

Matt looked like a younger version of his father. "Talking with Debbie." She was Paul's and Gary's longtime secretary. "Discussing the Carl Merton news."

"What news?"

"Didn't Dad tell you? Merton's being investigated by the SEC for fraud. He's suspected of running a Ponzi scheme."

Normally unflappable Betts gaped at her son. "What does that mean for Crown City Partners?"

"We could be investigated too, for money laundering."

"When did this come out?"

"Over a week ago. I'm surprised Dad didn't tell you. We also found out that Merton's ex-wife took out a restraining order against him. Rumor is he threatened to shoot her and her boyfriend."

Betts recovered her composure, stoically absorbing the bad news. She watched as Gary walked with Annabelle toward the house, guiding her with his hand on her waist which slipped down to caress one of her butt cheeks. The stolen gesture was brief but Betts saw it and so did Paul, who was walking behind them. He was focused so intently on Gary and Annabelle that he didn't notice his wife and son standing just inside the door.

Matt said, "Dad."

Paul turned. "There you are. And there's my bride." He gave Betts a kiss on the cheek. She responded with a chilly smile.

The Crown City Partners offices were on the sixth floor of a building on the corner of Lake and Green in downtown Pasadena. Betts had decorated the suite for the holidays with her usual panache. She encouraged the employees to add personal ornaments to a huge Scotch pine tree in the lobby. Fresh garland and twinkling lights were strung around the nest of cubicles and the office doorways. Tables in the lunchroom were laden with goodies sent from clients and vendors and Betts' homemade treats.

Gary and Matthew were in Paul's office, discussing the Carl Merton problem.

Paul was at his desk, which was adorned with silver-framed photos of his family and pets. On the credenza behind him was a collection of awards and commendations he'd received through the years.

Gary was sitting in one of the two leather guest chairs, drumming his hands against the arms. Matthew was leaning against a filing cabinet by a window.

"We need to act now to separate ourselves from Merton," Gary said. "Are we going to wait until the feds subpoena our books for crying out loud?"

In contrast with Gary's agitation, Paul was calm. "We have nothing to hide."

Gary stood and began pacing. "We can't afford a whiff of controversy. Our reputation is everything. Word about Merton's problems is out. John Barber and Tyler Williams called me about pulling their money out of Crown City over this. Both of them together amount to less than two million bucks. We can take that hit, but if more people bail out, especially some of our big guys, we could go belly up."

"Annabelle says that Merton had planned to go big into TechGen," Paul said. "Not having Merton's investment will sink TechGen's second round of funding."

"We'll find other investors," Matt said. "What else is Merton invested in?"

"He's got a couple of million in a few first-round deals," Paul said.

"We can cover paying him out," Gary said. "I'll break the news to Merton that we have to sever our business relationship, today if possible. He should understand our situation. If he doesn't, too bad."

"Make sure he doesn't have a gun with him." Matt looked out a glass panel beside the office door that gave a view of the cubicles where the associates worked. "What about Annabelle Hill? She's been with us for six months and hasn't brought in any clients other than Merton. Is she for real or is she a plant by Merton to launder his dirty money? I don't want to speak out of turn, but I can't help but wonder why you guys overlooked her sketchy resumé. Was it her great legs?"

Paul said, "I'm not making any apologies for hiring Annabelle. She's smart and capable and she brought in The Merton Group. If it wasn't for Carl Merton's investments, we would have had to lay off even more folks this year."

"Annabelle's a sweet kid," Gary said. "She's mortified about this Merton fiasco. She's worried about CCP and her own future. She just bought her first house."

"Did you see that brand new BMW convertible she's driving?" Matt asked. "That model sells for over a hundred thousand dollars. We're not paying her that much. Is Merton giving her kickbacks, or is their relationship even more personal?"

Paul and Gary looked at each other and said nothing.

After a minute, Gary said with conviction, "Annabelle's too close to Merton for comfort. We need to let our investors know that we've cut all ties with Merton. Annabelle's got to go. Let's give her three months' pay and call it a downsizing." He headed toward the door.

Paul raised a hand. "Hold on. I'm not convinced we need to go to extremes at this point and divest Merton's money and fire Annabelle too."

"When do we make a move, Paul?" Gary said. "When Merton's in prison? What if Merton throws us under the bus to get a deal for himself?"

"We haven't done anything illegal," Paul said.

"Tell that to the judge," Matt said.

"Firing somebody before Christmas is cruel," Paul said. "Feels a little vindictive to me."

Gary stared at Paul. "What are you getting at? You think I want to fire Annabelle because of a personal issue?"

"I'm just saying that the timing is cruel."

A mirthless smile spread across Gary's lips. "Have you been drinking Kiki's Kool-Aid? I am not having an affair with Annabelle or any woman. Sure I flirt with women. I *like* flirting with women. It doesn't mean anything. Kiki won't let it go. Her insecurity is oppressive. Look, my sole motive for firing Annabelle is this: I *need* Crown City to thrive, Paul. I'm not sitting on a mountain of family money and neither are any of our employees. People's livelihoods are at stake."

Matt watched his father from the corner.

The only response that Paul showed was a slight tightening around his eyes. His voice remained measured. "Of course I want Crown City to thrive, now and into the future. Why else did I bring my son into the firm?" He didn't touch the family money issue. Gary went down that path only during their worst disputes. Paul had grown up in an upper-middle-class family, but when he'd married Betts, he'd become rich and it still felt awkward to him. "Why don't we take a step back and let the situation breathe? We can certainly give it the weekend."

"No later than Monday." Gary left the office.

Once Gary had closed the door, Matt moved toward one of the chairs facing his dad's desk. "Have a minute?"

"For you, always. What's up?"

Matt hesitated before speaking. "Is there something going on that I don't know about? I've never seen you and Gary at each other's throats like this. We've never had any question of impropriety with the firm. Even things with Mom—I feel like something's off lately with everything."

Paul took a deep breath. The slight tension disappeared and he again conveyed being in control. "Everything's fine, Son. Sure, business has been tough. Tempers have been running high. Now there's this Merton thing. Your mom...Well, you know Mom. She always gets stressed out during the holidays. Does too much, trying to make everything nice for everyone else." He smiled. "We're all hanging in. Doing better than hanging in. Next year's going to be our best year ever."

Matt nodded but didn't seem convinced. "What about Gary and Annabelle? Sounded to me like he was protesting too much about not having an affair with her."

"I've known Gary for a long time and sometimes he doesn't think with the head that's on his neck. However, if he says he's not having an affair with Annabelle, I have to accept that as the truth. I can't put all the blame on him for hiring Annabelle without thoroughly vetting her and The Merton Group. She's an engaging, charming, and capable woman. I agreed with Gary that she'd be an asset to the firm. Still, I think it's wise to give it the weekend before making a big decision that will be damaging for her."

"I admire that about you, Dad. You always put other people first." Matt got up from the chair.

"Are you bringing your girl over for dinner on Sunday?"

"Absolutely. Right now, I'm going to the gym and try to clear my head. See you later."

"You can count on it. Close the door, please, when you leave. I have a couple of calls to make."

When Paul was alone, he sat back in his chair and rubbed his hand across his face. The strain that he'd tried to keep under control during the meeting returned to his eyes. He felt trapped by forces bigger than he, feelings that were foreign and deeply troubling to him.

Kiki opened one of the big doors of The Derby and was momentarily blinded when she stepped inside the dim restaurant from the bright glare of the hazy December day. She told a hostess behind a podium, "I'm just going to have a glass of wine at the bar. I have time to kill between appointments."

She walked past cabinets and walls full of horse racing memorabilia and entered the spacious cocktail lounge. It was quiet, as the horses weren't racing at Santa Anita racetrack. Only a few people were at the long bar and the cocktail tables.

Kiki's stretch leather jeans and snug gold-and-silver metallic top attracted the barflies' attention. She climbed onto a stool and looped a lock of blond hair around one ear, showing off a sparkly red earring in the shape of an old-fashioned Christmas tree light. She ordered a glass of champagne from a young, male bartender.

While the bartender was getting Kiki's drink, she glanced around. She stopped to squint at a couple at a table tucked into a corner. It was Betts Engleford with a man she didn't recognize. Plates on the table were pushed aside as if they'd finished having lunch. They were drinking coffee.

Kiki turned around and picked up her champagne. Intrigued, she leaned back for another glimpse. The man was tall with salt-and-pepper hair and looked to be in his fifties. They could have been having a business meeting except that Betts' and her companion's body language suggested something more intimate. They were sitting close together, engaged in intense conversation.

"What's Betts doing way out here? I've never even heard her mention The Derby," Kiki wondered aloud under her breath. She was here only because she'd had her Mercedes serviced at Rusnak and was early to meet her dressmaker, who lived in Monrovia. She risked another peek at the corner table. Her eyes widened when Betts' companion picked up Betts' hand and held it between both of his. Betts caressed his cheek with her free hand. For a second, Kiki thought they might kiss, but Betts returned her hands to her coffee cup.

Kiki's was still wide-eyed when she returned to her champagne. "Never in a million years—"

"Ma'am?" the bartender asked her.

"Oh. Nothing. Just talking to myself."

Kiki was debating whether to go over and say hello or to pay for her drink and slip out when Betts and her friend started to leave.

As Betts approached the bar, she saw Kiki. "Hi. What a surprise."

"Hi, Betts. This *is* a surprise." Kiki slid off the stool and she and Betts hugged. Kiki gave a big, expectant smile to the stranger. Up close, she saw that he was good-looking in a more rugged way than Paul. He was wearing slacks and a light blue dress shirt with no tie.

"What brings you out here?" Betts smoothed her hair.

The man said nothing and seemed a little amused as he looked from Kiki to Betts.

"I had my car serviced and I'm waiting for my dressmaker. She's fitting me for a killer dress I'm having made for the Valley Hunt Club New Year's Eve party."

"Oh. Nice." Betts pulled down the hem of her red-and-green tartan cardigan sweater. "Well—See you soon."

Kiki stepped in front of Betts. "And who did you have lunch with today?"

Betts appeared awkward, demeanor that Kiki rarely saw in her. "Oh. Of course. Ah, Forrest Curry, I'd like to present my friend Mrs. Kiki Sumner."

He held out his hand to Kiki. "I'm very happy to meet you."

"A pleasure. How—"

"I've gotta fly, honey." Betts started walking. "I'll call you."

Forrest nodded at Kiki, released her hand, and followed.

It was nearly noon on Monday and Annabelle Hill still hadn't shown up for work, even though Debbie had left a message that Paul wanted to see her in his office at nine.

Paul was trying to go over financial statements but was having a hard time concentrating. He had taken the weekend to decide what to do about Annabelle and announced to Gary and Matthew that he'd concluded that terminating her employment was best.

Gary gave a quick knock on Paul's open door before entering his office.

"You're back," Paul said. "How did it go with Merton?"

"It went, but not well. I met him at the Starbucks in the Paseo. Glad I did it in a public place. Handed him the check. He got back all his money and then some, but he still started yelling, saying he's not a criminal. Ending our relationship with him makes it look like he is... This is revenge. His face turned bright red and he's spitting all over me while he's talking. Everybody's looking." Gary raised his hands, happy to be out of the situation.

"What did you do?"

"I turned around and left. I started walking down Colorado Boulevard and he followed me. Get this. He yelled out, 'Did Annabelle put you and that partner of yours up to this? She's adding insult to injury?'"

The color drained from Paul's face.

Gary continued. "I'd had enough. I pointed at him, the sawed-off runt, and said, 'Carl, this conversation is over. You got your money back. I never want to see you around the Crown City Partners office or bothering any of our employees.' Like the little bully he is, he backed down. Just stood there, red-faced and sweating. I went to my car. I took a moment to calm down and then I called our investors who were troubled by the whole thing and told them we're no longer doing business with The Merton Group. They were happy to hear it."

Paul was silent for a few beats before realizing that Gary had stopped talking. "Definitely."

"Have you heard from Annabelle?"

Paul shook his head. "I called her house and cell phone. No answer. The documents and the check for her severance pay are ready. Maybe she had an appointment. Still, you'd think she would answer her cell. Maybe someone tipped her off about being terminated today."

"I can't imagine who. The only people who know are you, me, Matthew, and Debbie. She's kept bigger secrets than this."

"Don't know. I hope she's okay. Just looking for an explanation."

Gary studied Paul. "If you think I have one, buddy, I don't. I told you before, my relationship with her is purely business. If Annabelle won't come into the office, ask Debbie to send her a certified letter with her check. Let's have the key cards to the suite reprogrammed and notify building security not to let in either her or Merton. Good riddance to both of them."

Paul toyed with his Mont Blanc pen.

Gary clapped his hands. "How about some lunch?"

Paul slipped his pen inside his shirt pocket and pushed up from his chair. "Sounds great."

They left the office building on foot and headed toward Smitty's on the other side of Lake. While they were standing with other pedestrians waiting for the light to change, Gary said, "Uh oh."

Paul turned to see what had gotten Gary's attention and saw Carl Merton rapidly walking toward them.

"Let's go." Gary grabbed Paul's arm and started pulling him back toward the office building.

The streetlight changed. The other pedestrians, seeing a situation brewing, quickly moved on. When Merton pulled a pistol from a pocket of his jacket, panic erupted.

Someone shouted, "He's got a gun!"

Gary had nearly reached the glass doors into the building lobby with Paul on his heels when a bullet hit the window of a ground floor yoga salon. There were more gunshots. Gary opened one of the doors, threw himself onto the ground, and shimmied for cover behind the lobby furniture. People were running wildly in the building and on the street.

Gary peeked from behind a couch to see Paul on the ground outside the door. Merton came up to him, holding his gun out. Paul put his hands up and crouched to get away from Merton but there was nowhere to go. Gary heard Paul pleading for his life.

Merton bared his teeth, spewing words that Gary couldn't make out. Gary bolted up and shouted to distract Merton, but it was useless. Merton fired several shots into Paul, shattering the glass behind him. Paul lay still.

Merton looked inside the lobby and saw Gary duck behind the couch. Merton didn't shoot at him, but turned and headed down the stairs to the now empty sidewalk and nearly empty street.

Police cars sped to the scene with lights and sirens. Cops with guns drawn, using their cars for cover, shouted at Merton to throw down his weapon and drop to the ground. After a moment's hesitation, he complied. He was quickly pushed face-down against the pavement and handcuffed.

Gary returned to his fallen friend in time to hear his last words. "Tell Betts I'm sorry."

Betts had heard about the shooting in downtown Pasadena by the time Matthew, Gary, and Kiki knocked at her front door. When she learned that Paul had been killed, she collapsed.

Police found Annabelle Hill on the floor of the master bedroom of her home in Bungalow Heaven, dead from gunshot wounds. Scattered around her body were photographs of Annabelle and Paul in compromising and shocking positions.

A year later, Betts and her children honored the one-year anniversary of Paul's murder. The following week, Betts treated herself to lunch at the Langham Hotel's poolside café. It was a mild December afternoon. Visitors there relished the California winter sun. The locals never tired of it.

Betts poured more Darjeeling tea from a small porcelain pot into her cup.

It had taken months and the help of a psychotherapist for Betts to stop blaming herself for Paul's and Annabelle's murders. She'd finally accepted that, regardless of her role in the circumstances that had led to the tragic events, Carl Merton was the one who had pulled the trigger.

She also stopped regretting asking her old college buddy, Forrest Curry, to have his investigation firm look into her suspicions that, Paul, who had uncharacteristically started taking long lunches and not coming home right after work, was having an affair.

She'd expected her marriage to change after Matthew and Jessica were on their own and had moved out for good. Steadfast Paul had never wavered during their marriage. He'd never even engaged in a serious flirtation. As for Betts—having an affair wasn't in her vernacular. When she sniffed that Paul might be up to something, she wasn't completely surprised and wrote the fling with Annabelle off to a mid-life crisis. Still, it had to end.

When she confronted Paul with the sordid photographs that Forrest's associates had taken, Paul gave Betts the shock of her life.

"I want a divorce," he'd told her. "Annabelle and I are getting married."

It came out that Annabelle had ended her longtime romance with Carl Merton to take up with Paul. She was moving up in the world, going from a skillful con artist to a wealthy and successful pillar of society, earning an entrée into the Pasadena private-club set.

Betts taunted Paul with what Forrest had found out. "Annabelle threw herself at you only because she wanted to use you as a patsy to bring Carl Merton and his dirty money into Crown City Partners."

Paul had again shocked her. "I know. That's how it started with Annabelle, but then we fell in love."

"*Love?* Are you out of your mind? You really think she *loves* you?" Betts had to sit down. Her head was spinning.

She had long taken care of life's details, creating a peaceful and happy home for her husband and children, setting up a barrier around them so they could flourish. When anything threatened to tarnish the family, she took care of that, too. She'd become adept at covering Paul's business and personal gaffes. He could be hopelessly naive. His affair with Annabelle had put everything at stake—their marriage, the business Paul and Gary had built, and the family name. Who knew how it would end up? But for the first time in many years, Betts couldn't do what she knew in her heart needed to be done. She didn't have the guts to take the next step.

"Hello, there." Forrest Curry pulled out a chair at Betts' table and sat down.

"Good afternoon." After a pause, Betts spontaneously leaned over and gave him a long kiss on the lips. It drew the attention of people nearby but for once, Betts didn't care if she looked unseemly.

When they parted, Betts giggled and rubbed her fingers against her smeared lipstick.

"Wow," Forrest said. "I've waited a long time for that."

"It's been a year since Paul's murder."

He picked up her hand and kissed her palm. "An acceptable mourning period. But I'm talking about the thirty years I've waited for you since your mother made you break up with me in college. I wasn't acceptable in Sarah's eyes. She pushed you to marry Paul."

"Ah, yes. Mother."

"She won't be happy that you're with—What did she call me, 'that rascal'?"

Betts knew her mother had been right back then. Paul was better marriage material than adventurous Forrest. Her marriage with Paul had been stable and productive if not exciting. When Paul wouldn't listen to reason and end his relationship with Annabelle, Betts had turned to her eighty-two-year-old mother for advice.

"Actions have consequences," Sarah Ludlow reminded her. She'd asked Betts for the damning photos of Paul and Annabelle. When the police asked Mrs. Ludlow how the photos ended up in Carl Merton's mailbox, she pulled herself erect and told them she did what she had to do.

Betts' friend Kiki liked to joke about being the last wife, but for Kiki, it was about money. Maybe because Betts had always had money, it had never been a motivation for her. It was a question of honor, legacy, and doing the right thing for the family. She was Sarah Ludlow's daughter, after all, but it had taken her mother, a last wife, to ensure that Betts followed in her footsteps.

"Mother's already guessed about you and me," Betts said.

"And?"

"She says it's a good time for a rascal in my life."

"Glad to know she likes a happy ending."

"She does." Betts added with a wink. "And a rock-solid pre-nup."

Margaret Finnegan

Genius Unleashed

THE USUAL GENIUSES HAD red and blue first-place ribbons on their science fair boards. The usual geniuses themselves stood in front of these testimonies to their brilliance and wore the nonchalant confidence of the high achieving.

Willie, not being a usual genius, did not have a ribbon on his board. Like the rest of the rabble, he stood by his project in lonely silence. Occasionally, he pulled at the too-large tie his mother made him wear and, when he thought no one was watching, gazed at passing girls.

The mother of a boy he'd played with in elementary school came up to him. "Willie! Look how big you've grown. I wouldn't have known you but for the name on your board."

"Hello, Mrs. Kleeve."

"Don't you love the science fair? What's your project? Show me."

Willie pointed to a box standing on a table. The box was full of sand. In one corner there was a pool of water, and, in another corner, there were some plants that looked like corn. In a third corner, an earth-colored blob kept banging against the side of the box.

Mrs. Kleeve crinkled her brow in the good-natured way that mothers of usual geniuses do. "Hmm. What have we here?"

Willie fiddled with the knot of his tie and looked down at his shoes. It took all his strength not to melt away like ice cream. It was just so embarrassing. His project was so simplistic; he saw that now. It was something a kindergartner could have done. No wonder he hadn't won anything. "It's a carbon-based life form," he said.

Mrs. Kleeve bent down and took a closer look at the blob. "Really? I haven't seen one of these in ages. Very unpredictable, aren't they? Still, there's always something to be learned from them. What's your question?"

"Given self-awareness and knowledge of its own impermanence, what will a carbon-based life form do?"

"And your conclusion?"

"Bang constantly against the side of a box."

Mrs. Kleeve straightened up and laughed. Willie felt his face grow hot. "Like I said," she said, "very unpredictable. Well, it was nice seeing you, Willie. You should come visit Howard sometime. I'm sure he'd love that."

Willie watched her walk over to Howard and his red-and-blue-ribboned board. God, he hated Howard. God, he hated everything to do with Howard, including his mother and his ribbon and his stupid self-contained expandable galaxy.

He looked over at his blob and frowned. He flicked the side of the box and sent a tremor running through it. The blob froze and then fell to the ground and gnashed its little teeth. Jeez. These were the stupidest life forms ever.

Mary Ellen Dilbeck slid up beside him. He felt her long hair graze his back. Willie liked Mary Ellen. She wasn't a usual genius for one thing. She was just a normal girl—normal, not ugly, and nice to him, which was a pretty much unbeatable combination. Plus, her breath smelled like the Red Hots she always sucked on. It made him a little dizzy, but he liked it.

"You see Howard Kleeve's board," she whispered with a roll of the eyes.

Willie shook his head.

"It's covered with equations and twelve-syllable words. He's so full of himself. And, of course, he's advancing to State. Ten bucks say Bello nominated Kleeve before he even saw his board. I say, if no one can pronounce some loser dude's title, the dude definitely shouldn't win anything."

Willie nodded. He tried to think of something clever to say, but all he came up with was, "Totally."

"What'd you do?" he added.

Mary Ellen pulled out the wand of her lip gloss and applied it without even looking. "Something lame," she said. "How about you?"

He pointed to the box. "Carbon-based life form."

She bent down and peered inside. "Ah—it's so cute. Biped. That's advanced."

Willie bent down next to her. "Not advanced enough. Bello gave me a fricking

B-."

Mary Ellen rolled her eyes again. "Mr. Bello is such a prick. I like your biped."

"Really?"

"Really." She put her hand in the box and picked up the blob— then she dropped it. "Gross. It peed on me."

"It's got issues."

"Why?"

"It has self-awareness and knowledge of its own impermanence."

Mary Ellen stood up. Her mouth was wide open and her face was turning kind of purple, and it wasn't a good purple. It was a bad purple, a judging purple, the kind of purple girls faces turned when teachers gave them bad grades and were forevermore cursed as evil.

"That's so mean," Mary Ellen said. "It's scared." She ran a finger across the back of the blob. "Poor thing."

"Just because it's self-aware doesn't mean it has feelings," said Willie, sounding sulky when he meant to sound funny. He smiled at Mary Ellen to try to make her understand, but that just made her purple face shine neon.

"It may not have feelings like we do, but it still has some sort of emotions."

Now it was Willie's turn to roll his eyes. "I doubt it," he said, which was exactly the moment he knew he had truly blown it.

Mary Ellen's mouth dropped even wider, and then she just walked away, just straight away, sending her long hair rustling in outrage.

Willie banged his head against the table. Then he banged it again and again. When he stood up his friend Martin was staring at his blob. "Dude," said Martin. "Why is your carbon-based life form humping the box?"

Willie looked over at the blob. He nodded. "Ahhhhh."

That night, even though the science fair was over and Willie was stuck with the fricking B-, he started to make another blob. His mother said, "What are you doing? You haven't even finished your math homework."

"It won't take long," said Willie.

"It better not. Math matters, you know. Math gives you options. Universities look at math grades more than anything else. Howard Kleeve is being recruited by top-tier schools—and he's fourteen."

Willie grunted.

"And you know why?" said his mother. "Because he's good at math, and he works hard. His mother told me he spends four hours a night studying math."

"Blah, blah, blah," heard Willie. "Blah, blah, blah. Howard ass-kissing Kleeve. Blah, blah, blah."

Willie took his carbon polymer clay and rolled it in his hands until it became warm and the brown mixture began to stick to his hands. Then, with his fingers, he formed the clay into another biped blob, a little smaller this time, about the size of his fist. The blob yawned, as if awakened from a long dream, and it stretched out its pudgy limbs. Willie gave it self awareness and knowledge of its own impermanence and watched as little drops of salt water leaked out of its eyes.

He deposited the new blob on the other side of the box from the old blob and let them eye each other from across the distance.

Sometime later, after Willie finished his homework and watched a little TV, he went back to the basement to check on the blobs. Right away, he could tell something was wrong. Something red was smeared all over the sand. The pool of water was tinted pink, and the new blob lay floating on top of it, dead.

"No," sighed Willie. He picked up the new blob between his thumb and forefinger and placed it face up in the sand. Its skin had gone gray, and its eyes looked like glass, and even though it was just a blob, Willie felt his skin crawl.

Then it dawned on him: Where was the other blob? His eyes followed the smear of red back to the old blob's corner, but the blob wasn't there. No, the blob wasn't there at all, but a little way down— toward the corn—there was more red. Willie's eyes followed the color to a barely vibrating quiver of corn stalks. He pushed aside the plants. There was the blob, trembling and leaking salt water and making strange, soft, guttural sounds.

"What did you do?" whispered Willie. "You killed it."

The blob trembled and leaked, trembled and leaked.

Well, this is ridiculous, thought Willie. These blobs are the worst blobs ever. Clearly, they can't handle any advanced psychological variables. Clearly, advanced psychological variables make the blobs go fricking nuts. That's what he should have told Mr. Bello. That's what he should have written on the board. Jeez. What fricking messes these blobs were. No wonder no one ever experimented with them anymore.

Enough was enough. This experiment was over. Willie picked up the smooth stone used as the basement doorstop and prepared to smash the blob. He lifted the stone high above his head. With a thud it hit the sand, sending grainy particles sailing in all directions. But the blob had moved. It had eluded the stone and now the blob was on its feet, running from side to side, tripping in the sand and standing up again and running some more. Its moan morphed into a shrill scream.

Willie watched the blob, its panicked arms flailing. He put the stone back by the door and regarded the blob some more. It was over at the wall now, pounding, pressing, jumping, looking for some means of escape.

Willie stood transfixed. He had never seen anything so pathetically desperate and frantic. Frankly, it freaked him out and made him want to eat pudding or ice cream. He'd even settle for stale, store-bought cookies. Didn't he have some stale, store-bought cookies? Hadn't he seen some in the cupboard? He would check it out. He would look for the cookies, eat them all, and then come back and kill the blob. Or maybe he would just kill the blob in the morning when it had calmed down. Absolutely. That was a much better plan. He would kill the blob in the morning. Decided, he turned off the basement light and left the screaming blob in the dark.

Willie did not kill the blob in the morning. He slept in and his mom woke him yelling, "Hurry up! You'll be late! Blah, blah, blah." After school he had marching band and homework. Plus, he had a couple of big tests to study for. So it was three days before he had time to deal with the blob. Even then, it was sort of an afterthought. He was looking for his gym shoes and went down to the basement to see if they were there.

They weren't. It almost seemed like the blob had been waiting for him. It fell down on its knees and started rocking back and forth. Willie bent his face toward the blob. The blob fell prostrate onto the sand.

"At least you've calmed down," said Willie.

Willie almost had to laugh. These carbon-based life forms. Too funny.

"Okay, little guy," said Willie. "If it's that important to you. But you can't be this pathetic. That's just sad."

Willie looked at the blob and thought. "How about this?" he said. He put his hand on the blob and pinched off a bit of clay. He rolled it in his hand, spit on it, added some more clay, and worked with it until he had another blob. This time, when the new blob began to leak salt water, Willie put the new blob down right next to the first blob and stroked its head, gently.

When the first blob lifted its stubby arms to attack the new blob,

Willie made a barrier with his hand. Then he stroked both blobs on the top of their heads. The old blob made another move to attack. Willie made another barrier with his hand and then stroked both heads.

The new blob toddled over to the old blob. It put its hand on the old blob's head and stroked it. The old blob froze. Little bumps popped up from its skin. It stepped back, confused. Then, tentatively, it took small, crouching steps toward the new blob. It ran a stubby hand on the new blob's waist. It brought its stubby nose close to the new blob and smelled. It ran its nose over the surface of the blob and something seemed to click in the old blob, something seemed to happen, and the blob ran faster and faster in circles around the new blob, touching and smelling it, until, suddenly, the old blob fell to its knees and wrapped its arms around the new blob, contented.

"All right," said Willie with satisfaction. "There you go." And he turned off the light and went in search of his shoes.

A week later, Willie checked in on the blobs. A third blob was now in the box.

"Cool," whispered Willie.

"No way," said Martin when Willie told him. "You made a reproducible carbon-based life form? That's, like, really hard. You should have done that for your science fair project."

"I know," said Willie. "Even Bello would have to give me an A for that."

"Bello's head would explode for that."

By lunch, Willie was a god. Everybody knew about his reproducing blobs. Everybody knew what an amazing thing he had done and what a usual genius he actually was. Everybody wanted to come see the reproducing blobs, but Willie's mother would have none of it.

"I don't want a bunch of kids, blah, blah, blah, blah, blah," she said.

Still, Martin came, and then a few other kids came, so at least people knew that Willie wasn't making things up. He really had done something cool. He really did deserve everyone's praise.

Well, everyone's praise but Mary Ellen Dilbeck's. Mary Ellen did not praise Willie. Mary Ellen wouldn't even talk to Willie.

"She still thinks you're mean," said Martin. "She's telling everyone that it's bad enough to give one blob self-awareness and knowledge of its own impermanence, but to give it to a whole species is just evil."

"Species? It's three blobs."

Within weeks, however, it wasn't three blobs. It was seventy-five blobs. Then ninety-two blobs. Then one hundred and twenty blobs. With each passing day there were more and more blobs. Blobs filled the box. More than that, they wreaked havoc on the box and on each other. They fought over water. They fought over corn. They fought over blobs, over even the fricking sand, which was everywhere, which was worthless.

Willie would enter the room. He'd turn on the light. His shadow would pass over them. Only then would they stop their reproducing, their fighting, their weeping of salty tears and gnashing of tiny teeth. Only then would they still themselves and begin to tremble and bow, tremble and bow. Only then would there be peace. But then Willie would turn around, his shadow would lift, and wham!—the blobs would go fricking nuts all over again.

"Unpredictable." That's what Mrs. Kleeve had called them, and that's what they were. That's exactly what they were. But that was just the beginning. The blobs were dangerous. They were greedy and self-ish. Yes, true, sometimes Willie witnessed intimate gestures of love and kindness. Mothers cradled babies. Strangers shared food, but that was nothing, that was incomparable to the constant grief they bestowed on one another. They beat each other for corn. They murdered for sand— fricking sand! They were obsessed with their own survival. It was as if they thought they were some valuable commodity, some precious gift, when they were a fricking science project. And not even a good science project—a B- science project.

It was enough to make Willie want to destroy the lot of them. "I mean, I don't even like them anymore," Willie told Martin. "They're totally annoying, and they take so much time. Every day I'm in there building onto the box, throwing them loaves of bread that they just fight over."

"Then get rid of them. They're just blobs."

Willie sighed. He knew. He knew they were just blobs. He knew they were just ephemeral short-lived whispers. But they depended on him. "If I adopt a dog," said Willie. "I can't just take it back to the pound if it pees on my carpet."

"Sure you can," said Martin. "People do it all the time."

"I made the blobs," said Willie. "I'm responsible for the blobs."

Martin shrugged. "Whatever."

Willie's mother was less easygoing. "Those blobs have to go," she told him. "They are stinking up the basement. I'm telling you, they smell. It's disgusting down there."

"Carbon-based life forms have simple excretory systems. It's their physiology," explained Willie.

"There are excretory systems and there is putrescence. Those blobs are putrescent. I want them out of the basement."

"They've got to live somewhere."

"Why? Why do they have to live somewhere? This was a science fair project. The science fair is over. And—since we are on the sub-ject—let me say this. They take too much time. Do you think Howard Kleeve is spending all his hours babysitting carbon-based life forms? No. Howard Kleeve is studying math. Blobs are not going to get you into a good college, Willie."

"Blah, blah, blah, blah, blah, blah." Just fricking shut up already, thought Willie.

"Out of the basement, Willie. Out of the house."

"Okay. Okay." Jeez. Like he needed this too.

He went down to the basement. He stared down at the blobs. He watched as they stopped what they were doing. He watched as they trembled and bowed.

"What am I going to do with you?" he said. "You're a lot a trouble, you know that?" Then he picked up some screaming baby blob covered in sand and shit and handed it to its screaming mother looking for it in the cornfield.

At school now, Willie did nothing but worry about the blobs. He couldn't kill them, but he couldn't just let them spread their nasty pink blood everywhere either. And now he had to get them out of the basement too. Where the hell was he going to put these stupid blobs? What the hell was he going to do? It was too much. It was too much for one boy to deal with. At lunch, he dropped his head onto his lunch bag and kept it there even when his neck began to hurt.

The smell of Red Hots made him look up. There sat Mary Ellen. Right next to him. She didn't look at him. Instead, she stared across the lunchroom. With a placid face that belied her biting voice, she said, "I hear you've got over three hundred of those blobs now. It's not right, you know."

He dropped his head back onto his lunch bag and felt his stomach sink down to his knees. "I know."

"You should do something."

He looked up to find her green eyes locked on his. "I don't know what to do."

"You've got to destroy them. That's all you can do. With the knowledge you've given them, they must be constantly suffering. They must be constantly miserable. No primitive life form can live like that. They'll go mad. They'll kill each other."

Willie gave her a shifty-eyed glance and looked back down.

"Oh. So they've gone mad already. Well, you really messed up, didn't you?"

Willie nodded. "I can't destroy them," he said. "They want to live. They're so scared. They're so afraid. All the time they're afraid."

"That's why you have to destroy them."

"No," said Willie. "There has to be another way."

Mary Ellen stared out across the lunchroom again. "I used to like you."

The stomach in Willie's knees dropped down to his toes, leaving an enormous black void in his entire body. "I'll fix it," he muttered.

Mary Ellen walked away.

If only there was a way to fix it, he thought.

When Willie got home the blobs were in full-scale revolt. The ones by the pool of water were throwing stones at a group wearing corn-silk necklaces. They didn't even stop when Willie looked down at them. They didn't even stop when he bent so close that he could see the blush on their cheeks and the gleam of their gnashing teeth. "Stop," he said. But they didn't stop. "Stop," he said again, this time shaking the box with his hands so that the blobs all fell over. And they did stop. They stopped and looked up at Willie. They stopped and started to tremble and bow, but then one of the blobs stabbed a sharp stick into another. Blood squirted like water from a toy gun. It splattered the blob with the stick, and the blobs raged and screamed and attacked one another once more.

Willie fell back. He shook his head. He squinted and rubbed the back of his neck with his hand. "I don't know what to do," he whimpered. "Someone tell me what to do."

Willie's mother found him in the basement, slouched in a corner staring up at the box, his fingers pulling hard on his hair.

"What's this about?" she asked in a voice she didn't use much anymore, a voice she'd used more when Willie was small, when everything she said didn't sound like blah, blah, blah, blah, blah.

He nodded at the blobs. "I don't know what to do with them. I created them. I owe them, but they're so—unpredictable."

"It's not like they have real feelings," she said gently.

He twisted his neck back and forth and his face contorted in pain. "They have feelings," he said. "They suffer. They want to live."

She went and peered into the box. Her nose twitched and the corners of her mouth pulled down in revulsion. She looked at Willie. "Do you want me to take care of this for you?"

He looked closely at his mother. He remembered when she did things for him. He remembered when he trusted her for everything. "Don't kill them," he whispered.

She straightened her back and crossed her arms. "Leave it to me."

He tilted his head. Not sure he wanted an answer, he stuttered,

"Wh-what will you do?"

"Remember the farm we took Blackie to when we couldn't take care of him anymore? They take mistakes like this too. It's a nice place. They'll be happy there. Like Blackie."

Willie felt his soul shrink inside him, and he nodded.

He was watching television and eating his second bowl of ice cream when she came home. She had a sort of sweaty, windblown look about her, and her shoes were covered in mud. He watched her pull them off one by one and drop them by the front door. Then he looked back at the TV, which was showing people in a house. The people, he couldn't place them, but they were talking and their words seemed hollow, far away, like in a fever.

She came and sat next to him, and when she did, she reached over, gave his thigh two quick pats, and then started laughing and nodding at the TV. He heard her, but he didn't. It was like the TV. So far away. He felt tears collect around his eyes, and he was so afraid they would leak out, so he blinked them back and stared hard at the people. Yes. He recognized them now. They were the funny people. The people he liked. The people who made him laugh. He took a bite of ice cream. Of course. He could tell now. He could tell what the funny people were saying. They were saying funny things. Very funny things. He would think about the funny things. He would laugh at the funny things. Like her. He would laugh, and she would laugh, and he would eat another bowl of ice cream. And that's how he would do this. For as long as it took. And it wouldn't take long. After all, they were just blobs.

Dennis Fulgoni

Thunder

Three Sundays in a row, bikers park in the cul-de-sac behind our apartment complex in South Pasadena—revving engines, laughing, cursing. Backfire explodes up Fair Oaks, echoes like M-80s off our window.

Sandy cradles our son in the middle of the living room. His eyes are like the black sides of Othello disks, the pupils nearly eclipsing the irises. He clutches the collar of her blouse with little hands. "I can't take it anymore," she says.

"Try to relax," I say, although my pinky twitches like a caught fish.

I lean back on the futon, read the paper. It's difficult to concentrate, but there's a feature in the travel section of the *Pasadena Star-News* about Chile, a place I've always wanted to go. A panoramic photograph, blue hills shrouded in mist. For a moment I'm there—wind on my face, sun on my back, gravel under my boots. I hike into the hills, disappear.

I wrote a poem about Chile once. It landed in a small literary journal. No payment, just copies. Still.

Sandy jostles Ene up and down on her hip. She's in sync with the sounds of the engines: boom, jostle, boom, jostle, boom.

"Sit down," I say. "You're scaring him."

"Maybe if you'd get off your butt and do something about it."

Sandy moves closer to the window. She does this cautiously, as if she were peering over the railing of a tall bridge. She narrows her eyes, cocks her jaw. It's a look she has more and more lately. Instinct says stay clear. But we live in a single apartment—living room crowded with futon and crib, small kitchen with zero counter space, even smaller bath (shower, no tub)—and there's really nowhere to go.

"They're having a picnic down there," she says.

I watch her over the top of the paper.

"Blankets under the jacarandas."

We'd thought about having picnics under those jacarandas. But with the kid, and packing everything up, it just seems like too much trouble. The trees are amazing though. Fair Oaks is lined with them. In spring, they produce purple flowers so opulent they look photoshopped. The trunks are gnarled and dark. Woody pods hang from the branches. I used to sit at the kitchen table and stare at them while I waited for poetic inspiration. They never inspired much, but they were a nice distraction.

"They're eating sandwiches," Sandy says, her voice sharp. Clearly sandwiches are the last straw.

She walks into the kitchen and stands by the table. It has a white mountain of student essays—setting as character in *To Kill a Mockingbird*—I've neglected all weekend. Whenever I sit down to grade, or write something of my own, Ene goes wild. It's nearly impossible to concentrate.

Sandy shuffles around the kitchen, tries to stay in motion. Sometimes this helps. She gathers the baby blanket over Ene's head. He squirms like an insect trying to escape a cocoon. He tilts his head back, wails.

"We should call the police," Sandy says. She kisses Ene on the forehead, then pulls him closer, the fat on her arms bunching. "It's okay, baby," she whispers.

She isn't going to call the police, and neither am I. We called them a few months back, when we first moved in, because a Russian couple in the unit downstairs got into a knock-down fight—screaming, breaking, the unmistakable sound of fist-to-flesh. The police showed up after the fight and the tires on my Kia were slashed the next morning. I missed a day of work over it, and was out two hundred dollars.

The revving and backfire grow louder. A wrecking ball pounds the walls. Sandy still paces, still bounces. Ene's a delicate child, spooks easily. Even in the womb he seemed frightened. In each ultrasound, right up to the ninth month, he crossed his arms over his face so that we couldn't make out his features. Back then, he was just a faceless apparition haunting the hollow pit of my wife's uterus. Now he's live and loud, ceaselessly hot and howling. Two, three, four o'clock in the morning, he's up and kicking, screaming.

Sandy stops pacing. "Take him," she says. "I'm tired."

Rather than hand Ene over, she sets him in the crib. It sits a few feet from the futon. As with everything in our apartment, the crib is over-large. It's like one of those lion cages at the circus. Ene stares at me, his face scrunched like a pug. I brace myself for one of his ear-piercing wails. He lets loose and it's worse than I expected: a hot wire dances in my ear and my brain bursts into flames. I stand up, walk over to the crib.

"Hey," I say. "Hey, Ene. Bene. Penne. Touché." I pat his head. He begins kicking his feet on the floor of the crib. The crib shakes, and I grip the railing till the veins in my hands jump out.

I walk across the living room and look out the window—a bird's eye view from our second-story apartment—to see the bikers for myself. I did the same thing the last two Sundays, but this time they've camped even closer to our building, and I have a better view. There's nothing special about them: black shiny helmets, leather jackets, torn jeans. Two men, two women. One guy is tall with a blond ponytail. He's holding a bottle of beer. He stands legs apart, cocksure. The leader. He tilts the bottle back and takes a long pull. It's not even noon, and I know this means trouble. Everything on the other guy is short—legs, arms, hair. He has tattoos all over his arms. He's the one making all the noise. He revs his engine, turns it off, fiddles with it a bit, revs it again. Even the way he sits on the bike—back arched, boot playing at the chrome gear shift, chin raised in defiance—screams dickhead. He's wearing silver sunglasses that wrap around his face. He looks like a bug.

One of the women is heroin-addict skinny and has sleek red hair long as a peacock's tail. She wears a T-shirt with block lettering I can't read from up here. The other woman has jet black hair and skin like bleached linen. She appears pretty, but I can't tell from this distance.

It's hard to believe the bikers have chosen our neighborhood. South Pasadena is a small suburb with Craftsman houses and a few apartment complexes. Just a few blocks east, in San Marino, sits some of the most expensive real estate in Los Angeles County. The floats from the Rose Parade slide right down our street on their way to the Rose Bowl in the weeks just before New Year's. There's a Starbucks down the street, and a Kinko's copy where I mail off my poems to literary journals every month and photocopy my lesson plans.

Not exactly biker territory.

It's not the best neighborhood I've ever lived in—I grew up on Hill Drive in Eagle Rock, where most of the houses were three stories and the streets were wide enough for touch football games with my friends—but it's not the worst, either. Before we married, Sandy and I lived in a loft in downtown Los Angeles. Runaway teenagers fell asleep on the sidewalk outside our window, and the air, for some unknown reason, always smelled like burnt flesh. I was taking seminars in poetry back then, writing so much my hand would cramp, and I seldom noticed. With Sandy's pregnancy we decided some changes were in order. We needed a better neighborhood. I needed a more stable occupation.

I stand at the window another minute, watching the bikers. Sandy wants me go down to the cul-de-sac and tell the bikers to leave. I've seen the documentaries on the Hell's Angels, the spilled blood and broken bones; they can deliver some serious hurt.

As if it might solve something, I drop the blinds, and the sound is startling. Rattlesnake in the bushes. The light in the room dims. Ene stops crying, a moment of reprieve. Sandy walks over, stands beside me, and takes my hand. The gesture surprises me, although I don't let on. It feels nice to touch her. Her hand is deep and warm and, for a minute, I'm back at the café we walked to after our first night together, four years ago: Sunday morning, light cutting through the window, warm coffee in our hands. Floating.

We watch the darkened window together for a time. Having our view of the bikers blocked makes their noises seem louder. I'm reminded of Carlos, a student of mine who's blind, and how he can always identify me outside of class—in the lunch area, say, or in front of the school—by the sound of my voice.

One of the bikers yells, "You're goddamn right!" The engine backfires again, and Sandy squeezes my hand so hard my knuckles crack.

Ene starts up again. Then his tears turn into spasms of coughing. After a time, he goes quiet and just sits there, blinking at us.

Sandy and I move over to the futon and sit down. She leans into me. I put my arms around her waist. It's amazing how much weight she's gained since the pregnancy. Her body is soft, nearly gelatinous. I try not to notice and certainly never say anything, but compared to photographs taken only two years ago—Sandy wearing a skimpy silver dress in Vegas as she holds up the two-thousand-dollar winnings of a royal flush on video poker; in a tie-dyed halter top, her tan midriff flashing as she rides her beach cruiser along the crowded paths at Malibu—she's almost unrecognizable. She nuzzles her head into my shoulder. My whole body begins to relax.

I lift my hand, look at my finger. It's steady and still. A little wetness seeps onto my shoulder, and I realize Sandy's crying. I try to remember the last time I held her while she cried, but can't. I feel annoyed by her tears, and want to move past them, get back to that floating feeling.

"It'll be fine," I say.

"No it won't."

"They'll leave soon."

"They'll be back."

"They're not breaking the law."

"Noise pollution isn't against the law?"

I run my hand along her arm, try to soothe her. "Let's put on the TV for noise."

"I don't want to watch TV."

"Let's just get the hell out of here then, go to the mall or something."

"Ene's exhausted. I'm exhausted. This is our home. We shouldn't have to leave."

"Tell me what you want then."

"Quiet. Peace and quiet."

"I want that, too."

"Do you?"

"You think I like this?" I point to the window.

Sandy inches away from me on the futon. "You must not hate it the way I do. Or else…"

"Or else what?"

"Never mind."

I look over at Ene's crib. He reaches up and wraps his fat little fingers around the bars.

"Sunday morning," Sandy says, wiping her eyes on her T-shirt. "The day of rest. What the hell's wrong with people?"

I certainly don't know what's wrong with people. I don't even know what's wrong with me. Why can't I be the kind of guy to go down and tell the bikers to leave? Why do I have to consider things from every angle? Why can't I just act?

Sandy puts her head in her hands and cries some more and then suddenly she's not crying but laughing. Her laughter is enormous, fills the room like a bright idea.

She used to do the same thing when she was pregnant: laugh and then cry, cry and then laugh. The unpredictability of her emotions during the pregnancy frightened me, although I never let on that it did.

"What's so funny?" I say, hoping to focus on the laughter, force it to the top.

"Nothing."

I give her arm a squeeze. "Tell me."

"I can't stop thinking about this stupid thing that happened at work one time."

I hadn't heard a story about Sandy's work in quite a while. I used to love them.

"Come on," I say, anxious for the distraction.

"I don't feel like telling stories."

I lean in, lay my hand on her knee.

"All right. Barbie doll heads," Sandy says, laughing harder.

"Barbie doll heads?"

"This guy came in to the E.R. once with Barbie doll heads in his stomach."

The story is vaguely familiar, like she's told it before. But even if it's a repeat, it's a relief to be focusing on something remote and humorous.

"He swallowed them, obviously," Sandy says, looking me square in the eye. Her eyes are moist and filmy from the crying. "And do you know why? Sex."

"Sex?" The word comes out of my mouth quick. It used to seep out slowly, the elongation of that middle vowel. Now it's all about the consonants, the sharp edges, the staccato.

"He liked to masturbate as he passed them. Said it was like giving birth."

"Fuck," I say, and just like that, we're both nearly doubled over with laughter.

"Only a man would equate childbirth and orgasm," Sandy says. "He was wearing a Harley shirt. That's what made me think of it, I guess."

Our laughter has made Ene happy too; he flashes a fleshy, toothless grin. His eyes are wide and happy, and I feel happy for him. I'm about to walk across the room and pick him up and bring him back over to the futon. But then I remember something, and I feel almost embarrassed saying it.

"*Grey's Anatomy!*"

"What?" Sandy stops laughing, pushes the hair back from her eyes.

"I saw that on an episode of *Grey's Anatomy*, honey, like six months ago."

"What are you talking about?" Sandy says. "That's my story!"

I'm about to tell her that it could happen to anyone, the lines between media and reality fusing in phantasmagoric mayhem these days; or that maybe somebody else from her work has a girlfriend or boyfriend that writes for TV and indeed it was her story that I saw on television; hell, every strange bit of trivia seems to be gobbled up and regurgitated quicker than you can say copyright these days. But before I can say any of that, the Harleys start up again—Crack! Crack! Crack!—and Ene falls back; he looks jolted, as if he's just been blessed on the forehead by some crazy evangelical minister at a tent revival.

Sandy stands, moves across the room. She lifts Ene into her arms.

"I'll go tell those bastards to leave myself!" she says, and I know as soon as she says it that I can't let it happen.

"All right, all right," I say. "I'll do it."

Now that I've said it out loud, there's no turning back. My pinky starts twitching again, and I grind my teeth.

"Forget it," Sandy says.

"I said I'll do it." I pace the apartment now, although I don't have a baby in my arms, and I realize I must look pretty ridiculous.

She watches me for a while. "Don't get into a fight or anything. Don't get hurt. Just ask them to leave politely."

"Okay," I say, trying to imagine how that's going to go down.

I stand up and grab my coat from the closet. I hold onto the sleeve for a moment, gripping it, before I take it off the hanger and put it on. It's a very short walk to the front door.

Outside, a March wind grabs at my face and it's nothing at all like how I imagine the Chilean wind will be. Last month, Los Angeles County broke the all-time record for rain, the LA River so swollen homeless people were washed from its banks. Now, it's as if everything is gasping for breath after a near drown, the plants and flowers like giant open mouths. A few cars roll by on Fair Oaks, but the city seems strangely barren. A stray plastic bag catches in the breeze, inflating and collapsing like a jellyfish.

I walk down the front steps and shuffle toward the cul-de-sac. I didn't think it possible, but the biker's engines are louder out here. Sonic booms. *Stay calm*, I tell myself. It's something you have to learn as a teacher: kids smell fear. I was so frightened on my first day that I pretended I was Al Pacino in *Scarface*. All machismo and bravado. Pathetic, but it worked. So now I'm hiking through the hills of Chile, backpack full of journals and pens. I'm the great travel writer off on an adventure, and the Harley engines are thunder behind a distant turquoise mountain.

As I approach the corner and see the jacarandas, I understand why the bikers chose our cul-de-sac to have their picnic: many of the purple flowers have fallen to the ground, carpeting the sidewalk. The little dead-end street is the end of the rainbow. I don't understand the bikers' insistence on revving their engines every five seconds. It's a chronic, lonely cry: *I exist, I exist.* I turn the corner and all their noises rush at me: Blam! Wrecking ball! Blam! Laughter! Blam! *No shit?* I hate them. I turn up the collar of my coat, glance at my shoes. They each have a pale blue stripe on the side that looks like a guppy fish. Sandy bought them for me when I complained the dress shoes I wore to work were giving me blisters. They're comfortable and sensible, but not suited for confrontation.

The tall guy, the leader, stands in the shade of one of the trees. He's got that aura about him I've read some generals in the wars have, the ones who take all kinds of crazy risks—standing up with bullets whizzing past them—because they just know they aren't going to be shot. He stands about 6'3" and has hard, knobby-looking muscles. He locks eyes with me for a moment, then seems disinterested and looks away. I watch his profile as he takes a sip from his bottle, a hefty sip. I wonder how many he's had.

Shorty is still squatting on his bike, revving the engine. He's got a square jaw, like a boxer, and tattoos not just on his arms but on his neck as well. His bike is painted cadmium red and has mango flames blazing along the gas tank. The chrome handlebars are so clean and shiny they could double as mirrors. Up close the revving engine is even more visceral; it vibrates the ground under my feet; popping noises crack my eardrums. I want to reach up and plug my ears, it's that loud, but I stop myself. Shorty leans back on his bike and wipes at his forehead with a gloved hand. He cocks his head, takes me in behind the sunglasses.

I turn away, stare at the other bike, Leader's, I imagine; it's parked along the curb: metallic purple, an insignia of a wild boar with handlebars for tusks. Beneath the boar, written in Old English-style letters, are the words: Iron Pigs. There's not a speck of dirt on either bike, and I can't help feeling a bit of admiration for things kept so pristine. I've always liked motorcycles, just not the people who ride them.

Heroin Addict is reclining on the grass, her face up to the sun. I see now the writing on her shirt says, "Bring it On!" Her red hair is so long the ends rest on the grass. Hottie is standing in the street eating a sandwich. She slips the last of the french roll into her mouth and licks her fingers slowly, one at a time. My eyes linger. Is she being flirtatious? Mocking me? I can't tell. Her hair is black as a cocktail dress. She wears a pair of tight Levis and a purple leather halter top that does its job. She watches me a moment, offers a smile, and I feel the sense of relief that a friendly gesture from a beautiful woman can bring.

Either of the bikers could kick my ass—maybe even Heroin Addict; and it's little consolation that in a slam poetry competition I could wipe the floor with them.

"Hello all," I say, trying to sound casual and friendly. But Shorty keeps revving his engine—it's so loud I can almost see sound waves in the air, blurring everything like heat—and nobody can hear me. The tattoos on his arms are an intricate matrix of spider webs. There are so many of them his arms look diseased. The tattoo on his neck is a playing card, the ace of spades, and when he leans over to adjust something on the engine, I notice he has a leather case clipped to his belt, a knife case. My skin crawls.

I wave, take a half-step forward. Stop. Keep my eyes on that knife case.

Hottie moves forward too. She bends over, grabs a fallen jacaranda flower from the sidewalk, spins it around with her fingers, the way kids do with sparklers on the Fourth of July, and tucks it behind her ear. The purple petals brush her cheek. She's even paler up close, tracing paper held up to a light.

I think of Sandy, how she hides herself with a towel when she gets out of the shower.

"Excuse me," I say, raising my voice. "May I speak with you guys for a moment?"

Shorty seems to hear me this time. He gives the engine one more rev, then turns it off. It sputters to a stop and the street goes quiet. Previously shrouded sounds rush out: the whisper of the jacaranda leaves in the wind, the distant beeping of a utility vehicle in reverse, and the shuffle of my tennis shoes as I shift my weight.

"What's up, Man?" Leader asks, pointing the tip of his bottle in my direction. The label is yellow, familiar. It isn't a beer; it's a root beer. The brown bottle drips with condensation.

"I live there," I say, pointing at our apartment complex. I've never seen it from this angle, and it's even uglier from the side: beige stucco, faded green paint peeling from the trim, the rain gutter hanging limp and ineffective from the wall. The window to our apartment is still closed, the blinds still drawn. I give thanks for that.

"It's Sunday," I say, "and my wife and baby are upstairs trying to rest."

Shorty's hand goes to the case. He holds it there, caresses the leather.

Heroin Addict says, "Spit it out."

"It's only 10 a.m., guys," I say, my voice breaking. "My little boy, Ene's his name, gets spooked from the sound of your bikes. Could you maybe leave? Or at the least keep it down?"

"What kind of name is Ene?" Heroin Addict says, shaking her head.

I think about my son's name. It's a palindrome. I like the simple beauty of it, the vowel-consonant-vowel. When I was researching possible baby names, I came across it as being derived from my own name, although the connection seems tenuous now, and I can't really articulate the lineage.

"It's a derivation of my name." I watch the bikers. "You know, his name is taken from mine."

"We know what derivation means," Leader says, and I wince. "Strange name for a boy. Don't other kids pick on him?"

"He's fourteen months old," I say.

"They will," Shorty says, grinning.

He runs his hand along the gas tank. A jacaranda flower sticks to the flames. He peels it off, but a tiny piece of purple petal remains. The flames look hot enough to curl the soft purple flesh into oily ash. He unbuttons the leather case and pulls out a buck knife. It's about four inches long, maybe not as long as I'd feared, but there's enough steel there to end a life. Very delicately, like slicing garlic, he scrapes off the flower petal. He takes pleasure in working the knife, twisting it ever so slightly with his thick wrists. He snaps it shut, grins at me, and slips it back inside the case.

"Ene," Hottie says. "I like it. It's musical."

I appreciate the compliment, especially from her, but the knife has seized my attention.

"So you want us to leave?" Leader asks.

"I'm trying to grade papers." I'm rambling, but I can't stop. "I've got a stack like this high." I hold my hand out at waist level.

"You're a teacher?" Shorty says. His voice is a rock grinder, three packs a day, no doubt, and I can't help but imagine all the teachers he must have pissed off during his short academic run.

"We mostly want to relax," I say.

"We'd like to relax, too," Heroin Addict says. "We've got jobs too you know."

"I know," I say, looking down, losing steam.

"Listen, Buddy," Shorty says, employing a reasonable tone. "I'm working on my bike here. We're having a little lunch. We'll leave when we're done. It's not like we're breaking the law."

"Noise pollution isn't against the law?" I feel the hypocrisy of the words as they slip past my lips.

"You call this noise pollution?" Shorty says. He turns the key, and the engine starts up again. He revs it, revs it, revs it, each time holding the throttle down a little longer: PAP! PAAP! PAAAPPITIE PAP!

I look at the apartment complex. The blinds are up, and Sandy is standing in plain view, holding Ene. Their faces are small and out of focus, but I sense their unease, which turns my own unease to fear.

I turn back around. Shorty is revving away, grinning like a jackal. "Shut it off!" I yell.

"Can't hear you."

I take a jerky step forward. "Shut it off!"

"Or what?" Shorty twists the throttle: PAAAAAAAAP!

"Shut the fucking bike!"

Instead, he flips up the kickstand, backs the bike away from the curb, and starts riding around the cul-de-sac. He does skillful figure eights in the street, revving the engine, laughing, sometimes dipping his bike so low it seems he's going to scrape his knees on the pavement. I hate to admit it, but he's good with the bike. He doesn't even seem to be moving the handlebars. The bike is like a professional surfer's board. It glides in the direction he wants without him really trying or thinking about it. He keeps on laughing, like this is the funniest thing in the world, doing figure eights in a cul-de-sac with a frustrated school teacher on the sidelines, watching. I can't hear the laughter, only see his mouth wide open, his Adam's apple moving up and down.

Leader steps into the street, waves his hands. "Kill it!" he shouts.

Shorty parks the bike along the curb without hesitation. Idling, his Harley sounds like a panting Saint Bernard. Shorty's demeanor seems completely changed, his face serious now. He gives me a hateful look and bites at his lower lip. He gets off his bike, takes a quick step toward me. He only comes up to my shoulders, but his body is thick as a tree stump. I watch the leather case on his belt; his hands; his eyes.

"Who the fuck do you think you are?" he says.

"Just leave." My voice is low now, quivering, a schoolboy's voice.

"I asked you a question."

The other bikers stand around, arms crossed, staring.

Shorty's eyes are hazel with specks of green. Sunlight glints off his thin lashes. *Who am I?* It's not a bad question. But the only answer that comes to mind is: *Fucked if I know!*

"I live there!" I shout, pointing at the apartment complex. "There! There! There! You're making too much fucking noise! My baby is about to have an aneurysm! My wife wants to jump out the window! Leave!" I point at the jacaranda trees. "These are our trees, not yours! Ours! So get on your scooters and leave us in peace!"

Shorty takes another step forward. I brace myself. His hand is reaching for the leather case. I see it all happening before it does: the knife—cold, sharp blade slipping between ribs; crack of bone; blood gushing, thick as syrup. I step back, wobbling a little. Shorty reaches out, places a hand on my chest. His hands are huge. Heavy. Like stones. I try to step back further; my heels are against the edge of the curb; there's nowhere to go.

"Boo!" he says, and pushes me backward. The push is minor, but I'm off balance and fall flat on my ass. Pain shoots through my spine; it's nothing compared to the flush of my face. I wait for him to pounce on me, hope for it. Any other outcome. Shorty laughs.

"Fucking teachers," he says.

Then he's on his bike again, Heroin Addict straddling the seat behind him, her skinny hands on his waist. He takes one last look at me—hate replaced by pity—and then, to Leader, says, "We'll be at Hooters."

He revs the engine one last time and takes off, tires squealing.

I put my head in my hands. My body is shaking.

"Shit, Man," Leader says, trying to hold back a laugh.

I stand, but I'm unsteady. I glance up at the apartment window, afraid they're still watching me. The blinds slowly lower and pretty soon the window is shrouded again. I stare at the blank white slate the blinds make in the window, like the empty whiteboards at school in the rooms nobody uses; I want to run off somewhere, seek shelter, hide away.

"Fuck," I say, wobbling a little.

Leader takes me by the arm. "You okay, Man?" he says, moving towards his bike. "Sit down a minute. You don't look well."

I lean against the seat of his bike. It's warm from the sun.

"You're not going to have a heart attack or anything?" Hottie says.

I catch my breath, shake my head. "Your friend is a little high strung."

Leader raises his eyebrows.

I run my hand along the chrome handlebars of the Harley and then caress the purple gas tank. "Nice bike," I say, meaning it. The power I feel just touching it surprises me.

"Get on," Leader says.

When I just stare at him, he says, "Go ahead."

I start to protest but then think *what the fuck* and climb on.

The seat dips down low. It takes a moment for me to get comfortable. I wiggle my ass around a bit—it's sore from the fall—and slip my feet in the little leather stirrups. Like this, I'm so comfortable I can imagine cruising for hours on end. I place my hand on the throttle. The rubber is like dough: soft, malleable, almost form fitting. In the headlight's chrome casing, I see a tiny image of my face and to the left Leader and Hottie, watching me.

"Pretty brave of you to come out here," Hottie says.

"My family was going crazy."

"Sorry about Todd," Leader says.

"His name is Todd?" I ask; a frat boy name; I think of those tattoos.

"He gets a little worked up when we ride. Otherwise, he's a damn nice guy."

"He doesn't happen to have a Barbie doll collection?"

"Don't be rude," Hottie tells me.

"Sorry. Inside joke," I say, staring at my hand on the throttle. I realize I'm gripping it pretty tightly, so I relax my fingers, settle back in the seat.

"I'm Marcella," Hottie says. "And this is Steve."

"Dean," I say, and shake their hands.

"What do you teach, Dean?" Steve asks.

"English."

"My worst subject."

"What do you do?" I ask him.

"Seismology."

"Earthquakes?"

"At Caltech."

I study Steve's face. "I've seen you on TV," I say. "You're the earthquake guy."

"Mostly I do calculations. When our PR gal is out of town, I'll fill in."

"Wow," I say, looking around. Everything seems sharp and clear, like when a fever lifts. "So is the big one coming?"

"The big one is always coming," Steve says.

"And you?" I ask Marcella. "How do you spend the hours between bike rides?"

"Accounting."

"Earthquakes and taxes, the two certainties," I say.

"If you live in LA," Steve says.

"So you guys just do this on the weekends?"

"It's how we blow steam," Marcella says.

"It's sure working for Todd," I say.

"He's our mechanic," Leader says. "He rides with us when he's not working at his shop. I don't think he really hates teachers or anything. Damn nice guy once you get to know him. Works magic with an engine."

I settle further back into the seat and feel great relief knowing these are respectable people. Hell, Steve and Marcella have better jobs than I do. I grip the throttle, twist it silently a few times, my fingers strong and steady on the rubber.

"Want to give it a whirl?" Steve asks.

"Serious?"

"Start it up, Man," he says, nodding to the keys in the ignition.

"Just turn it?" I say.

"Yeah, Man, just turn it. Keep your hand on the brake, okay, and leave it in neutral." He puts his hand around Marcella's waist and she moves in and lays her head on his shoulder. It's a natural, tender gesture, and I'm jealous watching it.

I turn the key and the bike jumps to life. The rumble moves through the seat and up my spine and down my arms. It's a giant vibration that rattles and shakes me to the core. Strangely, the engine isn't so loud when you're on it; not so annoying. I'm guessing Steve is right about Todd's magic because the hum of the engine is steady and sure. I turn the throttle a couple of times, feel the high octane potential of the mechanical beast. It would be so easy to fold up the kickstand and pull the bike away from the curb. I doubt Steve would even stop me. The apartment window is still shrouded by the blinds. Open the blinds, Sandy, I think, Open them! I want her to see me on the bike talking to Steve and Marcella. But the blinds don't open, so I close my eyes and imagine what it would be like to barrel down the highway, weave in and out of traffic, hit the open road. There would be another town, another city, state after state. Maybe even Chile? Who knows? Either way, always new sky. I take a deep breath, open my eyes.

"Take it around the block if you want, Man," Steve says.

"No thanks."

"You sure?" Marcella asks. "Once you try it, you might be hooked."

"I'm sure," I say. "But thank you." I turn off the engine and step off the bike.

"Thanks, guys. Really, you have no idea."

"No worries, Man."

"Stay for a while, if you want," I say, waving my hand around as if I own the cul-de-sac.

"We will," Steve says, "If we feel like it."

"Right," I say, and walk quickly back onto the sidewalk through the fallen purple flowers and down the cul-de-sac. I lift my hand and slap at one of the dark, gnarled branches.

I take the steps to my apartment two at a time. When I open the front door, Sandy rushes over. "Thank God you're okay," she says. "I thought he was going to kill you."

I brush past her with a smile, lift Ene from the crib. He's quiet now, his face still streaked with tears. He looks at me like he's never seen me before. I drop to my knees, then spin him around so he's lying on my back, his little arms thrown over my shoulders, around my neck. I begin to crawl around the living room. Slowly at first, then faster. I make the noises of the engines: "VROOOOOOOMM!!!! VROOOOOOOOOOOOOMMM!!" I'm practically shouting. Ene begins crying, softly at first, and then at a pitch so high it rivals my own.

"What are you doing?" Sandy says. "Stop it! Please, you're scaring Ene."

I go faster.

"Dean, for Christ's sake!" she shouts.

I make a sharp turn and double back the way I came, heading right for Sandy.

I hope Ene has the sense to hold on.

Jill Alison Ganon

I Am the Jolly Ant

WHEN THE DOORBELL RANG, Aggie, wearing a white cotton nightie, was sitting at the end of one of the pine benches at her dining room table, vacuuming ants from the floor with the drapery attachment of the vacuum cleaner. Thirsty, diligent columns of ants were a prominent feature of the parched Pasadena autumn. August had come and gone and she had privately congratulated herself on making it through the summer without an ant conflagration. This was no accident. A casual winter and spring housekeeper, she became vigilant with the onset of heat. Not a stray grain of sugar. Not a nugget of kibble. Aggie was forty-eight years old and this was her family's fifteenth year as transplants from New York to Southern California. It was their twelfth year in this sprawling hundred-year-old house with its camphor trees and the heady scent of jasmine in the front yard every spring. Now, lethal and patient, she paid close attention to the ants as they appeared in a disciplined column from below the six-paned dining room window and marched down the wall toward the floor. She did not raise the hose attachment to the loden wall, choosing instead to thumb through the architectural magazine on the table, saving annihilation for those members of the column who reached the floor and made the fatal ninety-degree turn toward the kitchen.

These tiny black ants were a fact of life in the summer: invader drones, lacking in detectable personality. They were not the zaftig black ant friends of her girlhood. Being the first in her home to awaken on Saturday and Sunday mornings was one of her earliest childhood pleasures. She would dress and open the unlocked front door and walk around to the side yard of her ivy-covered brick house. A path of slate paving stones ran along the length of the house. She was methodical in her examination of the underbellies of those stones. Beginning with the first one, she would use both her sturdy arms to pull up the gray slate slab, the better to watch the busy world of the ants that made their trails beneath the flat, heavy stones. Activity was steady and varied—ants carried, prodded, groomed, rolled, communed. Only the slugs and tiny snails were ever still. The ants seemed to her to be busy and friendly and she believed that by ignoring her and going about their business they were somehow telegraphing their welcome; their comfort with being observed. After a while she would lower the stone back into place and move on to flip over the next heavy slate tablet. She never turned over more than one stone at a time, disliking the stress of dividing her attention between ant worlds. She rarely observed more than three stones worth of ants before she got hungry and returned to the house hoping that her sister would be awake and ready to watch cartoons and eat Ritz crackers with jam, or if it were Sunday, that her father would be up and about the business of preparing kippers and eggs. She imagined that if a giant were to lift the flat, heavy roof of her home, she and her family would satisfy him with their pleasing ways and their industry. She had been a happy child—serious, but happy.

Aggie answered the door. The FedEx man handed her a pen and she signed her name next to the line he pointed to.

"Hi. How about a cold drink today?"

He handed her a FedEx Pak and smiled. His teeth were very white. He'd been on this route for five or six years and they'd grown accustomed to sharing a few words.

"I have a thermos of iced tea in the truck. But thank you."

"Sure."

"I should tell you—this is my last day on your route. We're moving up to Seattle to be near my wife's family with the kids and all. I'm staying with the company—just moving out of town."

Aggie assured him that it sounded great for the family and he would never lose his California roots.

"Yeah, but it's gonna be really different. I grew up here. It's gonna be different forever."

Different forever. The moment last September that she took the jury summons from her mailbox marked such a day, though she had failed to recognize it for what it was at the time, seeing it instead as a sort of milestone—a transfer of her duty as a mother to her duty as a citizen. Over the years of raising her two sons she had filled out at least four such summonses with her crisp, calm message: she was the mother of two children, the only one available to take them to and from school, and to care for them after school. She appreciated the court's patience, and she would be happy to do her duty as a citizen when her children were no longer minors residing at home. And the state of California had been fine with that. The very day this jury summons arrived in her mailbox, Aggie had returned from taking her youngest son to college back east. She and her husband and son had flown to Boston, and only she and her husband had returned. Well, thought Aggie, they certainly hadn't wasted any time. She noted the day she was directed to begin her jury duty and wrote it on her calendar. Citizen Aggie.

The courtroom was austere and reassuringly official. The flags of the United States and California flanked the judge's bench. Aggie had dressed thoughtfully for this day—a burgundy blouse, darted in front and back, with an austere black wrap skirt, expensive cordovan flats and wine-stained matte lipstick. Admiring her as she'd buttoned her blouse that morning, her husband suggested that maybe she needed to get out a little more. She'd laughed, but she felt embarrassed, caught at caring too much about a public service that others loathed and considered an intrusion on the important events of their lives. He'd grabbed her hand as he left their bedroom before her. *"Give me a call. Let me know how it goes."* He loved her.

Aggie sat silently among other prospective jurors. She was curious about jury duty. She'd been a decent debater in high school and college and several teachers and professors had suggested that she consider "the law" as a profession. She never gave that idea any serious consideration. Preferring to follow a more artistic muse, she became an illustrator, eventually specializing in detailed botanical and zoological illustrations, working for many years with an Italian publisher of university textbooks. For the last ten years she'd found success as the illustrator of an award-winning series of children's books about a brother and sister who dreamed themselves into adventures in fantastic, imagined eco-systems.

Finally, jurors and spectators were instructed to stand as the judge, a woman no older than fifty, entered the room. She explained that this case involved a charge of murder with special circumstances, which in the state of California meant the possibility of the death penalty or a sentence of life imprisonment without the possibility of parole. Therefore, said the judge, looking out over them with dark, intelligent eyes, prospective jurors needed to be "death qualified." The court had to determine if each potential juror was capable, if necessary, of imposing the death penalty based on the rule of law and the facts of the case. Sitting there, a yeasty fear rose from Aggie's stomach to the back of her throat. She wanted to throw herself on the mercy of the court—*don't make me do this.* She wanted to be in bed next to her husband, telling him about her close call; how she'd almost had to serve as a juror for a murder trial. How she'd thought she could do this but she was wrong. She wanted to lie.

In addition to death qualifying, the judge or either lawyer had the right to challenge any prospective juror for cause, and either side could also make several challenges, excusing a juror without offering a reason. Listening to those questioned before her, Aggie realized she was still in control of her fate. She could frame her responses to the judge and the lawyers in such a manner as to either have herself dismissed or commanded to serve on this jury. When called upon to speak, she answered carefully, but without falsehood. She'd glanced at the clock just as it was her turn to be questioned by the judge. It was two-thirty. *Tooth hurt-y…time to go to the dentist… Get it, Mom?* Many years ago, it had been her eldest son's favorite joke for a week or so. She could not clear her head of the image of his hands; fingers rigid with joy, splayed out in front of his narrow chest, making her a gift of his joke. *Get it, Mom?* The judge addressed her directly, "Ms. Smith, will you please be seated in the jury box."

The third day of testimony, juror number three, a young Hispanic woman, clasped her hand to her mouth as the prosecution finished positioning enormous color placards of the murder scene on two easels before the jury. She drew a severe look from the judge, and placed her hands in her lap. Aggie looked at the accused murderer, Marcus Rich— charged with lying in wait to slash the throat and repeatedly stab Peter Molonov, a twenty-year-old, first-generation Russian-American boy who had embarrassed him in front of a cluster of giggling girls at a bar three days before the murder. Rich was twenty-three, white, and had a lock of shining honey-colored hair that hung over one eye and softened his facial features. He was slight, scrawny even, and he looked very young. She had to work hard to think of him as a man. The prosecutor apologized to the jury for the hideous tableau—a triptych of poster-size color photographs showed a young man lying on his back on a linoleum floor, his arms akimbo. He had long dark hair and dark, wide-open eyes. His throat had been cut. His white T-shirt read "Don't Be A Dick" and was saturated with blood stains where the four-inch blade of a paring knife had entered and left his chest and abdomen five times. His body was covered with and surrounded by candy bars, presumably scattered from the overturned shelves of the 7-Eleven that was the scene of the murder. With a laser pointer, the prosecutor indicated individual M&M's in the bloodied shoe prints that circled the body and disappeared behind the counter. In the last testimony of the day, the prosecution introduced into evidence an empty, crumpled bag of M&M's found in the defendant's pocket at the time of his arrest. Forensic officers, the prosecutor told the jury, had sprayed a protective perimeter of pesticide around the body in order to prevent an assembled column of ants from making a grisly picnic of the crime scene.

Appearing to listen and follow instructions, Aggie wondered if any other jurors had secretly pushed up on their toes, the backs of their thighs lifting, disengaging from the hard wooden bench—fleeing and floating as she did—*good Aggie, thoughtful Aggie*—flying over America, to Denver and St. Paul and Boston and Miami. *Citizen Aggie*—peeking into courtrooms and bedrooms and bars and alleyways where people were kissing each other and killing each other and hiding from each other and eating candy. How could it be, in all these cities where mothers stared rapt with love at their babies, that if you were to lift the roof of the courthouse, in any one of them, in all of them, you might see giant poster boards of young dead boys afloat in polka-dotted pools of their own blood. Boys killed by other boys. Yet, people dreamed and danced. They laughed, fucked, communed. They continued.

Each day that first week, Aggie made the trip from her home to the courthouse and back again. By the second week, she and her husband had established a schedule. She came from the courthouse and he came from work and they met at a favorite restaurant and drove home afterward in separate cars. Her husband, knowing his wife and the rules of silence for jurors, was respectful of her privacy, asking only about how she was faring. Was she all right? Yes, she assured him, she was fine. On Friday, they ate at home. He grilled salmon while she made a salad and they sat at the dining room table eating their dinner and sipping their wine. They talked about their sons and they talked about his work. He was the architect and contractor of a project that was converting an enormous downtown warehouse into retail space and apartments, one third of which were to be dedicated to affordable housing. His client was a prominent Los Angeles developer who had begun to make overtures to her husband about quietly abandoning the affordable housing segment of the project.

Aggie listened as her husband considered his responsibility to deliver the project as mandated. Getting this job had been a coup for him: an unprecedented step up in his career. She worked hard to focus on his voice: to remain in her body. Later, when they made love, Aggie, floating near the ceiling, looked down at the solidness, the aloneness of their two bodies, each seeking its own recovery from intimacy. She hovered above the bed, thinking—it is one thing to leave my body, but it is another thing entirely to lose the will to return to it. She felt the beginning of the end of herself.

On the day before closing arguments, Peter Molonov's mother was not in the courtroom. The word was that she had experienced chest pains the night before and was being held for observation at the hospital. Aggie felt free for the first time to look at Marcus for more than a fleeting moment. She watched as he filled pages of his yellow legal pad with sketches—of what, she could not say—but she could tell that he was focused as he worked quickly in pencil, stopping occasionally to erase something, wiping the pink shavings off his paper with a tissue. His attorney placed a hand on Marcus's arm and he laid down his pencil until he could stand it no longer, and the pencil crept back into his hand. Witness after witness confirmed what she knew, what they all knew. This was a guilty man. A young, damaged, guilty man who had stood on a toilet in a stall for twenty-five minutes before emerging at ten minutes after midnight to nod at the bewildered Peter Molonov who'd thought he was alone as he locked the door and began to walk back behind the counter to close out the register. The grainy surveillance tape registered Peter Molonov's shock as he careened out of the camera frame with Marcus Rich's arm hooked around his neck.

The jury deliberation took two days. Juror number ten, a retired LA Unified schoolteacher, and at seventy-three, their senior member, had been elected foreperson. This was her second time seated in a capital murder case. She requested at the beginning of deliberations that they refrain from voting until at least the second day when they would write *guilty* or *not guilty* on a folded piece of paper. Their first vote, ninety minutes into the second day of deliberation, was ten to two. Aggie, barely able to remain in the room—floating now more frequently than not—noted with surprise that she was only mildly curious about who the other holdout was. Who, she wondered, was as eager as she to ignore the truth?

When they broke for lunch, juror number three sat with Aggie under the shade of a large ficus tree outside the courthouse. As they ate their sandwiches she touched Aggie's arm and sought Aggie's downcast eyes. She confided her secret—she was three months pregnant. She was a janitor at the Los Angeles County hospital. A co-worker had explained that the hospital would pay her wages if she did jury duty, so she had come to the courthouse hoping to be chosen; hoping to get off her feet for just a few days. She crossed herself and her tears flowed. Aggie moved closer and put both her arms around the weeping girl. It's all right she said. *You and your baby are going to be all right.* The weight of the two lives in her arms pinned her to the rough grass keeping her from flight, and she was thankful.

After returning from their lunch break there was a brief discussion before they voted a second and final time, writing in pencil, folding their oblong pieces of paper in half and pushing them along to the foreperson for tabulation. Twelve unfolded pieces of paper formed a single messy pile and the bailiff was summoned.

Within minutes, they were back in the courtroom. The verdict was announced. Aggie, hovering above her body as the jury was polled, watched herself respond—guilty. It was unanimous. Juror number three crossed herself, and cried quietly, indifferent to the judge's gaze. Mrs. Molonov wept behind her two hands. Marcus Rich, standing beside his lawyer, held his own murderous right wrist and hung his honeyed head.

The penalty phase of the trial required the jury to hear information that had not been allowed as evidence during the guilt phase of the trial. The prosecution presented first. Marcus had stolen his foster mother's car and totaled it in a police chase; he had been thrown out of six foster homes for acts of violence; he had broken into a teacher's car and placed a pile of human excrement on the driver's seat; as a youthful

offender he had knocked a gas station attendant out cold in the commission of a robbery; he had slashed the tires of a girlfriend's car while
she sat terrified behind the wheel; he had robbed the weeping Mrs.
Molonov of her only son, her good American boy who worked at the
7-Eleven to make the money he needed to attend community college.
"He killed my baby." The judge, her chest rising and falling beneath
her robes, asked Mrs. Molonov if she needed a glass of water. "No,"
she said. The bailiff escorted her to her seat. The prosecutor turned to
the jury. Marcus Rich was a bad child who had become a bad man, and
now, it was time for him to pay with his life.

Aggie saw her immediately upon entering the courtroom the next
day to hear the defense present its factors in mitigation. She was a
woman of perhaps seventy in a royal blue dress with an enameled daisy
brooch worn above her heart. She had fine silver hair framing her face
in what Aggie's grandmother used to call a finger wave. She was pow-
dered and lightly rouged and kept one hand on a black leather purse
at her side. On her lap was a small artist's folio. Her name was Sarah
Wright and she had been Marcus Rich's fifth-grade teacher. Sarah
Wright was seated in the witness stand. When she had known Marcus,
she told the jury in a steady voice, he had been a good boy. Back before
all the trouble had turned him into the person they were describing
today.

Marcus was the youngest child of a troubled family. Damage had
followed young Marcus like an obedient pet into her fifth-grade classroom. The rumors and then the proof of every type of abuse; the drinking, the joblessness; the father, accused and convicted of the rape of
a thirteen-year-old friend of his eldest daughter; the discovery that
he had been raping his younger daughter as well. Marcus, gagged,
stripped, and strapped to a dining room chair all night for talking
back—watching, mute, as his father walked from his sister's bedroom
and out the front door for a smoke. The dissolution of the family after
the father's imprisonment as the mother boozed and finally fled the
three children, who were placed in different foster homes. This was

the silent ten-year-old in whose notebook Mrs. Wright discovered the drawings. Drawings that came to win him two regional 4-H blue ribbons. Drawings of animals and flowers and insects done in a fine, decisive hand. And each drawing with a merry title written within quotation marks in a flowery script. In another family, Mrs. Wright told the jury, he would have been seen as the prodigy that he was. She turned her head to face the judge.

"I would like your permission to share this young man's art work done in the year he spent in my classroom." She looked at Marcus, who looked down at his own two hands finally mute on the table before him.

"You were a good boy, Marcus. You were once a very good boy."

Aggie tried and failed to prepare herself for the shock of what she knew was coming. The bailiff passed two sketchpads into the jury box, handing one off to juror number one and the second to juror number seven. Aggie waited for the sketchpad to reach her. The first drawing was of a pine cone on a forest floor. It was titled *Quiet the Forest* and it was a botanical after the style of the Victorian naturalists, though Marcus could not have known that. At ten, he'd had the observational skill of a trained naturalist. The next was a wasps' nest, followed by the bark of a eucalyptus tree, followed by the first of a series of near photographic depictions of ants. Ants in a column; ants on a slice of jam-covered bread; a third one called *I Am the Jolly Ant* covered the page but for the lines leading out to block script defining the jolly ant's anatomy—antenna, mandible, brain, aorta, cleaning hook, petiole, femur, tarsus, heart. The jurors passed the sketchpads along to one another.

In Mrs. Wright's classroom he had not been up to any mischief beyond the usual grade-school hijinks she always saw in boys—water balloons in the school yard, the occasional squabble over taking turns. He was usually one of the first chosen to play yard sports, and might even be called a leader in some respects. "In fact," she said, "In light of the terrible goings-on at home, Marcus caused remarkably little trouble in school. I would say he was quite contained." She paused for a moment, lost in her thoughts. "There was," she said, "the matter of the next-door neighbor's cat"—the defense attorney was on his feet. He asked Mrs. Wright if she might elaborate a bit more on Marcus's exceptional artistic ability. Well, said Mrs. Wright, even the school district's psychologist had come to agree that Marcus was gifted and that drawing was a healthy emotional outlet for him.

Aggie received the second sketchbook. There, among sweetly titled sketches of sparrows and flowers, was the cat. The next-door neighbor's cat. The dead cat. It had no title. Aggie recognized murder on the page—the cat on its back, posed on a bed of dead leaves, its head flopped off to the side—the wound across its throat in dark velvety pencil showing only a slight pooling of blood; its eyes open and tongue lolling stupidly from an open mouth. Aggie fled her body, and entered Marcus Rich's body. She felt his syrupy blood in her veins. She knew his murderer's heart; this broken boy who'd begun killing animals as a child and had been waiting for so long to die. She stared at the drawing. The judge excused Sarah Wright, who stood and left the witness stand and took her seat once again. She would not leave the courtroom without collecting Marcus's sketchbooks.

The next thing Aggie remembered hearing was the judge's instruction, "If you believe from all the evidence that death is not justified, then you shall fix the punishment at life imprisonment. If after the most careful examination of the evidence you conclude otherwise, you have no alternative but to sentence Mr. Rich to death."

Aggie spent a quiet weekend at home with her husband, who was going through the motions of moral outrage about his dilemma. Saturday evening they sat facing each other in their comfortable living room. There was no longer any ambiguity on the job site. The developer was handling the city and he needed Aggie's husband to play ball or leave the game. He'd need to make design modifications on what were no longer affordable units with the tacit understanding of a significant bonus at the back end, or severe consequences to the arc of his career if he failed to be a team player. Aggie, no longer concerned with remaining in her body, watched herself nod sympathetically, pretending to believe her husband had not yet made his decision. She wondered how long it would take him to tell her what she already knew—that he had decided to play along. She floated back to her body. "I'm tired, sweetheart," she said. "I'm going to lie down." He watched her leave the room.

On Sunday, Aggie and her husband spoke with both their sons at their respective colleges. They were fine. Aggie thought of her kitchen filled with her sweet boys and their friends. Her husband found her weeping after she'd hung up the phone. He took her in his arms. "It's going to be all right," he said. "I'm going to work it out." She wanted to tell him that she wasn't worried about him. That she wasn't really even there. Instead, she wept soundlessly in his arms, and then, even though it was not yet two o'clock in the afternoon, they both had a drink.

Jury deliberations in the penalty phase of the trial began on Monday morning. Mrs. Wright's moral authority had not been lost on any of them. Was there some psychological disorder that made Marcus more susceptible to provocation; something that could ultimately explain, excuse, or justify the behavior that led to the commission of his vile crime? What was the likelihood, even in prison, that he might respond to treatment—or if provoked, lie in wait to murder again? The psych evaluations held few surprises. There had been an intervention by the Department of Social Services in the spring that he spent in Mrs. Wright's fifth-grade class. His first two foster families had both been recognized for excellence at the state level. Both knew they were taking on a great challenge by welcoming Marcus into their homes; both had been prepared to love him. His second foster family had petitioned the state to begin adoption proceedings. The slyness of his violence toward his foster siblings had been his downfall. The jury foreperson led them through the sentencing process. They began their deliberations with two uneven columns—one held eight checks and the other, four. Two days later, Aggie, the lone straggler, joined the three others who had marched one by one to the lengthening column recommending that Marcus Rich be sentenced to death by lethal injection.

It was mid-October when the weeklong penalty phase of the trial ended. An automatic appeal had been filed in the District Court of Appeals, catching the attention of the national media because of Marcus's statement that he would not cooperate with efforts on his behalf. He was guilty, he said, and he wanted to die. A reporter told Marcus that the average time between sentencing and execution in California was eleven years and ten months. Marcus's reply was that he intended to be gone well before that, causing prison officials to place him on round-the-clock suicide watch. Aggie's bouts of weeping had continued after the trial and the sentencing. She was spending less and less time in her body now, and that body seemed to be shrinking to accommodate her diminished presence. Her husband tempted her with take-out delicacies from her favorite restaurants, but she only picked at her food. The only thing that engaged her at all was her work. She had been asked to provide an illustration for a German publisher's nature book for children, and had proposed painting a colony of ants. The publishers were delighted with her preliminary sketches and her husband, happy to see her engaged, playfully bought her an ant farm that she placed on her drawing table and observed daily. Her sons came home for Thanksgiving with their shaggy hair and their sloppy ways and Aggie managed, with their help, to pull their traditionally casual, bountiful dinner together, and to speak to her son's friend about his planned travels to Spain in the spring, but both her boys saw the change in her and worried. Aggie brushed aside all inquiries.

It was a week and a half before Christmas when the first letter arrived. Stamped with notification that this, and all communication from inmates was read by prison authorities and any communication returned to this inmate would be subject to review by same.

Dear Citizen,

Thank you for your letter. I am interested in animals and would want the gift of an ant farm. I asked and they

may even say yes. I don't know how you know about me.
I know they wrote about my trial in the papers, and my
drawings and all, so maybe that's how. I would like some
ants to watch and draw as I am not much for books and I
don't care for my hour a day in the television room.

Yours Truely,
Marcus Rich

Over the Christmas holiday, Aggie realized she needed to tend to her fearful family. She sat down with her husband and her sons in the wintry California sun of their living room and told them she knew she'd not been herself and that it was some kind of middle-age woman thing from which she'd emerge. She told them this, knowing it would cause them to retreat, to turn away from that foreboding cave that held only mysteries for boys and diminishing returns for men. Her younger son, braver than the other two, shook his head from side to side as if anticipating an answer to his unasked question—*Are you sick, Mom? Are you going to die?* Churlish mother, cruel citizen. Love stung her eyes and she fought the wave of tears that threatened to drown her, to drown them all. Her husband took her hand, "Mom is going to be okay. Everybody has a rough patch now and then."

"Go on," she said to her family. "Give me a minute, and then I'll get lunch together." They rose as one, her husband leading the haphazard column of three. Wiping her eyes with the front of her starched cotton shirt, she noticed that she was there; present, in her body, watching their retreat.

The prison authorities operated at their own ponderous pace. Aggie imagined the giant fortress, with her letter carried in the mandibles of one worker and passed along to the next. She had signed her first letter to Marcus, *Sincerely yours, A Citizen.* Beginning with his first, and in all his subsequent responses, his salutation began, *Dear Citizen,* and ended with *Yours Truely, Marcus Rich.* She told no one about her correspondence with him. By mid March, Aggie had received permission to send Marcus his ant farm and the ants to inhabit it. The ants had a life span of several months, so she secured permission to replenish the supply of ants and the sand they lived in as needed. The 24-hour suicide-watch video surveillance of his cell proved a boon to his request to secure the ant farm there. No opportunity to shatter the plastic unit and use the shards to injure himself. Aggie's next missive contained a drawing pad and five art pencils that Marcus was allowed access to for three hours each day. *It is very human of them,* he wrote to his Citizen Correspondent. She had made a decision at the very beginning not to correct his spelling or vocabulary, it would simply not be *humane* she thought to herself, smiling for just a moment at her little joke.

The German publisher wanted her to do two more illustrations— one, a spider web in a hollow tree above the ground as the ants carried out their work below, and the second, ants swarming a piece of rotting vegetation above their subterranean nest. In May she received a letter from Marcus with a drawing enclosed—the first he'd chosen to send her. It was the life cycle of an ant.

Dear Citizen,

I thout you mite like this. I think it is the best one I've done so far. Did you know that ants go through stages like a butterfly? I just learned that even after all these years I been drawing pictures of ants. I guess I figured they just had an ant mother and came out of her as a tiny ant baby. Too bad for them they werent a butterfly, but they're just an ant. I'm getting even more of those letters from girls who want to see me. One girl wrote, when is your birth-day? I'll bake you a cake. I got a pile of six letters now with girls who want to marry me. But I would never marry no one. And I am going to die before too long any-way. You are nice to care about a murderer like me.

Yours Truely,

Marcus

In June, her closest friend spoke sternly to her. What was wrong, she wanted to know. "Are you ill? What the hell is going on with you? You do seem better than you were but I don't understand. Is it me? Are you mad at me? Are you having an affair?" It was a weekday evening and Aggie had finally accepted her friend's invitation to get together. They were in a coffee shop where they'd been a hundred times before and Aggie felt trapped. Seen. Her flights from her body had become less frequent, and now, when she wanted to leave and let the hollow Aggie respond, she was heavy, leaden, unable to flee.

"Do you remember last fall? The murder trial?"

Of course her friend remembered.

" I'm corresponding with the defendant. With Marcus Rich."

"The murderer?"

Her friend was incredulous. What did they write to each other? Did her husband know? Was it sexual? Was she all right? Did he know where she lived? That she had been a member of the jury? Aggie fielded the assault and answered without lying.

"I'm telling you now because he is going to be executed and I…"

The word hung there and Aggie felt herself begin to rise out of her body, the feeling familiar but not comfortable—larvae, pupae, adult, bursting from her body, watching herself continue the conversation while winging, winging her way out and into the night air.

Marcus's automatic appeal had been denied and now it was a matter of going through the state and federal habeas corpus petitions that were not confined to the transcripts of the original trial. California had a fast-track appeals process that allowed for petitions all the way to the California Supreme Court to be enacted simultaneously. Aggie noted Marcus's story's devolving presence from the first page to the back pages of the first section, to a paragraph or two in the "LATExtra" section of the *Los Angeles Times*.

In his letters, which now arrived with drawings more often than not, Marcus was little affected by the attention.

Dear Citizen,

You probably know about my appeal being denied. Now they got to go through these other steps but I don't have to do nothing myself. I am wanting to stand up here like a man as I see myself and die for what I done even if all the Jesus people and what not say I shouldn't. They are making protests and getting themselves in the paper for me. I know more then they know. I'm scared but I'm not if you know what I mean. My ants that I got are dead now but for three. They must be the smartest three or the strongest. What do you think?

Yours truely,
Marcus

The telephone rang. It was her friend.

"Hello."

"Aggie, are you dressed?"

"No."

"You told me you wanted to be dressed by 10 a.m. every morning this week."

"So I did."

"It is after eleven."

"The FedEx guy was just here and I answered the door in my nightgown this late in the morning. I fear he thought me lacking in industry."

"I fear he was perfectly delighted to find you lacking a bra."

"I'm going to get dressed."

"I'll pick you up in an hour."

"Okay."

Her friend sighed and spoke, "You're going to get through this."

"Okay."

When her friend arrived promptly at noon, Aggie was sitting on the front porch swing. The FedEx Pak that had arrived that morning was on her lap—opened, but with its contents still inside. Her friend swung her camera bag off her shoulder and sat down next to her.

"Well look at you. Dressed and ready to go. I was sure I was going to have to come in and haul you out. Where's your sketchpad? Do you want me to get it?"

Aggie looked over at her friend. So clear-headed. So completely herself.

"It's here."

Aggie gestured to a large satchel purse on the low table in front of them. Instinctively, together, the balls of their feet pushed off and the swing rocked gently, catching the hint of a hot Santa Ana wind. They both looked straight ahead. Her friend's bare shoulder touched her own. The table was covered with a fine coat of dust.

"We should get going. This is going to help. I know you and this is what you need right now."

Aggie looked at her watch. Marcus Rich was to be executed on this hot September day at 4 p.m. The date and time of Marcus's execution had been announced as dictated by law, two weeks ago. The story had migrated back to the front page because of the precedent set by its speedy implementation. Her friend had called her late that morning asking if she'd seen the paper. Did she know? *Did she know.* You are not going through this by yourself, said her friend. After their first somber talk her friend had reluctantly agreed not to tell anyone else about Aggie's correspondence with the death row inmate. The inmate she had sentenced to death. No, her husband did not know about the letters and drawings and Aggie insisted that it remain that way. Aggie had stared across the table at her friend. "I'm telling you because I know I need to tell someone, and tag, you're it. You have to promise me."

Fierce Citizen Aggie. In the end her friend had succumbed because she knew in her kind heart that Aggie was right. Crazy—but right. Today, they were going to drive to the desert where they would spend the afternoon sketching and taking photographs in Joshua Tree National Park. It was their remedy, taken as needed. They'd done it a dozen times over the years. They'd go for dinner at the only decent restaurant in town and take rooms in a little dive where they'd drink a bottle of decent wine and gab until one or the other of them began to yawn. Sleepy citizens. Aggie's friend pointed at the package.

"Is this the delivery you got this morning?"

Aggie reached into the FedEx Pak and took out what she knew she was going to find there. The ant farm slipped easily out of the package. She placed it upright on the dusty table and opened the letter that had arrived along with it, reading to herself.

> *Dear Citizen,*
>
> *You can see these ants are all dead now just by the act of nature, so I did them no harm by sending this along to you. I got no need of an ant farm no more and I got to thinking maybe you have a kid or somebody who might get a kick out of having some ants to watch. Maybe you would like to study up on some ants. Did you know all them worker ants was girls? Maybe you didn't know that but it is true. You can get new ants and new sand too. Do you have any kids? Just wondering.*
>
> *Yours truely from your friend,*
> *Marcus Rich*

Aggie stared at the ant farm. The sand next to the red plastic farmhouse quivered—and the black head, followed by the tear-shaped thorax of a lone living ant emerged from beneath the bodies of a dozen comrades. Aggie was unaware that she was holding her breath. The ant's first two legs scrambled for purchase, and propelling itself forward, its shining black abdomen came into view. Now, all of its six legs freed, the ant stepped over the bodies of its comrades. Antennae waving frantically, the ant turned its head from side to side.

"Aggie? You ready?"

Aggie sucked in a pillow of air and reached down for her satchel purse. She placed Marcus's letter inside.

"Yeah. Sure. Let's go."

She watched from above as they walked toward the car and got in. Citizen Aggie off to the desert with her friend.

Veronica Gonzalez Peña

The Sad Passions, an excerpt

Claudia

I T WAS 1960 AND we hitchhiked through the middle of the
United States. We slept wherever we could, on floors mostly,
in the backs of bars or stores, barns or garages, wherever people
would put us up. Just like that, like people without a home,
with nothing to show of where we came from. Like hobos or ramblers
or de-centered beings, beings without pasts and no notion of futures
because it's not like we thought about those things and no one asked
us questions, no one cared about our pasts or about our coming plans.
He'd just pull out his guitar and start to sing his Mexican songs of love
and yearning and eyes would turn dewy and soft and we would all sing
along and sway and sip at beers and then after awhile they would show
us our room or barn or storeroom, a blanket to lay out on the floor.

We got picked up in Dodge City, late at night. He came upon us
in his car, the sheriff, though he didn't turn on the flashing red lights
and then he stepped out his door, his gun at his side, and he cocked his
head while he asked us questions in the beam of his headlight. Like
someone very curious, like not a sheriff at all, a cat eyeing a bird, his
head cocking from side to side. Side to side to side. And that look of
his made me think that he liked us, and I guess I was right, I guess

he really did because he let us sleep in the jail, though not together of course. He could get himself in trouble for that, he said. So he put M in the men's jail and me in the women's jail, though we were the only ones there. The sheriff said it wasn't good us wandering the streets in the middle of the night, and so we slept there, the doors locked though we weren't locked up.

And I remember as I lay on my cot, a musty blanket the sheriff had brought for me from who knows where, I remember thinking then that the sheriff hadn't been making eyes at me. It wasn't me that he had liked, cocked his head at. My blanket smelled of dampness, of long wet nights, though it was dry and I turned my face from that smell and up high toward the tiny window in that cell and it was as if I could see M in his cell, see them, see them talking, whispering secrets, late into the night. I closed my eyes and tried to sleep though my mind ran circles and my heart raced, the door locked, damp smelling blanket, the sounds of the night, life rising and falling all around me, crickets and cicadas and all those other deep dark insects and hot breezes running through the weeping willows, or dusty ash trees, or sycamores, or whichever those trees of Dodge City are, the wind whispering mournfully through them, their leaves, outside the jailhouse, whispering leafy secrets, nature's susurrations, deep into the night.

In the morning the sheriff woke me with a shake and then he took me to where M was but M didn't even reach out toward me when he saw me walk in, barely lifted his eyes, so I turned away from him for a long hurt moment, and then I sat, trying to swallow my anger, though all I ever really swallowed with him, though it seems stupid to say it, was my pride, my legs crossed under me yogi style, close to M but not touching, and for a while we all three sipped our coffee together, like friends or neighbors, without asking too many questions, without talking too much about the previous night. Then the sheriff cleared his throat and in a low slow voice he did begin to inquire, about us, what we were doing, what we had planned. We didn't tell him too much though. We'd just gotten married.

Weren't we awful young? He asked.

Yes, we were awful young, should have waited, M said, should have thought better before acting.

What were we doing in Dodge City? He asked.

Well, we had gone to Kansas City where M had a friend and we'd stayed there on this friend's couch until our money had run out, and then for a little while longer while I worked a job cleaning a bar that this friend's landlady ran. I didn't like the cleaning part, but that bar was a place to go, a place to be and I liked that, the clear direction it gave.

And then we stopped talking.

What I didn't tell him, what I didn't tell that sheriff was that one night a woman came up to M while we sat sipping at drinks in that bar and she bent down into him, her breasts near his face, and thanked him for the beautiful necklace, completely ignoring my presence, her hand playing at her own neck which was bare at the time; and later when we were alone and I showed my anger and then cried at M he said, What, do you think you're the only one I ever had? And then cruel and with a smirk he began to name each one. I threw myself at him then, my nails bared, and when he laughed I broke a bottle and threatened him with it and when he laughed louder I lunged at him but he just grabbed my wrists and held me hard and then he was not laughing anymore; the next day I quit my job at the bar, though the landlady had been kind, had stroked my hair as she talked softly to me. And though at that time I mostly didn't understand her, her English, she had said things to me in that soft warm voice whenever I cried. But I was glad to be leaving; that friend of M's had beaten his wife. Not every night, you understand, but enough to terrify. And the wife, that girl was so quiet and mouse-like there was nothing I could ever say to her; I was afraid of being her, becoming her, though with pity I would smile at her from time to time. Once or twice, while she cried, I stroked her hair, like the landlady at the bar had stroked mine.

So with no jobs and no money we left Kansas City and began to hitchhike our way back to Mexico City. And it had been good again; I even told myself it'd been the place, that city, that Kansas City had been the badness I told myself; and I was hopeful once more, because it had been good again, so far, our voyage home, no one bothering us and people taking us in like they had.

I have to tell you now, make it clear right now, that it wasn't me, not my idea. I just followed him; I'd never done anything like that. I followed him because he knew what he was doing, M said. He said he knew what he was doing; barely twenty and he'd been hitchhiking for years, had moved all over two countries for years like that, since he was ten, he said, or maybe it was even nine. The sheriff told us to be careful on our voyage, not everyone was like him; it was clear he wasn't talking to me. And anyway, we already knew that. He hadn't had to say it. He hadn't had to say anything; I knew it all, the way he looked at M.

You have to understand. It wasn't my doing, wasn't my fault. I'd never done anything like that, wandered around like a stray dog, like a person with no home, with no past. M was so gorgeous. He played the guitar and sang his songs so sad or loud and joyous and everyone came close when he sang though his voice was not a beautiful one; he was alive and had eyes like an angel, blue and clear as water, the Irish eyes of his mother, her wry smile on his lips at all times. It was like he had borrowed his mother's mouth, her eyes, and though I hated her, and always would, I followed him with no reason, like a girl who had lost her mind. I'd started following him in Mexico City almost two years before; he lived three blocks away and had befriended my brother, Felix, and when I first saw M standing there in that group of boys my middle melted; then when he turned to glance at me for just one weighty second—his liquid blue eyes pulling at me—before quickly turning and feigning indifference, I didn't know how I would ever take my eyes off of him again. In the midst of that group he stood laughing and teasing; my brother was there too, surly at the edges as always, but they all disappeared, even the black hole that was Felix, all seemed to fall away, so that it was as if it was only M standing there in front of me, floating before me, the others having vanished from right in front of my eyes. My middle melted and then forever my head remained not right.

But it was all his fault. It wasn't me, I tell you. I wasn't like that. I'd grown up in a very strict household, though no one could say I was innocent because I was always the wild one, the one who took risks, the one who ran and climbed trees and fell and injured myself. I was always the one with the outrageous friends and the loud laugh and the anger at my sister for being so quiet and perfect and well loved by my father. My father who was now gone.

My father was serious, was a businessman, and was directed and clear, not like M's father who was himself a sort of vagabond, who skulked and hid and lived in secrets and half lies. It was his father who first took M to Kansas City, when he was eight or nine. But when I met M I didn't really know anything about his father, his family, the stories, of which I became a scandalous part at a later time. My own father managed a bank and was so straight and right and proper in his dealings that when a German lumber giant needed someone to go into business with him in Oaxaca, he went to my father. My father, who had always been so clear and serious in all aspects of that German's interests at that bank; my father, who seemed to know the ins and outs of Mexican money, my father who could also drink, and joke and laugh. I will put up the capital, the German said to my father, and you will manage the enterprise. We will be partners, he said. It was more of a statement than a request and my father said yes. A German had helped him before at least once.

I was about to tell you about my mother, she is (she's now very old, but still alive) the granddaughter of French immigrants, but now I feel I should first explain to you about the German who so long ago helped my father. Before he was even born. This is how it was, in Zacatecas, near the silver mines. My paternal grandmother was a tiny woman, and my father was big in the womb. Everyone said she would lose him, at five months it was already clear. This was a long time ago, 1909, you understand. She stayed in bed, but somehow it was believed she might lose him even then.

There were two daughters at home, my aunts, and so they, without complaint, stepped into most of the management of the house, though they were still young girls, twelve and thirteen at the time; they knew their mother would lose the baby if they didn't learn how to stay on top of it all. Even worse, their mother herself might be lost. So they told the cook what to prepare at every meal, and made sure the housekeeper kept things orderly and they tended their mother themselves, dressing her in the morning even though she never left the bed, feeding her, knitting and reading with her, bathing her at night. The German doctor made a sling for the baby. It sounds very simple, *is* simple nowadays, I suppose, but they all acted like he was a god, this doctor. He made an elastic sling, and maybe it was the elastic that made it fantastic in those days, elastic in 1909 only recently invented for clothing, fantastic, the fact that it gave. He adjusted it to her groin and every week or so he would come see her and he'd adjust it again, and so she was able to keep the baby inside. And then when it did come out it was a boy. A beautiful boy with those two older sisters who'd had to grow up when he was still in the womb so that by the time he came out they were miniature adults, had been caring for him already for nine months; and then there was also his mother and a grandma and that cook and the maid, all right there in that one house, all those women. Babying him. Well, he'd never had to do anything, you see, my father. The gorgeous boy. The golden one.

So, many years later, when this lumber man, the German lumber man, offered to move my father from Mexico City to Oaxaca, to make him the partner in this great enterprise, my father said yes right away and left his job at the bank. This was a sign, he believed. Because a German had given him life.

My mother was a granddaughter of a French engineer who had come to Mexico to help set up the Mexican railroad. My mother's young life had been incredibly cloistered. She'd still get excited by candies and balloons at fifteen. 1931 and a balloon was all it took. And she was moral, had principles. When she found out my father was cheating on her with the maid in Oaxaca she threw him out. He had grown distant and cold, was coming to visit us in Mexico City less and less, and when she found out why this was she threw him out. You must understand, nobody ever threw them out for cheating with the maid. Every man cheated with the maid; this was Mexico, 1950, so it was a pre-ordained fact. Plus, it was in another state. Nevertheless, she threw him out and then she raised all of us on her own. Her own parents had long since died, tragically both of them. Philippe Durand had been bitten by some kind of infectious horsefly and died a month later, his daughter only five. Her mother died nine years after that and then my mother was raised by her aunt.

And this part gets very confusing, because her mother had already asked her sister, "If I ever die," she had said, "you must take my daughter." And her sister pushed right by her and into the kitchen while in a rushed voice she said, "Yes, of course I would take her, but please do not talk like that." And then just a week or so later my grandmother contracted a fever and she did die. How had she known? And her sister, my mother's aunt, did take my mother in. But we all know that a mother and an aunt are not the same thing. Especially when a girl is fourteen. They just are not the same thing, a mother and aunt.

My sister and I—I don't at all like her, you might as well know it now, so you probably will not be hearing much about Sofia from me—my sister, Sofia, and I went to visit my father in Oaxaca, two or three times, my brothers refusing to come along because they hated my father's new woman. When we did go to visit, this is how it was: He was a silent man, spoke very little unless it was to command, even at dinner during which he merely gestured and grunted as that new woman held forth on some inane topic—she was very dull—while absently passing him the various dishes and sauces he pointed at. He merely gestured at what he wanted and she stupidly placed things in his hand.

I watched him as he ate, chewing hard like him.

After a short nap my father would set off to work again and in the afternoon we were allowed to follow. When we set into the woods there was dark and there was moist. My father trudged, trudged, ahead of us and we always kept him in sight—he might disappear, we both feared—even when we seemed fully involved in something else. So that we were this: a serious man who walked with the heavy monster steps of slightly arthritic knees—moving forward through his toil, in what he professed to be the straightest of possible lines—and two small girls, circling about him, stopping to chase and catch and dig, to look and observe and wonder and fall back, and then run forward again to catch up and even get a little ahead of the insistent plodding steps of that man, our father.

I guess what I'm saying, what I'm trying to explain, is that this wasn't what I'd been brought up for. Sleeping in jails in Kansas. It was thrilling, yes, the wandering. M was beautiful, drew people to him. People wanted to be around us, to help us. They looked at him like that. But it was his fault. Everything to come was his fault. Julia. All of it. Everything that came later. Everything that would eventually happen, Julia. Don't ever forget that. Though things had started out well, the trip to Kansas City exciting, almost immediately it had all begun to get confusing, what he would get involved in on those dark nights, skulking like his father, his friends and the gambling, the long list of women. Those drawn dark nights. But on our trip back it seemed good again; I thought we had left the confusion behind and again it seemed like he was mine. But only for a short while. A tiny little while. Because again things started feeling not right. We would get into a new town and M would disappear for long stretches of time. And then my mind started slipping in ways I didn't remember it doing before, in ways I didn't understand, and in these different towns I panicked; my mind would slip and my heart would race and I would panic. In these many different towns the dust tasted the same, the thick hot air, the sun beating, that sun beating down hard; and I cried and I cried. My thoughts started running in circles; these towns were all the same place. We would stay in a town for a day or two and then we would move on, but were we really moving? Were we really going anywhere at all? Getting any closer? All the towns were exactly the same. Was it in fact the same place? My judgment grew confused, my mind slipping, my heart racing for no reason at all, palms sweating, breath coming in heaves. He had a bit of a streak, then, and so we stopped in Amarillo for a while and on the third day there he gave me money to buy some groceries, things for the little hotel room we were staying in. He was lying in bed, propped up like a sultan, completely worn out from another late night, and when I approached him on that third Amarillo day he didn't want me to touch him. I looked at him with broken eyes and then I walked to the store instead, the dusty hot streets, and I came back thirsty from eating that dust and empty-handed except for a pretty little dog collar I'd found. I'd seen it in a shop window on the way to the groceries, so pretty and bright. But when I brought it home for him—it was a gift—he was mad. It was red leather, studded with diamonds, fake of course but so pretty. Luminous like his eyes, I told him. Bright and clear like the water which was his eyes, I told him; I was so thirsty and still he yelled at me while he held it in his hand. What the hell was I doing spending his money on a leash and a collar for a dog we didn't have? I blinked three times to make sense and then I tried to look into his eyes, those liquid blue eyes, I am so thirsty, I said to him, I need a drink, I said to him, but he just came up to my face and he grabbed the bag from my hands and stormed out with it so he could get his money back. And, confused, I stood there and I cried, staring at his receding back.

It was soon after that I started not sleeping; I paced and paced all night. I tried crying, but my eyes would not cooperate, so that there was no relief, now, a blank, nothing to let out. I tried screaming, my voice stifled. He would be gone sometimes for days at a time and so I had no one to run to. No one to find and to whisper to, no one to warn that there was somebody coming, someone was after us; I didn't know who, don't ask me who I would have said if he had asked; I had no idea, had not seen their faces, could not see their faces, but I heard them sometimes, whispering, and I knew that they were there, knew they were going to descend when I was not looking; and so I looked and I looked. I had to keep looking. I searched and I searched. I tried screaming. I would stand in the middle of the room, sometimes, and it would finally come to me, my voice, and so I would scream at them to come out, to just come now. I could not take it any longer. I would no longer wait! And sometimes, with my voice, this same voice, I yelled for them to go away. Get the fuck out of here!

In Galveston he took me to a hospital. It was not really a hospital, I don't think; no one there was there to help out, there had been no oath taken in that place. He slapped my face when I scratched at him and he pulled me into the car though I was kicking and when he got me there he spilled me out and they scooped me up off the pavement and they took me in and they tied me down. They tied me up liquid and held me down solid and shoved something cold and hard into my mouth and then they gave me those shocks in my head. They held me down tight and tied me up hard and gave me electricity shooting into my head and he watched them while they did it. I was seven months pregnant with our first baby, you understand; I don't think I've mentioned that. Did I already tell you that? I was pregnant. And I held on to Rocio with my steel legs gripping tight. I'd been sporty, the wild one, remember? And I was strong and I gripped my legs tight like clamping hard steel. And he, he let them do that to me. He watched while they did it.

It was his fault, I tell you. It was all his fault. Everything. All of it. I was not cut out for that life, that skulky wandering life.

Then, still drooling, he drove me back in another one of his borrowed cars—Where did all of those cars come from? From whom did he borrow those cars?—to my mother in Mexico City. He dropped me on her doorstep, savagely spilled me out there too, and she picked me up soft and then she fed me gentle with a rounded spoon and she lovingly wiped away the drool while I stared straight with my eyes all full of blankness for many many months; to me she sang each night and then it was months before he came back, Rocio already squirming about in my mother's overly engulfing swallow me up arms when he finally came back.

Denise Hamilton

The Lady of the Canyons

S UNSET WAS THE BEST time to run trails.

After the heat of the day, cool air eddied in the hillside canyons and Monica flew along the silky-dusty paths, her feet barely touching the ground.

Like always, Sirius loped at her side.

Monica knew every curve and straightaway, every incline and descent of these hills. The knowledge was hard-won, embedded in skin and sinew, a living map winding up her long, tawny legs.

People said it was dangerous to run alone through the mountain range that stretched from the blue Pacific through the hills of Hollywood to the sprawl of Colonel Griffith's park.

Especially at night.

They said a mountain lion might get you, or a pack of hungry coyotes.

Monica was more leery of two-legged predators.

And there were those too, because this was urban parkland in the middle of Los Angeles.

Still, she could handle it.

Sirius would defend her. And if that didn't work, she hoped she could outrun them.

Above her, the sky swirled in tangerine and tween pink, fuschia and grape Kool-Aid.

She passed an elderly Chinese couple in hiking boots descending quickly to the trailhead.

The man carried a six-foot walking stick fashioned from a dead tree branch.

California oak, thought Monica. Two years ago, a magnificent one had toppled in a storm not far up the path.

"Getting dark," the woman called in a sing-song voice. "You turn 'round soon."

"Thanks, I'll be okay," Monica said, clasping a hand to her heart and inclining her head as she ran past.

Another half mile and her breath grew ragged as the trail rose. It was a long incline, zigging and zagging, almost vertical at times, but eventually she emerged onto a promontory at the eastern end of the Santa Monica Mountains. From this perch high atop Colonel Griffith's park, she could see parts of Nando's Valley, Glendale and the downtown Pueblo of Los Angeles.

Below her, the Los Angeles River curved like a cerulean snake, the water shimmering as it caught and reflected the sun's last rays. A series of white stone bridges spanned the river. The city sprawled below her like a fever dream; skinny glass and steel skyscrapers, street grids clogged with traffic, hills studded with cantilevered homes. Past the northern flats, the Verdugo Mountains reared up, already drenched in purple shadow.

By a trick of the fading light, the Verdugos looked almost close enough to touch.

Monica wondered what it would be like to run *those* trails, and what adventures might await along its rock-strewn paths.

So close, and yet she'd never set foot there.

She never would.

Their upper flanks were wind-scoured and bare compared to the lush and coastal Santa Monica Mountain range where she ran.

Little wonder she felt at home in her bones here.

Far below her, the Old Zoo was a hive of activity.

Years ago, the Los Angeles Zoo had moved north to bigger quarters, leaving caves hollowed out of stone and the ruins of animal enclosures. Like most places made by human hands that lie fallow, the Old Zoo vibrated with strange energy.

And it drew visitors.

Each summer a theatrical troupe set up in the clearing and performed free Shakespeare under the stars. Monica had found their production of *A Midsummer Night's Dream* particularly resonant.

But now it was October, and carnival music drifted up, spooky and discordant.

She saw circus tents and tractors and bales of hay. Behind the scenes, actors were applying white face makeup and fake blood, wriggling into costumes, revving chainsaws.

She'd seen the signs on her run, a spectacle called "The Haunted Hayride."

Soon, carnival-goers would line up to buy tickets and then screams of fear and wonder would echo through the canyons.

Monica herself had little use for such cheap parlor tricks.

Still, it pleased her to see Angelenos venturing into the wilder redoubts of Colonel Griffith's park at night.

On full moon nights, the Sunset Stables even led horseback rides over the Hollywood Hills to a Mexican restaurant at the park's northeastern edge in Burbank.

Monica knew from experience that the place made a mean margarita.

A few of those, and you swayed easy in the saddle on the ride home.

Colonel Griffith's park was at its best then, a remote and timeless world where the lonesome yip of coyotes and the smell of leather, warm horseflesh, and sagebrush could transform you into a frontier scout or a mission padre or a Chumash maiden hastening to meet her lover from an enemy tribe.

Yes, the park was a jewel, the green and living lungs of a traffic-choked city.

Monica sighed and peeled off the main trail, looping west toward the Observatory and the Hollywood sign.

Her feet moved effortlessly, blood pounding a rhythm to her brain, her limbs strong and powerful, winged and fleet.

From time to time, Sirius crashed into the brush on mysterious errands, re-emerging down the path, redolent of rosemary and sage. They both smelled of the trail—dirt and sand and chalky clay, dead leaves underfoot, the pine and eucalyptus and pollen.

She moved inside the rhythm of flight, her mind floating free, meditative.

The miles passed under her feet.

Sometimes the trail was wide; at others it was a narrow foot-path. And sometimes it was only a faint animal trail, meandering over hillsides and up rock-strewn precipices so that her thinly shod toes grasped for purchase on crevice and rock.

The coyotes were starting up now with eerie yips and answering barks, then full-throated polyphonic howls. They didn't scare her. She knew that one or two coyotes could evoke a baying pack as they threw their voices across the echoing canyons.

Besides, it was only the evening barking, as they passed on news about the most promising hunting grounds and where each pack was headed. The coyotes didn't want to tangle with her, and she respected their autonomy and left them alone.

As she summited the hill—at last! at last!—Monica found herself on a ridge, the canyons plunging steeply on either side. Up so high, she felt the joy of a hawk that drifts lazily on warm air currents. Visibility was great in this back country. Far ahead, a dark blur on the path slowly resolved into two riders on horseback.

Seeing her approach, the horses nickered in welcome.

"You lost?" one of the riders called. "It's gone dusk and we're miles from the nearest trailhead. Want a ride back to civilization?" He patted his horse's neck. "Smoky here won't mind another passenger."

Smoky whinnied and bent his head in agreement.

Monica liked horses and they liked her.

She liked their warm soft flanks, their velvet muzzles and large inquisitive eyes, their comforting animal smell, the way their powerful muscles rippled under skin. She didn't even mind the pungent fruity droppings that littered these trails, slowly decomposing back to nature.

"I'm good, thanks," she said.

But her stride slowed.

Her gaze lingered on the beasts and their riders, young guys with Nudie's cowboy hats, handsome in the TV-actor way she saw so much in the hills above Hollywood.

A warm tingling began in the pit of her stomach. She liked the one in the checked shirt with red piping and mother-of-pearl buttons. He had a rough, raw-boned look to him. She pictured them cantering along these trails, the touch of his hand on the small of her back as they dismounted, the Mexican serape he'd lay out under a tree.

It had been so long.

With a rueful smile and a wave, she glided past, then sped up, shooting off down the trail like a coyote who spies autumn's last squirrel.

Soon, she heard only the wind soughing through the gnarled bushes and the scuff, scuff of her shoes against dirt, Sirius running silent beside her. The path curved and swung out to a viewpoint and there, suddenly, was the LA basin.

Far below, lights winked on street by street. She raised her arms and felt she could command the flow of light, conduct its movements like a neon symphony.

She thought of the orchestra warming up right now at the Hollywood Bowl, the magnificent concerts she'd seen there, the sound rising in waves to bless the canyons.

Humming snatches of Bach, she conducted the music inside her head and the lights below as she ran, until her arms balked at fighting gravity and fell back into the old piston-pump.

At her approach, small creatures slithered and scurried into the brush. Larger ones froze in place to watch her pass, more curious than afraid. Overhead, the screech of a hunting bird, the flap of mighty wings. And from a nearby canyon, the probing, tentative hoot of an owl sending out a signal flare. *Is anybody there?* And an answering hoot, bouncing off a far-off canyon.

A veritable hootenanny, Monica thought, cracking herself up.

She was at one with the hills, the trail, the animals, the mountains. This was her dominion.

Her mountains.

Each canyon with its own personality: Laurel was folk songs and floral-print dresses and the sweet acrid smell of weed. Runyon was dogs and non-stop chatter about agents and pitch meetings. Topanga was incense and vegetarian restaurants playing Pachelbel's Canon.

Some days, Monica would stand, freckled and sunburnt on the edge of the Pacific, listening to the crash and roar of the surf. The air had a vetiver marine salt smell that mirrored the tang of her skin after a run.

Other days, she'd run northern paths to the edge of Nando's Valley or east into the vast expanses of Colonel Griffith's park.

Occasionally she caught glimpses of him, a stout mustachio'd man in a dark woolen waistcoat and felt hat who still hovered on the periphery of things. He favored the high places, from which he'd gloomily survey the park he'd deeded to the people of Los Angeles.

Once she found him weeping atop the walls of his Observatory, a bottle of whiskey clutched in his hand. In his alcoholic delirium, he mistook her for his tragically disfigured wife.

"Your face! You are beautiful once more," Griffith J. Griffith shouted as he staggered toward her, his face radiant with tears. "Dearest Mary, I wasn't in my right mind when the revolver went off. Please say you'll forgive me or I shall go mad."

But as he drew closer he realized his mistake. "You are not she," he cried.

And then he began to dwindle, growing more faint and transparent until he disappeared altogether and Monica, who hadn't drank enough water that hot summer day, thought she might be hallucinating from dehydration.

But there were other, stranger things.

Like the homeless woman Monica had seen sprawled below the bronze statue of Griffith on the park's southeast edge at Los Feliz, howling and keening like a madwoman.

That wasn't so unusual in and of itself.

But the woman's ragged and faded clothes had once been richly tailored. And she wore fancy lace-up, heeled boots patched with Velcro.

Her face was completely obscured by a black lace veil, and though her words were muffled, Monica thought she was saying "Oh, Griffith" in a mournful voice.

Sensing Monica's presence, the woman turned.

"Behold what he did to me," she said and lifted the veil.

The right side of the woman's face was a puckered mass of scar tissue and her right eye socket gaped empty while her left observed the world with a terrible, unfathomable gaze.

Desperate to look elsewhere, Monica ducked her head and dug into a pouch for coins.

When she looked up with a fistful of silver, the woman was gone.

That day, Monica ran twice as hard and long to banish Mary Agnes Griffith's ruined face from her mind.

But still it haunted her nightmares.

Dark had descended fully now.

The path curved and dipped into a recessed canyon.

Somewhere below floated Hollywood, a palace of desert mirage and dreamscape.

The cool air wicked away sweat and her thin leather shoe soles were marvelously supple on the uneven paths. Sirius was off on one of his errands.

She ran past a shack.

The hills were full of these mysterious places: pumping stations; fertilizer sheds; nineteenth-century Spanish adobes; generating stations; reservoirs. And mouldering shacks with smashed-out windows whose purpose and utility were lost to the mists of time.

Sometimes, the old ruins were inhabited by squatters and other wayfarers, and she'd have to be careful. Then there was the Mission Bar, an old adobe tucked into an overhang in the mountains, which drew a strange crowd.

It was darker down here, as if night and mountain shadow conspired to enhance the blackness. But Monica had excellent night vision, and could navigate the path with only a sliver of moon and the stars that shone brighter here away from the city's electric grid.

Indeed, she scoffed at flashlights and headlamps, which she'd seen once near Supple Veda's Pass— a group of midnight runners traversing the mountains on a full moon, hooting and hollering and pawing the ground with their thick, rubber-wedge heels, scattering wildlife for miles around.

She'd shimmied into a tree and watched them stampede past, fascinated and a little repelled. Then she hopped down and caught up with them, merging undetected into their midst.

It felt unexpectedly good to lope along in a big friendly pack.

Monica matched strides with a guy who looked her up and down, intrigued by what he saw. And she made it easy for him, casting shy smiles from under her wild-flowing hair.

"You one of those ultra runners?" he asked after a few miles.

She laughed dismissively. "The ones who run 150 miles through Death Valley in July? Nah. Not nearly. I just have fun."

"How many miles d'you get in each week?" he said, and she imagined falling into his sea-blue eyes and floating there forever.

She named a number and they chatted easily about the things that obsess those who run and bore everyone else silly. Eventually she got around to asking if he came here often to run the trails, but he told her he was visiting from out of state.

At this her heart deflated. But she hid her disappointment and accepted some of the energy gel he offered and even gave him a handful of pignoli nuts from the bag slung across her waist.

When he asked for her number, because he got down to LA a few times a year and maybe they could see each other again, she told him she was in a relationship. It would never work, she told herself. For a moment there, she'd pictured them running free under the moon, and how she'd show him all her secret places.

The guy said that was too bad and then he grew quiet. Eventually, he fell behind and she ran on, then bombed down an animal path that looped back to the main trail. Ducking behind a rock, she watched them run past again, eyes seeking out her young man, and she had to restrain herself from calling out, "I'm here. I lied to you. I'd love more than anything to see you again."

The path ascended steeply and Monica pushed herself hard to expunge the memory.

Her breath grew labored but her feet spun beneath her, pushing her up step by tortuous step. Soon she'd reach the top and the lactic acid pumping through her legs would ease.

A foul smell hit her.

Sometimes hunters came out here to hunt deer illegally, leaving the bodies to rot.

Pumas were more efficient.

After bringing down prey, they'd gorge on the thigh and breast meat, eating in precise horizontal bands.

Once the choice flesh was gone, coyotes arrived to eat their fill.

Then the giant birds who'd been circling overhead awaiting their turn— buzzards, eagles, hawks, falcons, crows—to peck out the eyes, the soft gelatinous bits, the hard-to-find crevice meat.

And after them the possums and skunks, the smaller critters, the clean-up crew.

And working almost invisibly from the inside, the insect nation.

She'd seen a deer stripped to white bone in two days.

Monica didn't hear the rustle above until it was too late.

From an outcropping of rocks, a shadow dropped onto the trail.

She screamed, knowing full well that she was miles from anywhere and no one would come to the rescue.

The shadow landed on all fours.

A mountain lion.

That she could deal with.

But there was no tail.

And as it straightened onto two legs, she understood.

Its arms spread wide in a menacing manner.

A Bowie knife open in one hand, the tip of its blade pointing right at her.

Blocking the trail.

Monica's foot hit the ground, dug in.

She froze.

After the rocking cadence of running, how unnatural to be still.

A rustle behind her, then coarse, lewd laughter.

There were two of them.

Monica edged closer to the outside of the trail.

She didn't want to get pinned against the hill.

If she had to, she'd run straight down the side of the mountain.

It wouldn't be the first time.

From below came the sound of crashing underbrush.

A head of greasy, lank hair popped up.

Then a black beard. A soiled denim jacket, filthy jeans. Biker boots.

So they were three.

An ambush.

The one in front said. "We watched you, girly. Taking the switchbacks, zigging and zagging, heading right toward us. All by your lonesome, too. Don't you know it's dangerous here at night. Bad folks about."

Monica said nothing.

The one in front fingered the tip of his blade.

"So Barry here," he inclined the knife to the guy behind her, "said to find a spot near the top of the hill. Said you'd be tired and out of breath. And just look at you, huffing like your heart's gonna bust loose out of your chest."

The man gave an evil smile.

She felt the circle around her tighten as the three men shifted their weight, ready to pounce if she made a break for it.

"Boys, let's take her back to the campfire."

Rough arms grabbed her. They set off down the trail, cracking lewd jokes, jostling her.

Something flashed in Monica's head.

"You lit a campfire?" she said. "Are you crazy? The brush is like tinder."

She thought they might hit her and tensed, ready to duck, but they only laughed.

"You're the crazy one, running these hills at night. A little fire's the least of your worries right now."

Soon she could smell the campfire, and then see it in the clearing. The men had piled large stones around it, but one spark carried on the wind and the Santa Monica Mountains would go up in flames from Malibu to Glendale.

She shivered.

The flames danced, illuminating two pup tents. Stacks of cans and cup-a-noodles. Sacks of white bread.

"It was my idea so I get her first," the one named Barry said.

"Tie her hands and feet, Lester," said the third.

They knotted her wrists with thick, coarse rope, then Lester bent to tie her ankles while Barry held her shoulders. She felt his belly press against her back and buttocks, grinding against her.

As Lester knelt at her feet, Monica leapt into the air, jerking herself backwards while her heels came up and kicked Lester hard in the windpipe.

Something in his throat snapped.

Her backward jerk knocked Barry off balance in mid-grind.

He staggered and fell and she landed atop him.

She pulled her wrists forward, then brought both elbows back hard against his face.

The pain shooting from her elbows told her she'd hit her mark. The biker gurgled then lay still, the bones of his nose lodged deep inside his brain.

Monica scrambled to her feet.

She twisted her wrists and hands in a series of quick movements. The ropes binding them fell to the ground.

The third biker stood, mouth agape, eyes bulging, as he stared as his dead friends.

He scanned frantically for a weapon, then grabbed an iron poker sitting in the fire. Its end glowed orange red.

Awareness washed over her: they'd meant to use it on her.

The thought sent a white mist of rage flooding her eyes so she could barely see.

She advanced on him, fists clenched.

The biker danced backward, brandishing the poker, screaming, "Come any nearer, witch, and I'll kill you."

From the underbrush came the sound of a body crashing nearer, then an otherworldly growl as Sirius burst forth. He leaped onto the biker's back and knocked him to the ground.

Mouth open and slavering, he stood over the biker, waiting for the command to tear out the throat of this man who dared attack his mistress.

"Sirius," said Monica, and he fixed her with his eerie, pale-blue eyes. "Spare him."

Sirius looked down at the man's exposed neck.

Saliva dripped from his teeth.

He whined and snapped the air once, then padded to her side.

"Thank you, my faithful companion," Monica said.

Then she advanced toward the man, Sirius at her side.

The biker tried to scoot away, groveling and whining in terror.

"Keep that fucking giant coyote or whatever it is away from me," he begged. "The boys and I didn't mean any harm. We were just having a little fun. It was a joke. We wouldn't have hurt you."

An angry growl rumbled deep inside Sirius's throat.

"Yes, Sirius. He's a liar on top of everything else. But never mind.

"We're going to let this one live, my friend. He's going to get his sorry carcass up and out of these mountains and he's going to tell all his low-life city friends to stay out of my dominion. He'll spread the word far and wide that his kind will not be tolerated here. This is a place of sanctuary. I am the keeper of these mountains. I watch over them. And if he dares to darken my door again, I won't be so benevolent next time."

Monica prodded the biker's leg with the toe of her leather-clad foot.

"Is that perfectly clear?"

"Y-yes."

"Sirius, you will accompany this loathsome piece of human trash to the borders of my realm. You! Get up. Now!"

She bared her lips and her teeth seemed longer. Her gold-speckled eyes shone in the moonlight. Her clothes were dun and gray and brown and silver-green, and her muscles rippled beneath the fabric, which seemed woven of leaves and bark and branches themselves. Yellow acacia flowers twined through her hair and she smelled resinous like sage and pine and eucalyptus and the chalky dust of the trail itself.

She'd need to stand for hours under the waterfall of the Western Arch to wash the touch of these men from her skin, with their greasy fingers and foul thoughts.

"And one more thing," she said, as the man got shakily to his feet. She leaned forward.

"Run," she said.

Rachel M. Harper

How to Lose Your Children

W HEN YOU WALK OUT of the house, leaving your three children behind, there is a part of you that thinks you will never go back. But it is a small part. Mostly you tell yourself that you just need a minute, just one minute to breathe, and once you feel your legs solidly beneath you, something that is just yours and meant to carry you alone, it's going to be okay, you're going to be okay, and you can go back to what you created.

But you don't.

It is the middle of the day and you just made lunch—hot dogs for them, rolled into flour tortillas because the whole wheat buns went moldy, and a salad with leftover chicken for you, no dressing—and the baby needs a nap soon and you promised the big kids you'd clean off the slip n' slide, and there are things to do around the house, things you promised your husband you'd take care of like call the phone company about the outrage of last month's bill; take down the birthday decorations from your daughter's party two weekends ago, a dental theme that you thought was impossible for an eight-year-old to imagine or execute; clean the spider webs from the front porch so they don't nest in the baby's swing; bleach the boy's baseball pants for the game on Saturday, when it will be ninety-five degrees and he won't want to play and you won't want to watch him, but because you paid for it and he's got talent or at least a waning interest, and you are a good mother and want to give him the opportunities your parents gave you, deserving or not, desired or not, you will force the entire family to go cheer him on.

And there's more: you need to defrost something healthy and interesting for dinner, something they won't complain they just had, something you won't read about the dangers of on that mothering blog that sends you e-mail updates you don't have time to read; re-frame the family portrait that slipped from the matte in the heat wave and now sits cockeyed in the corner of the frame, exposing the cardboard lining behind the matte, making you feel cheap and lazy every time you walk by it, like you left an old pair of underwear soaking in the sink before a neighbor's unexpected visit.

So much to do, yet not enough to keep you there.

Three steps out the door and you hear someone calling your name: "Mom-my," not a name really, more of a condition, a label that sounds most days like an accusation, but you don't turn around. "Go back inside," you say over your shoulder, and even though you can tell them apart in the dark by the sound of their breathing, you don't even know which one it was.

After, more to yourself, you say, "I'll be right back," but even then, at the edge of your yard, the grass thick like it's manmade—so different from the grass of your childhood, silky and dark like spinach, always cool beneath your feet—you question whether you're telling the truth. Will you be right back? Will you ever be back?

The heat of the driveway surprises you, gritty like a beachside parking lot. You are barefoot, you now realize, and the complete lack of surprise surrounding this fact, the bitter truth of it, makes you smile. Of course, you think, why would you stop to put on shoes? Why take care of yourself when there are so many others to take care of?

You keep walking. The sidewalk is partly covered by fallen magnolia leaves, the underside soft like suede. These are the same leaves your kids collect and use as tickets to the shows they produce each afternoon in the backyard, your ears ringing from their pitch-less voices, yet proud that twenty-first-century kids can still use their imaginations, can play for hours without batteries. Your heart pounds in your chest, as if you're running uphill. You fight the urge to hold your breath. Instead, you inhale; feel the butterflies land at the bottom of your stomach as you remember how much you love your children.

But still, you keep walking.

Ahead, beyond your neighbor's house, you see the distant San Gabriel Mountains. Now you have a focal point, a goal, as you imagine those peaks to be your destination, tell yourself you're taking a scenic hike, the kind your neighborhood is known for, instead of abandoning the three human beings you intentionally brought into the world. The foothills are famous for cultivating poppy fields and bobcats, suburban legend boasting about the bobcat who took a baby from her carriage while her mother was gardening. You're not sure how the story ends because you refused to keep listening, but the words *bobcat* and *baby* and *mother* and *garden* were enough for you to know it was a warning not to have a baby or a garden, though you didn't heed either piece of advice. You also knew intrinsically that it was the mother's fault, not the bloodthirsty bobcat, though he had the two-inch incisors. No matter what, it is always the mother's fault.

Before you had children, you thought the most difficult part would be when they were babies—the diapers, the night feedings, the constant worry. In fact, those were the easy years. With babies, you don't have to answer questions or mediate arguments. You don't have to supervise their homework and their playdates, clean pee off the toilet seat, toothpaste off the walls, and blood from surprise nosebleeds while they sleep; you don't have to shop three times a week to keep them in pretzels and pasta and crackers shaped like the alphabet, things you're embarrassed to put in your cart but will later save you hours of complaint and refusal.

You thought motherhood was a territory, a place to stake your claim and plant seeds, watch them blossom, when really it's a negotiation between border states. You didn't realize there would be so much unrest. Before them, you and your husband barely argued. Not about time or money or responsibility, you argued about silly things like your ex-boyfriends wanting to meet for coffee or a coworker who texts too late at night. People don't make you jealous now, but time does. His Wednesday night card games, basketball playoffs in the neighbor's den, a conference in Dallas that puts him on a three-hour flight all by himself and gives him four nights in the air conditioned silence of a chain hotel. When he sits in the driveway listening to NPR after his commute, waiting for the story to end. You could slap him across the face for that—as if you ever get to complete anything. A conversation, a meal, an article, an argument. That is the problem with motherhood—your life becomes a To Do list you never get to complete. The satisfaction of a job well done, of being done at all, constantly eludes you.

Your only hope for accomplishment is escape.

Your only escape is in the bathroom.

Reading *The New Yorker* used to be something you did to keep up with colleagues, but now it is a strategy, a ploy that buys you a few moments of solitude. You distract them with snacks and sneak off to the bathroom like you used to sneak off to smoke in high school, the magazine tucked under your arm like contraband. Five, or god forbid, ten minutes alone, is worth the hassle of installing the key locks yourself, the occasional knocks from the little one to make sure you're okay, the strange looks as you sheepishly exit, lighting a match in your wake. You'd exchange anything for this solitude, let them think you have dysentery, that you're throwing up the four ice cream sandwiches you just ate, anything is better than the truth, which is this: you need to pretend, for a few minutes every day, that they don't exist. You need to know you have the option of escape. That you are something more than, something beyond, their mother.

You have walked two more blocks without realizing it. You don't turn around, but if you did, the roofline of your three-bedroom Craftsman would be visible. You would see that your house looks peaceful from this distance, and fake, like an architect's model of a typical suburban home, and you wonder just how typical you are—how many mothers have left their children unattended? How many other women have traded their name for a label they don't recognize, playing a part with lines they can't always recite?

You feel your phone vibrating in your pocket. The screen says your husband's name, yet has a picture of the baby kissing you. How sweet. You send it straight to voicemail by pressing the "reject" button, then see that you have three missed calls from him. A text reads: *Call me. Now.* Another one: *Are you okay??* You drop your phone back into your pocket.

A car passes by, slowing down at the corner. The driver looks back to see if he knows you. You look away. You don't want to be seen.

The street is suddenly quiet, unfamiliar. You stop short, stubbing your toe on a crack in the sidewalk, the concrete split by the roots of a tree you cannot name. The surface is still hot under your feet, though the sun is barely a suggestion in the sky. What is it about the desert, you wonder, that allows everything to hold such heat, yet never explode?

The phone vibrates again. You pause mid-step, half your body wanting to keep going, the other half ready to face what you've done, to explain, to justify. Your mind races to make up a story, something he will buy without too much effort or apology. Instead, you draw a complete blank. You wonder if you are out of words. You wonder if you are out of your mind.

You hold the phone in your hand. You feel his desperation, feel your own. You look at the picture of your baby, read your husband's name like it's a foreign text.

You press "accept," and hear your husband's voice before the phone is even touching your ear.

"Julia, are you there? What the hell happened?"

You start to speak, but instead of words coming out they go in. You swallow them in a gulp with the hot air. Your finger slides over the power button and you disconnect the line.

Seconds later, as you round the bend on Prospect, a street you can't afford to live on, you hear a familiar sound: the annoying jingle of the ice cream truck. The clown-shaped speakers that assault you with "The Star Spangled Banner" every day at exactly 3:45 p.m., predictable as an alarm clock, have found you. You stop cold, fury mounting. The sound makes you want to hurt someone, to forget yourself and become a criminal. You imagine screaming at the driver, threatening to slash his tires so he doesn't ever come back to your street, writes this block off as being borderline, beyond the god-like grasp of gentrification, but then you realize this isn't your block, and you're not on your street, and this truck, this mobile merchant, this man who deals with dozens more children in a day than you do, has as much of a right to be here as you. Probably more.

As you pass the truck, you glance at the stickered window, opened just a crack, yet large enough for a child's hand to slip through. Though trying not to look, you can't help but see the hobbled back, the loose off-brand jeans, slick with wear, and most surprisingly, the expression on the driver's yielding face, his cloudless eyes, and your heart breaks with compassion as you realize he is of your tribe, like a teacher or social worker: he knows the burden of a life spent sustaining children.

For that you walk over and give him the only money in your pocket, a twenty dollar bill, and tell him to keep the change in exchange for half a dozen ice cream sandwiches, wrapped in the same thin paper as the ones you devoured in high school, studying for geometry exams you aced in vain, never using the math aptitude that made your father so proud, instead studying Religion and Theater Arts in college, things that made you interesting at cocktail parties but had yet to get you a job paying more than $40,000 a year. But what did it matter in the end, when you married young and well and had left those dead-end jobs for the glory of motherhood?

"Hope the kids enjoy 'em," the driver says as you walk away, the ice cream sandwiches tucked under your arm and melting against the heat of your abdomen, hollow now that your womb is empty.

The kids.

Hearing them mentioned in a collective, like they are a destination, some fun-filled place you'd visit, makes you think of turning back.

You are filled with a sudden longing, a pure, clean desire to hold them, to feel the snap of their limbs bend around your neck, the weight of brimming bodies in your arms, yet inside you know it's too late.

You are no longer a mother; you are a monster.

Who else would leave their children home alone? To walk the streets like some addict? You hear the refrain in your mind like a nursery rhyme: you don't deserve to have these children, to be anyone's mother, when you can't even take care of yourself. Because if you could, you wouldn't be here, would you?

You carry the ice cream sandwiches, damp with sweat. Together they feel like a wet book under your arm, a book you might have written, your autobiography perhaps, if you had the time or inclination to create something outside of your own body, if you could remember who you were.

You pass a familiar house, one you've often dreamt was your own, and spot three children playing together on the front lawn, children that could belong to you. A boy you imagine as Max is holding the baby, a head full of soft curls, while a girl named Bailey or Sasha taps the cat with a stick, making them all laugh when the cat falls over, chasing his own tail. As you look at them now, knowing they are someone else's children, some other happy family, you think how easy it is to be kind to strangers, to smile and wave, to offer them melted ice cream sandwiches as you pass by, comforted by the fact that you aren't responsible for their happiness or well-being. That you don't owe them anything at all.

Naomi Hirahara

The White Tuxedo

OUR CIRCLE WAS SITTING on the grass having lunch, when the PA system rang out with feedback. Jack Lau stood on the cement stage and raised the microphone to his dry, cracked lips. He was wearing a fake down jacket, a little bit big, and jeans, a little too short. "I want to protest the use of senior class funds for the prom." Jack's eyes rapidly blinked. "I think that instead of a dance, we should spend the money to sponsor a Vietnamese refugee family."

A few football players pelted Jack with crumpled potato chip bags. Jack continued on, a smirk deepening on his face. My friends in our circle on the lawn began to laugh.

"What is he, Vietnamese?" someone said. "He probably wants the money for his relatives."

I looked down at my tuna sandwich.

"Nah, I think he's Chinese," someone else added.

"Whatever he is, he's gross," Laura concluded, crossing her long, white legs on the grab grass. "He has to make a big deal about everything."

I silently agreed. He was a reject: ugly, uncoordinated, and oily hair. He didn't have much going for him, yet week after week he would set up the PA system and start spitting out something unpopular.

The worst thing was that he thought I was his friend. He approached me the first day of high school, three years ago. "Are you Chinese?" he asked hopefully.

"No, I'm an American." What a creep. He acted like a guy fresh off the boat, a FOB, as we third-generation Japanese Americans would say. My mother could hardly speak Japanese, much less me. Ever since then, I knew enough to stay away from him, but time after time, he would talk to me, thinking that we shared some special bond—being among only a handful of Asians in this mostly white Catholic school.

I looked past Jack to the tables next to the cafeteria. My eyes moved through the Pendleton shirts and letterman jackets, and there, finally I saw the shock of chlorine-whitened hair. Terry Nelson. My stomach felt queasy and wonderful at the same time. We worked together on the senior class council. I had known him since junior high, when he stood only a few inches taller than me. At that time, his nose, whose long arch bent at the middle, seemed more nerd-like. But over the past three years, his body began to take shape; lean muscles emerged, and somehow his off the wall humor became popular.

"Let's get some milk." I got up and looked at Laura.

"You have some—" Laura looked at the carton on my notebook.

"Come on." I grabbed Laura's elbow and we began walking toward the cafeteria.

"Hey, short stuff." A ball of paper hit my shoulder. Terry was grinning, his nose looking slightly crooked.

I couldn't think of a snappy comeback. "Hi." My heart beat through my body and my face felt red. "Mr. Gonzales really gave it to us yesterday in calculus. 'No talkin', no talkin', if you keep talkin', you'll be walkin' out of here.'" Terry fattened his cheeks to look like walrus jowls.

"Yeah. I thought he was going to separate us," I remembered.

"The dynamic duo? Naah, he doesn't have the guts. You might sit on him or something."

"Terry Nelson, I'm not two hundred pounds!"

"You're not? Then two hundred fifty?"

I solidly hit Terry's arm. I could feel a muscle under his vinyl jacket.

"Oh, hurt me, hurt me."

"Come on, Laura, let's go." I feigned anger and walked toward the lawn.

"Oh, hey, Cathy," he called after me. "Remember we're manning the prom ticket booth tomorrow at lunch." Those words rang in my ears. Laura hit me squarely in the ribs as we walked to our circle. "I think he likes you, Cathy," Laura whispered. "I think that he might ask you to the prom."

I was almost afraid to think about it. When I was alone in my bedroom or in the bathtub, I would imagine him leaning over me, his white hair sloping over his forehead, his metallic blue eyes looking at my face. Then he would dip down and press his lips against mine and I would feel his wide shoulders and feel safe. Then I would shake myself and wipe those thoughts away. Why set myself up for something that probably would never be? I didn't go to the last Christmas dance, even though I spent hours putting red and green tissue paper decorations on the walls of the women's club. The prom would be the same way, I told myself. There were plenty of girls, the *soshes*, tall with thin, pointy noses. Who could blame Terry if he chose one of them?

I was thinking all these things going to English class when someone stepped in front of me. I looked up. It was Jack Lau. "Oh, hi, Jack. I guess we might be late to English."

"Yeah." He walked next to me, moving his notebook from his right hand to his left.

I sensed something different about Jack, a tentativeness that got me nervous.

We walked silently to class until he suddenly blurted out, "You want to go to the prom with me?"

I began walking faster. Please God, don't do this to me, I thought to myself. "I can't," I said, out of the corner of my mouth.

"Why not?" Suddenly he seemed more aggressive, as if he were challenging me to give him a good reason. "Are you going with someone else?"

"I thought you were against the prom."

"It's the money allocation that I object to," said Jack. "But if we're going to have it, I'm going."

I didn't say anything, hoping that no one would notice that I was walking down the hall with Jack.

"Well, who's your date?" He started again.

"I didn't say I was going."

Jack's pasty face looked especially white, and his eyes twitched nervously. I felt as though I were falling; tumbling into a deep, dark hole with a gigantic, sticky cockroach scrambling after me.

"You don't want to go with me," he stated.

You're getting the picture—I said to myself. *Just leave me alone. I have enough things to worry about.* Jack kept following.

"Then who else is going to ask you?" He asked just as the bell rang.

I ran toward the door to English class. "Who else, Cathy?" he shouted.

Terry Nelson—I felt like screaming at him. *Terry would ask me, wouldn't he?* Or did I misinterpret the looks, the light punches on the arm, the teasing? I couldn't stand thinking of Terry going with someone else—especially the popular girls with color-coordinated clothing and bored looks on their faces. Terry had gone to the Christmas dance with a girl like that. Later, I heard that Terry had a terrible time; she left the dance early to go out with a local policeman. Terry learned his lesson, I told myself. He would want someone dependable like me.

Sometimes I would just laugh it all off. Who knew what the guys at this high school wanted? Who cared? We would graduate in a few months; I could enter college with a new identity. I heard about the tight friendships and romances within the brick dorm buildings—the late-night parties, the crazy pranks and the all-nighters. But maybe I would remain the same old Cathy, just plopped down in a new place: a slightly older version, still probably surrounded by friends but actually alone.

The next day I tried not to think about lunch and sitting with Terry at the prom ticket booth. I was trying so hard that I barely reacted when Terry asked me to prom just before calculus. I was dumbfounded. "Hey Cathy, are you in shock? Wake up, do you need some mouth to mouth?"

"Watch it Nelson, or I might just stand you up," I laughed, the sound rolling from my throat and dancing on my tongue. It had happened. Someone wonderful had asked me out. Now I could join in and talk about trying on dresses and buying boutonnières and finding shoes that I could dance in. I would be there, holding Terry's hand and resting my hand on his stiff tuxedo, and wondering what would happen after the prom.

My mother immediately noticed that I was in a good mood that evening. "Don't expect me to pay you for washing the dishes." She sipped some coffee at the kitchen table. "*Hakujin* families require their children helping out at home. We don't give you an allowance like they do, but you get everything you need."

I didn't even try to pick a fight with her. Mom had all these theories about white people from doing bobs and perms for elderly women at the beauty shop. Her moods about them went up and down. Sometimes she would brag about a customer who had a new yacht or had just returned from a cruise in the Bahamas. Other times Mom would come home with a dark expression on her face. "Those *hakujins*," she would say, exasperated, and mutter something about being evacuated from her home in Pasadena to the desert during World War II. I didn't understand much of what she said, but knew I shouldn't ask.

Mom silently stared at me for a minute. I rubbed the soapy sponge on one of the plates, watching the little specks of spaghetti sauce disappear.

"Mom, I need a dress." The request came out so easily from my lips. "A dress for the prom." My mother looked strange, as if torn between laughing and crying. We never talked about boys, dating, or sex. When I learned about conception in sixth grade, I was horrified. I couldn't imagine my thin-lipped mother and quiet father touching each other, especially in that way. She brought her coffee mug to the sink.

"We can go to that cute store at the mall. You know, the one with the daisies on the sign," she spoke quickly. "They might have something your size—Well, I'll probably end up hemming it anyway." She was off in her world, thinking about sheer fabric, pins, and needles. As an afterthought, she asked, "Who are you going with anyway?"

"A guy called Terry Nelson. He's real nice. We work together on the student council."

Mom paused. I could see the thought bubble above her head, "Oh, a *hakujin*." "Well, come on," she finally said. "Let's go. The stores close at eight." I was only too happy to leave the dishes in the sink. Mom filled the spaghetti pot with water. "We'll just let this soak."

The weeks went by quickly and before I knew it, I was at the prom, swaying to "Stairway to Heaven." I moved slightly to avoid Terry's boutonnière. He looked down and smiled. "You look really nice, Cathy."

I felt hot, and looked down at the wooden dance floor. I stared at a pair of thin ankles poking above a pair of bright pink shoes. I looked up and it was Laura. She caught my eye, and waved her magenta fingernails at me. Her date was a football lineman, with knotty ears and a thick neck. He moved his large hands up and down Laura's back, even after the song ended.

I excused myself to go to the restroom. Terry squeezed my shoulder. "I'll be sitting over there," he said, pointing to one of the round tables.

As I moved through the crowd, girls who had never said much to me before smiled and commented on my dress or my hair. It was like we all belonged to one team. We all knew the plays and were executing them throughout the night. This camaraderie was new to me, and I relished it; the way it infused my movement and conversation.

I spotted the shine of the gold women's bathroom sign down a hallway and turned. "Cathy," I suddenly heard. Jack Lau appeared in the hallway. Dressed in a white tuxedo with long tails, he had a drooping white carnation stuck in the buttonhole of his lapel. I knew that he had stolen the flower from one of our table centerpieces.

What was he doing here? And who was his date? I noticed the stiffness of his tuxedo and knew that he had not danced at all that night.

"You did a good job on the prom," he said. "The place looks great."

I didn't know what to say. "Thanks. Sorry, but I've got to go." I gestured towards the women's bathroom.

"Yeah—ah—you want to dance later?"

I just stared at him.

"It doesn't have to be a slow dance." I looked past Jack onto the dance floor and I saw Jack's friends bouncing up and down with their dates. The tallest one, Alfred, was known for pickling lizards for herpetology class.

"I can't, Jack. I came with someone. You know?"

Jack's face fell, his eyes looking bleary and wet. "I know. I know."

I shrugged my shoulders apologetically and walked towards the bathroom. I hated doing that, but the cost of being seen with him was greater to me than the risk of hurting him.

As I walked back to our table, I noticed Terry and Laura sitting together and talking. "Thanks a lot, Terry," she was saying, "You're really a good guy." When they noticed me, they became silent for a minute. Laura then smiled widely, her fuschia lipstick outlining her big white teeth. "Havin' fun?" she asked, picking some lint off of my hair.

"Yeah," I mumbled. *What were they talking about? Was I just a charity case?* I tried to slow my thoughts down.

"Did you see Andrea? I can't believe she would wear something so low-cut." Laura's voice took on a new tone as she critiqued a few of our friends' outfits. In the background, the band announced that they were going to take a fifteen-minute break.

I started to feel a pang in the pit of my stomach and then a wooziness spreading throughout my body. Laura's date returned to the table. Wrapping his thick arms around Laura, he started to whisper something in her ear.

I looked away and saw a flash of white on stage. Jack was walking toward the standing microphone. *Oh my God*, I thought. My heart started racing and my stomach felt even worse. *Come to your senses, get off of there. Lord, please don't let him say anything about me.*

Jack adjusted the microphone. A few people noticed him on stage and began to boo. "Since this is our last social activity before graduation, I wanted to say a few words about this whole class. I hope that your lives will improve once you get out of high school, because right now, you guys are a sad, sad group."

Everyone was watching Jack with angry and tense expressions. "That stupid Chinaman," sneered Laura's date. Laura giggled, her face suddenly resembling a mask.

"Get rid of the Chinaman. Get rid of the Chinaman," chanted the crowd. A few of the chaperones headed towards the stage. I felt as though the whole room was spinning with my classmates' ugly faces and chanting seeping into my skin. I ran out of the room into the hotel garden. I felt like disappearing into the blackness and never coming back. I felt a hand on my shoulder.

"Are you okay?" Terry's face looked tender and serious, an expression so rare for him, that he looked totally different.

I'm not one of them—I wanted to tell Terry. *I'm not like Jack.* But as the jeering resounded from the dance floor, I recalled my childhood classmates pulling up the sides of their eyes with their index fingers and laughing at me—"Chinese, Japanese, dirty knees." I wanted to yell and pound my fists into their large bodies, but I instead I walked past them, pretending not to hear. I couldn't have stopped them; they were bigger than me. *It'll be different when I'm grown-up,* I comforted myself. This didn't happen to adults.

"Are you okay?" Terry repeated. His eyes looked sad and guilty, and I noticed that they were actually more gray than blue.

I tried to smile. "I just needed to get outside."

"Yeah, me too." Terry looked at me awkwardly. I glanced toward the stage and saw some adults grabbing the cloth of Jack's white tuxedo. People were standing on chairs and clapping.

Terry came up close to me and his hands felt clammy against my back. I felt numb. It wasn't supposed to be like this. I wanted to like someone special, and I wanted him to like me back. I felt angry and cheated, and for the first time in a long time, I wanted to sit in my mother's lap and cry.

But I didn't move. In the darkness, Terry stroked my hair, and I felt a strange stirring inside of me. *Wasn't this what I wanted? To be alone with Terry?* All I could think about now was the boy in the white tuxedo. Terry smiled and leaned over to my lips. As I tasted my first kiss, I heard the final cheers from my classmates at the prom.

Christopher Horton

Three Visions

L ET ME DISAPPOINT SOME of you right away—these were not revelatory or apocalyptic visions. On the other hand, if they were, I'd have to ask you to send money to a post office box to hear them. Although one of my grandmothers supposedly had visions—and I could use the money. Anyway, I'm not a visionary. I'm just an ordinary overeducated, underemployed, irreverent guy. That's part of the reason I never fit in in the Midwest. I always knew that, even when I was just a kid. And only irreverent. I was sure there had to be some place that was at least a little closer to paradise.

And then I saw it. On TV. Because that was the only place to see things if you were a small-town midwestern boy born further back in the last century. And there were only four channels. So my first vision of paradise was seeing Pasadena on a warm, sun-dappled, pleasant New Year's Day. Although there's a limit to how sun-dappled an image on a black and white television can be, it still looked pretty good if the snow drifts piled up outside your window and the wind blew so strange. I mean, there was a parade. And clean-cut kids in shirt sleeves. And a football game. Back then, it was a football game in which the lumbering challenger from the Midwest would annually be lacerated by the smooth and silky Pac-10 team. Like a fencer with a rapier opposing a tackling dummy. I got used to it after awhile.

I kept that vision through college. I knew a guy there who came from Pasadena; well, San Marino, but it seemed all the same to me. Of course he was a tall, lanky guy with blond hair down to the middle of his back. And he was going to become either a rock star or a lawyer. Three guesses and the first two don't count. Anyway, he talked about his bucolic childhood of soccer games, Frisbee golf, and guitars in a tone that reinforced all my media-fed conceptions.

Then I moved to Los Angeles. No good reason. Well, graduate school. In the arts. Like I said, no good reason. That's so not the same as moving to Pasadena. Except for the sun-dappled part. And I didn't go out there because I didn't know anyone there. LA itself is overwhelming to learn. All these streets and all these pseudo towns with separate names. But you have to learn—people said, "In New York, people have secret restaurants; in LA, people have secret ways to get places." Since this was at the very end of the dark ages, I used to sit with the *Thomas Guide* and listen to the traffic reports on the radio. So I knew where Pasadena was—just past where the 134 turns into the 210. Which, quite frankly, sounded like a miserable place to be, according to the morning traffic reports.

Anyway, besides going to school, I landed a gig with the Pepperdine system. Just so I could afford protein once in a while. Man cannot live on Restoration drama alone. Pepperdine has mini-campuses everywhere and, thanks to the *Thomas Guide*, I found all of them: scenic Malibu, sort of scenic Long Beach, not so scenic West LA and Encino, and Westlake Village, which looked like a Pine Valley set on *All My Children*—I always felt like I might be hunted down, killed, and eaten in Westlake Village. Anyway, after all those travels, I had a seminar at the Pasadena location. I drove down Colorado Boulevard for the first time. It was pretty quaint, although not at all as restored—or expensive—as it is today.

I found Pepperdine Pasadena. Then at least, all these mini-campuses had the same hallway décor—beautiful framed old black and white pictures of the local area from way back when, some as far back as the nineteenth century. I like old pictures and spent a lot of time looking at them. And, in West LA or Encino or Stepford—er, West-lake—Village, I'd think, "Wow! You can't even tell it was the same place." But, at Pepperdine Pasadena, having driven down Colorado Boulevard, I saw these shots of that street around 1900 and thought, "Yup, that's exactly what it looks like."

Little did I know that that was the last hurrah for my first vision of Pasadena as the essence of white-bread America. I made some friends in my program and one of them had a party at a big old decaying Victorian house he'd rented on Lake Avenue in Pasadena. Not that there's a lake within miles that I'm aware of. It's a coastal desert, you know. Just saying. So I went out there. Lake Avenue itself then stood on the tipping point between arching upward into something too-too very-very or continuing to plummet into a slum. You could see the house itself had been grand around 1900 but it was a collapsing rental now; the second-story floors listed badly, and the hallway had settled in the opposite direction from the bedrooms. So it was like walking on the deck of an ocean liner during a fierce storm. My friend was off somewhere so I met the roommates and received a new vision of Pasadena. Because people are strange when you're a stranger. Which I was.

This massive guy George was interesting in a *Big Lebowski* kind of way. And his upstairs room reeked of very kind bud, both smoked and green. I wasn't that much of a pothead but one did learn those things in college then. George was ABD from Harvard. He didn't seem that interested in his dissertation though. The internet was nascent then, mostly e-mail—he was prattling on about the idea of some sort of "mall" online where people could go from "store" to "store" and buy things. For a second I thought he would have fit in on Venice Beach before he veered off into talking about profits to be made, which didn't really interest me. Or, I reckoned, the denizens of Venice Beach. I guess you can tell that I didn't become a dot com mogul. George was absolutely right of course and, at that point, he was ahead of his time. But George didn't become a dot com mogul either. He was more into sitting in that room.

Right then, there was a reason to prefer sitting in that room. A very hot blond woman around thirty, in a little black dress topped with a striking metallic necklace. George saw me eyeing her, leaned in, and conspiratorially whispered, "See that necklace? It's cryogenics. When she dies, they're going to cut off her head and freeze it until they can revive her." Uh-huh. Thus the expression, the lunatics are on the grass.

To reinforce that thought, George then lit a joint. I took one hit to be polite, while murmuring something about having to get back to reality. I grabbed my beer and headed into the hallway. Since I really had sailed, I shifted my weight correctly to compensate for the steep reverse sag in the floor. An Asian girl coming out of the other bedroom apparently had had a landlocked childhood. She tumbled into a heap. Or maybe it was the four-inch stiletto heels. Who can say? It had already struck me that there were a lot of pretty Asian women running throughout the house. In four-inch stiletto heels. They never were on camera when I used to watch the Rose Parade. There you go.

I stuck my head into the other bedroom. This long-haired guy, Ned, bellowed a greeting in a thick Jersey accent and beckoned me in. If I'd known he wanted to tell me, a perfect stranger, the woes of his life, I wouldn't have done it. Don't you hate people like that? He lit a joint—I threw my hands up on that score and gave in to peer pressure. Actually, given the screed he then launched into, it was probably an excellent choice. For him too, since he was one of those nervous, jumpy Jersey guys instead of one of the tough, abrasive ones. Ned's story was pretty short—once you weeded out the profane, the misogynistic, and the perhaps dope-induced irrelevant tangents about rock music and his mother. Which I will. He'd been in the Philippines for no apparent reason—not even graduate school in the arts—and became besotted with a Filipina prostitute, whom he married and brought to Pasadena. After an appropriate interval—in the legal rather than decent sense— she left him in favor of practicing her craft in her happily adopted country. Ned viewed this as the great tragedy of his life. I wasn't so sure about that, but I began to suspect that the number of Asian girls in stiletto heels in that house overrepresented their share of the Pasadena demographic.

Coincidentally enough, this chat also turned to talk of cutting off heads and putting them in freezers. That was when the smart rat decided it was time to desert the sinking ship. I therefore leaped from the listing quarterdeck of the second floor and swam—figuratively accurate given the joint—back to the seemingly saner confines of Hollywood. That of course is saying something. Both Ned and George had said they loved it in Pasadena and were planning on digging in. My new vision of Pasadena was of an asylum housing a multi-ethnic collection of arguably interesting but drug-addled loons whose insanities were too offbeat in a non-hipster way to be suitable in Los Angeles proper.

I kept that vision for a couple of years, partly because I assiduously avoided returning to the scene of that crime. And my next trip only fortified my perspective. A different friend wanted to go to some cool counterculture event that he couldn't really describe. Nor could he describe where it was. It turned out to be in Pasadena. It was the Doo Dah parade, which apparently did start out as a counterculture alternative to the Rose Parade. But it had evolved into a display and glorification of the kind of insanity that wasn't hipster enough for Venice Beach.

At least that year, it featured entries like the BBQ & Hibachi Marching Grill Team, the Shopping Cart Drill Team, and the Bastard Sons of Lee Marvin. I never saw any of them at Venice Beach—and maybe you're thinking that I, who at that time was ABD in Restoration drama, should have understood the nature of spectacle. Well, we haven't talked about the onlookers. Some just flaunted eccentric outfits, and some of those wouldn't have been out of place in that old picture of Colorado Boulevard that I had seen at Pepperdine. But, too close to me in the crowd, there was this apparently deranged guy. A burly, strong one—that's the worst kind, you know. He had a shaved head and was screaming, "Stop shopping!" Over and over again. "Stop shopping!" I edged away. Nobody else in the crowd even seemed to notice. In fact, near as I could tell, he was there with two soccer moms and their children, all apparently indifferent to this performance. So this was normal?

You know, where I grew up, people used to say, "There's an education in being kicked by a mule." They also used to say, "There's no education in being kicked by a mule a second time." On the way back, I reckoned they might be smarter than me, even though I had more, well, education. So I pretty much decided that I was really done with Pasadena.

For a while, that was easy. I finished my dissertation and set off on the nomadic life of a young man without tenure and a PhD in *Stuff Nobody Cares About*. Eventually, I became a not-so-young man without tenure and a PhD in *Stuff Nobody Cares About*. Then, in Chicago, I met a woman, and we fell in love. Hey, I was at least as surprised as the next person. She was from Pasadena. But she didn't seem insane. In fact, she was a doctor. Of medicine. Instead of philosophy. And by then I had become convinced that man does not live by a graduate degree in Restoration drama alone. Even if that man liked tofu. Which I don't.

So now I have a third vision of Pasadena. A homespun one. Because it's the place where I live. In truth, this vision is more like my first than my second. In fact, I hear tell that in more than one hundred years, it has never rained on the Rose Parade.

Sean Howell

The Parade

I T WASN'T UNTIL THE float had already nuzzled itself up against the bleachers that Fish—experimenting with a cigarette on the roof of his father's apartment building, pleased to be so high above the grand civic machinery churning away far below—looked down. The sight of the foundered float was so odd—its underbelly exposed to the world as music continued to play tinnily from its speakers—that it took him a moment to realize how it had gotten there; to understand that it must have come adrift somehow on the slight declination out front. He couldn't believe he had missed it; he didn't hear anything until a man's agonizing wail cut through his early-morning reverie. The wail itself, even more than the downed float, seemed to threaten the proceedings: it was as though the atmosphere of the festival had been pulled in an instant into the vacuum of that cry—as though it was the wail, in fact, that had produced the disaster, not the other way around. A small crowd was coagulating around something in the street— the wailing man, Fish guessed. He must have jumped off the float and broken his leg.

Sucking at his cigarette and scanning the street below, trying to take it all in at once, Fish spotted a girl in a white dress pushing through the sidewalk crowd. She turned into the grass alley beside the grandstand where the float had beached and vanished underneath it. Fish blinked, ground his cigarette into the concrete, checked his breath, and hurried down to the street.

Below the bleachers, through a tangle of aluminum crossbeams, he watched the girl circle under the float, a strange light in her expression as she examined it. She froze suddenly, aware of his presence, and turned her gaze on him. She cocked her head, looking as though she was about to smile or ask him something, though she did neither.

"Hey," she said in her husky voice.

"Hey Sam," he said. She sat down in a puddle of flowers and patted the grass next to her, like she'd been expecting him all along. He looked around, as if seeking better options, then sighed and picked his way through the scaffolding. He rubbed his hands together, blowing into them.

"How are you cold?" she said. "It's one hundred frigging degrees."

A mechanical squirrel, one of the float's several forest creatures, glowered down at them out of depthless coal eyes, its buckteeth bared, like a captor examining its prey through slats in a cage. A white polyvinyl sheen was visible in sections of the puffed-out cheeks where the flowers had been scraped away. Chicken wire arced out of its left nostril.

"So," Fish said. "What's going on?"

"Just watching the parade, man."

"When did you get in?" he asked.

"Hm?"

"When did you get here?"

"I don't know. Few days ago."

"Where are you guys staying?"

"Ritz."

The wailing had stopped; Fish couldn't tell whether the man was still out there. Walkie talkies blipped on and off not far from where they sat, flat voices filtering through. The same Bob Marley song that had been playing from the float all the while started again from the top.

"All right," Sam said. "Come on."

Back in the sunlight, they slipped into a corridor between two office buildings. Sam wrapped her fingers around Fish's arm; he bent his elbow only slightly in accommodation.

"Where have you been, man?" she asked. "Why haven't I seen you yet?"

"I didn't know you were around," he said.

A man in a suit flickered across the mouth of the corridor ahead.

"What'd you do last night?" she asked. "D'you get wasted?"

"Did I get *wasted*?"

"I know what you did. You walked up and down Colorado Boulevard, hoping to run into somebody you knew, wishing something crazy would happen to you. Wishing you'd meet a girl. Then, when nothing happened, you went home, took a sip of your dad's Johnny Walker, had second thoughts, put it away, watched TV and went to bed." She peered up at him for a moment, then looked away, satisfied. "*My* night," she said, "was a *mess*."

"How's school going?" Fish asked.

She let out a laugh, leaned in, and wrapped herself tighter around his arm.

They ended up in an alley that sliced between backyards, fragrant with discarded Christmas trees. Sam stopped in front of an ivy-laced gate next to a white, barn-style garage, released her grasp on Fish's arm, and looked up at him, expectant. He set his jaw, then sighed, unlatched the gate and held it open for her. She executed a brief curtsy as she stepped into the backyard.

"It's sort of the same," she said, as Fish closed the gate behind them. "It's weird. That it's the same. You know?"

She wandered into the yard, pausing to run her hand over the wooden slats her dad had nailed into the side of their oak tree to form a ladder for a rope swing. She started to head toward the house, then hesitated, turning her attention to the garage. The peculiar light came into her face again. Fish followed her through the door at the right side of the structure, as if drawn by a string.

"Well, this is different," she said. And it was: the space had been completely rearranged, transformed. Where before everything was oriented toward the big barn doors, now the door Sam and Fish came through represented the main entrance. If Sam hadn't seen it from the outside, if she had woken up here, she never would have believed it was the same place. A new wall had even gone up, carving out a narrow nook behind it.

The room was populated with well-worn objects, each of which seemed dense with history: warped photographs, hand-carved figurines, a short shelf of hardback books, a wooden case stacked with scuffed baseballs. Large canvases in humble frames rested against the barn doors. It appeared as though they, too, might have been discovered at yard sales and antique shops, rescued from dumpsters—though the narcotic aroma of oil paint and the big easel holding another canvas, the faint outlines of some structure just visible beneath a coat of black, revealed them to be the creations of the man who now lived here. Everything in the room seemed half-finished, in the process of becoming something else. The canvases themselves seemed to depict this process: they contained vast warehouses with romanesque columns that sheltered trains, dirigibles, skyscrapers hung from wires, in the process of construction or deconstruction, preparing to be shipped, or stored away for good.

Sam paced across the room and picked out an old photo of a boy in an oversize Little League uniform, pounding a fist into his glove.

"All-American as shit," she muttered.

Fish lingered near the door as Sam flipped through books on the shelf, as she rummaged through drawers, spun an old black globe on its axis, lifted the phone from its cradle—"Sorry ma'am, Mr. Van Gogh isn't here at the moment. This is his mistress. May I take a message?" He tried to find other candidates for his attention—the baseballs, the figurines, even the speckled paint on the floor, which, he observed, had mingled with older, automotive oil stains. But his gaze kept tacking back to Sam, as if he hoped by its force to either pull her out of the studio and off these people's property, or to appropriate some of her confidence, her easy ownership of this space, for himself.

Now she was staring at a framed poster of a painting that hung above a slovenly couch against the side wall. The painting depicted a woman in a blue hat and overcoat, looking at something just out of frame. Sam cocked her head, studying the poster as if she knew the woman and was trying to determine whether it was a good likeness. Then, with the care of a professional art handler, she lifted the frame off its hook.

Fish glanced at the open door behind him. When he looked back at Sam, he saw the lunar glint of the bronze dial the poster had concealed.

"I wonder if they changed the combination," Sam said.

Fish glanced again at the cheerful sliver of yard visible through the doorway. He wondered if the click of the alley gate would be audible from here.

From behind him came a sharp intake of breath. From the safe, Sam withdrew two stacks of bills, a stripe of white around each, and held them up to Fish. "We're rich," she said. He accepted the bills in the same way that he might have taken her books from her while she bent to tie her shoe.

She pulled out two more stacks, then another, and another. Then came the jewelry. Fish felt the cold stare of the law on his back.

"Hey, this is—look, this is—" He looked all around.

"You are such a *chickenshit*. Were you always such a chickenshit?"

"I'm uh," he said. "I'm going."

"It's *mine*," she said. "Look." She grabbed him by the wrist. "*Look*."

The stuff she was holding out to him was little kid jewelry: fake stones, flimsy chains. The stuff in Fish's hands was of the same caliber, he realized. The bills were printed on smooth paper: photocopies.

Sam returned to the safe. "This stuff is *great*," she said. "I can't believe I *forgot* this stuff."

As Fish set the piled loot on the table nearest him, one of the baseballs fell off its perch, cracked against the floor and bounded across the room. "Shit," he said. He chased it down, scooping it to his chest with two hands, and set it back in its place.

"All right." He turned to leave. "Happy New Year."

"Hold it right there," Sam said. She held a toy gun at hip-level, her stance wide, the barrel aimed at Fish. "Don't think you're getting off so easy." Fish stared sullenly at her. Sam raised the gun and got him in her sights. "I've killed men tougher than you before," she said.

He put his hands up, took a couple of laconic steps toward her, then lunged forward, seizing her wrist and prying her fingers from the handle. In one graceful motion, as if she had been expecting exactly this, Sam let go of the gun, executed a pirouette, and pressed Fish against the wall. She ran a finger along his jaw, regarding him with the same look of appraisal she had bestowed upon the painting, and shot her tongue into his ear.

As Sam's cold fingers crawled under his shirt, Fish shut his eyes and tried to summon the wind-blown terrain of their shared childhood; to stand on the bluff from which he had originally envisioned this moment. But as he pushed her into the nook— as she pulled his hand to her breast, mapping the recesses of his mouth with her insistent tongue—he realized he had never imagined it as much more than a burst of color on the horizon, an interplay of light and smog.

"You killed that float, didn't you," he said.

"So what if I did."

They groped to the floor in the muddy darkness. He had managed to roll her dress down just far enough to wriggle a hand under the cup of her bra when he felt her go rigid. Footfalls sounded in the main room.

Lying on top of Sam, feeling the slow steady expansion of her stomach under his, Fish realized that, for the first time since he had seen her from the roof, he felt calm. His mind seemed to clear. For a moment he even forgot who the girl underneath him was. Whatever threat she represented to him seemed to have migrated into the other room. He felt her turn her face away.

He heard the tinkle of a can of paint thinner, the graze of a brush on canvas— uneven at first, increasingly regular as the painter settled in. It was going to be a long siege.

Lifting his head, Fish realized that the nook he and Sam had stumbled into was in fact a storage area. Stacks of canvases were filed into a wooden frame that receded into the depths. He could just make out part of the painted surface of one of them. It contained a shadowy form, its edge articulated by a rust-colored streak that cut across the canvas before vanishing into the depths. It could have been the lead edge of a boat; the wing of a prop plane. Or a spaceship, stowed away for some future age. Far below, the inhabitants of some nameless metropolis, dwarfed by the structure behind them, went about their day.

Michelle Huneven

Interest

NED'S DAUGHTER CORAL NEEDS $30,000. She wants to buy a house.

He has hung up the phone from their conversation and now stands in the kitchen of his duplex in Carpinteria. He smears his own homemade fig jam on a saltine, eats it, and thinks.

He has the money, of course. That is not an issue. He has his home, fully paid for, plus $978,600 and change according to his most recent statements—and they're a week old. Not bad for a retired schoolteacher. His money is in treasury bills and Franklin funds and several bonds. A few thousand in CDs. And he's carrying three mortgages, is looking for more. He does not believe in the stock market—who needs it? He makes a sweet side income from those mortgages. Interest payments, month after month. Balloons at the end. If they can't come up with the cash, he ends up with the properties. Guaranteed.

Another cracker. The sweet jam and the salt and the grit of the fig seeds make him eat another, and another. He will bring some fig jam to Coral, and a square tube of saltines. Some pleasures come cheap.

It is not surprising that Coral has turned to him when she wants to buy a house; he is something of a mortgage broker. Only she doesn't want a mortgage. She wants a down payment. No financial gain in that. She has found a house, or rather, her friends are trying to foist one on her. These friends have singled Coral out as their ideal buyer, or so they say. They claim to have put their heart and soul into remodeling the place and now that they've outgrown it (a toddler followed by twins), they want a friend to live there: Coral. More likely they have heard that Coral is an heiress and are eager to take advantage of her. They claim to be offering her the house at ten percent under asking price, but what they are asking is a fortune, even in this housing bubble.

Coral, his youngest, has always been credulous, extremely easy to talk into things, and impossible to talk out of them. He heard it in her voice when she described the house—drought-resistant garden! orchard! clerestories!—that she's deep in their thrall.

He would like to help her out. Her life is lonely.

A house in the suburbs may not be the solution.

He takes a jar of fig jam from the cupboard and puts it on the table, where he will see it tomorrow morning, and remember to take it to her.

Funny, he thinks, driving north on Lake Avenue in Pasadena, that Coral would want to live so near the old home place. Even he has moved away. And his older daughter, the daughter he'd been closest to, Diana, has always lived far away: Paris, Oslo, now Montclair, New Jersey. He would've thought that Coral, with whom he has always struggled, would be the one to go far afield and that Diana, his pet, would be nearby.

The old neighborhood is looking trim and bright, the small yards mown and blooming. No mystery there: interest rates are low, people are borrowing, fixing up their places, as they always do during a bubble. Later, they will have to pay, of course, with interest. Upwardly adjusted interest.

His daughters, while intelligent and even talented—Diana is a musician and Coral a museum curator of "installations"—have both chosen difficult lives. Neither is well off. Nor have they managed their meager finances well. He likes to say that one (Diana) spends too little, and the other (Coral) spends too much. When they were young, he claimed that having daughters was like a stream of pure affection running through his life. Now that they're out in the world, living their own lives, those affections are thinner, duller, directed elsewhere. He's been hoping for grandchildren, but neither of Diana's marriages produced any, and Coral, at 33, remains single.

He brakes to turn onto Orange Blossom Street. Diana too had once asked him for a down payment, for an apartment in a co-op in New York City. He had flown there and was shocked by her choice: a dim one-bedroom unit on an airshaft for a quarter million dollars that Diana insisted was a bargain. He had to point out to her that the initial outlay in these situations was just the beginning. This building was old, and the monthly fees, already astronomical (somebody was pocketing a tidy sum), would only increase—and there would be assessments for new electrical wiring, new plumbing, new furnace, new elevator, new carpeting for the corridors; the list was endless. He was forced to refuse Diana's request for her own good. Since then, she has moved to Montclair. He wants to visit her there, but so far, they can't seem to arrange a time. The orchestra keeps her busy, so much so she rarely even phones.

He checks the paper with the address. 2980 Orange Blossom Street. The number has a familiar ring, and of course, he knows the street, which is looking tidy and smart, each house freshly painted, lawns mown, hedges clipped. Orange Blossom has always been one of the better streets in this neighborhood, its wooden bungalows built in orange groves during the teens as winter cottages for well-off midwestern asthmatics and tuberculars. After WWII, the cottages became popular starter homes for young professionals. He and Eleanor had looked at a home on this street but had bought further west, for considerably less. For what two schoolteachers could afford.

Coral stands in the driveway of a green bungalow. Behind her is a big black Jaguar. Somebody has money. The house itself strikes a chord; he sees past the new paint job to recognize the home of a boyhood friend. Except that the driveway should be on the west side, and this driveway is on the east.

Coral, spotting him, waves and rushes down to meet him. In her brown skirt and straight long hair, she looks like a religious Jew, except that her arms are bare, and she wears strappy sandals. She wears the same skirt in solid black at her museum openings downtown. He has stopped attending; the drive from Carpinteria is too long, the so-called installations—piles of wood chips, a room filled with tiny paper umbrellas, another empty with piped-in computer tones—do nothing for him.

Hi Dad, says Coral. Thanks for driving down. You're looking dapper.

His heart lifts. Up close, she smells good, and her skin is tanned and clear. She kisses his cheek and taking his arm, pivots him around to face a front yard full of cacti, long grasses, and gray bushes. Rocks. It's a small patch of scrubby desert. She leads him through the thick of it on a path of compacted decomposed granite.

Coral is only five foot three, shorter than her own mother. Neither of his girls, he has to admit, are lookers. Diana has grown into the spitting image of his own grandmother, complete with Grandma Ulla's tics and giddy laugh—eerie to hear that laugh again after forty years. And Coral has the air of an orphan, or a religious penitent. She dresses only in solid colors and her hair is eternally straggled and droopy. Eleanor had fought long wars with that hair, taking Coral to countless salons, sending her money for cuts and permanent waves only to have it appear again and again long and lank and naturally separating into strings. At her museum openings, noisy, swank affairs with the city's wealthiest art patrons, there is Coral and her hair, a waif's limp locks.

Neither daughter has had success with men. Diana had tried a Korean husband for nine years, but he proved alcoholic. Then, she had married a Syrian psychiatrist she met in Damascus; they moved to New York and he divorced her minutes after his green card arrived. Coral has never married and has had a long string of boyfriends, every one of them what Eleanor called a wounded bird. And really, if she buys this house, any man who sees her front yard would be warned off: it's far too eccentric. What's the matter with lawn?

Coral, her hand grasping his arm, pulls him up the stoop, onto the porch and into the living room, where the name arrives. Yes. This is Jeff

Granger's old house. Jeffrey Granger! How many times had he dashed up these front steps behind Jeff, letting the screen door slam behind them. And Peggy Granger's voice ringing out, The door, boys, please!

Sorry Mom!

Sorry Mrs. Granger!

How tiny the living room looks now, and how different: the walls are painted the color of cinnamon and a terrible gold-orange that makes the space dark and unappealing.

Jarrod did research and found all the original Craftsman colors, Coral is saying. And he refinished all the wood, himself. Feel it, Dad. Smooth as skin.

He runs his hand over wainscoting. Eh.

Two bedrooms flank a narrow bathroom. The smaller bedroom, at the back of the house, Jeff's old room, has a single bed with an old-fashioned white bedspread, the kind with wicking that looks like a frosted cake. An oak desk and tallboy, nothing more. This simple room from another time pleases him.

This is your room, Dad, Coral says, whenever you come for a visit.

In the kitchen, the Realtor waits for them at the kitchen table. The owner, clever Jarrod, is wisely nowhere in sight. His agent, a woman in her fifties, has short bottled-blond hair, red nails, and a crisp directness. Strands of gold and pearls loop over her breasts. If these people intended to sell to Coral, why did they bring in an agent? He could've handled all the sale details for no fee. Or a very modest one.

He lets the agent give her pitch. She does, in fact, address his concerns. Copper repiping. Updated electrical. Furnace new three years ago. Also the roof. She goes to fetch some documents; apparently, it's her Jag in the driveway. He musters respect, then, for a fellow real estate professional. Returning, she hands him a list of comps for the neighborhood, no doubt doctored or at least selectively edited. He has an idea then: if he can get the agent alone, he means to ask, since he is essentially representing Coral in this transaction, if she will split the commission with him. That way, he can earn a little back—approximately $6,000 by his calculations—and offset the full loss of the down payment. He requests her card.

She prattles on about inspections and sewer lines. It has been sixty years since he sat in this kitchen, and he combs it for details to match his memories. He would swear that the Granger's kitchen was on the opposite side of the house, but his mind is slowing reorienting itself, the remembered kitchen swinging around to align with reality. The Grangers, he recalls, ate on thin, flowered china; there was always a tablecloth, and their sink was white porcelain, not the dark gray, chipped stone at the house now.

The agent and Coral stand. He follows them into the backyard where the redoubtable Jarrod has also revived and augmented the orchard. Peach, plum, and apple trees, loaded with green fruit, are evenly spaced in rows. At the back of the property are three aged orange trees. He looks over the rear fence; in all the backyards up and down the block, he can trace the vestigial rows of the original orange grove that once stretched back there for acres. As a teenager during the Depression, he and Jeff Granger had stolen buckets of oranges from that grove and sold them door to door further down the hill, making enough for a ticket to the movies and a bag of day-old pastries from Laidlaws. Once, on an endless Sunday afternoon in June, when the Valencias were ripe, he and Jeff and Jeff's brothers had juiced dozens and dozens of oranges. They had scrubbed and rinsed the Granger's bathtub, then filled it to the brim with orange juice. Ninety gallons, he figured. All the neighbors had come over with pitchers and helped themselves. At a time when nobody had any money, he and Jeff had cheered everyone up, letting them take as much as they wanted.

He stands between two old trees with their smooth lizard-gray trunks, and takes a deep breath. How many nights had he and Jeff Granger slept out here in a green canvas pup tent! This dusty-sour scent—of pulverized orange rind and dirt and blossoms, the smell of the orange grove floor—brings wave upon wave of sensation: Peggy Granger's warm dry hand on his arm, her lovely black curly hair, the smell and starchiness of the clean clothes she gave him to wear when he and Jeff muddied themselves in the canyon. She'd given him a whole bag of clothes, in fact, which he took home proudly, pants and shirts Jeff had outgrown, all of them ironed and folded and good for many more wearings.

What do you think, Dad? Coral's dark green eyes are focused on him with an eagerness that disturbs him. He wishes for a knob or a dial to tone down her intensity. Her face looks pointy, desperate. In her bloom, there had been a touch of beauty, a trace of Slavic cheekbones and almond eyes from her mother, but that has faded. She'll age, he sees, as a sprightly, difficult woman, eager yet on edge. Her mother was similarly high strung. Quick to turn on you, to lash out. He has to watch his step.

I'd like to have a word alone with the Realtor, he says.

They walk to the driveway and stand in front of her car. He clasps the chrome Jaguar hood ornament, warmed by the sun. Since I am acting as my daughter's agent, he says, I would be curious to know what percentage of the commission you would be willing to offer.

The Realtor's red-tipped fingers twist in gold chain and pearls. Oh, but Mr. Tilgman, she says, there's a misunderstanding. I am your daughter's agent.

I see, he says. Well then.

I have to think this through, he tells Coral on the stoop. I will let you know what I decide.

He is already on the freeway when he sees the jar of fig jam, undelivered. The square column of saltines. Securing the Mason jar between his thighs, he pries off the lid, dips in the crackers, eats and dips again, all the way home.

That night, he writes Coral a letter.

June 12, 2001, he begins, and the words pour out of him. To set the stage for his decision, he begins with his years as a teenager during the Depression, when he worked at two dairies in Altadena, juggling two and three jobs at a time, wiping udders, hauling bottles, loading trucks, starting at 3 a.m. with the first milking. He dropped out of high school for a whole year, he writes, so that his parents would not lose their little wooden house down on Casitas which, although not nearly as nice as a house on Orange Blossom, was still a home worth saving.

It may also interest you, he writes, that I am not unfamiliar with the property you showed me today.

He describes Jeff Granger as older, taller, stronger but not so bright. He tells about the buckets of purloined fruit, the bathtub of juice, and the clothes Peggy Granger gave to him, so clean and neatly folded.

Long forgotten details stream through his fingers, and who best to receive them but his own daughter. A legacy, of sorts.

He tells her that he and her mother had once looked at a house on Orange Blossom, a house beyond their means. They did not buy it, and lived to tell the tale.

As she will. This house she likes so much, he regrets to say, is far from ideal, financially or personally. She can't see it now, she has been too well versed in its alleged virtues. She is infatuated. A cooler head—his—knows that it is too expensive for what it is. The resale value is low; the property has no curb appeal thanks to the eccentric desert yard, and a dark, gloomy interior is never an easy sell. As an aside—this occurs to him as he writes—those same qualities (gloominess, eccentricity) could discourage suitors who, naturally, would be interested to see what kind of home she makes.

Even if you and I differ in these matters of taste, he writes, *even if the house were indeed perfection itself, keep in mind that we are in a housing bubble that will shortly pop. Buy now and, in a matter of months, you could easily owe far more than what the house is worth.*

When your mother was dying, he writes, *she told me to take good care of you and your sister. Although you may not see it now, that is exactly what I am doing.*

On impulse, he adds a caveat, a generous one which he may well have to make good on: *The house will no doubt languish on the market for some time to come,* he writes. *The price will come down considerably. I wouldn't be surprised if it comes down as much as 30%. If and when it does, I'd be happy to revisit the issue.*

And still, he keeps writing.

I should add that single women are notoriously poor risks, and even if I provided you with a down payment, it is unlikely you could qualify for a loan. And really, paying interest, any interest, is never a good idea.

In due time, you will be able to afford to buy a home flat out. You are an heiress, don't forget.

He tries to reread the letter, but he has written for so long, his eyes are tired. He folds it and sticks it in an envelope and walks it to the mailbox and raises the little red flag. The next day, when he goes to get the mail, the flag is down, the letter is gone, and the box is full of letters and statements addressed to him.

Walking back to the duplex, it comes to him that he has made a mistake. A mistake and also an omission: Jeff Granger lived on Boston, not Orange Blossom Street. And those clothes, those folded shirts and creased pants? He brought them home and his mother stuffed the whole sackful into the incinerator.

In the days, weeks, months to come, he cannot find Coral anywhere. Her phone is disconnected, all correspondence—letter after letter expanding upon and re-explaining his position—is returned to him unopened, stamped *Moved, No Forwarding Address.* No matter when he phones the museum, Coral is in a meeting. Diana refuses to discuss it. He has called the blond Realtor twice; she claims no knowledge of Coral's whereabouts. She does tell him that nine bids were made on the Orange Blossom house. It sold for twenty-five thousand dollars over asking price.

He finds some comfort there. When the housing bubble pops, his daughter will not be the one underwater with a crazy loan.

She will get her house, and it will be interest free.

At odd moments, in his chair, or washing up after a meal, at night as he drifts toward sleep, he does recall with some pain the single bed with its candlewick spread, the simple, old-fashioned room he might have occupied in his daughter's house.

Ron Koertge

Stoner & Spaz, an excerpt

SINCE I'VE BEEN PRETTY much treading water all day, the marquee of the Rialto Theatre looks like the prow of a ship coming to save me.

I limp past the cleaners, the paint store, City Scapes Furniture and step up to the ticket booth. A real one. Out in front where it's supposed to be, not buried in some mall next to a Foot Locker.

And inside sits Mrs. Stenzgarden. Her dress has flowers on it, she single-handedly keeps the rouge trade alive. She wears huge earrings like starbursts.

"Hello, Benjamin." Her finger hovers over the red button. "One?"

"Since it's Monster Week, do I get a discount?"

She glances up from the horoscope magazine she's been reading. "I don't think I understand, dear."

"Just a little joke, Mrs. Stenzgarden. Forget it."

"How's your grandmother?"

"She's fine. I'll tell her you said hello."

"Tell her I said hello."

Right.

Ticket in hand, I make my way past the posters for Coming Attractions, lit top and bottom by long, dusty, flickering bulbs.

It rained this morning, so I'm extra careful, but looking down at the tiles that lead to the big double doors isn't exactly a hardship. They are a very cool turquoise and black. My grandmother walked on these tiles when she was a kid. In fact, she's on a committee that wants to preserve things like this theatre, that red box office, these tiles before another mini-mall moves in selling acrylic nails, kung fu, and discount vitamins.

The lobby of the Rialto Theatre smells like butter from the Paleozoic, and so does Reginald: ticket taker, popcorn maker, projectionist, owner, and manager. Reginald of the world's most awful comb-over, Reginald of the bad teeth and worse breath.

"Hey, Ben. Not a bad crowd, huh?"

"I dub thee Reginald the Optimist. Now rise, go forth into the land, and promote positive thinking for your king."

Reginald grins, showing me what looks like part of the keyboard of a tiny, decaying piano.

Maybe ten patrons lean against the wall or sink into the once-plush couch. I know most of them by sight. They're people who don't own a VCR or don't want to. Or if they do own one can't get it out of its box. Misfits and Luddites. Castaways and exiles. And all of us alone. Whoever said no man is an island has never been to the Rialto on a Friday night. And I can't help but wonder if I'll be here in ten, twenty, or thirty years, dragging my foot down that street I've lived on all my life toward another movie I've seen before. Thoughts like that can drive a man to drink.

So I buy a Dr. Pepper from the Goth who works the concession stand. She has a lot of black eyeliner and a down-at-the-corners mouth that says, *How can you think of snacks when everything's so bleak?* I'm just paying her when somebody behind me says, "Hey, loan me a couple of bucks."

"Pardon me?" It's Colleen Minou. Everybody at King High School knows Colleen. At least, everybody who wants weed.

"I said loan me a couple of bucks." She flashes a hundred-dollar bill, then glances at the kid behind the counter. "Ms. Cheerful here is not going to break this for like one Jujube. I'll pay you back at school."

I dig in the pocket of my khakis. "Okay, but —"

She snatches the money and points through the smudged glass while I take in the rest of her: ripped tights, an off-kilter skirt the color of a lime snow cone, leather jacket, and over that a ragged denim vest. She tosses my two dollars on the counter. "Keep the change." Her hair is tufty and ragged. She's as pale as a girl in a poem about maidens and moonlight. Then she looks at me. "You coming?"

"In a minute." In your dreams.

First of all, no way am I gimping down the aisle during Monster Week while the lights are still on. People will think I'm part of the show. And second of all, no way am I sitting by Colleen. She is nothing but trouble.

I wait through the previews, then slip between the musty velvet curtains and into the last row. I see Colleen roaming the theatre. I shrink into my seat, but she vaults my legs (oh, to vault anything just once!) and settles beside me. She shows me the yellow box of candy. "What'd you get? Let's share."

"Shhhh."

"What? There's almost nobody in here but you and me. What'd you buy?"

"Dr. Pepper."

"Gimme a sip." She grabs my little cup, slurps at least half of it, and hands it back to me.

"Got anything else?"

I reach into the pocket of my windbreaker and show her the apple my grandmother made me bring.

She sneers. "No thanks, Adam."

"Can you talk a little softer?"

"Did you hear," she hisses, "Willard got into it with the Sixty-ninth Street Vatos?"

"When the movie starts you can't talk at all, okay?"

"Did you hear they're supposed to be bringing in dope-sniffing dogs? Did you see any dogs around school today?"

"Take it easy."

"Yeah, yeah, right. I'm a little amped." She glances around, fumbles in her purse. "I'll be right back." She heads for the side door.

"Now where are you going?"

"Like I'm going to blaze it on Main Street."

"You can't smoke marijuana in the alley."

"Why not?"

"Somebody'll see you."

"So? I'll give 'em a hit."

"I meant, they'll see you and tell somebody."

"Are you kidding? Anybody rats me out is going to have to deal with Ed. I'll be back in a minute."

"Take your stub."

"Like I know where that is."

I'm going to move, I really am. Crouch in the front row. Go into the men's room. Go home even. But I don't. And pretty soon she's tapping on the door with the classic red Exit sign above it.

I open it just enough so she can slip in, hoping Reginald won't see me, hoping I won't have to explain what I'm doing, hoping he'll believe me because what would I do if he banished me from the Rialto?

"That's better." She slides down into a nearby seat until her knees are higher than her head. "What are we seeing, anyway?"

I sink beside her. *"Bride of Frankenstein."*

"No shit? I thought it was something about a wolf man."

"That's tomorrow."

"Like I care. Anywhere I don't have to do Ed is fine with me."

I am all of a sudden totally conscious of my body. My left elbow is touching hers and it's like being plugged into a wall socket.

Not that it's some big horndog charge, either. I don't mean that. It's the way she's talking to me. *To* me. I know what sex is. Guys in the hall talk about it. Or girls acting tough. But I only hear things, see? I get them secondhand. On the rebound. Life as an eavesdropper.

"Hey." She nudges me. "Are you nodding out on me?"

"No. I was just thinking that *Bride of Frankenstein* is as good as *The Wolf Man.* You're not, you know, missing anything. You'll like it."

"You've seen it?"

"Oh, sure."

"So what are you doing here?"

"Oh, I check out the way the set is dressed or how James Whale uses his camera. He was a cool guy. Gay before it was okay to be gay. His suicide note said, 'The future is just old age, illness, and pain.'"

"Are you gay?"

"No! James Whale is gay."

"Whatever." Colleen yawns. As the movie starts, she leans into me and goes to sleep.

I have to admit, for once I don't watch the camera angles or the warty villagers in the background. I concentrate on not moving, on breathing evenly, on just generally what it's like to have a girl's head on my shoulder. Any girl. Even this girl. I look around the Rialto and see two or three other couples snuggled up. But for me it's the first time. Even if it doesn't really count.

Colleen doesn't wake up until the monster gets a look at his bride and howls.

She clutches at my arm. "What's going on?"

"Elsa Lanchester is just scared. Frankenstein wants to, you know, start the honeymoon immediately."

"You're kidding."

"No, she's his bride. The doctor made her for him."

"So does he jump her bones?"

"Do you really want me to tell you?"

"It's not going to be good, is it?"

"Colleen, it's a monster movie."

"Fuck that. I'm out of here."

I always sit through the credits. I am always the last one out of any theater. I even make a point of being last. I stay in my seat until everyone else has shuffled past. Then I turn my back, too, on the comforting dark.

But this time I follow Colleen. Or try to. By the time I get out of my seat, up the aisle, and through the door, she's camped on the curb.

"Hey." She motions for me.

I try to stand up straight. I try to hold my arm so it looks like it's maybe just sprained. I try to stroll over to her.

"Don't you want to see the end?" she asks.

"I know what happens."

She pats the curb beside her. "Want to sit down?"

"It's hard for me to. And then once I'm down it's hard to get back up."

"What's that thing you've got?"

"C.P." I say.

"Oh, yeah." She stands and brushes at the back of her tiny skirt. "At least your right hand works." She grins. "You can jerk off."

There it is again: those eyes of hers looking right into mine. Nobody ever looks right at me. Nobody talks about my disability. Nobody ever makes a joke about it. They talk toward me and pretend I'm like everybody else. Better, actually. Brave and strong. A plucky lad.

"You can't, like, have an operation or anything?"

I shake my head. "But when I was little I did this Bopath technique stuff and some biofeedback and a lot of physical therapy. It could be a lot worse. Did you ever see *My Left Foot*?"

She glances at my shoe.

"No, not my left foot. *My Left Foot*. The movie. The Christy Brown story where everybody thinks the guy is a vegetable, but he's really smart and he types stuff with his left foot because it's about the only part of him he's got any control over."

"The whole movie is about him typing with his foot? That must have sold a lot of popcorn."

"Actually it did okay. Everybody likes to see people triumph over adversity. And he had some serious C.P." Colleen just plays with her Marlboro for a while, inhaling deep, then blowing perfect smoke rings in the still air.

"Does it hurt?"

"What? My leg?"

"Yeah. Leg, arm, the whole human unit. Does it hurt?"

"No, not really."

"So then you're okay."

"Are you kidding? While every other guy raced to grade school with his pals, I rode the little bus with kids who drooled on my shoes."

She points. "Those are fucked, by the way."

"My grandma buys these shoes, okay? She thinks if I'm well-dressed, nobody will notice half of me doesn't work. I'd wear ten-dollar sneakers forever if all my toes pointed in the same direction."

"You get out of P.E., don't you?"

"Yeah, but —"

"I hate P.E. It makes my chest hurt."

At school, I'm The Invisible Man. So I'm not used to this—talking to people, I mean. But I like it.

I take a deep breath. "Did you, uh, like the movie?"

"It was okay, I guess."

"The monster and Elsa Lanchester weren't really compatible. Some critic I read once said the Frankenstein and the blind hermit made the best couple."

"You read about movies?"

"Uh-huh."

"For a class?"

"No."

Colleen lights a fresh cigarette off the old one. "Are you some kind of brainiac?"

"No."

"Ever read *The Great Gatsby*?"

"Sure."

"Tell me the plot, okay? Just what happens. I'm supposed to write a report or review or something."

"Now?"

She scratches her head, using all five fingers. "You're right. Call me and tell me the plot." She digs in her purse, comes up with a gnawed-looking Bic, then writes her phone number on my wrist. I like how she holds onto me with her free hand. Grandma pats me a lot, but nobody ever touches me.

Then she yawns. A big yawn. I can see the fillings, all silver, in her molars. "I don't feel so good. Give me a ride home, okay?"

"I can't drive with, you know, the way I am. I'm waiting for . . . somebody."

"So I'll wait with you." Colleen coughs hard, spits into the gutter, then leans to inspect it. "Man, is that supposed to be green?"

In a way, I can't wait to climb in Nonnie's spotless Cadillac and get out of there. Go home and watch the late show like I always do. But I want to stand here in front of the Rialto, too. All night. And listen to Colleen. And have her talk to me.

"Is this it?" Colleen asks as Grandma oozes up to the curb. "Cool."

She opens the back door and clambers in. I make the introductions as Colleen gropes in her bag for cigarettes. I mime a big no, then shake my head.

"Why not? This boat's big enough to have a smoking section."

Grandma glances into the rearview mirror and asks, "Have you and Ben been friends long, dear?"

"Actually, my mom won't let me hang with Ben anymore. He does all this scary stuff like hand his homework in on time and read the assignments. I tried to reason with him. I said, 'Ben. Are you crazy? You've got your whole life ahead of you.'"

All of a sudden, Colleen puts one hand on her stomach, taps Nonnie on the shoulder with the other. "Pull over, okay. And I mean now."

We are barely stopped when Colleen throws up out the window. She falls back, and wipes her mouth with the back of one hand. "Fuck. I better walk the rest of the way."

Getting out of a car isn't easy for me. I have to handle my bad leg like it's a big, dead python. So Colleen doesn't wait for me to be polite. She scrambles out on her own, then leans in my open window. Her breath is sour. "Call me. I mean it." Then she wobbles off down the street.

My grandma lets her forehead touch the steering wheel. "What a horrible girl," she says to the speedometer. "I didn't realize you even knew people like that."

"I don't really know her."

"Why is she acting so peculiar?"

"She's loaded."

"On drugs?"

"Not Jujubes. Not anymore, anyway."

"Why in the world did you invite someone like that into my car?"

"Grandma, we just bumped into each other at the movies. It's no big deal."

"Did she ask you for money?"

"No," I lie.

"She didn't recruit you to traffic in narcotics, did she?"

"Well, she did give me this big bag of baking soda to hold for her."

"This is no laughing matter."

"Grandma, Colleen's a stoner. She won't even remember this tomorrow."

"Well, I'm certainly going to try and banish it from my memory."

Not me, I think. No banishing for me.

Jim Krusoe

Hmm

I AM A LIMITED man. Clearly, this is an irrefutable statement because all men are limited, but how many of us are able to admit this fact, are able to visualize the ceiling of our possibilities, are able to say to one's own self, as I did recently: "My friend, you are not a bad person, but neither are you especially good, and I am sorry to inform you there are plenty of occasions you will never rise to, dozens of simple explanations you will never even think."

All this, by the way, is just to preface the highly personal events I am about to relate which took place some years ago in a strange city, a place where I knew no one and did not speak the language but where, as sometimes happens, I had been given to understand I might conduct some business.

So I had been in this foreign place, this city, for about a week, having taken a room in the largest, but by no means the most luxurious hotel, and still the outcome of my trip remained uncertain. In fact, the very evening I am referring to, I was sitting in my hotel room at a small desk, trying to measure the success of the previous days by writing down on a pad I kept by the reading lamp, a series first of minuses, then pluses, then more minuses and more pluses, and so on and so forth, when I heard a knock at the door.

Opening it, I saw what appeared to be an unusually lovely woman, who, speaking to me in my native language, said, "Quick, I need some help with my husband."

As she was clearly agitated, I asked no more questions, but shutting the door to my room for a moment, pulled on a warm robe and hurried with her to her own room, just a couple doors down the hall from mine.

The second we opened her door it was clear that her husband needed more than help. His mouth was open, his eyes were rolled back, and his tongue was the color of well-done meatloaf. I remember thinking that unless I was very mistaken, he was dead.

"I don't understand it," the woman exclaimed. "He was ill when I left him, but certainly not this…" She bent over the body, and began to sob, and as she did I couldn't help but notice that her robe parted just enough to reveal the surprising resilience of her breasts, each about the size of an acorn squash.

"This is worse news than you can possible realize," she went on to tell me. "For reasons I can't explain right now, but which have to do with the international diamond market, it's imperative that no one realize my husband has died tonight. I must be seen leaving this hotel with him, and be witnessed getting on the train to _____sburg." (Here she named a neighboring city.) "I would not ask this of you if things were not so desperate, or even if I knew anyone else in this city or spoke the language, which I do not, but would it be possible for you to don one of my husband's suits and walk out of the hotel with me as if we were husband and wife? We can then take the train to _____sburg, check into a hotel there, and you can have your luggage forwarded. No one will suspect a thing, and needless to say, I will make it very worth your while."

She looked up from the floor where she'd been kneeling and, pulling her robe close to her chest, she blushed. "I didn't mean that," she stuttered, then added, "even though I'm bound to say I find you quite attractive."

I looked around the room. It was a shabbily genteel version of my own, except that where the wallpaper of my room consisted of crisp bouquets of blue and red flowers, the faded print around me at that moment repeated the pattern of a deer looking backwards as it leapt away from its pursuers, two fierce and large brown hounds. My business in town, as I have said, was at that moment mixed, so looking around me once more and throwing all caution behind me, I turned back to her. "Yes," I said, "I will help."

The trip to the station was uneventful, though the woman seemed in a state of near panic. The dead man's clothes fit nicely, and were even a cut or two above my own exacting standards for material. The only difficulty I encountered were his shoes, which were surprisingly tiny. "The feet of a gentleman," I told his widow, and she nodded gratefully. So I replaced them with my own shoes, and, wrapping her husband's in a parcel, tossed them out the train window at the first tunnel we came to, about midway in our journey.

Our new hotel, alas, was not even the quality of the one we had left, but we were both exhausted, so much so that when we were told the only room available contained but one double bed, I readily agreed, confident that on entering it we would both be fast asleep in seconds. However, here I found myself pleasantly surprised. That is, whether from the strangeness of our surroundings, or simply because it's what people often do after funerals, we made love, not once, but often.

The next morning it appeared that some of the tension that had covered her face the previous night had disappeared. She looked calm, and even more beautiful than when she had been wearing the makeup of danger and of stress. I resolved to stay with her, especially now as she had no one else to help her, for as long as she needed. After a hearty breakfast we made love once again—a saner, more reflective sort than the night before—and when I told her of my decision to accompany her for as long as she needed me, after a brief pause, during which she thought things over, she agreed.

The days flew by. We would stay at a hotel or a *pension* for a few days, then one afternoon she would return from shopping or a restaurant and tell me she was being watched, and so we'd move. Thus we traveled from place to place and town to town, living, as we did, off the large amount of capital I had brought with me to do business in that first, momentous city. She rarely mentioned diamonds, or even jewelry, for that matter, and it was hard to miss the fact that she wore no jewelry of any sort next to her silken skin.

For three months we lived in this enchanted dream, until one evening, over a light supper in our hotel room, I was forced to tell her I was out of money. "Either we will have to return to the town where my business is located," I told her, "or separate for good."

She looked momentarily startled, and I was alarmed to see a touch of her original agitation returning.

"Wait," she told me, putting down her wineglass. "I have an idea. It's a long shot, but it may just work. I want you to lie here in this room, right on the floor and pretend to be dead. Whatever you do, don't move until I return."

It was an easy enough request—as a matter of fact, I used to practice that very thing as a boy, much to the alarm of my neighbors, who would frequently find me slumped in a mock-accident in a drainage ditch or hanging from a tree limb.

"Now," she said, "play dead. And you need to hurry!"

So I quickly lay down on the floor, stretched out my arms, shut my eyes, and waited. I heard her walk to the door, open it, and then shut it after her. Then I heard the click of her heels as she headed down the hall, then the door opened and shut again, then nothing.

Time passed—of course, it had to—first minutes, hours, and eventually, judging by the alternating periods of light and dark, whole days. All the while I stayed very still, and breathed as slowly as I could.

More time passed, and my lips became dry and cracked, and then more time. I could hear the buzz of flies as they drew closer, and then feel them tickle as they settled on the corners of my mouth and on my eyes. Exactly how long I waited I cannot say, but after a week or so I resolved that if she had not returned by evening, that very day would be my last. That evening I stretched, crawled to the sink, and poured myself a glass of water.

After that I remained in the hotel room for two more days, just in case. Finally I had to admit defeat. I left town and returned to what remained of my former business, which is to say practically nothing. I struggled to return it to its previous health, and failed. I began to work for others, lost those jobs, took new ones and, scarred by my ordeal, lost those too.

And in all the years that followed, I never saw her until last week, when, as I was hobbling down a sidewalk in hopeless pursuit of a bus which had ignored me, I turned and spotted out of the corner of an eye, a woman even more ravaged, more wretched than me. Her hair had mostly fallen out, her legs, once slim and long were bloated, and her clothes were old and torn. And as I starred at her, she recognized me also.

"You fool," she said, as she took care to aim a gob of spit in my direction. "If only you had waited one more hour."

Scott O'Connor

Untouchable, an excerpt

T HEY COME IN THE abandoned hour of the night, moving through quiet arterial streets, empty intersections, past gated storefronts and darkened windows, homeless men curled into bus stop shelters, prostitutes walking the desolate concrete stretches.

They come in a pair of white Ford Econolines, identical vans, flanks unmarked, windowless and blank. They sit parallel at stoplights and the drivers raise their eyebrows at each other and yawn, sip coffee from Styrofoam cups, roll forward when the lights change, toward the motel, the apartment complex, the house in the hills.

There is always someone waiting when they arrive, someone standing in the driveway or doorway, looking more than a little shell-shocked, still not quite able to believe what they've seen, that what has happened has actually happened. The police have left, the coroner's people have left, but someone slipped them a business card on the way out, passed along a company name and phone number and told them to call and wait. Mothers, husbands, wives, motel night clerks, apartment managers, security guards. Whoever was unfortunate enough to be the one to open the door, to walk into the room and see something they will never forget.

They weren't going to call the number. There was a moment after all the noise and commotion, after the police and the coroner's people left, when the person waiting in the doorway was alone in the new silence of the place, just outside the room, a moment where they thought they could handle it themselves, thought they could take care of things quickly and efficiently, that it would be the right thing to do for their son or husband or tenant or employer. That it would be unpleasant but possible. But then they remembered the sight and the smell and the profane mess, the horror of the thing, and they dialed the number on the card and spoke to a sweet-sounding old woman who took their information and told them that help was on the way.

The white vans pull to the curb, engines cooling, ticking in the stillness.

Two men get out of the first van, stretching and yawning in the bad light. These are not the kind of men the person in the doorway expected. The person in the doorway is not sure what kind of men they expected, but these are not those men. One of the men is tall, buzz cut, with full sleeves of multicolored tattoos. The other is short and gym-built, with a thinning cap of flaming orange hair. These are rough-looking men, truckers or sailors, heavy-lifters, men who look like they're in the habit of breaking things, dropping things, banging around in small rooms. They do not seem equipped for the subtlety and reverence required for the task at hand. The grandmother on the phone had used the term *technicians*, had said that she was sending a *crew of technicians*, but these men do not appear to have the degree of precision that the term implies, the level of scientific expertise.

The person in the doorway considers redialing the number on the card, canceling the job, dealing with this themselves. But then there is the memory, that first moment when they opened the door and came upon the scene in the room, the unspeakable thing. So they do nothing, they hold the business card and wait as the men move to the backs of the vans and pull out their equipment, red plastic buckets, squeeze bottles and spray cans, wire brushes and putty knives, roll after roll of paper towels.

Another man, the driver of the second van, steps down onto the sidewalk. He approaches the person in the doorway, walking slowly, head down. He is terrifically fat. He has a graying ponytail that stretches down between his shoulder blades and a thick, bushy mustache that turns up at the ends. There is a name for this type of mustache, an antiquated style, but the name escapes the person waiting. Remembering it seems important, suddenly, proving that they are still capable of simple acts, putting names to things. It seems like this would restore a level of normalcy to the night, having a name for it, that style of mustache. But the term is just out of reach and they are left at a loss, again.

The two men at the vans are pulling on blue paper body suits; they are pulling on rubber gloves. They are duct taping each other's suit sleeves closed around the gloves. They are pulling safety goggles out of the vans, plastic-and-rubber respiration masks, a box of disposable surgical booties. More duct tape for the pant cuffs of their suits, a man standing on one leg, balancing with a hand against the side of a van while the other rolls the tape around his ankles.

They look like something out of an old science-fiction movie. Moonmen. They look like moonmen.

The fat man approaches, the fat man arrives. He is even bigger up close, towering, damp-browed, breathing heavily from the short walk. He smells of cigarettes and coffee. He looks down at the scuffed toes of his work boots. He is about to speak and the person in the doorway has absolutely no idea what he is going to say, what anyone could possibly say on this night, standing outside after the police and coroner's people have gone, after the facts have been given and recorded, the known details. The person has no idea what's left, what words would still have a shred of relevance, what words wouldn't fail, utterly.

The fat man nods and looks up and speaks in a low, rich rumble. What he says is, *I'm very sorry for your loss.*

And maybe this is the moment when the person in the doorway cries or screams or lets loose a fusillade of vulgarities, a seething mass of profanity and loss. Maybe this is the moment where the person falls to their knees, dissolving into guilt, sobbing convulsively, and has to be helped up by the fat man, held under the elbows and lifted, gently.

Maybe this is the moment when the person hits the fat man, when they punch the fat man in the chest, just to put a physical action to the feeling, just to strike some kind of blow. Maybe this is the moment when they speak in tongues, when they resurrect a primal language, finding comfort in the acceptance of extreme things, babbling in God's own voice. Or maybe this is the moment when they say nothing, when they stand silent, when the weight of the thing that has happened finally settles upon them, and they sag a little, in the shoulders and knees, the smallest thing, the way they will sag from now on, the way they will carry this night in their bodies from this moment forward, and maybe this is their only response to what the fat man says.

The moonmen pass inside, carrying their equipment. Their blue paper suits crinkle and shush. The fat man stays for a few minutes, and maybe he says something else and maybe he doesn't. Maybe he just stands and waits as the person in the doorway gets used to the sagging weight, their new posture, the slight adjustment in bearing. Then the fat man returns to the vans and pulls on his own moonman suit, gathers the equipment the others have laid out for him, passes by the person in the doorway, and enters the motel or apartment or house in the hills.

And maybe this is when it comes to them, when it arrives unexpectedly, the lost identifier. Maybe this is when they remember. The name of the thing. The fat man's facial hair. Maybe it comes to them then, just like that, a gift.

Handlebar mustache. The name of the thing is handlebar mustache.

David Darby hauled his gear down the narrow hallway and up the stairs to the fourth and top floor. Jerry Roistler followed half a flight behind. They set their buckets down outside the numbered door and waited. Bob Lewis was downstairs speaking with the person who'd been waiting when they arrived. The apartment manager, Darby guessed, a harried-looking man with a gold hoop dangling from one ear. Bob would get whatever information he felt necessary for the job, probably more than he needed, then he'd come up and look at the room and give the manager an estimate, a timeframe for completion.

Darby could already smell the job on the other side of the door. The room had sat for a while. A week, he guessed, maybe longer.

Roistler winced at the smell, pulled on his respiration mask.

"What do you think, Tattooed Lady?" Roistler said, voice muffled by the mask. "Vectors or no vectors?"

"Not interested."

"Five bucks says vectors."

"No interest."

"With that smell, five bucks says *mucho* vectors." Roistler worked his knuckles, his neck and shoulders, an irritating sequence of firecracker pops. Darby ignored him, listened to the stairs groan as Bob lumbered up to the top.

"Apartment manager was in Reno for a week," Bob said. He pulled a loose strand of tobacco from his mustache. "Came back to a phone full of messages about the smell."

"Nobody called the cops?" Roistler said.

"Older people in the building, mostly. Keep to themselves. Nobody called anybody until it was time to complain about the smell."

Bob pulled on his mask, lifted the instant camera out of his bucket, unlocked the door with a ring of keys the manager had given him. He would take a picture of the room before they started work, what they called the *Before* photo. He stepped into the doorway, filling the frame.

"Studio apartment," Bob said. "One main room, small kitchen off one side, smaller bathroom off the other."

He lifted the camera to his eye, snapped a picture. The light of the flash echoed back out into the hallway. The print slid from the face of the camera, slowly developing. Bob pulled the print, shook it with his free hand. Darby strapped on his safety goggles, picked up his equipment, and entered the room.

The trick of the job is to forget what had happened. The trick of the job is to acquire as little information as possible about the site, the former occupants, the current occupants, the thing that happened there, and then to forget that information. Not to see the big picture, the whole story. There is no big picture, there is no whole story. There are only details that need to be sprayed, scrubbed, bagged, disposed of.

The trick of the job is to use an alternate vocabulary for these details, a list of terms developed over the years by the technicians, sanitized for their own protection. Once inside the room, there is no blood, or skin, or hair, or teeth, or chunks of brain, heart, lung, stomach. There is no evidence of violent death, self-inflicted or otherwise. There is no detritus of a human body left to decompose for days or weeks. There is only fluid and matter; there are only spots, stains, leakage.

The trick of the job is not to listen to the people who are waiting in the doorway, in the driveway, in the parking lot when the vans arrive. Often they will have a lot to say, a lot to explain. It is important to understand what those people do not: that there is nothing to explain. There is just fluid and matter. There are just spots and stains. There is only a mess that needs to be cleaned up.

Remember those things, understand those things, and the job is possible. The room can be cleaned, finished, set right. Remember those things and the picture taken once the job is complete, the *After* photograph, will show evidence that the trick is more than a trick. It will show what has been achieved through hours of spraying and scrubbing and scraping and bagging, what future occupants of the site will believe, safe and unsuspecting. That the trick of the job is now the new truth of the room:

Nothing happened.

The recliner would have to be disposed of. That much was immediately clear. The recliner was a lost cause, soaked in fluids and studded with matter. Once Bob came back up from the manager's office, they'd need to wrap it and carry it down to the vans. After the cleanup was complete, they'd drive it to the disposal facility with the other red biohazard bags full of all the other things they couldn't salvage, contaminated items that were impossible to clean.

The carpeting around the recliner was dark with dried splotches, stipples trailing out toward the wall a few feet behind. Darby pulled a spray bottle from his bucket, squirted the liquefying enzyme across the first splotch, softening the dried fluid, creating a low mist around the recliner. He gave it a few seconds to burble and hiss, then pulled a fistful of paper towels from a roll and soaked up as much as the towels would hold. He red-bagged the towels and sprayed the next splotch.

Roistler came into the apartment carrying the fogging machine. He closed the door behind him and shut all the windows, sealing them in. He set the machine down in the middle of the room. The fogger would flatten all smell in the room, years of cologne and cooking and cigarettes and a week's worth of fluid and matter sitting in the heat. It also helped with the flies, though it didn't do much about the vectors.

Roistler had been right. There were *mucho* vectors. Flies gathered almost immediately at a job site, and given enough time, flies laid eggs that became vectors and vectors multiplied at an alarming rate, squirming around in any fluid and matter they could find. A week was more than enough time for a complete generation of vectors, maybe two.

Roistler flipped a switch on the fogger and the machine jumped to life. Darby could feel its low rumble in his knees, vibrating through the floor. The machine chugged and pumped, releasing a thin white mist in a steady stream. Roistler said something Darby couldn't hear, then laughed at his own joke.

Darby sprayed another splotch at the foot of the recliner, tore more paper towels from the roll, scooped the softened fluid. There were sharp shards of broken glass near the toe of his work boot, the remains of a shattered vodka bottle. There was another empty bottle on the TV, a third lying on its side on the bed. Darby caught himself, stopped himself from looking around the room. He narrowed his vision, refocused on the recliner.

"Darby," Roistler said. "Look at this."

Roistler was standing at the bookshelves on the other side of the room, inspecting picture frames and detective paperbacks, anything that could have been hit with flying fluid or matter.

"Darby, look." Roistler raised his voice to be heard over the fogger, through the hood of Darby's suit. He was holding something between his thumb and forefinger, dangling it for Darby to see.

Darby didn't look. He nodded like he'd looked, nodded and grunted loudly as a false confirmation that he'd looked, because sometimes that was enough, sometimes that satisfied Roistler and he'd get back to work without any further conversation.

"Darby, look. You're not looking."

Darby didn't look. He nodded and grunted and scooped the last of the fluid from the carpeting. It wasn't going to be enough. The carpeting would have to be disposed of. He picked a scoring razor out of his bucket and started cutting the carpet into record-album-size squares, pulling the squares loose, stuffing them into a red biohazard bag.

It was already hot in the room. Darby sweated in his suit, used his forearm to lift his goggles a half-inch from his face, clear the condensation.

There was a large, shrieking splash of fluid on the wall behind the recliner. Above the fluid was a fist-size hole that had contained the discharge of the weapon used. The discharge would have been taken by the cops, but there would still be other things in that hole, things that clung to the discharge as it made its way from the recliner to the wall.

Darby pulled a plastic dustpan from his bucket, sprayed the stain on the wall with disinfectant and held the pan underneath to catch the fluid as it ran. The disappearing stain revealed more matter stuck to the white paint, little wads of what could easily be mistaken for colorless chewing gum. Darby kept the dustpan pressed to the wall with one hand, tore more paper towels with the other, picked the matter from the wall. Sprayed the entire area again, wiping it clean.

He carried a short stepladder in from the hall, climbed up to the hole, sprayed disinfectant and shone a flashlight around inside. Tough to see what the situation was. He grabbed a wad of paper towels and pushed his hand into the hole. Came away with enough on his towel to repeat the process a few more times.

Roistler stopped talking. Bob was back in the doorway. Darby tilted his head toward the recliner and Bob nodded. They tore long sheets of black plastic from a four-foot roll and wrapped the recliner, Bob rocking the chair one way and then the other while Darby pulled the plastic tight. They each took an end and carried it out of the room, down the hallway to the staircase, the gaps under the doorways shadowed as they passed, eyeholes darkening, a few doors cracking open along the way, braver souls, long faces peeking out, older men and women, mostly alone, one per room, nightshirts and pajamas, woken by the sirens and the sounds of people and equipment trampling through the building, fearstruck now by the two moonmen. They pinched their noses when they saw the recliner. The recliner didn't carry much of an odor, but they saw the hoods and the masks and a chair bound in plastic and thought that it must smell, assumed that it must stink like cellophane-wrapped meat gone bad.

Down the stairs, third floor, second floor, the recliner heavy from the liquid weight it carried. They stopped at each landing for Bob to regain his breath. Finally they were out the front door of the building into the early light, the sun-gathering haze. Bob wedged a wooden block into the doorway to keep it from shutting, locking them out. Darby covered the floor of the first van with a large sheet of plastic and they lifted the recliner up and in.

They peeled off their gloves, pulled back their hoods, took off their goggles and masks. Breathed deeply. Traffic was starting to thicken on the freeway overpass a block away, headlights and taillights in the gloom. Bob readjusted his ponytail up under his hair net, pulled the tape from his wrists, rolled his sleeves to get some air on his skin. His moonman suits were special-ordered for his size. One of Roistler's favorite jokes was to open a new shipment of suits at the garage, rummage through the box and announce that the supplier had refused to make Bob-size suits any more, that the techs would have to sew two large suits together to make new Bob-size suits.

Bob looked at his watch. "What do you think? Three hours? Four? We're back at the garage by ten?"

Darby nodded. He looked up at the apartment building, a gray stucco slab, counted up, counted back, looking for the light, the closed windows of the room.

"Which is it?" Bob said. "Three or four?"

"Three."

"Fifteen bucks on three?"

"Sure."

"Dinner on three?"

"Sure."

Bob tapped his watch, marking the time. He pulled two new pairs of gloves from a toolbox, handed one pair to Darby. He closed up the van and Darby kicked the wooden block loose from the front door of the building as they went back inside.

Darby stood in the center of the room, pulled off his goggles and mask, pulled back his hood. The cleanup was complete. Roistler was hauling out the last of the redbags and equipment; Bob was settling the paperwork with the apartment manager downstairs.

Midmorning light through the windows, soft orange and yellow. Citrus light. The beginning of another hot day in a string of them. Too warm for this late into October. He tore the duct tape from his wrists, retrieved the camera from where Bob had left it on the table by the TV.

The room had no smell, thanks to the fogger. There was a blank spot where any smell should be.

Darby lifted the camera to his eye, stepped back toward the door, getting as much of the room in frame as he could. There was a small, hard knot behind the bridge of his nose, the kernel of a headache that spread quickly out toward his temples, the back of his skull. A rushing in his ears, a loud white noise that threatened to fill the room. This had been happening for a while now, this feeling that came upon him when he was making his final check of a site. A nagging disquiet. The feeling that the room was unfinished.

He looked for something they had missed, some detail that would be discovered in days or weeks, after the carpeting had been replaced, after the wall had been patched and repainted, a telltale sign that would betray the secret of what had happened here. There was nothing. The room was clean, the job was done.

He tried to shake the headache. He held his breath to steady his hands and snapped the picture. The room flashed white.

Liza Palmer

Walter and the Ice Cream Truck

I REMEMBER WALTER USED to drive his truck up Montana and down Fair Oaks at about ten miles an hour. He would stop traffic just to let a child buy a rocket popsicle for two cents less than the price quoted. But, with chocolatey fingers and a red mouth, the child thanked old Walter and the parade of patient motorists continued on their way. For they had all been that child at one point in their lives. Walter's faded yellow ice cream truck filled our community with the music of Donazetti, Wagner, and Bach. And on Sundays we got the Winans and maybe a little bit of Sister Aretha. It depended. Day after day, we waited for that music to come floating down our street. Streets lined with billboards of expensive athletic shoes and various liquor companies touting the beauty of the lush life.

I was twelve years old during the summer of 1994. I lived in a house just off of Fair Oaks right by the carnicería. When I got home from school, mom would lay out a dollar for me, so I could meet up with Walter over on Raymond. She said it was less crowded than Fair Oaks, and we knew more people. Meaning she felt that now even Walter's ice cream truck was getting too dangerous. It was to join an ever-growing list. I could no longer go to the carnicería because of the pay phone out front. That and the bus stop, which was inhabited by people she didn't like the looks of. I resented my mom then, but now I can see why she limited me.

I got home from school and let myself into the house. Mom worked until about seven at the hospital so I would usually try to have dinner started. I could hear Reverend Green levitating down my street and I was entranced. Walter was in rare form today. I dropped what I was doing and scrambled for my dollar. Something was special. Reverend Al Green and it wasn't even Easter. I slammed the door behind me and locked the three locks it took to sequester the two people who hid so blindly behind it and proceeded to follow Walter. Down the streets and through the rows of barred houses I ran, feet barely touching the broken sidewalks.

Walter stopped his truck on the same corner he always had. I met up with Ayanni at the corner and we bullied our way to the front of the line to the dismay of Walter, who by now was giving us that look. He ignored us and let Alexus go in front of us. Alexus, who was always last in line because her attention span was about two seconds long. She would always forget why she was in line and run off after some butterfly. Ayanni and I conceded and allowed Alexus to go. When it was finally our turn, I stepped up to Walter and smiled my guilty no-teeth smirk and slipped him my dollar.

He loomed over me like Zeus and started in. "Now, you know my lambs aren't supposed to be turning on each other. You, of all people, Eve. Alexus is small, barely three years old if she ain't a lick and you are almost a woman. Respect, Eve."

It seemed almost odd to me that he even said my name. Usually he would just call us his lambs. I knew he knew my name, but I had never heard him say it. It seemed unfamiliar. First Reverend Green and now this. I ordered my usual rocket pop and apologized.

"I'm sorry, Walter."

I unwrapped my popsicle and Walter laughed. His laugh filled my whole universe and with the exhalation made the sun hotter. I turned around and he just shook his head. And as the red popsicle bled over my knuckles, I walked back to my house.

I walked back to my house and threw away the discolored popsicle stick. The experience with Walter was disconcerting only because I had known him as one thing for so long, any change was alien to me. Walter had such a distinct aura surrounding him that when he was having an off day, barometers fluctuated. I started in with my homework and waited for mom.

I walked to school with Ayanni the next day and she mentioned Walter. We both felt uncomfortable. Walter had driven these streets for so long, what could be different. It's always been the same kids. Children of parents who were once children he molded. The sidewalks had never been mended and the mountains never moved. The market and the Church of the New Life stood as wonders of our world, never budging.

Walter knew these streets better than anyone. He drove them straight for four hours every day. Even Sunday. But, as I looked onto these streets, I guess I knew what Walter had seen.

For as he drove past our satisfied faces now drenched in the colors of the horizon he also drove past poverty and hopelessness. When Rodrick Holloway was shot Walter had just driven by him, waving and telling him he looked skinny. When Jason Beckwith was being harassed by the police for jaywalking, Walter could be heard a block away: the sounds of Sister Aretha playing as a soundtrack to the demise of his innocence. When Alicia Grundy came home after losing her job at the market, Walter could be heard. That morning it was Lady Day.

As this community crumbles, we all hear Walter driving through us. With the sounds of something so ethereal, it quiets me. He shoots feeling into our hearts through music. Through laughter. Through consistency.

You don't have to think about why the day is so beautiful. It just is.

Victoria Patterson
Half-Truth

K ELLY BRUSHED HER TEETH and, for a second, terror passed through her. The feeling was almost physical, as if Owen, her six-year-old son, was sitting cross-legged on the bathroom floor, staring at her with that familiar look, gauging her emotions. She spat toothpaste and saliva in the sink, washed her mouth with water, spat again. She dried her mouth with a towel that smelled like grape shampoo, taking deep breaths.

When she checked, Owen was in his bed reading *How I Became a Pirate*, his leg extended from his comforter. He set the book down, spread open to keep his place. She saw the seriousness of his face, and because his bangs were combed back—damp from his shower and ridged from the comb—it made him seem open and vulnerable and adultlike all at once.

"Blue Bear," she called softly, hands cupped around her mouth, "where are you?"

The corners of his mouth lifted, but then he was serious again. "Happy Meal toy," he said, "a long time ago."

Owen had cried for Blue Bear only a few days before when he'd come down with the stomach flu, and that was when they'd first noticed the stuffed animal was missing. Owen had vomited three times— twice in the toilet, once on the floor—and although one full day and night had passed vomit-free, she knew that he lived in dread of it happening again.

She sat at the edge of his bed and he moved his book so she wouldn't disturb it. Just in the past month, Owen had stopped sleeping in her bed, but they'd broken the rule because of the flu, and his attachment to Blue Bear was connected to his sleeping alone. This was his first night back in his bed.

She watched the slight lift and fall of his chest.

"You were brave," she said.

He stared at her.

"I know how much you hate to throw up," she said.

"Mom," he said in a world-weary tone, continuing to stare, now with what looked like pity—maybe compassion; and then, after a pause, he said, "I didn't have a choice."

His answer surprised her. She hated how he sometimes refused to let her be the parent. Why couldn't he fake being a child, same as how she had to fake being an adult? Now that she was in her twenties, Kelly better understood the consequences of being a teenage mom, knowing that this defined and shaped her life more than anything else. She tried to hide the emotion on her face, remembering how Owen had begged her to sit in the bathroom every time he'd felt nauseated, and how he'd cried and panicked and even cursed, making his voice a grim mockery of hers: *goddamn, goddamn, goddamn.*

When Owen's first-grade teacher had said that Owen seemed detached, the school had tested him, and instead of scoring low, as the teacher probably expected, he tested advanced, especially in reading. Kelly got a jolt out of knowing that her son was smarter than the sons and daughters of the doctors and lawyers, the parents who were married and stable and already sending their children to tutors. If Owen was detached, it only meant that he was bored. And now his teacher smiled and said good morning, instead of ignoring her; or worse, giving her what she'd come to think of as the *Too Young to Be a Mom* stare. Still, her pride was offset by the sense of being in way over her head.

Owen's hand went under the comforter to his stomach, as if he might gain an indicator as to whether he'd be nauseated again.

"You can't get the stomach flu twice," she said. When this didn't help, she added, "You're not going to throw up."

"How do you know? How can you be sure?" He was shaking his head. She leaned over and just as she was about to kiss his lips, he turned his face so that she landed at his ear. "Blue Bear is gone," he said, eyes directed at the wall. "You won't find him."

Even though—in retrospect—Kelly got pregnant in an attempt to hold on to Nick, maybe even to save him, by the time she was four months along, she wanted Owen to be a girl: to cut all connections and reminders, including the commonality of male sex. Yet Owen looked like Nick, even more so the older he got: full bottom lip, hazel eyes, features that had attracted her to Nick in the first place.

Nick had only held baby Owen three times. By court order, he wasn't allowed visitations until he was clean. She was disappointed that he didn't fight her for visitation rights, same as he hadn't sued for custody. She would have won if he had. Kelly never injected heroin like Nick, only snorted it to accompany him, and then sobered up at seventeen when she became pregnant. She finished John Muir High School with a swollen belly, while he dropped out and moved from his home to the streets.

After Owen was born, she was relieved to discover that she loved her son—a straightforward love, different from how she felt about Nick; that other kind of love, it made her crazy, jealous, and irrational. It took from her life. What she felt for Owen was bound with guilt and responsibility. It provoked a desire to protect and nourish that was deep and real, and it came from her.

At around three years old, Owen started asking, "Mommy, do I have a daddy? Where's my daddy?" She'd been able to sidetrack him with vague and broad responses. But in the last year, unsatisfied, he started asking more questions, and after consulting with a child psychologist and her parents, she decided to be as honest as possible. She explained that Nick was a sick man, addicted to drugs—by this time,

Owen knew in a general way about drugs—and that she was sorry because he was no kind of father.

Owen started pointing to various men on the streets: "Is that him? That my dad?" And sometimes he'd shout, "There he is! There's Dad!" Her heart would thump each time, like Nick was really there, but then she'd see a businessman crossing the street or a construction worker wiping his forehead. Finally, in order to stop Owen's outbursts, she found a photograph that she'd used as a bookmark, the only one she had—Nick walking toward her, his hand held out. Right after she'd taken it, Nick had said, "Stop," and took the camera from her.

Owen, sitting on the couch when she handed him the photo, held it in both hands, close to his face, and after a fixed pause, his only comment: "Dads should not have long hair. All the dads I've seen—Jim's dad and Blair's dad, all the dads—they don't have long hair." And then he set the photo in his lap and gave her a look: repugnance, anger, grief. An acknowledgment—right there in his eyes—that he felt sad and responsible for her.

A month or so later, as if he'd been thinking about it all that time, Owen asked Kelly if she'd ever used drugs, and she said a long time ago, but that she didn't any more. Three days after that, Owen asked, "Do you see him?" and she said, "No, no way. I don't want to see him," which was a lie. Not only had she seen Nick, she thought about him constantly. Since then, there'd been no more comments or questions from Owen, and she knew that Owen was protecting her—she could see the questions in his eyes. And the guilt pressed, a weight. God, the way he sometimes looked at her! And what made it worse was that she was certain Owen knew that she'd lied—just like she knew when Owen had taken more chocolate chips, after she'd told him no more.

Nick had come into Vons earlier that week and waited in her line. When it was his turn, he didn't have anything for her to scan, not even a pack of gum; instead, he handed her a small folded piece of paper. *Nice Sweater*, she read, and then she watched him walk out as she tugged on a thread of the white pullover she was wearing over her Vons uniform. Nick paused at the door to flash one of his rare smiles at

Toby, the mentally challenged grocery bagger. She was relieved when he left, but at the same time, disappointed.

The last time he'd come into Vons, maybe three weeks before, was because she'd called Nick at his friend's house, sought him out after not seeing him for more than a year, with the excuse that she wanted to tell him about Owen. Showing Owen the picture of Nick had sparked feelings she'd thought she was done with, feelings that were waiting for her to catch her breath from Owen's infanthood, for her to have more time to think about Nick.

The next thing she knew, she'd found herself in the back of the alleyway, behind the produce trucks and the garbage bins where no one could see them, showing Nick photos of Owen from her wallet. He admitted that he'd recently watched Owen at school recess, from across the street, until the recess monitor had noticed him. And when she saw that he was crying, tears slid down her own face. He put his hand under her shirt, and she didn't stop him. As it was happening, she knew that she would never tell anyone. He was high, although he was doing his best to hide it as he put his weight on her, his face pressed into her neck; she let her fingers touch the side of his face, through all his hair. She let herself breathe him in, smelling his sweat and skin, taking him all the way inside, wanting to carry him away with her, even when she knew she was supposed to hate him. She was more than an hour late back to work, and she agreed to work a double for the cashier who'd covered for her.

Kelly could imagine what her parents would say: "You' re risking everything, all your hard work, for a nobody, a nothing. Hasn't he done enough to mess up your life?" They helped pay for her apartment in South Pasadena, so that she could raise Owen in a solid school district. She was taking night classes twice a week at Pasadena City College. Her friends set her up on blind dates—a young lawyer, a tax accountant. She'd sensed the men judging whether she was pretty enough for their efforts, and hadn't returned their calls. She'd only had sex with Nick, couldn't imagine being with another man, desiring another man; and while normally this might be considered good, discretionary, and modest, she knew that her family and friends didn't think so. It was as if they were waiting for Nick to die from an overdose, or in some other violent manner, confirming their good sense. She didn't blame them. Her mom made her attend a church singles' group, men and women in their twenties and thirties, already scarred and bitter from divorce, but covering with vague smiles and talk of Jesus.

Fifteen minutes after Kelly told Owen goodnight and then looked one last time for Blue Bear—under Owen's bed, in the closet, beneath the couch, and behind the refrigerator—Owen came to her bedroom. Even in the darkness, she saw that he was naked—most likely discarding his pajamas during a bathroom visit; she imagined them crumpled on the floor—and that his expression was worried.

Kelly scooted over to give him room. It struck her as near impossible that his penis—as innocuous as his fingers and toes—would become a man's penis.

He made a wheezy noise, forcibly breathing through his nose. He'd always been a loud breather. "Can't sleep," he said, taking his place in her bed. The distinctiveness of his voice connected them, reminding her of how she could spot him instantly in a crowd of kids—a flash of knowing—even before she could distinguish the tip of his head or a swing of his arm.

Their faces were close, and his eyes assessed her. "You okay?" he asked, and he seemed like an old man peering at her. "You okay?" He spoke sincerely. His breath was a little bad, even though it smelled of toothpaste. "I can tell when something's bothering you," he said. "Your eyes." He smiled, an extravagantly bizarre little smile, and then adjusted his head on the pillow.

She turned from him, stirrings of resentment. She wanted to tell him: *You should see your eyes.*

"You're not supposed to worry about me," she said, talking to the ceiling, using the refrain that his preschool teacher had told them a few years back, when an adult had first noticed his hypersensitivity and his sense of responsibility toward Kelly. Once, when Owen was missing Kelly, the teacher told him to draw a picture of a rainbow for his mother. Instead, he'd drawn Kelly with blue squiggles of tears running down her face. The illustration had upset Owen so much that he'd started crying uncontrollably, and the teacher had finally called her to come get him.

"Remember," she said, "you're the kid. I'm the parent."

He snorted: part laugh, part acknowledgment. She turned to face him, traced her fingertips on his shoulder and arm. He propped himself on his elbow.

"Mom, is Taco in heaven?"

Taco, her parents' Chihuahua-beagle, had been buried three years ago in her mom and dad's backyard after a cancerous tumor had distended his stomach, killing him. Owen asked questions about Taco's death to illicit the same comforting, unvarying response, as if they'd agreed upon one consistent security-inducing platitude.

"Taco is in our hearts," she said, thinking of all the lies and half-truths that people told kids to make life and death palatable. Santa Claus and the Easter Bunny and the Tooth Fairy—preparations for bigger lies. That was why she'd wanted to be honest with Owen about his father—though now she wondered if she should have lied, or come up with some other story that wouldn't be as painful for her, and for Owen.

"Nothing really dies," he said, finishing for her, "because it lives on in our hearts forever."

Owen was sleeping next to Kelly, his arm wrapped around a pillow, when she had that terror feeling again—but this time it wouldn't go away. At some point she managed to fall asleep.

She startled awake before the alarm went off, her skin wet with sweat. Owen's body was pressed against hers, his fingers tangled in her hair, his arm flung across her chest, a leg pressed against her thigh. She recognized the feeling. She wanted away, wanted out. At the same time, a sickening sensation: Owen would always be with her. Every day. No matter what.

That morning at work, Nick came in, and when it was his turn in Kelly's line, he just stood there. He was high—his eyes black dots. Money, he mouthed, so that the people behind him wouldn't hear. When he walked away, a sweat broke at the back of her neck.

She went on her break, and he was waiting, leaned up against the wall with a leg bent, foot on the brick, his pants sliding down his hips. She saw him the way others saw him—skinny, pathetic. Still, she had a twenty-dollar bill in her sweater pocket, and she let her fingers touch it as she walked to him.

The black vinyl seats of her old Cadillac were cracked from the sun, a yellowish cushion showing through. The air-conditioner barely worked, she turned the key in her ignition and there was a whooshing noise. She'd already given him the twenty, and he was leaned forward, fiddling with her radio.

He kept fiddling, not looking at her. He radiated an energy that drove everything and everyone else from her mind.

"It doesn't work," she said.

He leaned over and picked up an old dented juice box, opened the car door, taking the juice box with him—she watched him throw it in a garbage bin as he walked from the parking lot.

She remembered being so lonely as a child and in adolescence, and for no good reason—her parents loved her, she had friends. Then she'd met Nick. Sometimes when he kissed her, it felt as if her chest would crack open. Their intimacy and passion and the recklessness of their relationship had crushed her loneliness and given her purpose and direction—and a sense of elation.

She opened her car door, a gust of wind passing, and she had to close her eyes because of the sun glinting off the other cars.

Nick came at Kelly's lunch breaks all that week, and they sat in her Cadillac and talked, mainly about Owen. She gave him money—fives and tens—without him asking. She pretended not to care, and when he offered her a sip from a small bottle of vodka, the kind they give on airplanes, he seemed confused when she said no. "It's not like you're using drugs," he said. "I'm not corrupting you."

Instead, she smoked Marlboro Reds, one after the other, the smoke lifting out her cracked window. She told him about the terror feeling, and he said that most fears have to do with mortality.

"The more I get used to my own insignificance," he said, "the less afraid I am. You know, the whole 'Dust in the Wind' concept."

They kissed, nothing more—long sweeping kisses—so that when she thought about him later, it seemed like she'd hallucinated that part.

She was used to talking about Owen, especially with her parents, but it was more gratifying with Nick, like she'd stored the information and now the one person who could really appreciate was listening.

She talked about Owen's dive-bomb hugs when she picked him up from school; and how, just yesterday, driving home from school, from her rearview mirror she'd watched him staring out his window; and he seemed so far away, so lost in thought, that she asked him what he was thinking. But he didn't even hear her, continuing to stare.

She told him that Owen used to be afraid of houseflies, but that now he was afraid of mannequins, believing they were frozen people that would come back to life, and so he refused to go to the mall. And how sometimes, when he was trying to fall asleep, he waved his right hand and fingers through the air, watching with half-closed eyes, making shapes, as if casting some sort of magical spells.

She told him about how he kept asking about Taco.

"Your parents' dog?"

"Mm-hmm."

"He died?"

She nodded.

"What do you tell him?"

She said that they had, over time, developed a story that they told each other—she couldn't remember who had actually made it up—about death not being death. How they had decided that nothing really dies.

Nick surprised her, saying, "That's not lying."

"I'm not telling him the truth."

"There's a bigger honesty," he said, "in making a person feel better."

That same week, each time Kelly drove Owen home from school, he made faces—nose-scrunched—for her to see in her rearview mirror, letting her know that he smelled the cigarettes.

But she was getting better at lying, hiding everything from her face. And when she thought about it, hers were little secrets: it wasn't like she was using drugs.

On Friday, Owen told her something that made her heart race. He said that he got sent to the principal's office because three bullies—third graders—had surrounded him and thrown handballs at him, hitting him on his back and on his head. He'd finally punched the ringleader in the neck. "I punched him really hard," he said. For a second, Owen said, the kid couldn't even breathe, hands at his throat. Then the kid ran to the office and told on him.

Owen said his conversation with the principal went like this:

"Why'd you hit him in the neck?"

"My mom told me I should stand up for myself. He hit me, so I hit him back."

"Your mom is wrong. She's very wrong."

"Don't say that about my mom."

"She's wrong. Next time, don't hit—come to the office immediately and tell me."

Kelly cashiered on Saturday and Owen stayed with her parents. On her break, she and Nick sat in her Cadillac, and she told him about the bullies and the principal. Nick said she had to confront the principal, and they got in a fight.

"You do it," she said.

"Right," he said.

"Then don't tell me what to do."

She didn't want to listen to anything Nick had to say. And when she looked at him—wearing a jacket to hide the marks on his arms—she was annoyed.

"Forget it," she said, and she hung her head.

"I have something," he said, and when she looked up, he was fumbling with his jacket pocket, leg extended. And out came a stuffed purple bear, twice the size of Blue Bear, with a tag attached to its ear. He passed it to her, and she got a flash of his grimy fingernails.

"You can make up some story," he said, "about how little Blue Bear had turned purple or something, like he was undercover, you know, hiding out."

She didn't remember telling Nick about Blue Bear, and she imagined him stealing the purple bear from Toys 'R Us.

Owen would never fall for Nick's story.

On Monday, Kelly found the principal standing near the flagpole, watching parents and kids, occasionally waving and calling out hello. As she walked to him, he acknowledged her with a smile. He wore a suit and tie, and she saw that his chin and cheeks had a flushed, raw-skin look, probably from a recent shave. It was cold, and there was a foggy morning drizzle. Some of the parents were using umbrellas.

"Owen told me what happened," she said.

"Sorry?"

"How he punched a kid and got sent to your office."

His head went back and he squinted. The drizzle looked silver, and a few children shouted until someone blew a whistle.

She told him what Owen had told her, including how the bullies were third graders and how he had told Owen she was wrong, very wrong.

"That didn't happen." He sounded almost apologetic.

Before she left, she had Owen come out of his classroom, and she spoke with him by the drinking fountains, underneath the extended roof so that they wouldn't get wet. She wanted to know if there were real bullies. But within a few seconds, simply by looking at him, she understood that his story had been an elaborate lie. "Am I in trouble?" he asked. His breath came out in little pockets of white, and he stared at her with solemnity. Before he went back inside, she tied his shoe.

As she drove to work, she thought about how she might punish

Owen for lying; but then she thought about her own lies, and about truth and lies, and even what Nick had said, about some lies being more like the truth. Learning to cope was connected, but she wasn't sure how—it was somewhere in that space between lies and truths, that confusion between ideas and instances.

For a moment, with a pang of excitement and dread, she wondered if Nick had been meeting with Owen, without the recess guard noticing. Was that how Nick knew about Blue Bear? It didn't seem likely. Then she thought crazily of bringing Nick home. But he'd be high, his clothes hanging off him, his tennis shoes held together with duct tape. And he wouldn't want to be seen. She missed Nick—longed for the person that he used to be. She craved that exhilarating sense of being in love. But he was someone else now, an echo of his old self, and she was someone else, too. She needed to stop seeing him. She remembered him saying, "I was born bad, I live bad, and I'll die bad," and how, as a freshman in high school, this had excited her; but now, as the mother of his child, it dismayed her because it was so pathetically stupid. He'd taught her that her heart was capable of being resilient and tough, but because it was connected to him, he might incrementally wear it down if she wasn't careful.

She gave Owen the purple bear, and he set it atop his stack of toys, uninterested, not even asking her where she'd gotten it. But then later, she watched him swinging the stuffed animal through the air, as if making it fly.

That night, when she checked on Owen in his room and saw that he was sleeping, a feeling of unrestrained and irrational happiness swept through her, and she let herself hold on to it, thick and unreasonable and tasting of hope, because the purple bear was at the foot of his bed.

Samantha Peale

Sixty per Bird

MARTHA ZELENKO MADE PAINTINGS of barns and farmhouses in Spain based on photographs she'd taken her junior year abroad. Each lonely little building made me shudder, as if she'd shown me her soul. I wasn't the only one who hated her for being so far ahead. When Martha turned her easel around, the whole class gasped.

"Mah mother used to wear a brown turtleneck sweater quite like this here color." Martha pointed to her canvas, the first one she showed us. You could hardly understand a word. Martha was from Virgilina, Virginia and her high squeaky voice was knotted and twisted by her rural accent.

"Mah parents died in a car accident last summer and I just can't stop thinking about that sweater," she said.

While our work was critiqued, Martha ate rusty-looking stews out of a plastic Thermos. She pushed her glasses up her nose with a dirty finger. "In Virgilina, mah home, the townspeople leave their old glasses in a wooden box at the library, over by the book drop. Anyone can help herself." Martha picked up a pair each autumn. She chose the lenses closest to her prescription and wore them until her eyes adjusted.

"These belonged to the children's librarian." She touched the greasy frames. "The headaches only last a week or two."

We all stayed far away from her. We were eighteen, ruthless and self-conscious, afraid to be associated with anyone peculiar. Martha established that she was the best painter among us before the first week of freshman year was out. But she was an orphan, poor, ugly, and awkward, with slimy hair and pilled acrylic sweaters. I doubt she made a single friend during the four years she studied in New York. After graduation she disappeared.

I was thirty-one when I moved to Los Angeles from Brooklyn. I'd been out of graduate school for two years and hadn't made much headway with my paintings or getting people to see my work. I'd become lazy and spent more time chasing boys and watching movies on my laptop than painting. I was bored and ready for things to be different.

A few artists I knew had come to California already and I'd heard the art world here was more open to outsiders, but it was still hard to get a foot in the door if you hadn't studied at CalArts or Art Center or UCLA.

I spent a week with a girl named Cassie who'd been a classmate but wasn't really a friend. She taught art at a private school in Pasadena and rented a big Craftsman house there.

"Remember Martha Zelenko?" Cassie said.

"I'll never forget her."

"She's in LA. She applied for a tenure-track job at UCLA and they wanted to hire her but she's just too fucking weird."

"Have you seen her?"

"Hell no. Martha's a creep."

Martha remembered me. She'd rented an apartment below an exterminator's office in a depressing little neighborhood overlooking an on-ramp to the 101. She had four rooms—her studio, a big square kitchen, and a bathroom. The largest room was empty.

"Why'd you decide to live here, Martha?" The walls of the bathroom were stained with mold and the grey linoleum floors were chipped at the seams.

"It's cheap. In February I sold two paintings and a drawing at a gallery in Echo Park and I haven't worked since. I was waiting tables out at the airport. It was a nightmare for me. You can't imagine."

Martha wore new glasses but she still looked like a strange underground animal, with chalky skin and wet feverish eyes. A dozen years out of Virginia hadn't made her any easier to understand. Her paintings were more staggering than ever. She painted people now, bumpy sweaty animal people, with dark beady eyes that stared out at you in fear.

"What's happening in here?" I pointed to the big empty room.

"It's for rent. I can't find anyone to take it. No one wants to live with me." She took a bottle of Hawaiian Punch out of the fridge and poured two glasses.

I didn't have a place to live so for four hundred and forty dollars a month I rented Martha's best room. The neighborhood turned out to be a hub of gang activity. There was gunfire every other night. Martha didn't flinch. The exterminator and his wife were pleasant to us. They moved the trash bins out of our yard to the side of the garage and took some rodent precautions on our behalf.

Martha had a picture in a group show in August, when any person with two nickels to rub together would be on vacation.

"It's better than nothing. I've got to keep going if I'm going to get any serious action. I'm not going to be one of the people who complains for ten years. I'll quit before then. Or shoot mahself," she said.

"That's what we all say," I said.

"We'll see what you say, Anne-Marie. You better get cracking. You haven't made a thing since you moved in."

I'd only been there two days.

Sunday afternoons Martha emerged from her studio to create the disgusting concoction she called Brunswick Stew. She stuffed chicken, tomatoes, corn, and beans in her crockpot and cranked it up until it turned into sludge a few hours later.

"Here's a big bowl for you," Martha said.

"Maybe this will help my painting," I said.

"In Virgilina we make it with squirrel."

I stifled a gag.

"We should have been roommates in college, Anne-Marie. College was a nightmare for me."

I sat on the porch or in our weird backyard—a puny cement slab, a few rose bushes, and a half-dead bamboo grove—and watched birds zoom back and forth between the ash and jacaranda trees in the yards on either side of mine. Black Phoebes, mostly.

"Why aren't you working, Anne-Marie?" Martha waddled over and dropped to the ground in a heap.

"How do I start? I can't remember." I was still under the impression that I was the one who was being nice by living with Martha beneath the exterminator, making myself available for breezy conversation in the yard.

"Why don't you paint one of those stupid birds you watch all afternoon? Mah goodness, you can pass the time watching those little things fly."

Martha had no shortage of ideas, but unlike everyone else I'd ever met in my life, she didn't volunteer them. She waited to be solicited.

"Get up off your derrière and do some work. What are you waiting for?" This wasn't rhetorical. Martha didn't have the gene for entropy.

"I'm waiting to be inspired by life in California." I thought this was a legitimate answer but a fiery look passed Martha's face and she practically hollered at me.

"Inspiration is bullshit, Anne-Marie." Martha couldn't be light and breezy either.

"You were born inspired, Martha. It's different for you."

"I was born poor and I saw mah parents get killed. That is different than being a debutante from the Main Line."

"I was not a debutante!"

She waddled back toward her studio. When she got to the hallway she made a sound, maybe an angry sound, a laugh, or a self-satisfied snort. I didn't recognize it at the time because I wasn't accustomed to be being openly disdained.

First, I drew Black Phoebes in a notebook, learning the shape of their little bodies.

"How's it going?" Martha ducked her head in my room.

I didn't look up. "You were right. Thanks, Martha."

Then I made a painting of the Black Phoebe that sat on a bough above our laundry line and caught flies. I sent the first bird painting to my mother for her birthday and she was delighted. She left two consecutive messages on my phone telling me how talented and generous I was and how she always believed in me and was so proud.

"Thanks for your nice messages, Mom." If she didn't hear from me within forty-eight hours after she called she started to worry and then her worry turned to anger. I had to be careful with her.

"I can't stop looking at it. I don't even like birds."

Three days later I got a thank you card from her with a snapshot of the Phoebe hung over her desk at home and a check for five hundred dollars.

"Would you make one for your Aunt Gillian?" she wrote.

I painted another Black Phoebe, this one perched on the neighbors' fence. I sent the picture to Aunt Gillian in Bryn Mawr and got a two-page handwritten letter and another check.

I started painting Black Phoebes on square canvases, small ones so the birds were life size, or larger than life size. Phoebes were only about five inches long. I could do two in a day if I started by eleven.

Within a month my room was lined with Phoebes. I began branching out into other birds. I sent photos of the paintings to galleries and I applied for every grant, residency, and fellowship Martha told me about but no one in a position of authority wanted anything to do with my birds.

"They're too pretty," Martha said. She'd had three promising studio visits since she made her mole-people and their dirt mounds darker and more barren.

"No, they're not." But I got a sick feeling in my gut and my throat went tight.

"They're songbirds. Songbirds are pretty. I don't know what you can do with them. How many have you done?" Martha said.

"Hundred twenty-five."

She shook her fat little head. I followed her advice and now she was telling me I'd made a mistake. There was no point protesting. Martha had a feeling for painting that our teachers had recognized, everyone felt it, and a keen awareness of how prettiness—physical-ity and materiality—factored into any situation. Unlike her paintings, Martha herself was a mess to look at. Living with her had afforded me an intimate view of the sad cycle of dandruff, nervous rashes, and plaid dresses that pulled across her soft stomach.

"What kind of bird is that?" Martha pointed to the canvases I'd done over the last week.

"Those are crows and ravens. Ravens are bigger, their caws are deeper, and their feathers creep down their beaks a bit. That one's an African Grey Parrot."

"Too pretty, Anne-Marie. If it matches the bedspread it's too damn pretty."

Martha picked up a picture of a Black Phoebe flapping over the laundry line, sallying forth to fly on a field of flat lavender grey.

"You can have one if you want it," I said.

She took the painting to her room and hung it over her bed. It looked great on the cold white wall.

We went out to the yard with bottles of beer and watched the sun go down.

"What's your plan?" Martha said.

"When I reach two hundred I'm going to find a way to present them. I don't know where though. Something will happen. My aunt loves hers. My mother calls her a bellwether."

"No disrespect to your family, but you have to change your game," Martha said. Then she played a stupid tune blowing across the lip of her beer bottle.

I couldn't stop painting the birds and I was too proud to ask Martha for a new idea. Also I needed to earn a living if I didn't want to end up back in Philadelphia or word processing in a law office with a bunch of men who played fantasy football and talked about the sporting events they Tivo'd.

The only place in Los Angeles that ever got crowded was the Hollywood farmers' market on Sundays. I submitted an application for a vendor's permit. I would pay the market five percent of the gross and a twenty-dollar stall fee.

I couldn't wait to have a small success with my art, too. I wanted Martha to be happy for me. It's embarrassing to think of that now.

I set up my wares on Selma, by the children's clothes, scented candles, Mexican jewelry and bags, kettle corn, handwoven rugs, and cheap summer dresses. I'd invested in wooden shelves and painted them a pale silvery-grey and arranged a clever display of the Phoebes with a shade structure covering the whole thing so I wouldn't cook my brain for five hours. I sold twenty-three paintings that first Sunday.

"Anne Marie, you can't sell your paintings in an outdoor market and then get a gallery," Martha said. "You'll ruin your chances at a real career."

"I charge sixty per bird."

"Stop it. Anne-Marie. You didn't go to art school and graduate school to sell your paintings to farmers."

"What's wrong with farmers?" I expected Martha to appreciate my ingenuity, not strive to perpetuate an elitist gallery system.

"Where do I start? The tobacco farmers I grew up around were ignorant, malicious, and violent. Mah father and his two mean brothers and his mean brothers-in-law. They all hated me and tried to tamp me down. I would not let them shut me down, Anne-Marie." She exhaled dramatically.

I didn't know what to say but Martha changed the subject.

She said she wanted to live near the water one day.

"There's no water in Halifax County," she said.

I've always loved looking at pictures of artists' rooms. Most photographs and paintings of studios show the space without the artist and you get the sense, in her absence, that it's possible to discover the details, the secrets that set her apart from everyone else.

Once I went into Martha's room when she was at the supermarket. As usual, the door was open. I had a burning curiosity to find something concrete that was unique to her, a detail that would reveal the source of her artistic excellence and singlemindedness. I didn't think it was wrong, or that she'd especially mind if she found me there, though in truth, we only spent time together in the kitchen or the yard.

Martha's twin bed was covered with a pine-green chenille spread. Beside the bed was a pink-and-orange striped rug with fringe at both ends. The rest of the grey linoleum floor was bare; a few books were stacked in the corner haphazardly. The dresser was missing most of its knobs. A metal office desk and chair she'd found on the street occupied the corner, beneath the window. She had two easels, one she'd brought from Virgilina and one she built herself. Both were empty. She'd painted the long wall white and that's where she hung the canvases she was working on.

Martha's aesthetic interest didn't extend to her room. Her studio didn't have any charm or beautiful curiosities or arrangements. Perhaps the pine spread or the way she lined up her slippers and clogs against the wall beside the door might one day appear special in a photograph. I got my camera from my room and took a few random pictures of the unfinished paintings, the desk, the bed, her shoes. Nothing in the room spoke to me. Martha's genius went straight from her brain to the canvas via her hands and it hurt to know that her psyche was simply worth more than mine.

My mother sent me a card with a snapshot of Aunt Gillian and her Black Phoebe hanging over the chair where she reads and knits. "Would you paint one for Uncle Martin? You know he fancies himself quite the ornithologist!"

Martha got a solo show at a gallery in Culver City. She painted around the clock. The door to her room was always open, the light blazing, Martha stood with her right hand on her hip, her dark eyes boring into those canvases.

Everyone from our graduating class who'd moved to Los Angeles and hadn't quit painting yet came to the opening. All three of them. The Ossendorf twins brought their bored boyfriends. They all taught adjunct drawing classes or worked in film production. They stood apart from the crowd and didn't say much to Martha, just a quick congratulations after they'd looked at her paintings. Her work had gotten bigger and more detailed, more abstract, and darker. I wondered if anyone remembered Martha's mother's turtleneck sweater.

I was the only one who went to the dinner afterwards. Martha introduced me to the gallery owner, a scrawny little guy named Malinowski.

"This is Anne-Marie, mah roommate." She didn't say we went to college together or that I was an artist too. It was an indictment.

I sat between Malinowski's wife and a journalist and we talked about the food. I couldn't believe how much I had to say about artichokes, it mortifies me to remember. We all toasted Martha.

The show hung for a quiet month. Then there was a review in the newspaper and another in a British art magazine with reproductions. Then everything sold—nine paintings and six drawings on paper.

I'd seen her prices. At forty percent—the gallery took sixty percent—she made at least thirty-five thousand.

I'd have to sell six hundred birds. This year I sold three hundred eighty-seven, averaging almost seven per week.

"I deserve every penny," Martha said. "Getting this far has been a nightmare. You have no idea." She closed the door to her room. There was no Brunswick Stew that week. Or the week after. Martha was out looking for a new place to live.

"I need my own space," she said.

In another two weeks she was gone. To keep the lease, I had to start selling Phoebes at the South Pasadena farmers' market on Thursday nights.

I don't know where Martha lives now, or if she's even in Los Angeles any more. I assume she's by water. She shows her paintings in San Francisco and New York and London.

I'm still painting birds in the apartment by the 101. They still sell at a regular clip. I've added hawks and quail to my repertoire, raised my prices fifteen dollars, and there are different sizes, too. Martha's room is available but I haven't found anyone suitable. It should be a painter but I don't really know anyone who paints. Cassie still teaches the brats in Pasadena how to make brown from red, blue, and yellow. The others have been swallowed up in prop houses and design firms. My family is proud of me and they tell everyone how I accomplish the impossible, and actually make a living as an artist.

Compared to Martha Zelenko, of course, I put square pegs in square holes—for a pittance. Whereas she's turned her nightmares into fame and wealth. How strange to think of Martha as rich. She was lucky to have had a miserable background because it gave her drive and material. But I don't want people to be repulsed by me while I clutch an old brown sweater. It wouldn't be worth it. I don't have nightmares, nor do I want any. I do regret giving her a Black Phoebe painting for free. I should have held out for a trade.

Gary Phillips

House of Tears

"THAT SHIT'S BAD FOR YOU."

"What? You're into tofu and brown rice now?" LZ snickered and took a long pull on his Slurpee.

English Johnny turned the late '90s Astro van left off Garfield and drove slow and steady along a side street. As evening approached, kids were still out on their scooters and bikes and there was even a knot of girls jumping rope while a boom box blared a 50 Cent song.

"I'm just saying," English Johnny went on, "we ain't getting no younger and you got to take care of yourself." He scanned from one side of the street to the other as he guided the vehicle forward.

LZ scratched his armpit. "Look, man, I'm happy you ain't no longer sniffin' up your profits in crank and you're clean and sober as a Oklahoma preacher. But let me worry about my own goddamn vices."

"Uh-huh."

LZ grinned. "Fuck you." He had more of his Slurpee and leaned out the window. "Hey, girl, what you packin' in there?" he said to a young woman in tight low-rise jeans walking past on the sidewalk.

"Fool, be cool," English Johnny said. "Sit your ass back down."

"Maybe you should be on speed again," LZ cracked, "you're too wound up." He jiggled his shoulders and bobbed his head to the beat that pulsed in him. The beat that had been banging about inside him since he ran away from juvenile hall.

"We need to be focused. That's all I'm saying. Your head's gotta be in the moment like Iverson before a big one." English Johnny took a right and checked the rearview.

"You know I ain't nothin' but game, home," LZ replied. He pointed through the windshield. "How about that one?"

"That'll do," his partner agreed and pulled to the curb, the van idling on the lonely street.

LZ got out and trotted over to a parked Trailblazer SUV. He crouched down and quickly removed the rear license plate. Looking over his shoulder and spying no one, he got up and did the same in the front of the car. He then attached those plates in the appropriate places on the Astro van. English Johnny put the tranny in gear and got rolling again after LZ settled beside him.

They rode in silence, the driver taking a couple of turns until he reached Atlantic Boulevard. There he went left, to the north, passing signage on stores in Chinese, Spanish, and English.

Finally, LZ spoke. "Dude like this ain't got no bodyguards around? A couple of 350-pound pork chop eatin' square-head bruisers all tatted up jus' praying for the opportunity to light into some sneak thieves like you and me?" LZ smiled at his imagery, showing teeth he cared for daily. You couldn't get anywhere with the honeys if you had nasty teeth.

"He's a recluse. Danielle says until the stroke, he rattled around in his castle by himself. Maybe had a call girl up there now and then or some session dude dropped by from the old days."

"Man got to get his Johnson waxed now and then," LZ observed. "Man go crazy if he can't have that. Get all backed up and shit."

English Johnny looked sideways at his compatriot. "That right?"

"I'm just sayin'," LZ nodded at the window. "But he was something in his day, huh? I remember moms would have her girlfriends over and after they got to drinking and get all misty-eyed about their teenage years, she'd break out that antique that played those goofy forty-fives. Then they'd get to finger-poppin' and tellin' more lies while they put on homeboy's hits."

LZ stared at English Johnny. "Bet you had a collection of his records, didn't you?"

"Still do, youngster. The Slauson Shuffle, The Love You Left, Quicksand—man, those were the cuts. If you didn't get a grind on a slow tune like Heart of Fire, you must have been one sorry chump." English Johnny looked beyond the windshield then reeled himself back to the present.

"When was that? High school?"

"Yeah." They were on the border of Monterey Park and Alhambra, and English Johnny slowed to a stop at the intersection with Emerson.

"You finish high school?" LZ asked, a tenth-grade dropout.

"Hell yeah." The other man pressed his foot to the accelerator as the signal changed to green. "Hell, I was even on the football and basketball teams."

"First string?"

English Johnny gave him a raised eyebrow. "You got to ask."

"Aw'rite, brah, cool." LZ had another long sip of his Slurpee. "So it's just Danielle up there with him, wiping his ass and chin."

"Apparently."

"And you think he keeps his shit there? In that mansion?"

"Know so."

"Danielle seen it?"

"Practically."

"Practically? What? She have a vision?" LZ chuckled at his joke.

"He's got a room and in the room is this stuffed bobcat, and…"

LZ halted in mid-sip. "A stuffed what? Like a lion?"

"Sort of," English Johnny frowned. "Well, I guess technically, it's more like a cougar."

"What the fuck, he's a hunter?"

"No, everything I've read says he's afraid of guns. When he was a kid his old man shot the old lady. The gun flashed right in front of his face, his mother's chest exploding, blood all over him. Traumatized him. In fact, that's how he got into music."

"You've studied up on him."

"Naturally." English Johnny checked his watch; the clock on the dash was broken. They were now heading west on Hellman and he'd turn north again when they reached Fremont. The cell phone rang and LZ plucked it off the narrow dashboard.

"We're almost there," he said after listening briefly. "Sure." He handed the cell to his friend. "Your squeeze needs to hear your voice so she can cream."

"You need to stop." English Johnny put the phone to his ear. "Hey, baby." He listened as he drove. "Oh, yeah, we're set. Is he awake?…I see. Okay, we follow the plan and we're gonna make out like a souvenir-huntin' Marine in one of Saddam's palaces." She said something else and he lowered his voice. "You know it." He clicked off.

"Where you two going after this?" LZ took his bandana off and buttoned his shirt over his breastbone. Absently, he flicked at the oval embroidered with the name *Steve* on the upper left side of the shirt.

"Danielle wants to go to London first because she's only seen it on TV or James Bond movies, and wants to know what it's like first hand. You know, Big Ben, red phone booths, cobblestones." He shrugged. His nickname had nothing to do with the capital of England.

"Yeah," LZ said, "go to Jimi Hendrix's grave and pay your respects."

"Hendrix is buried here."

"Here—wasn't he from there?"

"Seattle."

"No shit."

"Nope."

"Huh," LZ reached under the seat and extracted a black Beretta.

"We're not going to need that."

"Safety first, son," LZ winked. And he tucked the gun away in his back pocket.

English Johnny weighed raising an objection but understood the lad needed a security blanket of a sort so why not. He could take care of things if LZ went off, though he didn't anticipate such a situation.

No, this was going to be one sweet operation. This was the set up he'd been on the road to since that time long ago when he stole his shop teacher's bad '67 Camaro—one of the limited Yenkos with a 427 engine. This was going to work, and nothing was going to derail his chance at a real payday.

The van took a right and traveled up an inclined street heavy with old oak trees, and from several houses, the air faint with the scent of onions and garlic cooking in butter. They crossed from Alhambra into the hills of San Marino.

"Hey, that was the street," LZ said, knocking the tip of his thumb against the side window.

English Johnny looked past him, straining to see the street sign in the gloom.

"That's it, I'm telling you," LZ repeated. "Where're your damn reading glasses?"

"My eyes are fine," he growled, reversing the van in a three-point turnaround. He started onto the street he'd missed, stopped, and put the automatic transmission into its lowest gear. They lumbered up the hill, the street swaying left-and-right as they neared the top. Behind them in the cargo area, canisters rattled in their harnesses.

"I've got it." LZ reached around and held onto the tanks.

The van topped the summit and they saw an opening partially hidden among leafy shrubs to their right. They went through that and followed a driveway that curved and sloped downward to a metal art nouveau-style gateway and arch. The electronic gate was open.

"I can smell it," LZ said.

"Don't start barking yet. I don't want to jinx this."

"It's ours, man." LZ gripped English Johnny on the upper arm. "You know it."

English Johnny's eyes widened and he guided the van next to Danielle's dark blue '77 Grand LeMans Coupe with the Hopster aluminum rims he'd put on the car for her. He breathed in deep and let the air out slowly.

"Ready?" LZ asked.

"Let's do this." His partner got out the driver's side and went around to where LZ had slid the side door back. They got the two oxygen tanks, heart monitor, dolly, mask and tubing, and clanking equipment bag onto the ground.

As LZ positioned one of the tanks on the dolly, he glared at some illuminated letters cut into yet another arch leading to a garden. "Fuck's that say?"

"Casa de Lágrima," English Johnny said, straightening out one of the casters on the monitor's cart. "House of Tears. That refers to his first album, which the critics liked, but it didn't sell."

LZ took in the massive Spanish-Moorish structure complete with turrets. "How many rooms in this mug?"

"Danielle said there are thirty-three."

"Damn." Together, they started up the walkway that jutted through the garden. "You sure this dude ain't Dracula?"

"You know what he spends his days doing? He watches re-runs of *Combat, Mannix*, and that goddamn *High Chaparral*."

"Those were TV shows?" LZ rolled the strapped oxygen tanks along on the dolly.

"Yeah, before your time. He's got all the episodes filed away on DVDs and gives her a list of what he wants played and what day."

"Does he listen to them songs he wrote and produced?"

"No, that's the funniest thing, he doesn't. According to Danielle, he never asks her to play them. And barely listens to the radio. Like he's forever shut out that part of his life." English Johnny pointed at a horizontal sliver of light that grew before them.

"There's my girl."

The men got the equipment through an entrance fronted by wide double doors while Danielle stood to one side. She wore a mid-thigh skirt and her sweater blouse was opened just so as to reveal part of her black lace bra.

"Ain't you supposed to be in white or something?" LZ set the dolly with its load against the rough-hewn wall in the circular foyer.

"Practical nurses wear what they want. And anyway, my patient likes the view." She cupped her large breasts in her hands and shook them, laughing.

"Long as he don't touch." English Johnny put an arm around her waist and pulled her close. They kissed and she wiped her lipstick off his mouth with her fingers.

"He awake?"

"He was dozing," she answered. "Rough day of watching his fuckin' shows."

English Johnny looked toward the staircase, visualizing what lay beyond. "Come on."

The trio proceeded up the stairs and English Johnny was struck with the absence of any evidence that the house belonged to a man considered one of the pioneers of sixties' and early seventies' rock and roll and R&B.

"Know what's odd?" Danielle whispered when they reached the mid-landing. "Today he started to make some notes."

English Johnny bored in on the closed bedroom door at the end of the upper hallway. "What?"

"Looked like he was jotting down some lyrics," she said. "In all the time we've been planning this, this was the first time I've seen him do that."

"We'll give him something to sing about." LZ ascended backwards, effortlessly pulling the dolly and tanks.

At the top, English Johnny gently pushed Danielle forward, his hand in the small of her back. She went ahead of LZ and opened the double wooden doors of the bedroom that matched, though smaller in scale, the main ones.

"Ian," she said sweetly, "the men are here from the medical supply." The room was spacious and made even more so by the paucity of furniture. There was a plasma screen with a VCR and DVD player attached. There was a large portrait in oils of a dark-haired woman, with a scowl and sizeable hoop earrings partially emerging from her tangle of hair. The painting hung on the west wall, and to the left of that was a raised oak bed atop a colorful throw rug, and a sturdy nightstand nearby.

In the bed reposed the former music baron. The thin man was bald, with a prow of a nose below recessed eyes, and stooping shoulders encased in blue silk pajamas. He lay propped against a thatch of pillows, and stared intently at the scene between actors Cameron Mitchell and Henry Darrow on his TV set. On a long low dresser tucked under a window were a series of foam heads, each with a different style of wig.

"Gentlemen," he said in the slightly slurred speech of a stroke victim.

"We'll just set this up, sir," English Johnny said, already heading toward the bed. LZ fell in step and they worked efficiently, as they'd practiced, getting the tank and monitor into place.

A pad of paper was on the nightstand. English Johnny noted the lyrics the man had been writing. Being a fan, he couldn't resist reading the words.

"I don't think it's gonna put me back on the charts." The man in bed looked evenly at English Johnny. He chuckled hoarsely until he started to cough.

"Now, now, let's let these men do their work and you rest, dear." Danielle attended to the man, making sure not to look at English Johnny.

"Maybe you should have some oxygen," she offered. "Dr. Sawyer did suggest it would be good at this time of the evening."

"Sure, sure," he rasped, gesticulating with knotted and blotched fingers that were more like the hinged legs of an insect's than a human's.

Danielle bent over more than necessary and slipped the oxygen mask with its elastic band around his head. The song man's eyes took in the offered view.

"'Bout finished aren't we, boss?" LZ gave English Johnny a crooked smile.

"Sure." English Johnny calibrated the dials on the heart monitor. He pushed the instrument toward the side of the headboard.

"The city burns at night past the windows of my four-on-the-floor," the former mogul mumbled into the mask. "I got eight starving cylinders and a hunger to match. Something's inside me girl, and it's no lark, but in this dark my name is called..." His eyes closed and his lips moved slowly, but no sound came out of his mouth.

Danielle slipped off the mask and shut off the valve. The tank contained a derivative of fentanyl, an opiate that induced stupor.

The three plotters exchanged glances and, as one, exited the room. There was a shorter hallway off the long one and Danielle led them past a set of tall vases filled with even taller elephant stalks. At a tee, there was a door with a hinged peephole.

"What up with that?" LZ said.

"I think it was a study at one point, and I guess if the man of the house was into his books or brandy, he wanted to know who was knocking and disturbing him." Danielle produced a set of keys and unlocked the heavy door.

"Goddamn," English Johnny said as the trio stepped into the room and Danielle turned on the lights. The chamber was in one of the turrets, so it was circular, a high ceiling over their heads. There was a set of stone steps built into a part of the wall that led to a second tiered platform. A low, rectangular bookcase on the platform overflowed with volumes.

On the ground level, part of the space was crowded with stuffed animals, including a murder of ravens on their perches, a mandrill posed in mid-swing, a snarling wolf, and the bobcat. There was also another section that had bunched together all manner of '50s-era toy ray guns in several glass-enclosed cases.

"All this shit means something to him? Or is he just another rich boy don't know what to do with his money?" LZ touched a bronze axe among a set of different types of axes grouped along one part of the curved wall.

"That's an Egyptian piercing axe," English Johnny rattled off. The other two gaped at him. "I told you, I read up on my man. There was a interview he did in *Vanity Fair* about sixteen or seventeen years ago and they had pictures to go with it."

LZ was in motion. "Well, that's really fuckin' groovy, but let's get busy."

English Johnny removed his torch from the equipment bag. LZ rolled in the other tank, marked oxygen, but actually containing acetylene. He and Danielle pushed the bobcat to one side. Its platform was made to look like a mountain path.

"That's heavier than it looks," LZ huffed.

The woman got down on all fours, running her fingers in the grout between the pavers.

"Here we go," she said, standing up. She pushed the ball of her foot on a particular tile and depressed it. They waited.

"Ain't part of the wall supposed to open up like in an old movie?" LZ looked around.

"I didn't hear a click or anything. You sure that's how he gets to his vault?" The anticipation in English Johnny was roiling acid in his stomach—he was neither a happy nor a patient man. He held Danielle firm by the arm.

"Yeah, baby," she insisted, pulling her arm loose. "That time the door to the peephole was loose and I looked in to see him stepping on that part of the floor and then he—oh."

"Oh what?" English Johnny said between clenched teeth.

"He walked," she turned to face the door, getting her direction right. "Ian went that way," she pointed, "toward the stairs. I couldn't see him then and I didn't dare stay at the door too long."

"The fuck." LZ charged close to English Johnny. "We doin' all this on your practically. This bitch never saw the money?"

"Your mama's a bitch," Danielle told him.

"Fuck you."

"Everybody relax." English Johnny advised. He tamped down his temper. "If he went toward the stairs, he went up the stairs."

LZ declared, "This is bullshit."

"No, no it can't be." Danielle looked up at English Johnny, who was now prowling about on the platform, his hands probing the bookcase. He hooted. "You were right, LZ, it's just like one of those Charlie Chan movies." English Johnny slid away a portion of the bookcase.

LZ ran up the steps, followed closely by Danielle. English Johnny was already in the exposed opening. Stepping on the paver had unlocked a paneled section behind the bookcase.

Danielle asked, "Is there a light?"

"Can't tell, but there's got to be." LZ bumped into something and there was a crash. "Hey, I've got something."

"All you got is one of his framed gold records. I already saw those. This," English Johnny said, tapping metal, "is what we came for." He swung his penlight onto their smiling, sweaty faces. "Get my tools."

"Bet," LZ scrambled out.

Danielle came beside English Johnny, placing a hand on his chest. She looked at the standing safe. "How much you think is in there?"

"Enough to keep you in thongs and Beemers, baby."

She put a hand on his tightening crotch. "So that's what excites you."

"You damn right." He put a hand on her breast and they kissed ferociously. They only stopped when they heard LZ approach with the cutting tools.

English Johnny got his rig set up. "You two get up front so you don't get any sparking or metal in your eyes." He flicked down his welder's mask and went to work.

When Danielle told him what she'd seen that day, peeking into this room, the idea had taken root. He looked up anything and everything he could about the reclusive music legend. It was already known that he'd had tax trouble in the past, and English Johnny found a couple of quotes from him attesting to his belief that the government had no right to the money he'd earned. In an article in a crumbling issue of *Teen Beat* he came across at a flea market, the first of three ex-wives was interviewed. She'd been the lead singer of the Sparrows, the girl group the legend guided to early success.

"He is one cheap, paranoid bastard," she'd said. "He grew up without and took to heart what his grandmother always told him about how the banks had ripped her folks off in the Depression. The more he got famous, the more he did lines of coke and quarts of booze, the more he felt everyone was out to get him."

The torch's concentrated flame made progress, burning a hole just above and to the left of the handle. The box was an old Mosler, and English Johnny had been weaned on specimens like this one.

More digging into the record man's life had produced his last interview. For a piece in *Rolling Stone* in June of 1992, he'd gone on about the riots that April and May here in LA. The quote that sealed it for English Johnny was the one where he alluded to the safe.

The idol maker's father, a Holocaust survivor and a jeweler back when the Fairfax district was solidly Jewish, had the safe in his shop, as English Johnny learned from a documentary obtained from the library. The impresario said that as he watched the smoke and the helicopters in the distance, he figured if the rioters should make their way up his hill, he'd roll down on them the only thing of value his shitheel of a father had left him.

The interviewer had pressed for clarification and the man answered, "Well, maybe I'll just take some money out of it and toss it over the wall." It was related in the article that he'd laughed uproariously at that.

"How's it going?" Danielle asked from the entrance.

"I'm almost to the pins," English Johnny enthused. Fine metal dust congealed on his mask. He suddenly glommed onto something that had been in the back of his mind. How did a stroke victim, a man partially paralyzed on one side of his body, move that bobcat to get to the tile?

Then the lights went out.

"Hey," LZ yelled.

"Deal with it," English Johnny commanded. "I'm not stopping. Danielle, use my flashlight. It's in my back pocket. Shield your eyes and come get it."

"Okay." She came forward haltingly. "I've got it."

"And take this." He'd put the torch on top of the safe, cutting down its flame. Its glow lit them in wavering blues and yellows. He passed her the Glock he'd strapped to his calf under his pant leg. "LZ has a piece. Maybe this is nothing, or maybe he's trying to pull some shit."

She didn't blink. "I can handle him."

"I know you can." She left and English Johnny went back to work. He didn't like sending her off to do his job, but he couldn't have any delay in getting this box open. The hole was completed. He used the reduced flame for light, and set about using his drill, hammer, and pointed chisel on the door's lock pins. Sweat gathered on his face and he had to stop and wipe the grime from his hands. The only thing he could hear was his tapping and drilling and grunting. There was the satisfying slip of the pin from the rotor, and the auger bore through just where he wanted inside the lock mechanism. Soon. Very soon.

The Pretty Boy Floyd-era Mosler opened silently on well-oiled hinges. And just like the fairy tale this job was—the castle-like mansion on the hill, the hermit, Danielle as his princess—there was the treasure inside the safe. Neat collated stacks of hundreds the IRS would, no doubt, be happy to know about were nestled inside the safe.

He reached for one of the piles and his hand jerked at the retort of a gun. His temples pulsing, English Johnny crouched and listened, his fist tight around his hammer's handle. Come on, somebody say something. "Danielle," he boomed. "Danielle."

Breathing deeply, he scooped the money into the equipment bag and got out of the room. There was minimal light coming through the high windows and he could make out enough to get back down the stairs leading from the hidden alcove in the turret. If LZ was up to something, wouldn't he have been there to bust a cap in him?

Once more in the larger room, every dark form was a potential enemy, every shadow a place where he could be jumped. The equipment bag banged against his leg; his other hand gripped the hammer. There were no more shots, no whispering, and no movement. English Johnny strained to discern the door they'd come through and walked purposefully to it. He was going home with this money.

Out in the dark passageway he stopped and listened. He started forward and collided with one of the vases, toppling and shattering it. Instinctively he crouched low, expecting...something, but there was nothing. He moved forward, feeling his way to the tee section. He stopped again. There was something, a presence. He put the equipment bag aside, wanting to use both hands and his hammer.

"Baby," Danielle said, the word thick with mucus. "Help me." She moaned. "Help me," she repeated. Squinting into the semi-darkness, he could see she was crawling in the long hallway, the one that led to the master bedroom.

English Johnny frowned, trying to make sense of things. "What happened?"

"He," she started but didn't finish.

Was it a trap? Were she and LZ in on it together? She was young and fine. When the three of them had been out, working on the plan, people usually assumed she was with LZ.

"Chris," she coughed, using his real name. "I know you're there."

Fuck it. He went to her, crouching down, keyed up for anything. She was on her belly, doing her best to drag herself along by her arms.

"What happened?" English Johnny had her face in his hands, her cheek cold like fish flesh.

"He whacked LZ alongside his head when we turned the corner."

"He? You mean—?"

"Yeah. He wasn't knocked out by the gas. I had the light on him and was bringing my piece up when he shot, put it right into my chest. Bastard shot me right in the tit." She laughed and coughed up fluid and blood.

"Where's your gun?"

"Dropped it, back at the door. God, it hurts."

"He's in there now? The bedroom?"

"Don't know," she managed weakly. "I need a doctor, honey."

"I'm gonna get you straight, sweetie. You hold on." English Johnny wasn't going to let some gimp get the better of him. Not now, not having come this far. He rose and walked forward. "Hey, faggot. You think you're better than me?"

"Come on in and find out," the man taunted through the door. "You think because I had a stroke I can't take care of a bunch of also-rans like your *F Troop* crew? You know what kind of shit I've been through for forty years in the record business? What kind of flesh eaters I had to deal with? You're nothing compared to that." He coughed then continued.

"Didn't it occur to you I might have your girl checked out? Find out about her record and known associates like you, Chris. You fuckin' loser, penitentiary bitch." He laughed. "Did you know I was a lifeguard when I was young? Still pretty good at holding my breath."

"Big man," English Johnny groused. He positioned himself next to the door, the hammer in his hand. He felt along the door, got set, then banged at the old-fashioned latch to bust it off. Two shots went through the door but he wasn't stopping.

"Come on, motherfucker," the sick man screamed. "You aren't gonna let a cripple beat you, are you, tough guy?"

The latch gave and the door creaked open slightly. English Johnny went low against the doorjamb, waiting and listening. If he were the other man, where would he be? He visualized the room as he'd remembered it, and looked to his left where the big TV was.

"Chris," Danielle called from the hallway.

The thief launched himself, two more shots rang out as he dove for the bed. One of the rounds caught him in the lower leg, right above the ankle. His momentum took him to the bed and he scrambled over to the other side, knocking the nightstand and doped oxygen tank over as he got to the floor.

Another shot went wide. His wound was on fire and English Johnny grimaced in pain. He used the bed as a battering ram. He shoved the heavy frame toward the large TV, and the man hiding behind it. More gunshots, wood chipping, and a round pinging off a metal surface.

The bed collided with the TV, which toppled over. There was a groan, and the clatter of the gun across the tiles. English Johnny moved as best he could, his leg spasming from the effort. He reached his target, trying impotently to get up from the floor from under the upset big screen. English Johnny hauled him erect and was surprised the scrawny man still had fight in him. A hand that had more strength than he would have imagined was around English Johnny's throat.

"You lousy fuck," the recluse said. "You think you can steal from me?"

"I earned this," English Johnny hollered, striking him. Only one side of the man's body had power and with the blow, he was through. His body collapsed inside his silk pajamas.

English Johnny grabbed at him. "You shot my old lady."

"I'd have shot you too if I had the chance." The one-time record producer was pale and shaking. He was through but wouldn't admit it.

English Johnny was about to hit him again when an approaching siren caused him to pause.

"What's a'matter, didn't think I'd call them, genius?"

English Johnny shoved the squawking man aside as if he were a child. His wobbly leg buckled. Straining, he got his feet under him. A hand clutched at his pant leg. He kicked the man who'd earned twenty-seven gold and platinum albums in the head and limped quickly away. Danielle had managed to sit up against the wall. She held out her arms.

"Help me up, baby."

He went past her to the equipment bag, bumping and stumbling into objects and bric-a-brac. He got the bag and turned. He'd have to pass her again on his way to the stairs.

"Chris," she wailed, using his real name.

"They'll take care of you, Danielle. They'll get you an ambulance and everything."

"You backstabbing mothafuckah. Get me out, Chris," she yelled. "Get me out of here. You wouldn't have shit if it wasn't for me." She was in tears. He was at the stairs.

"No," a new voice hollered.

"LZ, wait," English Johnny began but didn't finish as the younger man tackled him and they went horizontal down the stairs to the mid-landing.

"You ain't taking that money nowhere." LZ was bleeding from his head and sounded woozy.

English Johnny got a knee between them and leveraged his partner off of him. He beat at LZ's head with the stuffed equipment bag.

"No, no you don't," LZ raged, lunging for English Johnny.

The gun punched a wicked hole in LZ's stomach and he fell back against the carved banister. English Johnny had picked up the Beretta LZ had brought in against his wishes. When the hermit had hit and dazed LZ, he'd apparently placed the piece on his nightstand.

"Sorry," English Johnny said, getting up and stepping over the wounded man on the stairs. "I'm very sorry."

"Man, that's fucked up. That's really fucked up." LZ's warm blood leaked past the hand held to his gut.

The siren was coming up the hill and English Johnny was barreling down the road in Danielle's LeMans. The San Marino cop car, a Caprice with crash bars, crowded the narrow incline. English Johnny went right like he was getting out of the way then veered left viciously, knocking the cruiser into a parked pickup. The cop on the passenger side aimed with his nine as the driver straightened the banged-up car. English Johnny decimated their side window with a blast from the Beretta.

As he'd hoped, the two cops ducked and that afforded him the opportunity to barge past, scraping the side of his car against theirs, screeching his way free. The cops put rounds in his trunk and punched holes in his rear window as he got to the bottom of the hill. There was another cop car coming. But there was another street and he took that. He wasn't sure where it led, but it was better than where he was. Any street leading down would get him out of the hills.

He tore through residential streets, past high-priced houses behind high walls. He was heading into Pasadena. Which meant a larger police force, and more resources. His leg bled into the worn mat. A police chopper searched for him overhead, its spotlight cutting like a laser through the foliage. He kept driving. Panic and fear gurgled his stomach when he got momentarily trapped in a cul-de-sac, but miraculously, he turned around and finally reached flat land.

The hunted man got himself oriented near the Caltech campus and bore westward. He took Del Mar hoping to throw them off by not taking a major street but already two black-and-whites were on him. At Los Robles he got lucky again and managed to beat an eighteen-wheeler heading south. The truck locked its brakes and the trailer fishtailed through the intersection as he roared past. This momentarily delayed the pursuit and gave him breathing room. On a side street he ditched the V8 and took off on foot.

His leg was on fire but he knew this was better than trying to escape in the moving target he was driving. In the near distance he could hear the traffic on the 110 freeway. He got to a cyclone fence, the freeway on the far side. Below, between him and the freeway, was Arroyo Seco wash. This being the Southland, it was a concrete river, its bed dry except in the rainy season. Access tunnels were cut into its sloping walls. There was one such opening just across the wash from him.

English Johnny threw the bag over and used what reserve he had left to clamber over the fence. He lost his grip at the top and came crashing down on the other side on his back. The whoosh of the helicopter and its spotlight suddenly swung into view, trapping him in its glare. Wrenching himself up, he grabbed the bag and ran, limped, skipped his way toward that hole. The zipper had worked loose and money began flapping loose from the bag. Caught in the light, the bills fluttered about with a green luminescence.

His side aching, his leg numb, English Johnny kept on. Overhead came the warning through the bullhorn. *Run*, he admonished himself, *run*. He was on the slope, he was almost there. He was pushing fifty and he was going to live like a pharaoh.

The rifle shot sent a high velocity slug clean through his hip, exiting above and to the side of his knee. He went down as if struck by lightning. But he held onto the bag, he held on to the money. He would never let it go.

"It's mine," he wailed. "Goddammit, I'm way past due." He dog-walked up the sloping wall but the second shot bore between his shoulder blades, exited his sternum and drove him back to the deck with thudding certainty.

His muscles lost control and his body ceased to respond to commands. It was all he could do to focus his eyes. Footsteps and loud voices reached him and with nothing left but desire, he reared up, staring at the tunnel hole. It seemed then, as they put hands on him and a foot slammed into the upper part of his back, shoving him down again, that the slot in the wall grew. His breathing slowed, his heart beat less and less, but he couldn't look away.

The hole loomed larger, telescoping toward him, blotting out the light and pain, darkness all about him. Then English Johnny could suddenly see clearly, tumbling along that long dank corridor, clutching his money, never to return.

Cynthia Adam Prochaska

Don't Cha

M Y MOTHER IS WATCHING the Pussy Cat Dolls now. Ever since she became blind in one eye, she has been watching more television and I wonder how it looks to her—the kittens with a whip, beating time to "Don't Cha." She is seventy now and obsessed by the *Making of a Doll*. Robin Antin running around bossing the doe-eyed one and the slutty one bragging about how she can sing rings around the other bitches. My mother tells me their names on the phone and says, "It fascinates me. I just can't explain it."

She even buys the album and I feel odd like when I was eleven and she asked me if she should buy black underwear for my dad. As if she is saying something to me that I don't want to hear. She says the music is really good.

"They're a phenomenon," she says and I know she is lonely, filling time with reality shows and *Lost*. Every night, she has her shows.

Last year she fell in love with a singer on *American Idol*, the pretty boy that stared straight into the camera and sang "Father Figure." She said it was creepy to be as old as she was and find him having an effect on her.

I picture her at the end of a long day, settling into her chair and tuning out the world. She weighs almost two hundred fifty pounds and she huffs when she walks. She holds the walls when she moves through her house because it is so painful.

In one of the episodes there is something about a swing, I think, that the girls have to swing on and sing. They have to hold their legs a certain way and belt out a tune. They all complain about how hard it is, to rehearse and still look tarty doing it. The bitchy one doesn't have a very good singing voice and the others are running around in what pretty much looks like underwear and trying to keep up "the image of a Doll" as the Robin Antin person puts it. "You have to project the image of a Doll twenty-four seven," she says. I turn it off after five minutes. It makes me sick.

Ever since my dad left, twenty years ago, my mother has been obsessed with things. First, it was Madonna. In a momentary fit of insanity, I had bought an album and jettisoned it at my mother's house. My mother took it to school; she brought it to play for her students. She was ahead of the curve; a week later Madonna was huge. It made my mom feel powerful, to know about something before it got big. Then Madonna kept reinventing herself and Mom was hooked. It was her claim to fame. She knew Madonna was a star before anyone else. And Madonna did in a month what Mom had been trying to do her whole life: become someone else.

Mom makes cookies for the guys who come to work on the beams outside her house. This is a sign of how bad things are. "They've been so nice," she said, "I just wanted to do something nice for them."

My mom is not a baker and never was one. Twice a year she made cookies for us and usually they were burned. She just couldn't be bothered after a long day of teaching school, unless there was some special reason. Usually, it was the first day of school or someone's birthday. Most of the time, she came home, poured herself a drink and told us to pick up the crap we'd left on the dining room table.

"Pick up your shit," she'd say, "Every day, I have to tell you kids to pick up your shit."

But now she was baking cookies for the handymen. I imagined her watching them with interest as they pounded nails into wood. She felt close to them, these people not in, but outside of, her home. It was a grandmotherly gesture, warm cookies on a plate tendered for their approval, a kind of flirtatious gesture to let them know she was there. Stuck in the house but not without curiosity.

These gestures had gotten her involved with her roofer years ago. He had come for a week-long job and before I knew it, she was having an affair with him. I could tell because of the way she said his name over and over again, and seemed eager to get rid of me, when he was there.

"Bob," she said, "lost his leg in Vietnam, but you wouldn't know it."

It ended after two months, when Mom finally got tired of the fact that he wasn't going to leave his wife. It was his bill that pissed her off most, though, the quoted price and then some. I guess since she was sleeping with him, she was hoping for some kind of a discount.

"Getting old is hell," Mom says. I drive her to the dip in the curb so she can get out of the car. She uses a cane, but still she walks so slowly, I have to stop every third step so I don't lose her in the dust. I feel like I am with the fat lady from the circus, who shuffles along with the speed of a glacier melting. I picture her in a yellow and red polka dotted dress and a big bow in her hair, and a barker behind her.

I am the clown alongside her, a sort of angry clown, buying tickets for the movie we will see, with orange tufts of hair sticking out like Bozo. I don't mean to be pissed off. I know it's not my job, but we are walking so slow, I feel like I have giant clown shoes on, dragging me back.

"Mom," I say, "I'll go ahead and get us seats." This is practical, I know, but it is also mean. I will be happy to walk at a normal pace, and sit down alone for a minute.

I should take her hand and walk alongside her, but I can't bear to. It infuriates me to see her so slow and needy.

"I'd like a drink," my mother says, when she finally makes it into the theater. "Would you be a dear?"

I am pissed because the trailers are starting, but I know she will whine and try to talk to me in the movie if I don't get her a soda. She'll talk anyway, because she has the DVD player mentality from seeing too many movies at home. She loves to talk about movies like she's in her own living room while she's in the theater.

"And maybe some popcorn," she adds, as I get up.

It's the indirect shit I hate the most, the "maybe's," but I go anyway, trying not to stomp in my angry clown shoes.

She is offering to show me the Pussycat Dolls DVD she got for her birthday and she is smiling, like she has a special treasure that answers all the world's questions.

"It's really quite good," she says.

She is amazed by the way they move, she says. The way they market asinine songs, is what I think.

"They have moves," she says, "that are incredible."

We are there with my daughter, her granddaughter, who is eight. And in my head I am asking myself what kind of message thigh-high boots and corsets will send to a child. A girl child. Women shaking their breasts and crotches at the camera as their only stock in trade. My mother, who took me to my first bra burning when I was ten, is trying to push the Pussy Cat Dolls on me.

"That's okay," I say, "I don't really need to see it."

Mom looks disappointed, and something in her face deflates.

"Okay," she says, "Another time."

The one time I watched the show, there was a moment, a candid moment, when the doe-eyed contestant admitted her feelings about being on the show.

It was one of those classic spiels about what a great opportunity this was and how important this chance to be a singer–dancer–sole survivor–on–the–island was to her.

"My whole life, I've been waiting for this moment," she said, in probably that most predictable, almost-scripted moment these shows have.

"But I'm nervous about Allie, because she's such a good singer."

Doe Eyes goes on to say that the Allie-person is a bitch, though, because she expects help with dancing, and she still treats everybody else like shit.

They show Allie fumbling through the routine and Doe Eyes giving her help.

"I'm not gonna help her anymore after today," Doe Eyes says, "because she just doesn't show any appreciation. I am gonna let her fail. I gotta start looking out for myself."

Then Doe Eyes looks in the camera and says, "She deserves to fail. That's it."

And I realize that I have misjudged her. Now that she is hardening her too-soft heart, I see that she will be the winner. I see that she will dig in her heels and repeat the words *that's it* as if to convince herself. She will clench her hand into a fist, tight with the resolve that she will not backslide and help Allie ever again. But I also know that fist and it may be weaker than she thinks. One look, the right word, a pathetic *thank you,* and her hand will unfurl, her heart will melt, and she will be right back where she started.

Wally Rudolph

Ocean Water

LAST AUGUST, THE POLICE caught up with me and Brafo in Elysian Park. He was driving a white city van and told us if we kept by the trees, we were liable to burn in our sleep.

He said, "These Santa Ana winds—they're unpredictable, gentlemen. Do what you want, but if they get goosed, LA burns to the ocean."

The man wasn't lying. All day, I had watched smoke choke the sun, and now, the east hills were lit up in white-orange cracks of damnation. The whole night horizon was an old, trembling war. Choppers and army cargo planes stirred mile-long hives of cinders; exploding pines delivered dazzled, charred flakes into the sky. The ash cut my throat and melted on my eyes like chips of black salt.

Brafo cackled like he always does and tied his blue hanky around his face like a bandit.

"What's so funny?"

The police spat out the words scared and set a hand on his big, black flashlight on his belt. He was an old cop for sure—dressed tidy with his little bit of hair mowed down to a crew cut. He licked his lips, and his eyes flashed. He was keen to tune us up.

Brafo said, "If this all going to burn, Mister, why don't you take us to the ocean?"

The police wiped his forehead with his fist, shook his head, and took a deep breath before he spoke.

"I ain't no damn cabbie. You in or out?"

He opened the van's back door. I pulled my bag across my chest and climbed in. Brafo didn't move. He and the police stared each other down under the street lamp. Brafo looked four times the old man's size. His boots were the size of house bricks, and he was tall—like he was hiding a horse under his long jacket. Brafo gave the old police a load of wild eye, and the police laughed right back. The world was fixing to burst with their fevers.

"Alright, alright, old man," Brafo said. "No beach—not tonight."

Brafo ducked down and stepped into the van. Before he could sit, the door slammed shut.

"Hey, hey, hey," he yelled, slapping his hand on the ceiling. "Be careful. I's rare, sir. Rare."

The van jumped into gear and sped out of the city park. I crouched by the back window and saw smoke and haloes on all the city lights. From the park's pink street lamps to the cars' headlights in the city, a thick dust filled the air in a silent, gritty squall. I turned to Brafo and tried to get him to see.

"This is something you're missing. There ain't one clear thing out there."

Brafo pulled his hanky down from his face and spit on the van's floor.

"A beautiful song, Berry, I heard before."

We drove past Dodger Stadium and wound up on the low end of Sunset Boulevard. Batches of Spanish strip malls filled the little back window. Glowing yellow signs with red block letters, lit-up green storefronts with pink script, dirty white billboards tagged up in blue, black, and purple scratched ink—I couldn't read a word. I recognized the letters for food, *comida.* The rest of the stores were all advertising the same thing: God knows what for however much we didn't have.

As we got into downtown, the road noise changed, and I figured we were rolling on soft, fresh-laid asphalt. The cracking bombs of street potholes gave way to that peaceful hum I could sleep to. The van passed another bum and came to a stop in a bus lane. The front door opened, and the policeman's steps knocked dull on the ground. I got onto my knees and watched the old police walk slowly up to the bum. The man had on a pair of bleached-out coveralls cut high to his ankles and nothing else. His hair was to his shoulders, and his beard was braided into little rubber band knots. He was drunk as ever—throwing his arms around, dancing with his bottle. Brafo still wouldn't move, but he wanted to know what I was seeing.

"What's he doing now?"

"The police is trying to convince the man like he did to us. He's pointing to the sky."

"And what's our man doing?"

"Oh boy, he's not having it. He's yelling something and pointing at the van. This one's all bowed up."

"And what's the police doing?"

"He's backing up. He's raising his hand—telling the man to stop."

"Get back from the door, Berry."

"Don't you want to know?"

"Sit here, and have some pekoe."

"You brought some drink?"

"Get over here, and I'll show you."

I got up and sat next to Brafo on the van's steel bench. He kept an eye on the back window while he pulled our plastic bottle from inside his coat.

"Leave a little for me," he said.

The yelling got louder and closer outside. I twisted off the cap and took a short pull of the pekoe. The drink scorched down my throat; I was coughing before it was down.

"Take it, Brafo. Take it back—"

Right as I held our bottle out, the van's back door swung open. Brafo grabbed it and stashed it back in his jacket. I couldn't catch my breath for the life of me.

"Quit your heaving, Berry. Always too much with you."

The bum got thrown in on his belly. His hands were cuffed, and he was kicking around like a fish.

"Give it back. If you gonna do it, give it back!" the bum yelled.

"Give the man his bottle," Brafo said to the police.

The door slammed shut, and I heard the bum's bottle empty onto the street. I already smelled vomit and piss on the new man. Looking on him in that square of light from the back window—flopping on the ground, scratching his face for a grip of steel floor—I don't know what I believed in anymore. We don't have a cent.

My name's Berry Prince, and I wish those fires burned California to dust. I never suffocated in my sleep like the police said I would. No, I watched my friend, Brafo, roll that crying bum for three dollars and some change. Brafo didn't take the bum into his arms like he'd done with me at my worst. He just kicked the man over with his boot and went through his coveralls—every single pocket—like the man was asleep, but he wasn't. Oh, what a night. The bum cursed and yelled. Brafo put a straight razor at his throat. I couldn't watch. The bum got quiet. I listened to the tires fuck the road; the brakes squealed in heat. I tried to remember when my life wasn't a rope of sand.

I met Brafo three years ago. He was squatting behind highway 110 just past Chinatown. I found him cutting red apples and soft, dark peaches into bits. It was the middle of the day, and he looked on me kind, so I sat down some yardage away and watched my man with his scabby razor chopping at that fruit.

"I never seen it like that before," I called out.

"What's that?" Brafo yelled back.

"Is you deaf?"

He called me over with his free hand. I smelled the fruit, and my mouth watered up.

"I ain't coming over there," I said. "You and that blade look mighty literate with each other."

"Come, it's better and sweet."

He picked up three squares of apple and tossed them at my feet.

"Better and sweet," he said again.

I walked over with my ration in my hands, and as soon as I sat down, I felt like a man lucky at cards. Brafo didn't look up. He kept chopping the fruit into bits and dropping it by the handful into a plastic jug.

"You'll see about this pekoe," he said.

His eyes were glassed over and bugged out—straight bloodshot on the whites. I thought he was flying on smoke, but then he poured hairspray into the jug, and I got his drift. He capped the jug and brought it over his head with both hands. He shook it slowly, humming through a smile. The jug got darker and darker till the juice looked like tea.

"That's just drink to me," I said.

"Nah, it's the pekoe."

Brafo held out the jug to me with one hand.

"Go ahead," he said. "You and then me."

I kept an eye on Brafo and tilted the jug back. The pekoe sparkled on my tongue—popped inside my mouth. It sweetened my lips and tore up everything on the way down. I coughed and spit up on the ground.

"Just a little the first time, yeah?" Brafo said.

My face flushed with blood, and I shook my head "yes."

I said, "My name's Berry. You're fine by me."

I swung the jug back whole hog; the pekoe spilled over my cheeks.

"Just quit now. You're wasting it," Brafo said.

I choked down four swallows, and they settled in my gut. My face burned under my skin.

"Let me see—"

Brafo grabbed the jug and took a short pull.

"There, that's all you need, Berry. Just keep your mouth wet."

I laughed and tried to stand up, but my legs broke at my hips and sent me to the ground. My heart danced in my chest, and I felt the ocean rolling side to side.

"Too much, Berry. Too much…"

I don't know how far Brafo dragged me that day. I remember

waking up feeling like I busted out of a cage. My lips were pudding, and Brafo was spooning me noodles from a cup. He showed me pictures of his family, and I counted their eight black faces over and over. He was a Ghana witch, he said. Back home, he drove a red jeep and ministered to the wild animals in his country. I told him I was a punk and a tramp. After that, we walked together—forgiven. We held the other's secrets close. We clutched them bitches like gold.

The police kicked us out in the middle of downtown by the diamond shops. I was thankful he hadn't put us out on the row. When we got out, the other bum didn't say a word. He just eyed us from the floor, and if I didn't know any better, I'd say he was smiling—all wide-eyed and twisted teeth.

Brafo didn't ask the police where he was going to take the bum, so I kept my mouth shut till the city van pulled away.

"Was you going to kill him?" I asked Brafo.

He didn't answer and got moving down Hill Street to Third.

"'Cause I was fixing to say, I ain't seen you pull a blade like that for a minute. You was a street bull in there."

Brafo turned around and pulled his hanky down from his face.

"I scare you, Berry?"

"Scared ain't the right word."

The air was hot and dry even for a summer's night. Sweat dried on my brow before I could wipe it. I looked up as we walked; smoke passed through the tops of the buildings, putting doubt into the sky like black does to water.

"He didn't have nothing is what it is," I said. "You knew he didn't have nothing when you looked on him. He was broke like us."

"Not like us, Berry."

Brafo was walking in those big strides like when he crossed the highways. I was trying my best to keep up—but with my bag and the air hot and sharp like I said.

"How's that?" I called up to Brafo. "How's he any different?"

"He's done, Berry—been done. You and me, we's fighting for it."

"That's 'cause you took a blade to his throat!"

I threw my bag down and took a knee in front of a lit-up gem store. I was having a time catching my breath, and all that precious sheen and gloss wasn't helping a bit.

"Berry—Come now."

Brafo was half a block up—all flesh and shadow under a stop light. I couldn't make out his face. I waved him on and sat down on the polished cement in front of the store. I heard cars but didn't see any lights. I heard shouting but didn't see a soul. I smelled smoke, and I knew the fire was miles away burning up the ground, the hills, the trees, the coyote and his songs. I felt Brafo's steps landing hard on the sidewalk. He crouched in front of me and took my shaking, teary face into his hands.

"Not like this, Berry."

I remembered my daughter and wife—my only relations to God. In this memory, I was a wastrel ghost. I haunted the rooms of our home, waiting to lash out like a shot wild beast heartless near its end. I beat my wife and child. I ripped their hair and slapped their faces till their cheeks swelled fresh and pink.

At night while they slept, I was that horrible man driving the streets, smoking *Tina* from a thin, glass pipe. I eyed faggots in Boys Town parking lots—just looking for something bent like me. I cursed myself in the day and worked my job; guilt soured my tongue. I kicked at the sheets while I slept and woke my wife—night after night— already deep inside her no matter how much it hurt. I was an uncomfortable man. I was a terror and a fraud. I said a punk and a tramp. I freaked cheap cigarettes and bags of dirty speed. When I was high, I laughed, and I heard my life and became sick in my pants.

I lost everything in nine days and awoke on the tenth in my stripped bed with another old man I didn't know. My daughter's room was turned over like we had been robbed. The bathroom fan seemed to shake the house. That afternoon, I put on a pair of jeans and buttoned a white collared shirt to my throat. I drove my car until it ran out of gas. I lived in my car until it was towed away. I never spoke to my family again.

Brafo picked up my bag and gave me a hand. He walked; I followed, dragging my steps one by one. We walked Third Street to the tunnel, and I still didn't speak a word. The sidewalk stopped. We crossed into the street, and I still didn't raise my chin. Tar streams dried on the pavement. A lone car of Mexicans honked at us as they drove by. The horn bounced off the tunnel's white tiles, making my ears ring—hexing my sight into shambles of worthless, orange light.

I asked Los Angeles to leave me with the fire. Let me fend with nothing but the pekoe in my chest. I wanted to see Brafo gnash and fight for his own like he'd done to that drunk man. I ran at Brafo with all I had. My feet barked on the city's street. I landed on Brafo's back. I yanked him to the ground.

"Not a chance," I screamed. "Never a chance for that man—"

I scratched. I cried. I kicked until I saw blood. I didn't stop until I was spent. I didn't stop until I forgot the body on the ground.

Andrea Seigel

Open House

O N SUNDAYS SASCHA ATTENDED open houses, but she wasn't looking to buy, just looking to look. Before she discovered the real estate section of the *LA Times*, she spent Sundays in the condo bathtub. When her fingertips looked ninety, she made herself get out. Her fingertips took about an hour to turn thirty-one again, and then she got back in. She sank her head under impressively hot water until her ears were covered. Using her toes, which were longer than most people's, she turned on the faucet. She listened, pretending for the first second of waterfall that someone was cannonballing in at the other end.

She squeezed her breasts together, pretending they were having a steamy affair. Then she jerked the more ethical breast away in shame; she'd make it sigh and say, "We can't do this. We're related."

She shampooed twice. Then, because she worried that she'd dry out her scalp, in frequent contact with permanent black dye, she shampooed her pubic hair twice. At Rite Aid she'd found small packets of intensive crème conditioner that read, *Leave on for THREE MINUTES*, which was the longest amount of suggested time that she'd come across yet. She conditioned her hair, rinsed, and then conditioned her pubic hair, raising her hips out of the water. She left the conditioner there for six minutes, calculating that that type of hair was in need of at least twice as much conditioning.

One Sunday, when there was nothing left to do but pass out, she passed out. Her head lolled back against the white tiles, and the water kept coming and coming, overburdening the bathtub. The water spilled out onto the linoleum floor and tumbled over itself to get under the door and onto the living room carpet. The carpet was a cheap synthetic material designed to resist stains. It wasn't having any of the water.

The water kept going, looking for someplace good to collect itself. It snaked its way over to Mark's bare foot. He was on the couch, watching his third DVD of the day. He worked on special effects make-up for feature films, and he liked to see what his competitors were doing with their monsters and open wounds. When the nose of the water poked Mark's nearest toe, his first thought was that the left side of his body was going cold and he was having a heart attack. He started to get up to go grab some aspirin, which he'd heard on a TV commercial might save his life. The weight of his body pushed him down in the puddle. The water covered his whole foot. He finally looked down.

"What the fuck?" he asked it.

He followed the trail to the bathroom, the water still coming. Throwing open the door, he was hit with the backdraft, a face full of steam. "Sosh. Sosh," he said as his girlfriend slowly materialized before him. Now that he knew where her cheeks were, he hurried over to smack them. When that didn't wake her, he rotated her body until her forehead was under the faucet, then switched the water from hot to cold. He pelted the space between her brows with the hard stream like he was boring the hole for a third eye. She flinched and came to.

Sascha looked over the edge of the tub. "I never believed those warnings they put next to Jacuzzis," she said.

"You okay?"

"Absolutely."

Mark rubbed the red blotch in between Sasha's eyes for her. "I just thought of an idea for a new monster," he said. "One with a third eye. But it's not just another eye, it's a whole person that's trying to come out through the guy's forehead. It's his twin. His unborn identical twin. They fused together in the womb, and the monster got the majority of the space, so the twin was subsumed inside him. But in the middle of the monster's distended eyebrows, you can see the twin's face trying to surface, and one of the twin's eyes has popped through on the outside. A little worse for the wear." Mark demonstrated the twin's effort, putting his hands flat in the air like he was a mime trapped in a box. He turned his cheek to that same, invisible wall, and strained against it. His eye bulged. "Like that," he said, then relaxed.

"Got it."

"You're my muse," he said.

"But who's mine?" Sascha asked.

"I don't think Aaron Brothers clerks need muses."

They used every towel in the house to soak up the water, but the towels weren't enough. They laid down an entire roll of paper towels and four rolls of toilet paper. The water instantly turned all the rolls to pulp. Sascha brought out her period panties, which were big and cotton. They didn't help the situation that much.

She grabbed the Sunday edition of the *LA Times* off the dining table. They'd subscribed to it for a year, but never opened it for anything other than movie times. She began pulling it apart page by page, offering up the sheets to the moat running through the condo. When the water swallowed each page, she dropped another one on top.

"Says here there's a dog that knows how to ride a skateboard," she told Mark.

"So do I," Mark said. "With less feet."

She arrived at the real estate section and pulled off the top sheet, which was also the bottom sheet. It floated down into the water and darkened. She pulled the second sheet and released. On its way down, she saw a house.

The house was already soaked by the time Sascha got to it, but she could still make out the details. It was a modernist house in Curson Canyon, and its face was made of panels of black glass. The row of panels rounded the entire front of the structure like bared teeth.

She wondered what it would be like to stand on the other side of those panels, and the answer she came up with was "a little bit diabolical." This was a house that a mastermind would buy. There was lots of outward-looking built into it, but no looking in. Silently, she read the text beneath the picture.

Sleek modernist w/ incomparable views. Not another like it. 4bds, 3.5baths. Open & social flr plan w/walls of glass to vu. Den w/wet bar, patio w/waterfall & koi pond. Open house 2-5 p.m. Sun.

This being a Sunday, Sascha realized she could walk right into that house. She could stand behind the expansive wall of windows and foster crafty thoughts about the people below. She could stick her finger in the koi pond and poke a fish in the back.

Sascha looked at her watch and found out it was ten until four. "This paper's useless. I'm going to run out and buy cheap towels at Ross," she announced.

The front door of the Curson house, which was less a door than a sliding panel, was open. A real estate agent stood in the foyer. "Welcome! Come in!" she shouted to Sascha was at the bottom of the long walkway, and Sascha said, "Hold on. I'm getting there."

When they were face to face, the agent pressed a sheet of statistics into Sascha's hands. The year the house was built: 2001. The square footage: 4,150. The number of fireplaces: 3. Sascha couldn't believe that it had never occurred to her to tour open houses before.

This was better than Halloween, which she'd always loved not for the free candy, but for the free glimpses. She'd look over the shoulder of whoever's dad as he bent over to drop a fun-size Butterfinger in her pillowcase. She'd check out the furniture, the lighting, the pictures, the ambience, the channel the TV was set on, and she'd ask herself, "What would it be like to live in there?" She'd give herself the good kind of chills.

Not that her childhood home was unpleasant, because it wasn't.

It smelled like wood polish. It was clean. It wasn't embarrassing. Her little sister was practically a mute, in the best possible sense, and her parents only fought about major things. But it had just never felt like her home.

The agent asked Sascha if she wanted a tour of the house, and Sascha was astounded that the tour was optional. She was allowed to go into this strange person's *ginormous*, expensive house without a chaperone? She could leave her fingerprints all over someone else's belongings?

"I'd really like to go at my own pace," answered Sascha, thinking the answer made her sound rich.

"Of course," the agent said. "Take all the time you need. If you have any questions—"

To secure her perceived financial status, Sascha asked, "I don't have to take the koi with the house, do I? I have my own. Hand-picked. They match the flecks in my eyes."

The agent shook her head, her bun unmoving. "That would never be a problem."

"Great," Sascha said, and bounded up the stairs, pretending she'd just quashed the last care she had in the world.

There was no one on the second story. First she went to the stainless minibar in the corner and opened the cabinets to see what the stranger kept on hand. There were mini bottles of every liquor ever made, with no signs of a favorite. Taking the baby Jim Beam, Sascha walked over to the wall of windows and stood atop Hollywood, chugging. The tinted glass turned the world silvery, and she ended up feeling not as evil as she thought she would. Instead she felt nostalgic, but not nostalgic for events from her past. It was a free-floating nostalgia, a filmy sense that there had once been, quivering just out of her reach, something better than Now.

"No wonder the stranger's moving," said Sascha to the glass. She finished her drink. Went to go put her finger into the pond.

When she returned to the condo, Mark paused the DVD he was

watching and said, "That took forever."

Spreading towels printed with coy fish over the water, Sascha said, "Well, that's because these had to be right."

From that point forward, Sascha never had another Sunday without a visit to an open house. She went to see oceanside California bungalows in Santa Monica and stone manors in Pasadena. She went to model homes in new developments in Agoura Hills, where she tried the designers' imaginary families on for size. In a three-bedroom two-story traditional, she walked around a living room garnished with framed photographs of an Asian mother, father, and two sons. The pictures seemed clipped from magazines. The family did not look related.

The imaginary younger son's bedroom was decorated to express his two imaginary interests: a. violin, and what Sascha could only identify as, b. schoolwork. There was a mobile hanging above the beanbag chair with baby, humanized violins. A bow rested on the dresser as though it had only just been put down. On the desk were two sheets of lined paper with unfinished math problem sets penciled on them, and above the desk were framed awards for excellence in Latin, spelling, art, and science. This kid was an academic all-star.

Sascha lay down on top of the periodic table of the elements bedspread, and shut her eyes. She pretended she was a twelve-year-old Asian boy. Clearing her mind of her own circumstances, she imported worries about report cards, cute girls, and showering after P.E. A man touring the model home walked into the bedroom, and asked, chuckling, "Taking a nap?"

Refusing to open her eyes, Sascha replied, "Just for five minutes and then I'll get back to my math."

One Sunday was Topanga Sunday. After writing five open-house addresses and directions on the back of a dry cleaning ticket, Sascha drove up the coastline and entered the canyon. Driving behind a jeep full of surfers, she watched the one in the back making wave motions in the air with his hand. She envied how thoroughly surfers were obsessed with the surf. It was never just a hobby, but an entire life. Up at 6 a.m. and out on the water, only then the day was worthwhile. This surfer, with his peeling red skin and hair on the verge of snapping, had just come from the waves, but he missed the waves so much that he couldn't help but make them with his hand.

"How nice it must be!" shouted Sascha out of her rolled-down window. Because the drivers were taking the canyon twists slowly, not wanting to die, the surfer heard her. He turned around. She could not make out his eyes behind sunglasses, but his chapped lips broke into a smile.

Sascha put up one hand, half to say, "Hello," and half to say, "Ignore me." The surfer flashed her the hang ten sign, then turned back around.

The first house on Sascha's list was high in the hills, and every driveway she passed had a rounded mirror at the end of it. The road was so erratic that the mirrors could only reflect the past five seconds. Pulling out of a driveway became an act of faith. The pavement thinned as Sascha's car climbed higher and higher, and soon it ceased to be pavement at all. To her left was a lush drop that she could easily drive off, and to the right was a waving, flagged "open house" sign pointing up a side path. The street wasn't on her list. She followed it anyway, winding in a half circle, and pulled up to a lone, contemporary house.

Painted a deep red, the house looked like three boxes of different dimensions stacked upon one another haphazardly. The edges didn't line up. No two windows existed on the same vertical or horizontal axis either, and the effect was of the house being in motion, a shifting Rubik's Cube, even though it was all straight lines. The boxes looked made of clay that hadn't dried yet, like you could stick a finger in a wall and leave a print.

Sascha walked up to the entryway, touching the cacti at the tips of the needles. The front door was a slab of wood in the midst of concrete, and she knocked. There was no answer. Cupping her hands around her eyes, she peered in the glass panel next to the door, seeing an empty living room. The floors were concrete too. She pressed her ear to the door and thought she could hear a dull whooshing inside of the house.

She knocked again. Maybe the realtor was sunbathing in the backyard.

After a minute, she noticed the doorbell—a red button sunk into its environs—and pressed it. From inside the house she heard an electronic chime. Then nothing more. Often the realtors left the front doors unlocked, so Sascha depressed the lever and pushed forward, asking, "Hello?" as she did.

The ceiling in the living room was the highest Sascha had ever seen in a residence. It shot straight across to the second story, which only existed in the far left half of the house. Lowering her eyes, she saw personal items flung haphazardly around the living room. They made her immediately uneasy. There was a lone shoe, a high-top Converse, underneath the glass coffee table. There was a pair of scissors on the mantle.

When people showed their homes, they rid them of these signs of daily living. They put away the old mail and took out the garbage and washed out their gargling cups in the bathroom. After that, they hid their valuables.

The sight of the shoe and the pair of scissors in plain sight produced in Sascha the jumpy apprehension that she had walked into the wrong house. Maybe she had turned off the main road too soon or maybe there was another house on this street that she'd missed. "Oh man, I'm standing in the living room of someone's real house," she panicked. A real house was one still in operation. Standing in it was akin to being one moral step away from a robber. Sascha felt like the police were on their way.

She was backing toward the front door when a guy in only a towel appeared at the top of the stairs. He spotted her immediately. "Oh!" he said.

"I'm sorry. I was just leaving!" Sascha yelled, feeling for the door handle. "I thought this was an open house, my mistake!"

The guy put up one hand and used the other to clutch onto his towel. "No, no mistake. It's open. I just didn't think anyone was coming."

"But you have a sign," Sascha said, heartbeat slurring.

"In the middle of nowhere."

He asked her to wait while he changed, and Sascha was still thinking that she should leave, except she wanted to see the second floor. And the backyard. So she said, "Yeah, sure. I'll just be here," took a seat on the soft, soft couch. She touched the toe of the Converse under the coffee table with the toe of her own Converse.

The guy reappeared, clothed, and jogged down the stairs, saying, "I'll give you a tour."

"You own this house, right?" Sascha asked.

"Right."

"Why are you the one showing it?"

In all the houses she'd been in—over two hundred now—Sascha had never had to look the homeowner in the eye. Real estate agents were necessary for negotiating offers and drawing up official papers, but mostly for acting as emotional middlemen. Agents listened sympathetically to talk of tearing down walls and replacing wallpaper. They laughed at the wallpaper, too, saying, "I don't know what they were thinking."

Agents didn't stop a prospective buyer from touching, from looking. If Sascha wanted to open a medicine cabinet to study its contents and an agent hovered behind her, all she had to say was, "I want to see the condition." Agents had no personal connection to closets. Once Sascha shut a sliding mirrored closet door on a real estate agent's face because she wanted to take her time looking at the homeowners's western belts. "Do you have any questions?" asked the agent from the other side, and Sascha said, "I just want to see the condition of the back of the door."

Sascha debated if she still wanted to see the red house if she had to walk around it under the guy's observation.

"I'm selling it myself," he said, sticking out his hand. "Neil." He was bald by choice. Sascha could still see the shadow of his hairline. Her gaze went to his arm when she reached out to shake, and she said, "You have no hair," before she thought the comment over.

"I was almost going to be an Olympic swimmer," he said.

"You must have a pool then."

"I do. What's your name?"

"I'm Sascha."

They walked through the dining room, out through the sliding glass doors. Neil had not only a pool, but a Jacuzzi as well. The pool was long, dazzling, and pristine, and the Jacuzzi had bubble jets. "The key's a little tricky. I'll show you," said Neil. Sascha shielded her view from the sun as he inserted the bubble key into the slot hidden in the concrete wall. "You turn it as far as you can to the right, then it seems like it's stuck. You twist it a tiny bit to the left, then right again. And it goes all the way." He demonstrated: there was a roar, and bubbles sprang up throughout the water.

"Right–tiny left–right," Sascha repeated.

"Just so you know," Neil said. "In case."

They toured the kitchen. Neil showed Sascha the new cabinetry and shelving, opening and shutting doors. "It's all custom, just put in last year."

"Why are you moving?" Sascha asked.

"I don't know if I am. You're the only person who's come to see the house so far." Neil opened a cabinet door, revealing rows and rows of glasses. "Do you want anything to drink?"

"No thanks, but, hey, really nice glasses," Sarah said. They were a light aqua, shaped like tall vases.

"They come with the house. I buy new kitchenware every time I move."

"I'll keep that in mind." Sarah nodded thoughtfully like she was an authentic buyer. Neil looked like he was close to her in age. She wondered how many times he'd had to buy new kitchenware.

"Shall we go see the upstairs?" Neil asked.

"Love to."

He showed Sascha the master bedroom shower, still wet, which had slate floors that she squatted to inspect more closely. Secretly, she was down there to look at the Aveda shampoo bottle in the corner of the shower. It was an expensive choice for someone who had no hair.

She decided to try again. "So why are you moving? Is there something you don't like about the house?"

"No!" Neil exclaimed, gesturing to the shower as proof. "The house is beautiful! The house is fantastic! Who couldn't love this house?"

"You?" Sascha suggested. "It's up for sale."

"Here, I want to show you something." Neil walked out of the bathroom and into the bedroom proper. He opened the door to the master closet, which was like its own guesthouse. Raising the dimmer, he said, "This closet is big and can hold anything you'd ever need." He lowered the lights and shut the door before Sascha could walk into it to study his other shoes. "But this closet is my favorite." They walked out to the hallway, where Neil opened a laminated-glass door, glowing a faint green, in the wall.

The extra closet was big—not master-bedroom big, but big enough for the chair in the middle and another five more like it. There were no racks or bars going across it, no winter jackets, no board games, no boxes; nothing more than the chair.

"You go ahead and take it," Neil said.

"Thanks. If I buy the house."

"I was talking about going and sitting in the chair now."

Sascha sat in the chair. Neil sat on the floor, pulling the door shut behind them. The sun leaked through the opaque glass, coating them in a diffuse light that looked like ocean water evaporated into dust. The closet was the perfect size for holding the light, for being completely and uniformly filled with it.

"It's strange," Sascha said, reaching forward to press her fingers to the glass.

"I sit in here sometimes," Neil said.

"If this was mine, I'd sit in here too," Sascha said. "This is what I imagine the light would look like right before I died."

"I know it can't be counted as an official room."

"I love it." She tried again. "Why are you moving?"

"You can't change bodies," Neil said.

Not wanting to leave the closet yet, Sascha tipped her chair back against the wall, resting her head. She didn't believe that Neil really wanted to leave this place. No agent, no preparatory maid service, no ad in the *Times*. He was fooling himself. That's why he was lucky that she didn't even have enough for a down payment in her bank account. Because if she did, she would trap him in an offer right that second. They'd go into escrow before the reality of the deal sank in. He'd lose the closet before he could fathom the magnitude of his loss.

"Maybe there's something else you can change," Sascha suggested ten minutes later.

She may not have had the money, but any Sunday now a stranger could come winding up the road, see the sign by chance.

"I'll show you the third bedroom. I converted it into an office," Neil said.

On the walls there were photographs of him competitively swimming, sucking in air mid-stroke. He was wearing a different swimming cap at every meet.

"So you were really good?" Sascha asked, pointing to him doing the butterfly.

"I still am. Just not as many people know anymore." He pulled a book of photography off a shelf and flipped to a picture of a man's back, flexed. Underneath was the caption, "Anonymous, 1998."

"That's me. Top secret," Neil said.

Because he wasn't rushing her, Sascha began at the left side of the bookshelf, examining his collection with painstaking attention. Silently, she estimated that they shared fifty percent of the same books. When she came to the third shelf from the top, she touched a leather book that looked out of place. All the others were modern. This one had a gilded rose on its spine. The print under the rose was so small and delicate that Sascha bent forward to read it. The book popped out at her. It flew off the shelf like it was aiming to jump into her arms.

"I didn't touch it!" she insisted, throwing her arms up, stepping away from the book, now innocent on the carpet.

"You didn't?" Neil asked. He showed her a remote control hidden in his palm. "I got the book at a magic shop. Spring-loaded."

Sascha clasped both hands to her heart, let go a giant breath. "I thought it was alive, like it had consciousness."

"Sorry if I scared you, but the moment was too perfect."

"That's some magic," Sascha said. She shut her eyes. When she opened them she said, "Time for swimming."

"I'll meet you out there," Neil nodded.

Sascha skipped down the steps two at a time, taking off her worn T-shirt as she went. Before taking off her shorts, she stopped in the kitchen and got one of the aqua glasses from the cabinet. Her choice at the icemaker on the outside of the freezer was *crushed*.

"Neil, you want something to drink!" she shouted up at the second floor.

His voice came down through the ceiling. "Whiskey, please!" Sascha pulled the bottle from the leftmost cabinet and poured the liquor over a bed of whole cubes. Taking each of their glasses in a hand, she slid open the back door with her foot. Her clothes were left in the house and outside: she was only in her best bra and underwear.

After taking a swig of her water, Sascha dove into the pool, making it halfway across before she had to come back up for air. She tread water, facing the inner sanctums of the hills, seeing no other houses.

"Watch," Neil said, having suddenly appeared at the opposite end of the pool. Begoggled, he also dove in, and when he resurfaced within seconds, he'd made it the entire length of pool without Sascha ever having seen him go past or under her.

"More magic," she said, paddling over to join him.

They decided to finish their drinks in the Jacuzzi. They'd warm themselves, then jump back into the pool and be shocked by the coolness. Neil slid in while Sascha did the right–tiny left–right with the key. As if it was synchronized, the doorbell rang, the chime tunneling out to the backyard.

"A friend?" Sascha asked, her hand frozen on the key.

"No," Neil said, drink not yet at his lips.

The two, hunched over, crept back into the house like rabbits on hind legs, joints bent. They moved like objects of prey. The doorbell rang again. As they crept through the kitchen and into the dining room, Sascha saw a shadow encroaching on the window next to the door.

"Someone!" she said.

A knock came and now, closer to the door, Sascha could hear at least two voices on the step outside. They were muted, but she heard, buried among one of the sentences, "Try the door?"

"Did you lock it after you came in?" Neil whispered as they crawled across the final stretch of the living room.

"No reason to," whispered back Sascha. The sensation she'd had upon entering the house had returned, except instead of the police finding her there, she now felt her heart seize at the thought of those strangers on the step making their way inside.

Sascha and Neil, on their knees, had made it to the door now. Neil pushed against the door with all his strength so that whoever was on the other side would have difficulty pushing in, and Sascha, slowly and quietly, reached up to the deadbolt lever and began to lock the door as invisibly as she could. When the lock fell into place, it made a small click.

Outside a man's voice said, "I heard that! I heard someone inside."

Their eyes bulging, Sascha and Neil pressed their backs flat to the door, gathered up their knees and their feet and pressed them to their bodies. "Small, small," instructed Neil.

To their left they heard the sound of hands against glass, the man cupping his face so he could peer into the house. Sascha and Neil held their breath without discussing it.

"I see shadows!" yelled the man to whoever was with him.

"What?" said a woman.

"I see you! I know you're in there!" he shouted.

Jervey Tervalon

Rogue Rules, an excerpt

1974

I DON'T WANT TO be anywhere near this part of town: black people been trained not to cross Colorado, to turn your ass around and head back to northwest Pasadena because ain't nothing good for you over there by them rich white people. The police don't want us here unless we're working on a garbage truck or cleaning houses. They'd think I was infiltrating, and if you infiltrating you might get put down, and even if I was infiltrating, fully intending to do nefarious shit, I wouldn't do it around here, because these neighborhoods scare the shit out of me. Like *Night of the Living Dead* happened and the fucking zombies ate everybody south of California off of Lake: you don't see a soul, just big ass mansions that are waiting for somebody to come close enough to grab and swallow them whole. Why you need so much room for so few people? Why do rich white people need so much privacy from each other: who are they hiding from?

Back to reality: if the police stop my van we'll have to stand for a search, and then they'll find the stash of stolen bikes I got in the back of the van; then I'd be doing life or something close to it. The streets down here don't flow right and I'm lost, nervous and sweating bullets. Finally, she points to a mansion with a gate that would make a penitentiary proud. She runs out of the van and tries to push the gate open.

"It's locked!" She shouts. "I'm going to have to climb it."

"I dunno, that's pretty high," I say, shaking my head. "Can't you push that buzzer? Shit, I'll push it for you."

"Last time I was here it was broken," she says.

Shit. I did my good deed, got this crazy Barbarella—so fine with her red hair and a face you see on magazine covers—home safe. I don't need to be doing this, risking everything, my van and five hundred dollars in bikes. I could just drive out to the Big Rock and just relax my mind and smoke weed to sunrise.

Rule 7
Be smart when you doing something stupid.

"Please wait for me," she says

"Be quick!" I say as dogs appear, barking like crazy. She sticks her hand through the bars of the gate and pets one of the huge Dobermans.

"Help me over," she says.

"Cool," I say. I sure ain't putting my ass on the other side of this fence without a M-16 in my hands.

I put my hands under her arms and she flows over the gate without a scratch and drops to the ground on the other side so quickly the dogs scatter in surprise.

"I'll be right back," she says, heading into the darkness.

Now is my chance to bail, get the hell out of here before shit gets bad, but then shit gets bad before I can do anything about it. Headlights, the sound of a big engine, and I know it's the police before I see them. I hide behind a hedge as the patrol car stops in front of the mansion. A lone police slips out with gun drawn. He surveys the scene, presses a button on the intercom then gets back into the patrol car.

I guess the intercom does work because the gates open and he drives in. I see Barbarella standing under the now-illuminated gate.

"Come on," she says. "Are you leaving? What are you waiting on?"

"I was trying not to get shot. Cops tend to shoot people like me."

"Come on, meet my old man," she says like I'm joking. She takes me by my hand and leads me toward the mansion. Up close it doesn't look that frightening—though it do resemble the Haunted Mansion at Disneyland—unless you're scared of the stink of money. We walk along a path heading towards the house. That must be her old man in the wheelchair talking to the cop. The cop reaches for his gun when he sees me. Damn, now I get popped, and the white girl gets tucked in bed.

"Daddy, this is my friend, Calvin. He gave me a ride home."

The dogs are gone, but now I get a pig glaring at me like he couldn't do nothing better than to shove a nightstick up my ass for being seen with a white girl.

"Sir," I say, like I'm back in the service, and stick my hand out the old man. He's frail and shrunken, but he shakes my hand hard like he means it.

"You served in Nam?"

"Yeah."

"What a crapped-up mess. What a bunch of idiots who ran that fiasco of a war."

"Yeah, that's it pretty much."

The old man snorts, "I was in Iwo Jima, lost the use of my legs."

He turns to the cop.

"We won't be needing you," he says, and turns his wheelchair around and wheels to the open doors of the mansion.

I stand there as the old man retreats into the mansion, his daughter following him. I don't know what to do and wait for the cop to say something since we've been left alone. He looks at me like I'm some kind of animal he needs to test himself against. I see myself clocking him, maybe I will, and then I hear the squeaking wheels and the voice of the old man.

"I have the bourbons poured and you're out here wasting time."

I nod to the cop, "Guess I'll be seeing y'all around."

He grunts, and I head into the mansion. I wonder where Barbarella is, feeling stupid because I still l don't know her real name.

I see a new woman in the hallway: she's straight-out beautiful, with long, dark hair pulled back into a long, fancy braid down her back.

"Mr. Ruston is in the library," she says, and leads me across a room big as a basketball court. I see the old man is sitting close to a fireplace big enough for me to step right into it without bending my head. He hands me my drink and downs one himself.

"Where did you find her?"

"In Zuma. I was at the beach and she came up to me asking for a ride."

"She came up to you, a complete stranger?" the old man asks, as though he wouldn't believe me no matter what I said.

"That's what happened."

"Did she pay you?"

"Yes, she did. For a bike I sold her."

He looked at me coldly, like he was waiting for me to lie.

"Are you a drug dealer?"

"No. I sell bikes."

"Can you take care of yourself, Mr. Johnny?"

"My name is Calvin."

"Can you take care of yourself?"

"That depends on what you mean."

"Don't bullshit me, Mr. Calvin. You got that look about you that you've seen lots of trouble, and you know how to handle it."

I shrugged and kept my mouth shut.

"Are you a man of your word?"

"I don't trust words."

"Don't be a smartass, Mr. Calvin."

"I'm not a smartass, Mr. Ruston. I sell bikes because I don't get much shit involved with that. I had all the trouble I needed a long time ago."

The old man looks at me for a long moment. "Was a man with my daughter?" He asks, flatly.

"Yeah, guy who looks like a drugged-out rock star and his pal."

"Those two pieces of shit." Old man Ruston's face reddens so much I thought I might need to call for his nurse.

"Yeah, that's my opinion of them, too."

"Goddamn them to hell!"

I nod like I know what's going on.

"Understand this, Mr. Calvin, this isn't about me. I've tried to keep Ashley safe; this bastard keeps coming back. But it's not just him; she needs someone to protect her from herself."

"I don't know what to say to that."

"Trust me, I've seen a lot of miscreants and dumbasses in my life and the local police don't measure up to even that standard. You coloreds have it hard in this country. Where I'm from, my Daddy trusted few white men, but the colored men who worked for him made his fortune."

His long-winded story tires him out. It takes a minute for him to catch his breath to continue on.

"I want to trust you with my Ashley."

"Me?"

"You. I trust my instincts and I get a good feeling from you."

"What do you want me to do?"

"Keep that son of a bitch away from her. He'll be up here trying to drag her back with him."

"I don't know. I got my own business to worry about."

"Screw that! You"ll be working for me, one of the richest men in Pasadena. I can set you up in this town."

The old man starts to cough, a racking cough that gets the nurse running in. She waves me for me to leave and starts to administer to him.

I wait in the marble-floored cavern on a little bench, too small for my ass, having no idea of what I would be doing, where I was going or what.

I didn't hear Ashley coming.

"Ashley," I say.

She frowns. "Call me Barbarella. I like that."

"What's the deal?"

"Deal?" she asks, smiling.

"Your daddy just offered to pay me to watch your back."

"Did you take it? If he wants to pay you, he'll pay you well."

"What the fuck is going on here? You comfortable with this crazy shit?"

She shakes her head and laughs. Then I look up and there's the nurse, but Barbarella is gone. The nurse gestures for me to follow her and she leads me to the second floor where the bedrooms are. She opens a door to a room that would make the Holiday Inn look low rent. I see this huge bed and suddenly I realize how tired I am. She pulls the sheets back for me; then she opens a closet and lays a robe and towel across the bed. She's one beautiful lady, brown skin, strong legs and ass, and dark hair, streaked with a little grey. I hadn't been sprung for a woman in years 'cause they got to be truly fine to be worth the trouble until I saw Barbarella, and now I see another woman that got me going. Life is nothing but feast or famine.

She finishes with the bed and turns toward me.

"Are you hungry?"

"I wouldn't want to trouble you."

"It's no problem. When you're ready I will have the cook prepare something."

"You run this house?"

"I'm Mr. Ruston's nurse. My duties are to keep him healthy. Please come downstairs when you are ready."

She leaves me alone in the big ass bedroom. Aching and tired, I close my eyes and try to sleep. Seems like I've been running for days; burned out and exhausted, but I still can't sleep even in the land of plenty.

Katie Vane

After School

S IX WEEKS INTO SCHOOL the new kid shows up at our classroom door. He's late, which is probably because his mom couldn't find where the classroom was. That happens to parents all the time. Our school used to be a church compound, so the grades aren't in lines like at the public schools; they're every which way around a big patio where we eat our lunch.

I'm so sorry, the new kid's mom says when she comes inside with him. She's really beautiful, like an actress, with red lipstick and smoky eyes. She's wearing high heels, which almost none of the moms do here, and a sweater that looks as light as a cloud.

We're in the middle of snack, so Claire tells her that's fine.

This is my son, Solomon, the mom says. We just transferred.

Solomon. That's the longest name in the class, apart from mine, which no one calls me by. Most of the time I'm called Minnie, because I'm small; and after the mouse, because I sneak around after school when there's no one to play with.

Solomon looks scared. He's taller than most of us, and skinny. When he tries to smile at Claire I see his teeth are crooked. Also, he's black.

My parents have told me how that last thing shouldn't matter, and really it's his teeth that bother me most. The two beside the front ones are pointed in, and it looks funny, like he's a vampire or something. I guess I'm not perfect, though. One of my front teeth is still chipped from the time I fell off a skateboard at recess, racing around the basketball court trying to beat the record. My parents won't cap it because they say it reminds me not to do that again.

Would you like to tell us where you're from, Solomon? Claire asks.

The new boy says something too quiet for us to hear. His mom has her arm around him, like she doesn't want to let him go. I can see he's got her nose, even if her skin is white, and his is a brown like rye bread. It makes me wonder what his dad looks like.

It's okay, Solomon, his mom says.

Echo Park, Solomon says, more loudly this time.

That's a long way, Claire says. I can tell she's excited because this is different. So what? My parents live only ten minutes from school, but at least I don't get stuck in traffic.

All right, you can come and take a seat, Claire says. We'll introduce ourselves, too.

Solomon's mom gives him another squeeze, and kisses the top of his head. See you soon, Sol, she says.

When she's gone he looks lonelier than ever. He sits down almost outside the circle we've made on the carpet, and puts his lunch next to his side and pulls his legs up to his chin with his hands tucked under the knees. We go around introducing ourselves, and since there're only eight names I hope he'll remember some of them, because it's not that hard. I say my full name and everybody laughs, like they always do.

Just call her Minnie, Sarah says. That makes everyone laugh again.

Solomon hardly says a word for the rest of the day. I think he looks sad, like a cat you leave outside too long, until it stops even yowling for you, and just mews to itself instead. I know what that feeling is like. I'm always the last one to get picked up from daycare, which means for an hour or two every day I don't have anybody to play with, and nothing to do except explore.

I keep myself busy sneaking into the unlocked classrooms, where everything is neat on the tables and the shelves, and nobody is there to make any noise but me. I like to look through the seventh- and eighth-grade students' books, and read parts of their stories, or go back to my old classrooms and look at the drawings the youngest kids make, which usually aren't as good as mine. That's okay. They're still learning.

If I'm in the classrooms for a while it makes me feel like the whole world has gone quiet, and there's only me left to breathe in it. Then when I go outside the smells are stronger, and the air is warmer, and I sometimes go to the lower playground, with the field and the big wooden play structure, and watch the cars come off the 210 freeway. There's so many cars and so many drivers to look at. I can hear bits of their music if it's hot and the car windows are down, or I hear the people inside talking to each other, or on their cell phones, even if it's illegal, and I feel like a detective putting the pieces together.

That's why after school I decide to look up Solomon. I do it on the slow computer in the daycare house, which is the only one we can use. I want to see if his mom really is an actress. It turns out she isn't, she's just an art dealer. But what's better than that is Solomon's dad is an artist and a musician, and it seems like he was really famous in New York.

I think that's funny because Solomon doesn't like art at all. He already got in trouble with our art teacher, Lien, because he wouldn't even do a collage. The most he did when she talked to him about it was draw a couple shapes and color in where they met with each other. That's it.

What he seems to like better is sitting near the window and watching the birds. There're mourning doves that land on the telephone lines, and finches and scrub jays, which make a racket from the trees.

It gets me frustrated, thinking how his dad is famous, and what I'd do for a famous dad, or a dad who does more than leave his dinner dishes for my mom and me to clean up while he reads upstairs. My mom's pretty annoying too. She's always talking about people at work I've never even met, and friends of hers who wonder how I'm doing, even though I don't remember them. My mom and dad both teach at a college where smart people go, people who like science and math. I don't. I bet it would be better to be living in New York. I imagine all the buildings I've seen in movies, and so much light, and people walking everywhere, and hundreds of museums, practically. What would it be like to know your dad made the art that hung in them?

James wants a turn on the computer, so I go to the library and look up Solomon's dad. He doesn't have a whole book on him like I'd hoped, but he's in a book called *The Diaspora: Contemporary African American Art.* Maggie, the librarian, takes it down for me.

All right, dear, she says, and goes back to her desk. She's used to me asking her for strange stuff. She can never remember I hate being called dear, though.

I haul the book over to a beanbag chair and sit. I like it in the library because it used to be the church building, so the light in the afternoon comes through the stained glass and colors the walls.

I get comfy and look for the right page. There he is: Solomon's dad. He's wearing a T-shirt and jeans, and no shoes. He's standing in front of a giant painting with red and black splashes across it, and white speckles covering those. Some of the splashes are dripping so they look like wings. Some of them drip so they look like blood. His face is Solomon's, only bigger, and with a goatee, and a mole on his cheek, and his hair is longer, and lumpy in places like cotton candy. He's black, too, but his skin is darker, more like pumpernickel bread.

I look at him, and I look at the painting. I don't know what makes it art. In my class, art is good drawings, like James does of cobras and tigers, or Mei's watercolors, which have flowers and dragonflies in them, or my story books, where I show the dragon Hiss chasing down another knight to roast inside his armor.

I give the book back to Maggie.

The next day at recess I find Solomon on the upper playground playing handball with himself. He has the pink ball, which used to be red, and it's shaped like an egg so it comes off the wall in different directions than you'd think.

Have you seen your dad's art? I ask him.

He's about to throw the ball, but he stops and looks at me. His eyes are his dad's, warm and black.

Yeah, he says.

What's it about? I ask.

He looks suspicious, like I'm leading him into a joke. I don't know, he says.

It doesn't look like anything, I say. Is it supposed to be something?

He shrugs, and throws the ball so it makes a wet smacking sound on the wall. When it comes off he can't get to it in time, so I chase it down.

Hey, I say when I come back. How come you don't like drawing in class?

My hand is messed up, he says.

I give him back the ball. How? I ask.

He puts the ball at his feet and shows me. It's funny that I didn't notice before, but the first finger of his right hand won't bend, and neither will his thumb. It's like he's always pointing with that hand, which maybe I thought he was.

What happened? I ask.

It's been that way since I was a baby, he says.

Why don't you draw with your left?

He shrugs again.

That's weird, I say.

He doesn't say anything; he just throws the ball against the wall. I get it again, and throw it back. We play a little longer together. But I have the feeling he wants me to go, so after a while, I do.

The next day Solomon comes over to me during free time and sits down.

You're good at drawing, he says.

I'm working on a picture of the dragon Hiss and the Maiden, who's a princess, although instead of spending time with unicorns like she's supposed to, she spends time with dragons. Hiss is a red and green dragon with a yellow neck, which is a sign of beauty because the scales look like gold coins. The Maiden is tall and comely, with black hair like mine, and green eyes like I wish I had instead of hazel.

Thanks, I say.

My dad can do stuff like that, too, he says.

Pictures?

Yeah, but he likes to do *ab-stract*.

That's how he says it: *ab-stract*.

What does that mean? I ask.

He hides the picture inside of something, he says.

He sounds like maybe he isn't too sure, himself, but I don't point that out. He's quiet then, just watching me color in the scales. Until out of the blue he says, Want to come to my house?

I look at him. When?

Tomorrow? He looks scared, like he knows I'll say no. I think about it, and it doesn't seem too bad to me, although I don't know what my classmates are going to think.

Okay, I say.

That night I read a story from the big fairy tale book I got for my birthday. It's about a princess whose brothers are turned into swans, and she has to make twelve shirts for them to change them back into humans, but she doesn't have time to finish the twelfth shirt, so when that brother puts on his, he ends up with a swan wing for an arm. I guess it's because of all the birds, but it makes me think of Solomon.

His mom picks us both up after school. Her hair is in a long braid over her shoulder, and she's wearing a vest with a fringe, and blue jeans that look like a bike ran over them, which is the style I guess. I think she's got to be the most beautiful mom at school.

It's strange being in a car so early after class is done, before there's even much traffic on the freeway. It's bright out, and since the wind this morning blew away the smog, the palm trees are shining along the streets. I like these windy days, when I feel like I could almost be lifted up and fly away over the streets and the buildings to the San Gabriel Mountains where you can smell the sage and see the stars at night.

Solomon's house is far away from school, almost forty minutes. It isn't the mansion I thought it'd be. It's nice though, up on top of a hill. There's a view of downtown, and in the back there's a yard twice as big as mine, with hedges all around it, and a pool on one side and a patio on the other. His mom goes to the kitchen to make us snacks, and Solomon and I sit by the pool and put our feet in the water. It's too cold to swim, but it's nice to splash and watch the sunshine break apart. Solomon's legs are skinny and light brown. The bottoms of his feet are yellow. My legs are pink from how cold the water is, and it makes me feel embarrassed somehow to see them that way, because his legs don't change color when it's cold.

His mom comes out with a plate of little cheese sandwiches, and a bowl of grapes, and two glasses of orange juice that's fresh squeezed.

The neighbors have trees, she says. I just love citrus.

Me too, I say.

Solomon's already eating. When we're done he takes me to the back corner of the yard, where there's a big oak tree. His dad has built a platform up in the branches that we climb to using a ladder. On the platform are some seat cushions, and dinosaur toys Solomon says are really old, and a shelf with books and binoculars and a magnifying glass on top of a pencil box.

I watch birds up here, he says.

He takes out a book and shows me: house finches, hummingbirds, scrub jays, red-crested parrots, mockingbirds. The only ones that interest me are the parrots, which look like they came from a pet store. He tells me the birds he's seen that are rare, because they only come through here on their way to somewhere else, like South America. Their names are funny: yellow-rumpled warblers and spotted towhees.

After he's done telling me about birds I tell him about dragons, even though I know about a lot of other things. Dragons are what I like the best. I tell him how Hiss hatched from a green egg, which means he's a good dragon, even though he eats knights from time to time. I explain the dragon council, and how the Maiden comes from a great kingdom next to the dragon plains, and that her world is full of strange beasts. I tell him how the dragon and the princess love each other even though the kingdom's laws forbid it.

Let's draw, Solomon says when I finish. He takes out a book of paper and the pencil box from the shelf. Inside are pens. I can tell right away they're nice, not like the markers in our classroom that are so dry they hardly make a color, or have their tips smashed in. These pens make perfect thin lines, and when I draw the dragon's horns they look sharp, and the scales look like dangerous crescents.

Solomon watches me until I'm done. Then he does his own drawing of a bird-dragon, with thick, scaly legs and a crown on its head. The lines he makes are shaky, but it's pretty good anyway.

You can draw, I tell him.

Not really, he says. But I can tell he's happy.

I take his picture home and he keeps mine. That night as I'm going to sleep I see him again the way I did when I was following him across the backyard. I see how his neck looked, smooth and brown, and his hair like little kernels on his head, only softer, and I remember how much I wanted to touch it. Then I get a funny feeling in my chest and I know I must like him. So I sit up. I take my journal from the table by the bed, and I write down, with the date, Minnie likes Solomon.

After that I have to stay away from him. I don't even tell my friends in case they tell him. Not that I see him spending much time with anyone else, except for Sarah, and that makes me like her less. They sit together at lunch. He trades his mango for one of her rice crispy treats, and she gives him her juice squeeze for a green tea. I wish I had something good to trade, not just my smooshed-up PB&J.

But Sarah doesn't spend time with anybody for long, and the next day she's sitting with James and Dylan, and Solomon is alone. I can feel him watching me when I don't sit at his table, but what else can I do? If I sat with him our legs might touch, or our hands, and then my skin would go pink and he'd know.

I keep avoiding him until a couple days later during math, the school secretary comes into our classroom and says something quiet to Claire. Claire puts down the chalk.

Solomon, she says. Will you please go with Naveen?

Solomon looks confused. He gets his things and follows Naveen out the door, and he doesn't come back. I wait and wait for him, through the rest of class, and daycare, although he never stays after school, until my heart feels like it's going to squeeze into a pulp. Finally when it's dark my parents come and take me home.

He's gone for another day before he comes back. I see him getting dropped off in the parking lot by a stranger, a woman with her hair in a bun and big silver earrings, who's driving a shiny black car. She waves and pulls away.

Hey Solomon, I say. Just saying his name makes my heart start jumping, although for the past two days I've been thinking maybe I never even liked him.

Hey, he says. He has his right hand in his pocket.

You were gone for a while, I say.

Not really, he says.

Well, a day.

Something happened with my dad, he says.

What?

He got arrested.

What did he do?

Solomon's face becomes angry. He didn't do anything, he says.

Then why'd he get arrested?

Because something happened near where he was.

So?

So, they thought it was him.

I don't get it, but he doesn't look like he wants to talk anymore. I shrug to show him that it's not a big deal, and we walk to the classroom together. Still it hurts my feelings when he picks another place to sit away from me during morning announcements. Now I guess I know what it feels like.

Claire teaches spelling before lunch. We're working on vowel combinations.

Who wants to come spell 'variety'? she asks.

Nobody says anything. We like to use the chalk, which we can only pick up with permission, and sometimes we can make it squeak so bad it hurts our ears. But we're hungry for lunch, and variety is one of our harder words.

Variety? she says. Solomon?

He gets up slowly. I'm nervous for him, because of his hand. Now that I know about it, it makes it harder to watch him write or draw, like I can feel the effort he's making, too.

He tries to spell it, and I think he's close. The letters are almost too shaky to read. The chalk squeals once like an old door, and all the kids start laughing.

Solomon drops the chalk.

Claire gives him her patient voice. Take your time, Solomon, she says.

No, Solomon says, and he runs out of the classroom.

Claire goes to look for him. While she's gone, James draws a lion on the board, and Sarah writes variety correctly, and the rest of us roll on the carpet and pant like dogs. When Claire comes back she says she couldn't find him.

He may need a little bit of space, she says.

But at lunch we still can't find him. He's not on the upper or lower playground, or in the bathrooms, or any of the classrooms. He's not in the office, or the daycare house. None of the other teachers have seen him. They're starting to look scared when a fifth grader runs over and says he just saw Solomon on top of the daycare house.

Suddenly everybody's looking up and pointing, the fifth graders and the first graders, all my classmates, the teachers, even Luisa, who does the hot lunch cooking. I have a cringing feeling inside, but I look up too, and see Solomon looking down on us. Then he disappears from view.

Solomon! Claire calls out. Honey, will you please come down?

Two of the teachers have already left to get the ladder, but I know it won't be tall enough. I've climbed the daycare house once, but I still had to climb partway down to reach the ladder when the teachers saw and came to get me. I got in bad trouble that time. They put me inside for the rest of the afternoon with no snack or anything.

Hank, the seventh-grade teacher, tries next.

Hey buddy! he shouts. We're getting the ladder for you so just sit tight, okay? It isn't too safe up there.

Solomon doesn't make a peep. The teachers keep calling to him, and the kids take it up, the older classes because they think it's funny, and the younger classes because they're trying to be helpful. Solomon doesn't come back.

The two teachers have the ladder with them now and they prop it against the side of the daycare house. It crunches just under the bottom of the windows on the second story.

Honey, Claire says, I'm going to need you to come down a little.

She's tying back her hair, and then she's climbing the ladder, even though she's wearing a long skirt and all the older boys are going to try to look up it. She gets to the top and waits a second before she says,

Solomon?

I have a better idea. The way I got up last time was using the drain pipe on the other side that takes you to a little roof over the door, and from there it's easy to pull yourself onto the real roof. So I sneak off around the side of the house that faces the lower-grade classrooms, until I'm where the drain pipe starts, and since there's no sign of Solomon down here on the ground I start climbing.

I'm breathing in bits of leaves and dust, and my hands are getting slippery by the time I'm high enough to get onto the lower roof. My arms start shaking then, because I know I'm pretty far up and this always scares me. But I pull myself over onto the real roof and there he is.

He's sitting near where the peak is, so no one can see him from below. He doesn't look at me even when he knows I must be there, but when I sit next to him I see he's been crying.

Go away, he says.

I can't, I say.

Why not?

I don't know if I can get down.

I'm lying, but it's a little true. I can feel how my stomach is still swooping, which lets me know it would be a bad idea to try anything right now, but I'd probably be fine.

Why did you come up? he asks.

I could tell him I like him, but what's the point if he doesn't like me? So I ask, How come you came up?

He puts his arms around his knees and squeezes. It's nice here, he says. I can see into the trees.

I like it here too, I say.

He looks at me. Are the teachers going to be mad?

They don't get that mad at you, I say.

He nods. I don't know if I can get down, either, he says.

It's easy, I say.

We sit for a little while, being quiet with each other. I don't know what he's thinking about, but I'm thinking about what made him upset in the first place.

Is your dad in prison? I ask.

Solomon makes a snorting sound. No, he says, like I'm dumb.

Okay.

You don't know how that stuff works, do you? he asks.

What stuff?

Nothing.

He's talking to me like one of the older kids, and it makes me kind of want to hit him, so I shove him with my shoulder instead.

Hey, he says. For some reason it makes him laugh.

I shove him again.

Stop it, he says. He's still laughing, though. Stop it, Minnie.

It's Minerva, I say.

No it isn't, he says.

It is.

Isn't.

We're shoving each other back and forth with our shoulders like we're rocking in a boat. I'm laughing so hard I'm afraid I'm going to fall over. The roof is warm under me, and the sun feels good on my hair, and there's a little wind playing with the tops of the trees across the street. It feels perfect.

We don't even hear the teachers moving the ladder, or Claire climbing up it, until her voice says all of a sudden from close by.

Solomon and Minerva, come down.

She's angry. I've almost never heard her talk like that before, and it scares me.

Minerva, I know you're up there, she says. I will call your parents.

It's not the best threat she could have come up with; I've never been grounded by my parents for anything in my life. I decide not to move.

This isn't a game, she says. You two need to come down, right now.

I look at Solomon. He has a smile on his face, so I figure everything will be okay. I stand up and go over to the edge, and I can hear the teachers saying warning things to each other, but I get to the little roof just fine. I'll have to get down on my belly though to get to the ladder, and that worries me. I've got the trembling feeling in my stomach still from laughing, and now from the sound of Claire's voice. It means my hands are shaking.

I'm squatting down to put my legs over when something gives out. I have a strange feeling, like I'm not falling but floating, or else the daycare house is going on forever, and there isn't any ground at all. I don't see Solomon but I wish I hadn't made him that shirt so he could just be a swan and rescue me. Instead I hit the ground so hard my eyes go dark. Something else has happened, too, but I don't know what it is until the darkness clears and I see my ankle. Then I start to cry. It doesn't look like it's mine anymore.

Claire rushes down and I see her face over me. Her lips look blue. She sits and takes my hand while the other teachers run to the office. Then somehow Solomon is there, and he's holding my other hand. The pain starts growing, so I squeeze it. I feel the pointed finger and the thumb, like a hook I'd hang my jacket on. I squeeze and squeeze, and he lets me.

It's okay, Minnie, he says. Minnie, it's okay.

In a while the teachers come back, and it's Hank who picks me up and carries me past the lower-grade classrooms, and the library, to the parking lot. My mom and dad are just pulling in. Their eyes look kind of crazy. Then I see Solomon's mom and dad get out of their car. Someone must have called them from the office before I climbed the daycare house.

Solomon's dad looks older than in his picture. His hair has gray in it, and his cheeks have sucked in. He's got the same look in his eyes my parents have.

Sol, he says. What is going on?

His voice is deep, and it could be gentle, but it's hard right now. I look at Sol, who's been standing next to Hank, waiting. I have a confused feeling, because of the pain that's swelling in my leg, but my heart is happy just looking at him, and I don't want either of us to go.

I ran out of class, Solomon says. Dad, I climbed the daycare house. I just wanted to be alone. And Minnie came up to help, and then she fell.

That doesn't seem true, but his parents turn to me, and it's like I'm stuck in the headlights. The look in their eyes is one I don't know. It's full of something; maybe love, or anger, or confusion. It's an *abstract*, I guess, and I just hope someday I'll understand it.

John Vorhaus

In English and Dutch

S O I'M ON THE set of this film I'm directing and the whole thing is going to hell on a Handi Wipe because for starters it's a period piece, but strictly low budge, and not even indie low budge but basic cable low budge, where the set designer's idea of Edwardian drawing room is Peel 'n Stik fleur-de-lis wallpaper from Home Depot and staple-gunned wainscoting with little dabs of, I think, Kitchen Bouquet to take the postindustrial shine off the staples. I tell her it all looks about as authentic as a plastic cow and she gives me this look like, *what do you have against plastic cows?* Meanwhile my production assistant has just refilled my mug with something hot and bitter, which makes it either coffee or my ex-wife, who is in her dressing room putting on prima donna airs laughably beyond her real actor stature: about a five on the *didn't you used to be?* scale. We shouldn't even be on the same set, of course, for our chemistry is currently on the order of hydrogen and sulfur, which, put them together, they smell like rotten eggs, not a bad metaphorical framing device for the final eighteen months or so of our garbage scow of a marriage. But this is film three of a three-picture deal I signed back in happier times when the thought of spending a dozen hours a day together in the close confines of a movie set didn't make me want to drink Drano.

Anyway, there's no hurry to coax Marye—yes, Marye with an e,

God help us—out of her cave because at the rate the grips are grip-ping, it'll be the better part of an epoch before she's needed on set. It's not that they're *wildly* incompetent, these grips, it's just that we're shooting in Fresno, where the production talent pool goes about teacup deep. They mean well, though, and they're nonunion, which fact, along with generous tax breaks and equally generous kickbacks, provides my overlords at Pizza Box Pictures with more than enough incentive to shoot here. Still, at the end of the day it's Fresno, and when your day ends in a manically depressive room at the Home Sweet Suites near the freeway, you pretty quickly come to realize why no one calls Fresno the Paris of the San Joaquin Valley.

Then again, no one's calling me the Truffaut of Pizza Box Pictures, so there you go.

To make matters worse, though admittedly there's not a lot of headroom in that area, this young producer nitwit is hovering nearby. His name is Josh—seems like all their names are Josh. He's trying to catch my eye, and I can see the words—*I still have some problems with the script*—floating over his head like a thought balloon, ready to burst and shower shit down on me as I sit here in my canvas director's chair with my name on the back—misspelled, and that's Fresno-qual-ity production services at your service. The Josh has a title of putative significance—Co-Executive Something—and an MBA from—I'm guessing—his safety school. Like the grips, it's not that he's evil, just criminally wet behind the ears and painfully aware that if he does nothing and says nothing then he's justifying neither his presence on set, nor his salary, per diem or—I'm guessing—existential sense of self. So he feels this need to "contribute," but his contributions, of story ideas or staging suggestions or even, bless his heart, alternate line read-ings, are about as welcome on this set as *staphylococcus aureus*, which I hear is going around.

He's oversolving the problem anyhow. This is a Pizza Box produc-tion, where "second takes are for wimps," and thrift is not just a virtue, but the company's whole economic model. Nuance, finesse, artistic vision: all of these things pale to insignificance beside the question of how many pages you can shoot in a day. You'd think he'd understand this, given that Pizza Box is the functional equivalent of Walmart, specializing in quickie remakes of public domain texts tarted into script by entry-level screenwriters and realized on film by "workman-like" directors like me. Or hack if you like. I don't mind the aspersion so long as the check clears. I've been out of work enough times to know that being in it is better.

So...problems. Grips who can't grip. Color-blind art directors. Actors who can best be described as "best available," which means, really, best available for scale. Plus Marye the harpy, coiled in her dressing room just waiting to spring forth and barf hammy emotion all over the set, with a text that says *I'm a lusty Edwardian widow in love with a much younger man* and a subtext that says, *Fuck you Bob Wouda*, meaning me.

Now here comes the Josh, clearing his throat with a little adenoidal bark and saying, "Excuse me, Bob?"

I point to the back of the chair and say, "Please, call me Mr. Gouda."

"That's not on me," he says defensively. "That's production services."

"No worries," I say, patting the canvas chair back with an understanding hand. "Gouda, Wouda, whatever. I guess they thought I didn't sound Dutch enough." The Josh looks pained, which gives me gas, so I move the conversation along. "What's on your mind, Josh? If this is still about the fencing scene, I gotta tell you, we really do need swords."

"It's not that," says the Josh. "Namir called. He needs you in LA."

"Great. Tell him I'll see him in three weeks when we wrap."

"That's not gonna work. He needs to see you now."

That's not gonna work? Namir Trumpleder is the head of Lederhosen Entertainment, the parent company of Pizza Box, with smarmy corporate tentacles stretching in all directions, including international distribution, format sales, arms deals, money laundering, sex trafficking, what have you. Okay in fairness, I don't know about those last few, but I wouldn't put them past any company with Namir's hand at the helm. The guy has gangster written all over him. But he's always appreciated my work ethic— lots of work, not much ethic—and has been my go-to guy in slim times ever since we were together at USC film school and he produced my senior short using local Crips for crew and, I'm pretty sure, paying them in cocaine. No one knows where Namir's family came from. Iran, Russia, and Israel are all possibilities, but Namir holds his passport pretty close to his vest. It's only known that his clan has money, lots of it, and that money is their religion. It is his passion for parsimony that made Pizza Box what it is today: an on-time, under-budget schlock machine.

That's why *that's not gonna work* strikes such a discordant chord. For me to go to LA will cost at least a day's delay in production, and in Namir's time-is-money math, production delays are right up there alongside rape and murder in the not-so-fun club. What could be so urgent that he's willing to waste his money—akin to spilling his blood—to see me face to face? I have a feeling it's not to tell me he's pimping me for a Humanitas Prize. So, with a certain sword-of-Damocles dread in my head, I give everyone the day off, hop in my shitbox Song Soprano and start driving south.

Limos? Drivers? At this chicken dance? Don't make me laugh.

Fast forward five hours, and now I'm in Namir's office, waiting for the big man to finish his business in his private bathroom behind his desk. His office is furnished with Pacific Design Center floor samples and decorated—if one wants to call it that—with posters from Pizza Box's greatest hits, including the misguided courtroom comedy *Trial by Jerry* and *The Pride Is High,* a stoned remake of *Pride and Prejudice* set in a seaside resort and shot in a Jamaican beach house that Namir bought for the shoot and, of course, kept. He has a little sign on his desk, one like you buy in those kiosks at the Glendale Galleria. It reads, *There's two ways to do things: My way and wrong.*

So the toilet flushes and out strides Namir in all his squat, bald, paunchy glory. He offers me a hand, which I hope to God he's washed, and beckons me to a low couch beneath the window. All of Namir's couches are low, and he always puts his visitors in them, while he either stands or sits in his tall leather desk chair. He likes to have the high ground. This time, though, he takes a seat beside me on the couch, which scares the living crap out of me, for if Namir is willing to surrender status that means I have zero, or soon will. From the moment he pats me on the knee and tells me how much he's loving the dailies, I know I'm toast.

He truly does love the dailies, and why not? They're plentiful and cheap, and they tell the story with a minimum of obfuscation and a maximum of cleavage. Namir calls this self-evidence to my attention, then launches into a litany of all the good work I've done for him down through the years, before turning the inevitable kiss-off corner and breaking into a chorus of, *It's not you, it's me*. Actually, it's not him, either. It's his son, Namir, Jr., who fancies himself not just a director but an *auteur*, which is going to be a huge problem for Namir, because the last thing Pizza Box wants on any of their pictures is a whiff of artistic integrity—that shit costs *money*. But the wife dotes on the son and Namir, for all his business bluster, is whipped like a truffle meringue. Junior wants a movie, and as mine is already in production, and therefore less likely to be completely clusterplucked by Trumpleder *fils*, I'm being let go. So there you go. One minute, I'm a journeyman director with no self-respect, prospects, or future, but at least a job, and the next minute I'm a journeyman director with no self-respect, prospects, future, or job. As Marye used to say, "Hollywood's a bitch and so am I."

"It's not the end of the world," soothes Namir. "You'll land on your feet. I'll make some calls." But he won't, I know. He can't. How does that call go? *Hey, buddy, would you mind hiring my longtime friend who I fired because my son is an effete poser with delusions of Soderbergh and my wife has me wrapped around her vagina?* No, what he'll do is subtly let it out into the community—where subtle, by the way, is defined as anything less overt than a full-page ad in the trades—that I was riding ineffectual shotgun on a runaway production that, thankfully, he was able to rescue with the help of his son, the second coming of Orson Freaking Welles. *Sad when a talent goes south*, he'll say, and then admit with a sigh that I was never that much of a talent to begin with.

Well, on that point I have to say, he's right. I mean, I thought I was, once, back in film school and after. I'd studied the greats, French

New Wave and Britain's angry young men, and copped every move I could, like a newbie in a skate park. Tried to incorporate that *style* into my work, you know? That style—the off-kilter shot, the unexpected lighting trick, something that tells the audience there's *vision* going on. But there's a certain statute of limitations on vision, and if you haven't realized yours by your fourth or fifth film, you can be pretty sure that you never will.

But I'm not bitter.

No, you know what, check that. In fact, I'm bitter as hell.

And what I do when I'm bitter is drink. Hard.

I drive off the studio lot where Namir has his office and, in an act of puerile protest, crumple up my drive-on pass and throw it out the window. *Littering! Ha! That'll show 'em!* By grace of bad timing, it's now the dark heart of rush hour, and I'm stuck with the sick prospect of trying to make my way from the badlands of Hollywood to the grotty East Pasadena flat I've been renting since the World's Ugliest Divorce netted me the double whammy of usurious alimony and *persona non grata* status in my own heavily mortgaged house. I could, of course, barstool away traffic time in any number of dank holes that dot the perimeter of Hollywoodland, but for the kind of drinking I plan to do, I know I'm going to end up very impaired, and the last thing I need right now is a DUI. So I'll delay gratification—no, blotification—till I get back to my neck of the weeds. There's a divey little joint just two blocks from my place that I favor. The tattoo girls call it home. I know I'll never get to first base with the tattoo girls, but still they're nice to look at.

I phone my production assistant back in Fresno, and her vapid prevarications make it clear that she knew I was tagged for the slaughterhouse before I did. Probably got a bump to AD just for keeping mum, the Judas. Next call is to my agent, Art Sardino of Sardino and Associates, where the associates are his wife who cooks the books and a half-wit Hmong secretary he shares with the bail bondsman next door. Once upon a time I was with the William Morris Agency. Well, once upon a time I had six-pack abs, so there you go. Art says he's shocked, *shocked!* to hear about my ill treatment, which means he knew about it, too. The good news is that Namir is honoring my contract. The bad news is it wasn't much of a contract to begin with. Art promises to get word out that I'm on the market again, and gives me every assurance that I'll be back on the earn in no time. With his clout, I'll be lucky to book a cat litter commercial.

So I finally arrive back at my apartment, hot, sticky, sweaty, achy, with a tickle in my throat that tells me that on top of everything else I might be coming down with that lovely golden staph. There's a pile of pent-up mail beneath the slot in the front door, and I gather it up and shuffle through it without much interest. I don't know what I'm looking for—it's not like there's a life-changing letter in there. Still, you can't resist: checking the mail is like checking your latest pan of gravel, hoping that, unlike the last ten zillion times you looked for gold, this time you'll find color in the grit. In among the flotsam of bills, credit card offers, and circulars from local drugstores, I find no items of interest and one item of bathroom reading, this being the latest quarterly newsletter of the Dutch-American Friendship Guild, an organization that promotes closer relations between blah-blah-blah, and chronicles the doings of Americans of Dutch descent. How I got on their mailing list I'll never know, but I find it amusing, in a random-access kind of way, to see that Ms. Pam Vogel has published a cookbook and Mr. Donnie Ring has invented a new process for milling green waste. Maybe I should send them an update on me.

> *Bob Wouda of Pasadena, California, announces the end of his not-too-promising-to-begin-with career. Now available for wedding videos.*

I grab some cash and head out into what is now night. Down the cracked sidewalk I trundle, to the corner of Colorado and Parkwood or Greenwood or one of those woods, where a relic old beer bar called Last Call weathers the ongoing hurricane gale of San Gabriel Valley gentrification. It's only a matter of time before this joint is a Jamba

Juice or Juicy Couture, but for now it's still the sort of dark refuge for lost souls where you can drink in peace, unmolested by modern music, pretentious trendies, or TGIF-style hostesses wearing unbearable layers of flare. The tattoo girls favor it for the same reasons I do: drinks are cheap, and no one checks your pedigree.

I spend my first scotch-and-a-half fuming at the awful unfair unfairness of it all. Oddly, I'm not mad at Namir. He's just being true to his nature. And I'm not all that mad at Hollywood, though it extends and withholds validation like a toddler teasing a kitten with a piece of string. You could say that Hollywood is just being true to its nature, too, constantly obsolescing and replacing the moveable parts on the sausage machines that grind grand ideas into lowbrow entertainment.

I'm not even all that mad at myself; those who say you have no one to blame but yourself rarely know what they're talking about. After all, did I not tread my career with measured steps? Everyone who's ever seen me on a set would rate me as *careful* and *prepared*. Okay, so maybe I'm not that magic with actors—I figure I do my job and they do theirs—and maybe I haven't been all that bold in my choice of material, but look: I've kept my head above water for more than twenty years, and if you can say that after a generation in this godforsaken youth-obsessed viper pit, then you've earned yourself something. Maybe not the respect of your peers, but at least a pension. At least some peace. I appreciate the difference between art and craft. I never had pretensions about art. I just wanted to practice my craft.

The jukebox is playing some hoary country fairy tale about how sex is better with love, so now I get to get all maudlin about my sex life too. When's the last time I got laid? There was that friend of Marye's who pity-banged me not long after the divorce. Well, pity; she may have been testing the waters for a rebound. In any case, it didn't work out, for sex with Marye during the grim, final Cheyne-Stokes phase of our relationship was so fraught with bitterness and obligation that it left me worthless in the sack, a fact Marye was never at less-than-enthusiastic pains to point out. And that sort of thing takes time to get over. So the question of sex has been largely rhetorical for me for longer than is healthy.

Imagine my surprise, then, when one of the tattoo girls actually strikes up a conversation with me.

We strike it up with each other, more or less, two lonely souls down drinking at the bar. I admire her belly tattoo, flames around her navel; she admires my ability to buy drinks. She tells me her name is Dawn.

"Is that Dawn with an e?" I ask. She doesn't get the self-referential reference, but it's only a bump in the conversational road—a wart we quickly burr down with Tequila Braindeath, a house-special drink that comes with a legal disclaimer.

It turns out that we have something in common—more in common, that is, than the adjacency of our barstools—for Dawn, too, was fired today.

"I work at this mom and pop print shop," she says. "I was giving pop a blowjob and mom walked in. Think I can collect unemployment?"

A charmer, this one.

But there's a calculus of alcohol, an inverse proportion between drinks consumed and common logic, so it's not too many drinks later before we're stumbling down the street together and up the surprisingly tricky outside steps to my apartment. She pauses to smoke a cigarette, leaning against the metal railing at the top of the stairs. Normally I don't go for smokers, but drunken bastards can't be choosers, and when she flicks her cigarette butt into the tired bushes below and turns to kiss me, I'm a ready teddy.

We go inside and get naked. I discover that her burning navel tattoo is part of a larger leitmotif of body parts on fire; flames lick her nipples and nethers. I emulate the flames. Things turn squishy from there, and I'm pleased to discover that neither empathy nor methodology have abandoned me completely. I am careful not to think about Marye just the same.

Later, we're lying in the dark, spent, the only light in the room the cherry glow of Dawn's next cigarette. "You weren't bad," she says, "for a middle-aged divorced guy." Thus damned with faint praise, I fall into a booze-drenched sleep.

I awake after dawn. Dawn is gone.

And later when I call the number she gave me, it's a Jamba Juice. So there you go.

The next days are a haze. With my orientation and expectation suddenly stripped from me, I feel adrift, like I'm having an out-of-body experience, only my body is two hundred miles away on a sound stage in fricking Fresno. It's not like I've never been shitcanned before, and it has usually turned out for the best, because by the time you arrive at a firing, everyone knows the situation sucks. Still I cling to the shards of my former life, no matter how badly they cut my hands. With the stubborn persistency of those blind to the writing on the wall, I reach out to prospective employers, letting them know that I'm back on the market. I call this particular brand of hell "banging my head against the phone," and once it was a strength of my game. I was just relentless and, in fact, had a magic way of easing past the underlings and reaching the right people, the choice makers. Now, though, the factotums are younger, savvier, more resistant to the oily charm of the cold call. Plus, I suspect, my middle-age desperation comes through on the phone. It's one thing when you're riding your film school cred to the inner sancta of Paramount or Warner's, quite another when you've been fired off a Pizza Box production and would now gladly grab any directing gig you can get, up to and including crime re-enactments for the Justice Channel. I bang my head against the phone just the same. I am compelled. Because there are two kinds of people in this world, people of *doing* and people of *being*. People of being, those lousy Buddhists, can feel good about themselves no matter what. But people of doing, of which I'm one, define themselves through their actions. If we don't have something going on, if we don't have a story to tell—to our agents, our peers, or ourselves—we're lost in a swamp of negative self-image. We suffer. We suffer and die. But my cold calls are a cold lead and my permanent abode is now *square one*.

Maybe I should just retire? I could, you know. Though Marye pillaged my main assets, my remaining meager resources would go a long way in—say—Nicaragua. But is that seriously an option? What would I do with my days? Shack up in some beach hotel, that creepy expat lifer that the local girls steer clear of because, you know, he's *that guy*?

So what does that leave? Just hanging around waiting for a *deus ex machina* to save me in the final reel? I've seen that story. Hell, I've shot that story. It's the lamest fiction in filmdom and I'm not going to hold my breath waiting for it to come true.

And I'm not going to give up. I'm going to investigate every obscure corner of opportunity. Craigslist. The DGA online classifieds. Even the trades. Sooner or later, I tell myself, something will wash up on my beach. I just have to keep combing. It takes faith to think that something will wash up on your beach. After all, there are a lot of beaches out there—why should something wash up on yours? Then again, you could see everything that has happened in your life so far as a function of that which washed up on your beach, by luck, fate, or circumstance. I mean, viewed through a certain filter, we're all living the butterfly effect, yeah? Suppose I didn't have a grandfather who was wet for Billy Wilder—so much so that he bought my father a Super 8 camera. Suppose my father had had some use for the damn thing and hadn't chucked it in a box in the garage, where some numb years later, inquisitive eight-year-old I found it. Suppose I didn't have a madly extroverted friend who wanted to star in a backyard version of *Bullitt*. Put it another way, if Grandpa loves pussy, I'm a gynecologist.

So you never know what's going to wash up on your beach. But it's there for a reason. All of it. Every bit.

And that may explain why I'm even hunting for leads in, of all places, the Dutch-American Friendship Guild Quarterly. This starts out as a bathroom read, but when you're trolling for opportunity, you tease it out of the tiniest nook, which is why this brief announcement catches my eye: "*In English and Dutch*, a joint project of Netherlands Film Fund and Cross-Cultural Purpose, in preproduction now, Arne Vangeld to direct."

The thing is, I know Arne. We met on a panel at some film festival, both singing the praises of cost-conscious (i.e. cheap) directing strategies. We're kindred spirits, fellow students of the *get in, get the shot, and get out* school. Maybe he needs an editor —I wear that hat as well—so I shoot an e-mail to the Quarterly, asking if they can hook me up with Arne's e-mail address.

The day floats away. I stroll down to Luigi Ortega's for lunch, my eye half-peeled for Dawn, who is nowhere to be seen. Later I stroll back. I think about taking a swim, but the pool, uncleaned since winter, remains greasy and thick with algae. God knows what creatures lurk in its murky depths. I swear I've seen fins. I call a few friends, but no one seems to be around. I leave messages for some; for others, not. With a rustle and a plop my mail arrives. I sort through it quickly. Nothing but dead trees. Time hangs heavy on my hands. For lack of anything better to do, I scrub my kitchen floor and *look at me,* I think, *I'm Cinderfrickingella.*

The phone rings. I assume it's one of my friends calling back, but when I look at the caller ID, it's a string of numbers I don't recognize, starting with 3130 and going on for way too long to be any number I know. I answer with a speculative, "Hello?"

A husky feminine voice asks in oddly accented English, "Is this Bob Wouda, the film director?"

"I don't know about *the* film director," I say. "*A* film director."

"Mr. Wouda, my name is Lia Geilis. I'm calling from the Netherlands Film Fund. In Utrecht?" She has a way of ending each sentence with a lilt that turns statements into questions. It's not an unpleasant sound; in fact, it is melodious.

"What can I do for you?" I ask.

"I have a forwarded e-mail here, from which I understand that you're trying to reach Arne Vangeld."

"Well, yes, but I mean, why—?"

"Mr. Wouda, I'm sorry to tell you that Mr. Vangeld has passed." I know she means passed as in passed on, but I can't help thinking she means passed as in passed on a project. "He was killed in Amsterdam last week. His bicycle was hit by a car."

None of this makes much sense. I mean, Arne is—*was*—Dutch-American like me, but it's not like we're close. Why am I getting this call? "I'm very sorry to hear that," I say. Then, at a bit of a loss, I add, "Um...thank you for letting me know?"

"Mr. Wouda, you seem to be aware of the project he was working on."

"Yeah, an indie film of some kind. I read about it in the trades." Well, trades in the loosest sense of the word. "I'd, uh...I just wanted to say congratulations." Okay, that's not a lie, exactly, just text and subtext. You never come right out and ask for the job.

"I wonder if you'd be interested in taking over for him."

But sometimes they come right out and offer? What the hell?

I tell Lia that I don't understand, so she explains in her mellifluous Dutch-English that Arne had been just about to start shooting when he was killed. Now down a director, the project is day-to-day. I know how expensive that can be. Some producer somewhere is dying by degrees. Still, it seems odd that this Lia person should be reaching out to me, of all directors in the world.

"What is the movie about, exactly?"

"It's the story of an American exchange student who comes to Holland and falls in love."

"Sounds lovely," I say, but I know I'm not right for it. Love stories are not a strength of my game.

"Sir," she pauses, and I can feel her awkwardness flowing down the long fiber-optic, "it's a peculiarity of the funding structure. This project requires a director of Dutch descent."

"Well, I mean," I say, "there must be plenty of those in Holland."

"I'm not being clear," she says. "It requires an American director of Dutch descent. The funding partner, Cross-Cultural, intends the film to be instructive for all the cast and crew."

"And you think American directors know something you don't know?"

"Sir, *I* don't think anything. But the funders..." her voice trails off. In that moment, I get it: all of it. For some bizarre reason, the people who put this project together saw value added in the American touch with a side of Dutch. In fact, maybe the whole thing was Arne's idea. I guess I just arrived at that well-known intersection of right place and right time.

Next thing I know, they're sending me a hefty retainer and a first-class ticket to Holland. So there you go. The *deus ex machina,* the lamest fiction in filmdom. I should reject it on purely artistic grounds, but that doesn't sound very much like me, does it?

Bob Wouda is working again. He's out of his depth, overseas, the very definition of stealing his paycheck, but steal it he will, because that's how he rolls.

In English and Dutch. We'll see how that turns out.

Lawrence Wilson

Old for California, an excerpt

S AY WHAT YOU WILL about Wales Branch and the many ways he had managed to undermine his own long-made plans to fuck up the Rose Parade—the fact was, perverse as they might be, at least he had some long-made plans.

While he was still in high school, still several years away from the millennial parade year that seemed best to shoot for—and that would be the year of Janey and her pals' Royal Court eligibility—Wales started ed doing some preplanning on the positive side. Because the fact was he loved a parade too. He wasn't all about how awful parades were— just how awful the Rose Parade was, or was now that it owed its soul to its corporate sponsors.

His ideal parade was still out there. Along with celebrating the Arroyo and Craftsman culture, von Karman, and Lamanda Park— Wales could abide a parade that celebrated the local fruit of the vine and flowers that smelled.

Ever since he was little, he'd known that the bloomingest Pasadena winter flower by far, easily outdistancing the fickle rose, was the prodigious camellia. He'd seen properties that had been abandoned or neglected for years with hundreds of blooms on their unpruned camellias.

"So, Mr. Florio, you're saying that none of the hundreds of camellias you've got here have a scent?"

Wales, sixteen going on twenty, had made a field trip, purloining his father's rattletrap, classic Corvair, to the famous camellia and azalea nursery in the foothills above Altadena, passing himself off as a Caltech student with a particular interest in botany. Though botany certainly is a science, the institute didn't have a real major in the subject, leaving the mysteries of horticulture to the aggie-oriented land-grant colleges; to the UC Davises and the Texas A&Ms. Wales had said on the phone, in a preliminary call, that he longed to talk to someone who really knew plant materials on a practical, not theoretical, basis.

Wales headed up Chaney Trail off of Loma Alta and, just below the Angeles National Forest boundary, found the driveway into the parking lot of the commercial nursery. Unlike every other nursery in town, Florio's sold nothing but specimens of the two flowering plants; one a bush, one a small tree.

A century ago settlers had found that both camellias and azaleas did particularly well in Pasadena's warm and dry climate; better, perhaps, than they did even in their native Asia. Frosts were infrequent here—except in the microclimate of the Arroyo floor, where it was several degrees cooler on winter nights: most parts of town had just two or three sub-freezing evenings a year, which both plants tolerated quite well, and neither needed much water.

Three generations of Florios had grown them exclusively here on a dozen acres. They had also hybridized almost one hundred varieties, leaving far behind their Japanese origins.

Wales tracked down one of the proprietors and introduced himself and his quest.

"So, Mr. Florio, you've sure got a lot of gorgeous camellias here—pink, white, red, and all the combinations thereof. But you're saying none of them smell—uh, give off a pleasant fragrance?"

The short, olive-skinned, balding man, wearing jeans and rubber Wellingtons and a faded long-sleeved khaki shirt, shook his head. "Not a one."

"And why is that?"

"They just don't. I never thought about it."

"But don't flowers need to smell to attract bees into their little pistils and stamens and whatnot so as to spread the pollen around?"

"Not really. Or bees can smell what we can't. Anyway, we take care of that. More or less artificial insemination I suppose. And—well, you know that *camellia japonica* is tea, right—black tea? Maybe the good Lord figured he'd put enough flavor in the leaves and didn't need no frivolous scent in the flowers."

"Mmmm—So you're the king of camellia hybridization, right?"

"Over 230 varieties developed right here by my brothers and me, and by our dad and uncles. And by our grandfather, back at the turn of the century."

"But you never tried to cross-breed a smell into one. Get an—I don't know—rose and work your magic?

"Like I say, never thought about it—and nobody ever asked."

"Could you?"

"How much of a stench are we talking here?"

"Big time—I'm thinking gardenia-size…"

"Jeez. Couldn't you have said—I don't know—azalea?"

"Azaleas don't smell either."

"Well, it's delicate little odor, I'll give you that."

Trying to play to Joe Florio's pride, Wales asked him if it wasn't time that—perhaps even more than the rose—his famous camellias became the true floral representative of Pasadena.

"Oh, sure. Should be the camellia parade, I've always said. Though Temple City's got their annual Camellia Festival, but, I don't know—it's kinda small time. Straight out of Iowa, with their little-kid king and queen. Off the record, that. We sell more trees in that town than anywhere else."

Wales recalled that there was an annual floral festival in that neighboring town to Pasadena's southeast, though neither he nor anyone he knew had ever been to it. It was a Mayberry-like shindig, sweet and not ready for prime time.

Wales looked out over the spreading nursery, specimen bushes marching over the hills as far as you could see, and turned back to Mr. Florio.

"But if we could—if you could—develop an odiferous camellia, and then cover a big float with tens of thousands of blooms, and have it roll up and down Orange Grove and Colorado with the scent just wafting off it, knocking the spectators out like Dorothy in the poppy fields in *The Wizard of Oz*—wouldn't that be special? A kind of career-capper, even?"

"Son, as you say, I'm already the king of the camellias. It may not seem like much to a Caltech kid who's been breathing that Feynman air for too long. Say, he was a customer, you know that? Dr. Feynman—lived down the street on Boulder Road. Knew him way before the Challenger commission, way before the Nobel, too. Salt of the earth Jewish fellow. Had a nice little garden. Always used to tell me, 'Joe, now here's a tree that DOESN'T grow in Brooklyn!'"

"Feynman was before my time," Wales said. "But I imagine he was a man who liked a challenge, Mr. Florio—just like you. So if you'll give this aroma thing some thought, I'll be in touch."

Erica Zora Wrightson

Bel Canto

THE FALL THEY ARE sent to live with the opera singer in the Altadena foothills, she stops speaking. It is autumn and, new orphans, they find themselves in a large house with a large man who sings and fancies liquorice allsorts and is worshipped by a smelly miniature dog. A window in the main room of the house frames the silhouette of an old church dusted with jacaranda blossoms and white ash that drifts down from the smoldering San Gabriels when the winds are hot and strong.

While her brother fashions weapons out of spiky pods from the sweetgum tree, she passes the time eating butterscotch drops in her room and sketching faces to the soundtrack of his arias, which quiver glass and course through all of the metal in the house till it rings. The swelling of the large man's chest and the shape his mouth makes when he sings warm her. She is a farouche girl, unaccustomed to the behavior of effusive men. Her father was a man of few adjectives and spoke only in low octaves. The singer breaks silence over and over without warning and she imagines his notes contagious, bouncing around in the immediate ether until they tire and attach to strands of her hair like small iridescent flies. In the full-length mirror on the back of her bedroom door, she examines her body, brushing the large tan nipples with her fingers to see them tighten like the mouths of sea anemones. As his solfège climbs, she takes to kneading the warmest part and the sounds siphoned from her mouth echo off the high ceilings in tones as foreign as the Italian lyrics trembling under her door.

At night, deep longing for home and the certainty of deciduous trees. She returns often to her memory of a picture from *The Ox Cart Man*, a book her father would read to her before she went to sleep. A farmer with a red beard and tall boots prepares for a trip across New England to sell the family's harvest—mittens and shawls knit from their sheep's wool and brooms carved from birch wood. His wife, daughter, and son help him pack the wagon tethered to a brown-and-white ox. Behind them, a green hill covered in crimson leaves, embosomed by a range of purple mountains. The picture nurtured a great sadness in her each time, knowing that while his children tucked spools of wool into the back of his cart, they were thinking of what she would later recognize as a great unraveling—the empty chair at the head of the dinner table, the kindle they'd gather alone, their mother's lonesomeness leaking like maple sap from a wood wound.

Contributors

PETREA BURCHARD grew up in DeKalb, Illinois and currently resides in Pasadena. She received her BA from the University of Illinois at Urbana-Champaign. She is the author of the novel *Camelot & Vine*. Past works can be found online at *Altadena Patch* and *South Pasadena Patch*, the 'Act As If' column at *ActorsInk*, and *Rose City Sisters*, where her story *Belinda's Birthday* was a 2009 finalist for Story of the Year. She blogs at *Pasadena Daily Photo* and is a regular contributor to *Hometown Pasadena*.

LIAN DOLAN grew up in Southport, Connecticut and lives in Pasadena. She received a BA in Classics from Pomona College. She is one of radio's Satellite Sisters and was a co-author of the *Satellite Sisters' UnCommon Senses* (Penguin, 2001), a contributor to the *Over the Hill and Between the Sheets Anthology* (Springboard 2007) and the author of the *Los Angeles Times* bestseller *Helen of Pasadena* (Prospect Park Books, 2010) which was nominated for Best Fiction by the Southern California Independent Booksellers. She has had regular columns in *O, The Oprah Magazine* and *Working Mother*. Her novel *Elizabeth the First Wife* will be published by Prospect Park Books in May 2013.

DAVID EBERSHOFF is the author of four books of fiction, including *The Danish Girl* (Viking, 2000), *The Rose City* (Viking, 2001), and *Pasadena* (Random House, 2003). His most recent novel is the international bestseller *The 19th Wife* (Random House, 2009), which was also made into a television movie. His writing has won a number of awards, including the Rosenthal Foundation Award from the American Academy of Arts and Letters and the Lambda Literary Award. His books have been translated into eighteen languages to critical acclaim. Ebershoff teaches in the graduate writing program at Columbia University. For many years he has worked as an editor-at-large at Random House. Originally from Pasadena, he is a graduate of the Polytechnic School. He now lives in New York City.

DIANNE EMLEY is a Los Angeles native who splits her time between Pasadena and the Central California wine country. She received a BA from UCLA and an MBA from the UCLA Anderson School of Management. She is the author of the *Los Angeles Times* bestselling Pasadena Police Detective Nan Vining thrillers, including *Love Kills* (Ballantine, 2010), and the Iris Thorne mysteries, including the forthcoming *Pushover* (Pocket Books, 2013), and is a contributor to the *Shaken – Stories for Japan* anthology (Japan American Society of Southern California, 2011). Her books have been translated into six languages. She has led workshops and panels at Thrillerfest, Left Coast Crime Conference, Bouchercon (World Mystery Conference), and the California Crime Writers Conference.

MARGARET FINNEGAN was born in Niagara Falls, New York and currently lives in South Pasadena. She graduated from Scripps College and received her PhD in U.S. women's history from UCLA. She teaches composition at CSULA and is the author of the historical monograph *Selling Suffrage: Consumer Culture and Votes for Women* (Columbia University Press, 1999) and the novel *The Goddess Lounge* (Lucky Bat Books, 2012). Her essays and short stories have appeared in *Salon*, the *Los Angeles Times*, *Family Fun*, *Word River Literary Journal*, *Chamber Four*, *Rose City Sisters*, and other publications.

DENNIS FULGONI was born in Pasadena and currently lives in the Highland Park neighborhood of Los Angeles. He received his BA from CSULA and his MFA in fiction writing from Antioch University. He has taught composition at CSULA and is currently the Title I Coordinator and Literacy Coach for Irving Middle School. His work has appeared in *The Colorado Review*, *Quarterly West*, *New Stories from the Southwest*, *Parting Gifts*, and *The Citron Review*. He is the recipient of an Intro Journals Project Award, a Kirkwood Award for Fiction, and a Special Mention in the Pushcart Prize. He is working on his first novel, *All Good Killers*.

Jill Alison Ganon was born and raised in Staten Island, New York and has lived in Pasadena for twenty-five years. She attended SUNY Binghamton. Ganon served as the managing editor of *American Bungalow* magazine and is the author of numerous nonfiction books including *Raising Twins: What Parents Want to Know* (HarperCollins, 2000), *Twins!* (HarperCollins, 2006), and *Hometown Pasadena* (Prospect Park Books, 2008).

Veronica Gonzalez Peña was born in Mexico City, grew up in Athens, Ohio and San Gabriel, and currently resides in the Mount Washington neighborhood of Los Angeles. She received her BA from UCSD and her MA from New York University. She has taught at NYU, the Pratt Institute, CUNY, UCSD, and California Institute of the Arts. Her novel *twin time: or, how death befell me* (Semiotext(e), 2007), won the Aztlan Literary Prize. She is the co-editor of *Juncture: 25 Very Good Stories and 12 Excellent Drawings* (Soft Skull Press, 2003) and her stories have been published in *The Massachusetts Review, New World: Young Latino Writers, Black Clock,* and *Animal Shelter.* Her novel *The Sad Passions* is forthcoming from Semiotext(e) in May 2013.

Denise Hamilton is a native and resident of Los Angeles. She received her BA from Loyola Marymount University and her MA in Mass Communications from CSUN. She is the author of five bestselling Eve Diamond crime novels, including *The Jasmine Trade* (Scribner, 2001), which was short-listed for the Edgar Allen Poe award. She also edited and contributed to the Edgar award-winning short story anthology *Los Angeles Noir* (Akashic, 2007). Hamilton is a Fulbright Scholar and award-winning journalist who spent ten years on staff at the *Los Angeles Times.* She still writes a perfume column for the paper. Her most recent novel is *Damage Control* (Scribner, 2012).

Rachel M. Harper was born in Boston, Massachusetts and currently lives in Pasadena. She received her BA from Brown University and her master's degree from USC. Her first novel, *Brass Ankle Blues* (Touchstone, 2006), was a finalist for the Borders Original

Voices Award and selected by Target for its Breakout Books Program. She has received fellowships from Yaddo and the MacDowell Colony and has published both fiction and poetry in *The Carolina Quarterly*, *Chicago Review*, *African American Review*, and *Prairie Schooner*. She has an essay in the newly published anthology *Black Cool* (Soft Skull, 2012), edited by Rebecca Walker, and recently adapted her second novel, *This Side of Providence*, into a television pilot. Harper is on the faculty at Spalding University's brief-residency MFA in Writing Program.

NAOMI HIRAHARA was raised in Altadena and South Pasadena and currently resides in Pasadena. She is the Edgar Award-winning author of the Mas Arai mystery series. Nominated also for Macavity and Anthony awards, the novels in the series include *Summer of the Big Bachi* (Bantam Dell, 2004), *Gasa-Gasa Girl* (Bantam Dell, 2008), *Snakeskin Shamisen* (Bantam Dell, 2006), *Blood Hina* (Thomas Dunne, 2010), and *Strawberry Yellow* (Prospect Park Books, 2013). Another mystery series with a female bicycle cop in Los Angeles will be released by Penguin Berkley Prime Crime in 2014. Her novel for younger readers, *1001 Cranes* (Delacorte Books for Young Readers, 2008), won honorable mention in youth literature by the Asian/Pacific American Librarians Association. Two of her short stories were included in *Los Angeles Noir* (Akashic, 2007) *and Los Angeles Noir 2: The Classics* (Akashic, 2010). She has served as chapter president of the Southern California chapter of Mystery Writers of America.

CHRISTOPHER HORTON was raised in Crown Point, Indiana and currently resides in Hollywood. He received a BA in European History from Northwestern University and attended the Neighborhood Playhouse in New York City. He is the author of the novel *The Great Big Book of Bitches (a love story)* and a collection of short stories, *Ode to Dentistry and other Mostly LA Stories*, and is currently working on his second novel, *Canyon Creatures*.

SEAN HOWELL is a Pasadena native. He is the author of a Kindle Single, *The Same Coachella Twice*, and is currently working on his first novel. His story "The Parade" was previously published in the *Santa Monica Review* in 2009 under a different title.

MICHELLE HUNEVEN is a native of Altadena, where she currently resides. She received her MFA at the Iowa Writer's Workshop. She is the author of four novels: *Round Rock* (Knopf, 1997), *Jamesland* (Knopf, 2003), *Blame* (FSG, 2009), and *Off Course* (forthcoming FSG, 2014). She has won a GE Younger Writers Award and a Whiting Award. *Blame* was nominated for a 2009 National Book Critics Circle Award. Michelle presently teaches creative writing at UCLA.

RON KOERTGE is the author of a dozen books of poetry and another dozen novels for teenagers. A recipient of two PEN awards, an NEA grant and other glittering prizes, he lives and writes in South Pasadena. After teaching at Pasadena City College for thirty-five years he retired and now teaches at Hamline University in St. Paul, Minnesota in their low-residency MFA program. His most recent work includes the poetry collections *Fever* and *Indigo*, both from Red Hen Press, and a crossover book of revisited fairy tales, *Lies, Knives and Girls in Red Dresses* (Candlewick Press, 2012).

JIM KRUSOE was born in Cleveland, Ohio and lives in South Pasadena. He teaches at Santa Monica College and in the graduate writing program at Antioch University. His first novel, *Iceland*, was published by Dalkey Archive Press (2002), and his others, *Girl Factory* (2008), *Erased* (2009), *Toward You* (2011), and *Parsifal* (2012), were published by Tin House Books. He has also written five books of poems and two books of stories, *Blood Lake* (Boaz, 1999) and *Abductions* (Nothing Moments, 2007). He has received an NEA fellowship and a Lila Wallace Award.

SCOTT O'CONNOR was born in Syracuse, New York, graduated from SUNY Brockport, and currently lives in the Eagle Rock neighborhood of Los Angeles. His novella *Among Wolves* (Swannigan & Wright, 2004) was followed by *Untouchable* (Tyrus, 2011), which received the

Barnes & Noble Discover Great New Writers award. The audiobook version (performed by Bronson Pinchot) was named by *Publishers Weekly* as its Fiction Audiobook of the Year. His next novel, *Half World*, will be published by Simon & Schuster in 2014.

Patricia O'Sullivan (ed.) is an Altadena resident and the associate publisher at Prospect Park Books. She received a BA in English from Barnard College and an MBA from the Drucker School at Claremont Graduate University. She is currently a doctoral candidate at the University of Liverpool.

Liza Palmer was born and bred in Pasadena, where she still lives. She is the internationally bestselling author of five novels, including *Conversations with the Fat Girl* (5 Spot, 2005), which has been optioned for series by HBO, *More Like Her* (William Morrow, 2012), and the forthcoming *Nowhere but Home* (William Morrow, 2013). After earning two Emmy nominations writing for the first season of VH1's Pop Up Video, she now knows far too much about Fergie.

Victoria Patterson was born in Whittier, California and has resided in South Pasadena for almost twenty years. She received her BA and MFA from UC Riverside and is a visiting assistant professor at UC Riverside and associate faculty at Antioch University. She is the author of the novel *This Vacant Paradise* (Counterpoint, 2011), a *New York Times Book Review* Editors' Choice. *Drift* (Mariner, 2009), her collection of interlinked short stories, was a finalist for the California Book Award and the 2009 Story Prize. The *San Francisco Chronicle* selected *Drift* as one of the best books of 2009. Her novel *The Peerless Four* is forthcoming from Counterpoint Press in fall 2013. Her work has appeared in various publications and journals, including the *Los Angeles Times*, *Alaska Quarterly Review*, and the *Southern Review*.

Samantha Peale lives in Echo Park. She received her MFA from The School of the Art Institute of Chicago. She is the author of the novel *The American Painter Emma Dial* (Norton, 2009), which is being developed for the small screen by Philip Seymour Hoffman and Emily Ziff's Cooper's Town Productions. Other writing has appeared in *Five Chapters*, *Narrative* and the *Los Angeles Review of Books*.

GARY PHILLIPS is a Los Angeles native raised in South Central where his experiences, ranging from community activist to delivering dog cages, provided material for his tales of chicanery and malfeasance. He is the author of more than twenty mystery and graphic novels, including the Ivan Monk and Martha Chainey series. His short stories have been featured in anthologies such as *Los Angeles Noir* (Akashic, 2007), *Black Pulp* (Pro Se Press, 2013, ed.), and *The Heroin Chronicles* (Akashic, 2013). His current novel is *Warlord of Willow Ridge* (Dafina, 2012), and he's developing a web series called *Midnight Mover*.

CYNTHIA ADAM PROCHASKA grew up in Claremont, California and has lived in Pasadena for the last eighteen years. She received her BA and MA in English Literature from UCSB. Currently, she teaches Creative Writing, Composition, Literature and Film at Mount San Antonio College. Her short stories were featured in the New Short Fiction Series in 2011 and have appeared in the *Santa Monica Review* and the *Florida Review*. Her poetry has been published in *inside english* and other publications.

WALLY RUDOLPH was born in Burlington, Ontario, Canada, raised in Texas, and has resided in the Montecito Heights area of the San Gabriel Valley for the past five years. In 2007, he was recognized by the Ford Theatre Foundation as part of its INSIDE:Reading Series for his collection of short stories, *The World's Princess*. More of his work can be found in the literary journals *Milk Money*, *Lines+Stars*, and *Palooka*.

ANDREA SEIGEL was born in Anaheim, California and is a resident of Pasadena. She received her BA from Brown University and her MFA from Bennington College. She is the author of *Like the Red Panda* (Harvest, 2004), one of Amazon.com's Top 10 Debuts of 2004, and *To Feel Stuff* (Harcourt, 2006), as well as the young adult novel *The*

Kid Table (Bloomsbury, 2010). In spring 2013 Lynn Shelton will direct Seigel's feature script *Laggies*, starring Rebecca Hall.

JERVEY TERVALON was born in New Orleans, raised in Los Angeles, and is a resident of Altadena. He received his MFA from UC Irvine and is the author of five books, including *Understand This* (William Morrow/Anchor House/University of California Press, 1994), for which he won the Quality Paperback Book Club's New Voice's Award. He was the Remsen Bird Writer in Residence at Occidental College and now is an associate professor at National University. His current novel is *Serving Monster*, available as a Kindle Book (2011). He is also the director of the *Literature for Life Project*, a literary/salon magazine.

KATIE VANE grew up in Altadena and currently lives in Mammoth Lakes, California. She received her BA in English from Vassar College, where she was the recipient of the Ann Imbrie Fiction Writing Prize, and her MFA in Creative Writing from Hunter CUNY, where she studied with Peter Carey, Colum McCann, Nathan Englander, Claire Messud, and Patrick McGrath.

JOHN VORHAUS was born in St. Louis, Missouri and currently resides in Monrovia, California. He received a BA in Creative Writing from Carnegie Mellon University and has taught at Northwestern University, the American Film Institute, the Writers' Program of the UCLA Extension, and the Australian Film, Television, and Radio School. He is the author of five novels, including *The California Roll* (Crown, 2010) and *Lucy in the Sky* (Bafflegab Books, 2012), and numerous works of nonfiction, including *The Comic Toolbox* (Silman-James, 1994) and *Killer Poker* (Lyle-Stuart, 2002). *The Texas Twist*, the third book in the Radar Hoverlander series, will be published by Prospect Park Books in 2013.

LAWRENCE WILSON is a native of and resident of Pasadena and is the Public Editor of the *Pasadena Star-News* and an editorial board member of the Los Angeles News Group. He received his AB in

English from UC Berkeley and his master's from the Thunderbird School of Global Management. He has taught news writing at the USC Annenberg School and created and taught an online journalism course for high school students for the *New York Times Knowledge Network.* He is a member of the Arts and Humanities Advisory Board at Claremont Graduate University and the *Daily Californian* Board of Directors, UC Berkeley. He is the Artistic Director of LitFest Pasadena. Some of his poems from the forthcoming *Twenty Surf Poems and a Song of Despair* were recently published in *Slake* and *The Berkeley Poetry Review.*

ERICA ZORA WRIGHTSON was born in Pasadena and currently lives in Los Angeles. She is a graduate of the College of Creative Studies at UCSB and received a certificate of merit from the University of KwaZulu-Natal in Durban, South Africa. Her essay "Artichoke" was listed as a Notable Essay in *The Best American Essays 2011.* She attended the poetry workshop at the Community of Writers at Squaw Valley in July 2011. Her work has been published in the *LA Weekly, Los Angeles Times, Slake, Squaw Valley Review,* and Tasting Table Los Angeles.

Rights and Permissions